CATRIONA McPHERSON

Dandy Gilver and the Reek of Red Herrings

HODDER

First published in Great Britain in 2014 by Hodder & Stoughton

An Hachette UK company

First published in paperback in 2015

1

Copyright © Catriona McPherson 2014

A CIP catalogue record for this title is available from the British Library.

Paperback ISBN 978 1 444 78552 4
eBook ISBN 978 1 444 78550 0

Printed and bound by Clays Ltd, St Ives plc

Hodder & Stoughton policy is to use papers that are natural, renewable and recyclable products and made from wood grown in sustainable forests. The logging and manufacturing processes are expected to conform to the environmental regulations of the country of origin.

Hodder & Stoughton Ltd
338 Euston Road
London NW1 3BH

www.hodder.co.uk

the Reek of Red
Herrings

About the author

Catriona McPherson was born in the village of
Queensferry in south-east Scotland in 1965 and
educated at Edinburgh University. She divides her
time between Scotland and California.

www.dandygilver.com
www.catrionamcpherson.com
Twitter: @CatrionaMcP

This is for Neil McRoberts, my old pal.

Acknowledgements

I would like to thank all the usual suspects, so that's Nancy Balfour, Kat Brzozowski, Hector Dejean, Suzie Dooré, Jessica Hische, Louise Kelly, Catherine Lepreux, Jean and Jim McPherson, Neil McRoberts, Marcia Markland, Erin Mitchell, Lisa Moylett, Poppy North, Eileen Rendahl, Sarah Rizzo, Francine Toon and Spring Warren.

Chris and Sue at Atkinson-Pryce Books; Nicholas, Alzeda, Jina, Erin and Bruce at The Avid Reader, Colin & Co. at Waterstone's in Edinburgh, Dave, Dan, Pavla and Mia at Goldsboro Books in London, my Sisters in Crime at Capitol Crimes and NorCal, my fellow Mystery Writers of America, my old and new friends at The Crime Writers' Association, the Femmes Fatales, the Criminal Minds, and the Scissor Sisters, who know who they are.

Also this time:

David Catto at the Local Studies Dept of Aberdeenshire Libraries in Old Meldrum; Marjory Nicholson at Macduff Library; Rosemary Sanderson, author (in association with The Banffshire Maritime & Heritage Association) of *The Herring Lassies*; and Susan Johnson at Driftwood in Pennan.

I

Although English is the finest language ever to rise up from the strewn remains in Babel, subtle yet piercing, mellifluous yet plain, and much as it pains me to give the Scots any cause for that unwarranted sense of superiority which it is their risible but unshakeable habit to display, still there are times when the language of Milton, Shakespeare and the Bible itself cannot furnish the moment and clothe the passing sensations with adequate words.

This was such a time. Alec Osborne and I were standing on a quayside at Aberdeen, the granite sparkling in the sun behind us, the sea sparkling in it before us, the stiff wind of a November morning tugging at our hat brims and whisking our coat hems up and around our legs like the petticoats of can-can girls in the last big number, and yet our cheeks were pale and our skin clammy as we worked our throats, swallowing hard and willing our troubled innards to subside.

'I'm absolutely . . .' said Alec, and I knew what he meant. He was more than sickened, more than disgusted, more than repelled. He was beyond the reach of English altogether.

'Scunnered,' I said. 'Me too.'

'It's preposterous, what he's suggesting.'

'Utterly,' I agreed.

'It's out of the question.'

'Indeed it is,' I agreed again.

Alec wiped his mouth with his handkerchief, then folded it and shoved it into his pocket, taking out his pipe instead.

'But we're going to do it, aren't we?'

'Of course we are.'

Alec grinned, settled his pipe in the side of his mouth and took my elbow to guide me back across the road and up the steps into Birchfield's Buildings, where Mr Birchfield waited on hooks to discover if we would bite at his bait or call for a bobby; I could see him quite clearly at one of the ground-floor windows, shifting from foot to foot and worrying at his beard with anxious fingers. The sight of him brought back another wave of horror, however, and I faltered.

'Second thoughts?' Alec asked, slowing his steps.

'Not at all,' I said, trying to sound stouter than I felt. 'Just that . . . our life is far from dull in general, but even so this has been a very strange day.'

It had started ordinarily enough. Granted, Mr Birchfield's letter had had its peculiarities but we have become used to that in the years, eight now, since 'Gilver and Osborne: servants of truth' screwed their brass plate to the railings. Figurative plate and figurative railings, but eight years is right enough, for we fell into detecting in 1922, when death touched our two lives and joined them together. Alec's young fiancée went missing from the house of a friend of mine and suddenly there we were, with a fire, a jewel theft, insurance fraud and murder. When the dust had settled and the broken bones had set again, we were detectives for good or ill and since then we have bumbled and bickered our way through the fog of countless crimes, solving most, giving up with the greatest reluctance on a few, and becoming friends.

Alec has not replaced the fiancée yet, despite some efforts, and my husband, Hugh, rumbles sometimes – I think George at his club teases him. But I am over forty, a matron with grown sons, and Alec is thirty-five. Odd that single men of thirty-five are a generation younger than married women of forty, but Hugh would rumble louder if matters were otherwise, I daresay.

So, old hands that we are, we took Mr Birchfield's excesses

with pinches of salt and were even amused as we reread portions of his letter to one another while coming north on the fast train.

'"A matter of the utmost concern to a great many good people who are ignorant of their interest in it and must remain so",' I had said. 'How can they be both concerned and ignorant? I don't understand him.'

'"Requiring discretion, confidentiality, and a fine feeling for the greater good",' Alec added. 'Which sounds a bit ominous if you ask me. The greater good as decided by Mr H. Birchfield, I'll bet.'

'"The harm and horror which would be visited upon countless innocents by any impulsive broadcasting of such matters as a common humanity dictates we preserve in silence." What can he be talking about? Horror? Harm and *horror*?'

'Horror for Mr Birchfield's wife and eight little children, I think,' said Alec. 'And harm to the man himself when it all comes out.'

'Ah,' I said. The conductor came into our compartment just then and I bit my lip until he had punched our tickets and left again, for I did not want to shock him. 'Blackmail. Do you really think a respectable Aberdonian merchant with a letterhead like the Albert Memorial would get up to that sort of nonsense?'

'A sovereign says so,' Alec declaimed. 'A sovereign says that Mr Birchfield, of Birchfield and Sons, distributers and exporters since 1871, had a cosy arrangement with an obliging woman until he forgot himself and put something in writing.'

'And shall we take the job?' I asked. 'We've always tried to keep away from seaside hotels and suchlike.'

'As far as divorce goes,' said Alec. 'But blackmail is another question altogether. I'll happily bang on her door and put the willies up her. I can't abide a blackmailer.'

'It's news to me that you've had cause to form a view.'

Alec grinned and wiggled his eyebrows.

'Let them try,' he said. 'I'd like to see them catch me.'

I was thoughtful for a while after that, gazing out of the window at the rolling fields. They were ploughed and bare this late in the year but no less orderly looking for it, if a little cheerless, punctuated only by wind-bent hawthorns and very occasional stone byres. If Alec had an arrangement with an obliging woman of his own he might never stir himself to marriage, and I should be sorry to see him grow old without children about him. Then I frowned as my thoughts caught up with me. If Alec, a bachelor, had a companion tucked away somewhere handy, what could anyone make of it anyway? Unless *she* were married. If so, I could only hope that her husband was indeed a blackmailer and not a crack shot with a hunting rifle.

'Do you take the bet?' Alec said, drawing my attention from the passing scenery and back to Mr Birchfield and his travails.

'I'll take your sovereign certainly,' I replied, with more ebullience than I felt; if one were going to gamble one should surely do it with a bit of flair.

An hour later, the sovereign was mine and I would gladly have given it back and ten more with it, to be spared the knowledge Mr Birchfield had imparted to us and the illustrations my fancy had supplied.

To begin with, he had sounded exactly like his letter.

'A delicate matter,' he had said, once we were settled in his private office, in the red studded-leather chairs, the door shut tight against all ears. He had even sent his clerk on an errand and checked to see that none of the harbour worthies were loitering under his window. 'And strictly speaking, you could say a police matter, plain and simple. I only beg you to hear me out before you act. I beg that of you.'

I could not meet Alec's eye. Of course a police matter should be taken straight to the police. Of course it should. On the very fingertips of the other hand, though, it is the

4

curse of the amateur ever to be forbidden the best of the fun and required to make do with such little matters as police ignore, so that at times one is practically coming along with a shovel behind the horses. And while all honest toil is noble, as the Bible and more recently the Russians have told us, still no one could resist a good bite at the juiciest meat when it was dangled so expertly.

'Of course we shall,' I said and noticed Alec sit back a little, happy to have the knot cut for him.

'Well now, someone has died,' Mr Birchfield began, rather chattily given the subject matter. 'This summer, in July or August most likely. Along the coast from here. At Gamrie. Or Gardenstown, I should call it.' Then he stopped.

'Who?' asked Alec. 'Natural causes, one assumes.' Of course one did not, but we had to observe the niceties.

'I cannot tell you the unfortunate creature's name,' Mr Birchfield said. 'For I do not know it. As to the cause . . .' This time the silence lasted even longer. 'If it was an accident, or if he was ill, or even if the poor soul had troubles he couldn't bear, then surely we'd all agree that it's a private matter.'

'But?' I supplied.

'Yes,' said Mr Birchfield, repeatedly performing a kind of genuflection comprised of patting his watch-pocket, refolding his perfectly folded handkerchief and pulling on his top waistcoat button until it seemed sure to give way. 'Yes, there is certainly a but, Mrs Gilver. Or an if, anyway.' At which tantalising moment he ran dry again. I sat forward to prompt him further but, seeing Alec give the tiniest shake of his head, said nothing and subsided. Mr Birchfield rose – he had only been perching on the front edge of his seat anyway – and crossed over to look out of the window at what he no doubt viewed as his domain: the quayside with its sheds; the harbour with its boats; the very North Sea itself with its treasure of herring, the pot of silver which had made Mr Birchfield rich.

'Let me start at the other end,' he said presently. 'It'll be easier understood that way. We had a complaint, you see. And Birchfield's prides itself on quality. We take complaints seriously when they come, and they seldom do. But, as I say, we had a complaint about a foreign object in one of the barrels. And then another one, abroad thankfully. And before we had stopped reeling, four more reports of barrels quite spoiled. All from last July. That is to say, all from Gamrie where July is the height of the season. Unusable and offensive. Noisome. Not at all what Birchfield's customers have been used to.'

'Oh God,' Alec said. I had yet to make the connection.

'And the thing is, sir,' said Mr Birchfield, turning all his attention to Alec like a compass to north, 'we reckon – the very few who are privy to it at all – we reckon there's only two to go. Three at the most. If we could weather it. If we could only weather two more . . .'

His little round of pattings and pullings looked fair to start up again; at least, he took out his handkerchief and shook it loose for refolding. 'It's not myself I'm thinking of,' he said. 'If it were all to come out then my business would suffer, it's true, but I don't think I'm being fanciful when I say it would spread beyond Birchfield's if it were known.'

'If what were known?' I asked.

'No, I don't suppose you are being fanciful,' Alec said.

'I have three hundred men, good hard-working men, arled to me at Gamrie and Macduff,' said Mr Birchfield.

'Arled, sir?' said Alec.

Mr Birchfield puffed out a thoughtful breath.

'Contracted, near enough,' he said. 'Three hundred men on fifty boats. Five hundred boats along this coast. More yet in the islands. Not to mention the gutting quines and coopers. And then arling aside there's the chandlers and boat-builders, and the shopkeepers and innkeepers and outfitters. They all rely on the wages of the fishing folk. Do you see, sir? Do you see?'

'But what does it have to do with the person who died?' I asked.

'And it's not as though times aren't hard already, I daresay,' Alec put in, in a musing sort of voice.

'They're not what they were,' Mr Birchfield agreed, although I could see how it grated on his businessman's pride to admit it. I could see that, if nothing else. 'And if the papers got a hold of something like this,' he added.

'Two more?' Alec asked. Birchfield nodded.

'The first spoiled barrel got sent back without us asking. After that we put the word out, if I have the expression right. We dressed it up as a new endeavour in giving full satisfaction. Money back on returned stock, all carriage paid for by us. And so we got the other three. And ah . . . piecing things together, as it were, we're only short two more. I can't sleep at night waiting for word that they're coming. Or for the loud knock on the door. It was my wife who suggested you to me. She reads the papers. She knows all about you.'

'I still don't follow,' I said. 'What have spoiled barrels of herring got to do with a dead man?' As I spoke the words, though, I began to see the first distant glimmers, like the scales of a shoal turning deep underwater, reflecting only the faintest gleam.

'Or perhaps three, you say?' Alec asked him.

'Maybe three,' Birchfield agreed. 'One of the ones we got back was rather . . . muddled.'

I was suddenly aware of a dreadful cold clammy feeling beginning to crawl up the back of my neck as though it bore the idea to my reluctant brain. And for some reason, the word 'muddled' was the detail above all which troubled me.

'A leg and an arm,' said Birchfield. I saw Alec turn pale. 'Well, arm and shoulder together really.'

That was when Alec and I bolted for the door, the fresh November air and quite the thorniest question we had ever had to answer in all our days.

Ought we have gone to find a constable? I still cannot say. Might lives have been saved? Hindsight, smug and unassailable, tells me yes. But as Mr Birchfield had seen so clearly, if a little conveniently, lives would have been ruined too: the lives of those fisherfolk, coopers and quines; the grocers and barbers and chandlers in each of the fishing villages strung out along the Banffshire coast like beads on a necklace. Not to mention the life of anyone who had ever boiled a potato, steamed some kale and poached a herring for his tea.

2

'It's a godforsaken spot to put off to in December, Dandy,' Alec said, poring over the ordnance survey map in my sitting room the next morning.

'But it's getting me out of the dreariest Christmas ever.'

I had agreed to travel to North Norfolk over Christmastime, where some Gilver relations were offering excellent shooting to entice the menfolk and a guest list which at the outset had sounded rather fun for me. Hugh and the boys were still a-twitter over the sport but a dreadful downward slide was underway socially. It is a familiar enough tale: someone – some pretty, witty guest of high value – had dropped out and been replaced by a thundering bore. News of the exchange had leaked a little, an entertaining someone else who had only agreed to come for the pretty wit had bowed out in turn, the thundering bore had suggested a tedious stop-gap and now all the prospective fun was draining away like bathwater and, in its place, every dullard with a gun was signing up. The thought of spending five days with the wives – who made their husbands look like Oscar Wildes, I had to say – was causing me such a sense of mounting panic that I had been half-considering a bout of fictitious flu.

'Besides,' I went on, 'it's either now or wait until next July, by which time the scent will be even colder and poor Mr Birchfield will have exploded from the tension.'

Birchfield had explained to us that now was our chance to catch the herring fishermen at home for once, not to mention the girls – 'quines' as he called them – who gutted and cleaned and packed barrels at the harbour. They were only rarely to be found at Gardenstown through the year, following the herring as they did and putting up in harbour lodgings at the end of each long day. Mr Birchfield, judging by his tone, found it romantic, but it had sounded a hard and comfortless way of life to me. Not only did the fishermen's travails speak loud and clear to anyone who has ever crossed the English Channel or North Sea on a ferry, but even the gutting quines and coopers earned every bit of their crust, in my book, slaving away at the catch as the boats came in and then trundling off in carts and charabancs to meet the men at the next fishing ground along the coast, all of them endlessly following the herring.

They set off to the Western Isles in January, across the stormy seas, going as far as Ireland some of them, spent a month at home in April which was the closed season, swept down the east coast throughout the rest of the year, from a start in May in the Shetland Isles, taking in July on the Banffshire coast, to a finish in November as far down as Yarmouth. Then, over Christmas, they came home to rest, mend boats and nets and, this year, be prodded and grilled by Gilver and Osborne by methods upon which we had yet to decide.

'Perhaps,' said Alec, sounding a little wistful, 'Birchfield will get news of the last two barrels very soon and decide to let well enough alone.'

'Well *enough*?' I said. I knew that my voice had risen to an unseemly pitch because Bunty stirred and looked at me. She was stretched out on the hearthrug, occupying an impressive portion of it for such a slender dog, and leaving only awkward little patches for Alec's spaniel. I shushed her fondly and she stretched her neck, gave that unearthly yawn which means she is about to sleep for hours and laid her head down again. I felt a pang as I regarded her. 'Slender' was kind to the point of dishonesty. She had been slender in her youth, solid in her middle years – although Dalmatians are not wont to turn into ottomans the way that Labradors do – and had begun to lose bulk at an alarming rate once she was past twelve. She was fifteen now and one of the farmhands from the Mains whom we had encountered on a recent walk had said she 'minded him of a scouring calf' and had asked 'was she right at the back end'. Bunty had turned away with all the delicacy one could after one's back end had been discussed by a ploughman, and we sauntered home. 'Sauntered' was a kindness too, like 'slender'; in fact, she tottered and I dawdled in order not to outpace her.

'Is she all right, Dan?' said Alec, like some wretched mind reader. 'She's looking terrifically spindly this last while.'

'She's fine,' I said. 'Good grief, Alec, I hope when I'm a spindly old lady you don't start wondering if I'm all right and reaching for a shotgun.'

'I never mentioned a shot—'

'Yes, well, barely a day goes by without Hugh mentioning one,' I said. 'I swear his fingers twitch whenever he sees her.'

It had long been Hugh's habit to take dogs behind the stables whenever they got decrepit and then to bury them in a corner of the park and immediately replenish the population with a new puppy. I could see the sense of it but I was sure that the threshold of decrepitude was on the move; the first of his black Labradors that I ever knew – the fabled Adder – was easily as rickety as Bunty and milky-eyed from cataracts too before Hugh saw him off and replaced him. These days he seemed to give up on a dog at the first sign of ailing, as though his pack were a regiment, with the old ones demobbed and fresh blood enlisted for battle.

'I'm certainly not leaving her behind, I can tell you that,' I said. 'I'd come back to a mound of turned earth and a lecture about sentiment. So I hope the Three Kings at Gardenstown has a nice warm stable and a lad who needs a bit of extra money.'

'I'm sure he wouldn't go that far,' said Alec. 'He's practical but he's not heartless.'

'This from the man who just used the words "well enough" to describe a dismembered corpse in barrels of herring,' I answered. I very much hoped that Becky, the housemaid, did not hear me. She had opened the door with the coffee tray as the words were leaving my lips but her face betrayed no emotion. Of course, when I was a girl, a housemaid's face would have betrayed no emotion if the corpse were being dismembered on the carpet and she had to step over bits of it to reach the table, but times are changing and Becky has been with us a good while, long enough for her own journey from slender to solid to scrawny to be well underway; easily long enough for her to venture a raised eyebrow if what she heard surprised her.

'You are right and I stand chastised,' Alec said, once we were alone again. I knew he was being deliberately soothing but I let it pass without comment. 'So. One leg and one arm to go. Or possibly a thigh, a calf and an arm.'

'And it might be years before they surface,' I said. 'It might have *been* years since they were hidden. I'm not altogether sure I understand how Mr Birchfield can be sure it was last July since he made such a point of the barrels not being dated.'

'They don't need to be,' Alec said. 'They're stamped with a harbour stamp and since the herring are at Gardenstown in July a Gardenstown stamp dates them nicely. And even if it didn't, he said he'd recognise the barrel. It's rather wonderful, isn't it Dandy, to think that a cooper's handiwork could proclaim its origin that way.'

I didn't find anything wonderful in any of it but forbore to say so.

'Still,' I persisted, 'it mightn't have been this *past* July. That's rather the point of salting the herring, isn't it? So that it keeps.'

'Ah, now, I've been thinking about this,' Alec said. I

shuddered; I had been trying not to. 'Mr Birchfield hinted that the adulterated barrels "made their presence known",' he went on. 'And that's sensible if you consider it, Dandy. I mean, a bit of salt might well preserve a cleaned and gutted herring but it wouldn't be equal to a chunk of meat the size of a—'

'Don't!'

'—haunch of venison, I was going to say. Much less anything that wasn't a haunch. Anything with offal attached.'

'Stop it!'

'And besides, we know it didn't work, don't we?'

'We do?'

'Because the first report was of a "foreign object", nicely vague. If it had been more recognisable—'

'I'm not going to tell you again, Alec.'

'You'll have to face it sometime, Dan. Best get used to it now. As I was saying, if it had been well-preserved there'd have been even more of an uproar.'

'It was well-preserved enough for Mr Birchfield to go into all of that detail,' I said, shuddering again. He had regaled us at some length with the skin's discolouration, the neat dismemberment at the joints, the lack of what he had called 'piscine nibbling', all supporting the theory of a very deliberate act, all knocking away my attempts to cling to a competing theory involving a shipwreck and remains caught in nets by unfortunate chance.

'Ah, but Mr Birchfield studied the things quite closely,' Alec reminded me. 'At least the first few. The . . . extremities. Whoever opened the first spoiled barrel, on the other hand, only looked close enough to see reeking lumps of nameless gore and mouldy herring.'

I stood, glared and stalked out. As the mother of sons, I have had to stomach a great many different sorts of unpleasantness over the years, from forgotten jam-jars of frogspawn (only discovered after the boys had returned for a new term at school) to experiments with Christmas-stocking chemistry sets (whose only attraction for Donald and Teddy was the promise of stink-bombs. I knew from the instruction booklet in one that cologne and saddle soap were possible, but as far as my sons were concerned, had every little jar in the box contained sulphur they would have been satisfied. Or that and some gunpowder anyway.)

So perhaps I should have been prepared for Alec to recover this fast from our shared initial horror and start poking around with a stick like any small boy, grown up or otherwise, who finds a dead seal on a beach or a drowned rat in a puddle. For some reason, though, I took his callousness hard, almost as a betrayal; ordinarily he was my ally in the face of men's brutality.

'Dandy?' Hugh's voice accosted me as I marched stiff with rage across the hallway, making for the stairs, my bedroom and true sanctuary. He was standing in the doorway which leads to his part of the house (I cannot help thinking of the business room, billiards room, gun room and library that way). 'Are you feeling all right?' he asked.

I stopped on the third stair and tried to make my sigh a silent one. Hugh is the product of a terrifically strict upbringing, one he has tried without success to perpetrate upon his own sons in turn, and in his view to go upstairs for any reason other than to change for dinner or retire for the night is a kind of Bohemian thumbing of one's nose at all that is decent and good and keeps the navy afloat and the trains running.

'I'm fine,' I said.

'Osborne gone, has he?' said Hugh, making me wonder for a moment if his concern at hearing footsteps ascending to the first floor was more than just a desire to preserve the Empire after all. Did he, could he possibly, listen out for furtive creepings when Alec was around? 'Only I wanted to ask if he could use some posts. I seem to have got some spare.'

'Posts?' I asked.

'You remember,' said Hugh, with his usual confidence. 'I'm fencing the deer out of that new planting, but the wire is sturdier than we thought and we've managed to space the posts at ten feet instead of eight.'

'How could I forget?' I said. 'No, he's still here. We've got a job starting actually.'

'Local?' said Hugh. Again I wondered if my gallivanting off with Alec *did* trouble him somewhere far under his tweed coat. Or perhaps he saw less chance of offloading his fence posts if Alec were travelling from home.

'Gardenstown,' I said. 'Can't Donald use them?' Going rather against the grain of the times, Hugh and I had bought the neighbouring estate to Gilverton a few years ago and, instead of throwing them in together, we had set our older boy up there with a factor-cum-steward of great experience to guide him and a tenant farmer of great wisdom and even greater independence to ignore him. Thus we hoped to provide occupation enough to keep him away from casinos, music halls and the army. He had not the brains for Oxford, poor boy, where Teddy, the little one, had just begun a month ago and to which, to judge by his letters – two of them so far – he was taking with abandon. Of the lectures and tutorials he had said only that 'they started jolly early' but about the major part of academic life, after tea and Friday to Monday, he had been much more chatty: saying that Somerville College was visible from his rooms and not as full of bluestockings as he had expected; that Oxford to London was a shorter train journey than he had dared hope; and if any tradesmen's correspondence turned up for him at home – Foyle's, Corney and Barrow, that kind of thing – perhaps I would forward them without Daddy seeing. Foyle's, a bookshop, was one thing (although I did wonder what the bookshops of Oxford could be missing) but Corney and Barrow I rather thought was a wine merchant. Besides, it was Pallister's decision. If our butler chose to put the envelopes by my plate at breakfast I might easily drop a napkin on them until Hugh had gone, but if he – Pallister, that is – were feeling starchy and gave them to Hugh then there was nothing for it.

'You'll have to learn to call it Gamrie as the locals do if you're to fit in,' Hugh said, drawing me back from thoughts of my younger son's dissolution and my slight maternal guilt over my older son's being denied it.

'How does one get "Gamrie" from "Gardenstown"?' I said, although I should have been past all surprise at the arcanery of Scotch pronunciations by now.

'It's not a corruption,' said Hugh. 'It's a different word. Clearly.'

'Perhaps to you, dear,' I said, 'but for anyone not brought up on Kilconquhar, Kirkcudbright and Milngavie the waters are always muddy.'

'Well, I envy you the trip,' said Hugh. I stared down at him, suspecting sarcasm, and then cocked my head to listen to the rods of freezing rain lashing against the skylight at the top of the stairs two storeys above our heads. As miserable as November can get in Perthshire, with lamps lit at breakfast time and mackintoshes still damp from one morning's walk when the hour came round for the next, I imagined that December in Banffshire would be much worse. All the rain and darkness, with a biting east wind too. Hugh caught my look and sighed. He made no attempt at silence, I noticed.

'Because of Lump House,' he said. 'You remember the Searles of Lump House, Dandy.' I shook my head. 'I know I told you about them. Searle's Circus? I saw it once and never forgot it.'

'A circus?' I said, surprised at his enthusiasm. I had had a run-in with a circus five years before and to hear Hugh on the subject then, Caligula himself would have walked out and written to *The Times*.

'In the ancient sense,' Hugh said. 'A circus of wonders, meaning an exhibition or museum.'

'Oh.' I was familiar with Hugh's tastes in museums.

'Rather interesting,' he went on. I could hear Alec's footsteps approaching very slowly along the passageway from my sitting room. 'Dioramas of curious nature, that sort of thing. Ghoulish, I suppose, but informative.' The slow approach was explained as Alec appeared. Bunty was with him.

'She woke and missed you,' Alec said. 'Good morning, Hugh. Has Dandy told you we're off again?'

'To Gamrie where the Brothers Searle practise their craft and display the results. She has.'

'And I'm taking Bunty with me,' I said.

'Really?' said Hugh, looking amused for some reason.

'What craft is this then?' Alec asked him.

'They are taxidermists,' Hugh said. 'Self-taught and rather dotty, but their collection is a sight not to be missed. I don't know whether they take commissions.' He gestured vaguely towards Bunty as he spoke.

I, for the second time in half an hour, found myself unable to speak, white with fury at one of my menfolk. The other of my menfolk though, if I can call him that, was with me on this one. Alec put out a hand and cradled Bunty's head.

'Who's a good old girl?' he murmured softly to her and her tail beat once against his trouser leg.

'Juicy case?' said Hugh, blithely.

'A corker,' I said. 'We're employed by a Mr Birchfield, a herring dealer from Aberdeen, to solve a missing person puzzle for him.'

'Aberdeen, eh?' said Hugh. He spent his college days there, which I have always found tiresome, for the perversity it takes to choose Aberdeen over Oxford or Cambridge is edging towards the pale even for Hugh. He certainly does not seem flush with anecdotes about the place. He was casting around now for something interesting to say and failing.

'He seems a most amiable and generous client,' I went on, filling the silence. 'I could probably wangle a barrel of his best herring out of him and send them down to you on the train. I know how much you like them.'

'I certainly do,' Hugh said, trying not to look startled.

'And I believe Birchfield's herring are something out of the ordinary,' I added.

'Well, that's very kind of you, Dandy,' said Hugh.

'Don't mention it,' I said, turning and beginning to climb the stairs to hide the look of pleasure I could not keep from my face. 'I'm going to fetch my mackintosh, Alec, to take Bunty for a walk. Are you coming?'

'I'll tag along,' Alec said. 'Yes, your mistress said "walk"! Look at that tail go. Plenty of life in the old girl yet, if you ask me.'

3

I wanted to believe Alec was right, but the long motorcar journey up to the Banffshire coast took all that Bunty had. I tried not to think of the days when she would stand up in the back seat with her head out of the side window, snapping at the wind and whining with joy as her ears flapped and the adventures in store came closer with every mile. This time she spent the trip curled on a blanket and barely raised her head, even when we stopped for luncheon.

'I hope she's warm enough,' I said, looking in at the window and dithering.

'She's covered in an eiderdown,' said Alec. 'She's fine. I, on the other hand, need a chair by the fire and a glass of something in the worst way.'

It was a particularly cold day, with that hard seeping chill I had come to know so well since I left my southern home and settled in Scotland. Rain and even occasional snow were not unknown in Northamptonshire, but my memories of a childhood there were made up of soft springs, gentle summers, smoke-scented autumns and crisp blue winters. I could not bring to mind a single day like this one, on which the sky was a great unpolished pewter tray that the gods had set down on top of the trees and an icy vapour rolled along at our feet. Even the lamplight of the little inn where we had stopped looked dim behind its fogged windows.

'I wonder if they'd make a hot water bottle?' I said as we bundled inside.

'Not if you told them it was for a dog,' Alec replied, but

I had already caught the arm of a passing maid and, partly for a shilling but mostly out of the kindness of her heart, she made straight for the scullery. By the time Alec and I were tucked into a table by the window, sipping our drinks and looking forward to our plates of stew, she was crossing to the other side of the lane where I had left the Cowley, holding not only a hot water bottle, but one wrapped in flannel to boot and something which looked very much like a sausage.

'If the Three Kings is half as snug as this we'll be all right,' Alec said, taking a huge glug of his whisky and settling back in his chair.

'Unlikely,' I said. 'For one thing, it's dry.'

He frowned, puzzled.

'The weather? East coast, you mean? All wind and no rain?'

'All lemonade and no whisky,' I said. 'Gamrie is a drouthy toon. A teetotal stronghold, you know. Presbyterian leavened with Plymouth Brethren. None of them drinkers. Or Sunday travellers either, for that matter. Our cards will already be marked for rolling up today.'

'Did you know that, Dandy?' Alec demanded, 'when you took the job?' I had to work not to laugh at the look on his face.

'I thought you knew it too,' I said, but he was not listening. He was already taking his wallet from his inside coat pocket and going to negotiate with the barman.

Successfully, of course. For one thing, Alec could charm the birds from the trees. Also, my shilling tip, news of which the maid had spread around her colleagues, had put us in good standing. Finally, of course, a publican was bound to share Alec's view that journeying into the interior, into the heart of Temperance, was the kind of emergency for which the licensing laws could most readily be suspended.

Full of stew then, armed with a bottle of whisky and a little keg of porter against the coming drought, and as warm as toast from the miraculous effect of leaving a dog, an eiderdown and a stone pig full of just-boiled water in the motorcar over luncheon time, we were pretty jolly as we set out on the second leg.

The day outside the Cowley was as cheerless as ever, it is true, and by the time we reached the turn-off for Gardenstown it was almost completely dark too and sprigs of frost were beginning to grow in the corners of the windscreen and creep over the glass, encroaching on all sides like vines covering a castle in a fairytale. I could feel the cold of the road coming all the way up through the floorboards, my stout boots and my thick woollen stockings and before long we had to stop, get down and rub at the head lamps to wipe away the rime of frost which had dimmed them to near uselessness.

Thank the Lord we did so for, at the Gamrie turn, the road, which had lain over the fields like an unspooled ribbon, changed its nature absolutely and without a scrap of warning. It hooked round a building which looked to be either a church or a school and then it began to drop. A minute later it hooked back again and dropped a little more. Then it narrowed, tilted up as though trying to empty us into the sea and turned into a nightmarish snakes-and-ladders adventure squeezing us between close-packed cottages on one side and a sheer drop on the other and presenting us every few feet with another impossible bend.

I should not have thought it possible to hurtle at six miles an hour, but that is what the little Morris Cowley did. My gloves squeaked against the steering wheel, the smell of rubber from the brakes and wheels filled our noses and even Bunty woke up and raised a quivering head to look at the blocks of granite flashing past her, just outside the window. To finish it off with a bow, there was a flattish patch near the bottom, causing me to relax, then one last vicious corner, so that when we did finally emerge from the mouth of the lane like a cork from the neck of a bottle, we were inches from the harbour. I stamped on the brake. The Cowley jerked to a halt and stalled.

Bunty would have slid off the seat but for Alec's lightning reflex. All those schooldays on the rugger field had not been wasted and he fielded her deftly as she shot forward and settled her gently back again. I stepped out on wobbling legs and leaned against the door.

On reflection we were yards from the harbour, not inches, but still my hand shook as I lit a cigarette and looked around in the headlamp light.

The working day was over, the harbour quiet and tidy, with creels and nets and pots of all descriptions heaped up in the shelter of the breakwater walls. There were not many boats: a dredger, a few fat little skiffs well-buffered with straw-rings against winter's storms and a small sailing yacht, but of the fishing fleet not a one. We had beaten them, as we had meant to, planning to bed ourselves in and be ready to meet them when the herring men and their lasses came home.

'No sign of the Three Kings,' Alec said, joining me. Then, as we both heard the sound of boot nails on the cobbles, we turned. 'Hie!' said Alec to a dim outline in the shadows. 'Hie there, my good chap. Could you tell us where the inn is?'

The boots stopped dead and a voice like a growl came out from the figure.

'Fit?'

'Um,' said Alec.

'He means "what",' I explained. The cattleman's wife at The Mains was from Aberdeenshire and I had conversed with her a great deal one measles-ridden winter, taking in soup and such things.

'We're looking for the inn,' Alec repeated rather louder.

'I heard you!' said the man. 'But you'll find no inn at Gamrie. Inn!'

'The hotel, he means, of course,' I said. 'The Three Kings Hotel, if you please.'

'Sounds like an inn to me,' Alec muttered.

'English, are ye!' said the voice, with withering scorn. 'Spitting on the Sabbath.'

'The innkeeper is expecting us,' I said.

'Dear save ye,' said the voice. 'It's halfway up yon.' And the boot nails rang out again as he moved away.

'Charming,' Alec said.

'Not a very auspicious beginning to offend the first man we speak to,' I said.

'And *who's* supposed to save us?'

'God, just as usual,' I said. 'But these northeasters would no more name him than they would the other chap.'

'I wonder if he commended us to God's mercy because we're English or because of where we're staying,' Alec said.

In all the time we were there we never found it possible to say. Certainly our southern origins were a daily affront to many, but it is equally true that I would not have wished a sojourn in the Three Kings upon the Kaiser himself.

It was indeed 'halfway up yon', on the single street of solid Victorian buildings in this village of corners, crannies and dog-leg lanes, but the turn into it was so tight if taken from below and the street itself so narrow that, in the end, we left the Cowley where it had come to rest and simply went on foot, hauling our small bags up one of the many sets of steps which ran like capillaries up and down the hill, connecting the pends and yards and snickets.

'Pity the poor postman,' said Alec as we paused to rest. 'It's a labyrinth.'

'He was probably born here,' I said. 'He'll be like a London cabbie. Oh, dear.'

I had just got my first good look at the hotel. It was the usual bleak stone tomb of a place, but such buildings can have their charms if enlivened. In this case the owners had worked at endeadening: the foot-wide strip of garden ground setting it back from the road had been covered in granite

23

chips and marked off with a low fence fashioned by looping black iron chains between spikes; a black front door was shut tight with a cardboard sign tacked to it reading *No vacancies, no hawkers, no food served, NO BAR*. Neither was there a knocker, doorbell, nor any apparent means of summoning the patrons. Alec stepped over one of the loops of chain to peer in at a window but, to match the raw-liver-coloured paint around the frame, there were raw-liver-coloured velvet curtains within, closed so tight I suspected they might be sewn shut.

'You did write?' said Alec. I nodded. 'And they answered?' I nodded again, then made a fist and banged hard on the black door. The sound was muffled and between that, the granite chips and railings and the dried-blood-red velvet curtains I could not stop a sudden flight of fancy that I was knocking on the sealed door of a mausoleum trying to wake the dead.

The dead woke readily enough. Almost before I had finished pounding I heard faint scuffles, then creaks and then saw a chink of light as the door was opened and someone held up a candle to the gap.

'Are you them?' said a voice.

Alec and I shared a quick look and then answered in chorus: 'We're them.'

'Aye, well, right then,' the voice said and shut the door again.

There were several unfortunate consequences of our failing to realise that it had been closed only to unfasten the chain before it was re-opened. For one, Alec stood where he was, and where he was was on the precious granite chips. Worse though, I responded by saying 'What the devil?' which counted as sailor's language in these parts (actually it was worse than sailor's language for I never heard any of the fishermen say anything half so ripe). Worst of all, as the door opened and the candle was raised I put a hand out to steady

Alec's step back over the chain – those spikes were nasty-looking – and there we were, a man and a woman, in the street, touching.

Euphemia Clatchie, sole proprietress of the Three Kings Hotel, writer of signs, sewer-shut of curtains and guardian of the granite chips, had never seen anything like it in all her days. Her face, owlish in the halo of candlelight, was frozen in disbelief and the light shimmered a little as her hand shook from the enormity. Then and there I decided that Alec and I were not friends and colleagues any more.

'Mrs Clatchie?' I said.

'*Miss!*' she hissed, as though I had insulted her. Perhaps I had; perhaps it is patronising to assume that another woman my sort of age must aspire to my estate.

'I'm Mrs Gilver and this is my brother Mr Osborne. I believe you're expecting us. Sorry we're late.'

'I was not! On the Sabbath? I thought you'd made a mistake with the date.' For a moment she just stared at us, and she had a marvellous face for staring; large protruding eyes, apparently lashless, that swivelled notably in their sockets as she looked from one of us to the other, cheeks like golf balls and a very small receding chin so that it appeared her mouth was hanging open, even when in fact it was firmly closed. Then there was her hair. It was the colour of a biscuit, or a cairn terrier, but the texture of candy floss which someone has just begun – only *just* begun – to spin into threads. I supposed that some of it was caught up in some kind of bun somewhere at its core but there was so much of it waving in wisps about her head like a sea anemone that one could never say.

'Well, here we are. What's to be done about it?'

'Ocht, away you come in then,' Miss Clatchie said.

'Is there a boy?' I asked her. 'Someone to fetch our bags? We've parked our motorcar down by the harbour.'

'There's no boy here,' said Miss Clatchie as though I had accused her of using some strapping lad as a warming pan.

'I'll get them,' Alec said. 'If you can furnish me with a key, Miss Clatchie? Or shall I just leave the door on the—'

She was horrified and leaned out to look up and down the empty street, where she must know everyone and where everyone must know her, as though at an alien city of brigands and thieves.

'I'll let you in again,' she said.

'Are you coming, sister mine?' said Alec, twinkling. 'I'll bring the bags but there's um . . . .'

'Bunty!' I said. 'You don't mind a dog, do you, Miss Clatchie?' It was obvious from the way the Three Kings was tucked into its roost on the hillside, with a higgledy piggle of fishermen's houses above it and below it, that there could not possibly be a stable here where Bunty could bed down on straw with horses' breath to warm her.

'A big dog or a wee one?' said Miss Clatchie and her eyes opened even wider. One almost wanted to hold a hat under her chin in case they popped out and fell. I scrutinised her expression for clues and then took a chance.

'An extremely large one,' I said. 'Wonderful guard dog.'

'Aye, fine,' said Miss Clatchie. 'I cannot abide a wee yapping thing. It can sleep in the kitchen.'

I bit my lip, planning to fight that battle later, but it turned out for the best in the end because when I began to follow Miss Clatchie into the warren of creaking passageways that threaded through the Three Kings I soon saw that a blanket on the floor in front of the kitchen range was the honeymoon suite and that Alec and I were much less to be envied.

My room must have been the drawing room once upon a time. It was cavernous, with two long windows facing the front and a fireplace of pink marble taller than I was. The mirror above was set at a compensatory angle and loomed as a result, making me think of pulpits and lecterns and, a little, of what would happen if its chain gave way, for it was a fearsome thing in gilded mahogany and easily five feet square.

Not that there was any call to stand before it, since the fireplace was cold and bare, the grate swept clean and not a stick of wood or a single cobble of coal anywhere.

'I've put a pig in your bed,' said Miss Clatchie, who was either psychic or had seen me shivering. I turned. The bed was high and narrow, a Scotch double, meant no doubt to help two people stay up out of the drafts and close enough for shared warmth in a freezing croft. It was tiny marooned in the middle of the floor in this place, with nothing but crimson linoleum all around it like Homer's wine-dark sea, not even a little mat to put one's feet on in the morning.

A meagre wardrobe on one wall and its mate, a meagre dressing chest, on the other completed the furnishings. There was not a chair, not even a stool, in sight. I tried a door beside the fireplace, expecting a cupboard but hoping for a cosy sitting room. Miss Clatchie stopped me, her voice so tense that her words came out like a series of barks.

'There's nocht in there. It's locked up tight.' Upon this Gothic note she drew me away to show me my brother's room and the 'doings'.

The doings were a narrow but high-ceilinged chamber shining from top to bottom with those nasty brick-shaped tiles – these in tobacco yellow – and lit in a coordinating tobacco-yellow glow by a gas lamp next to the bare window. There was a line painted round the bath to rein in one's excesses with the hot water and a row of enamel pails set alongside it. I eyed them.

'Don't the taps work?'

'Ocht, aye,' said Miss Clatchie. 'I just bid you ladle out what you can before you pull the plug. It's good water for the floors.'

After this, even Alec's room could not shock me. It was upstairs again under the eaves and the ceiling of it was open to the sarking – the boards which line a roof in these parts and give the roofers something to nail the slates to. I was sure I could see a glint of slate here and there. This was not a room, but an attic, the bed no more than a campaign cot.

'Is there nothing downstairs?' I asked Miss Clatchie.

'The rooms downstairs are for ladies,' she said.

'Surely my brother, though,' I coaxed.

'My own room is down there,' Miss Clatchie whispered, as though she expected Alec to wake in the night maddened with an ardour that could not be contained if he were on the same landing but which would ebb at the thought of some steps.

Alec took it cheerfully enough when he arrived, only stopping off in the other attic rooms to collect extra blankets, which he heaped up on his cot until the whole thing was the shape of a pioneer's wagon and almost as tall.

'Supper in the front room in a half an hour,' said Miss Clatchie as she met me returning to the ladies floor.

'I shall be ready for it,' I said. 'Shall I ring for my bags to be taken to a boxroom when I'm unpacked?' Then I looked around at the acres of linoleum and went on: 'Or shall I find a corner to tuck them away in here somewhere?' In truth, I hoped that they would warm the place up a little, with memories of home or indeed as a windbreak for some of the lustier draughts.

We were too cold and tired to dissolve into giggles half an hour later in the front room and for Alec a disappointing meal is always a grave matter. We managed therefore not to disgrace ourselves as Miss Clatchie entered with her tray. I had hoped that cooking would prove to be her metier, since housekeeping, small talk and personal adornment were clearly of no interest, but the plates she set down, jostling them slightly to fit them onto a card table which was set up in the window for us, put those hopes back at naught again.

On each plate was a pastry roll filled with sausage meat, two pieces of boiled floury potato – evidently one large potato had been sacrificed to feed both of us – and a mound of cabbage prepared the way my sons refer to as 'in flaps', that is to say torn into irregular sheets and boiled until slimy. There was a china jug of water, a plate of exactly two slices of bread, a dish with exactly two pats of butter and a bowl with an apple and a pear over which we were presumably to do battle when it came time for pudding.

'Well, we can improve things a little,' Alec said, as soon as Miss Clatchie had left us again, and he stood, lifted the card table and walked away with it. I thought for a moment he was going to take the whole lot back to the kitchen and lecture Miss Clatchie on her shortcomings but he only went as far as the fireplace and set it down.

'Why light a fire and then maroon us at the window?' he said. 'Especially with the curtains shut.' He came back, moved the chairs and then seated me. 'We can swap places at half-time and roast our other sides,' he said.

'Thaw, perhaps,' I answered, 'rather than roast, but yes, good idea. I don't suppose there's any coal in that little brass box thing?'

Miss Clatchie, coming back to retrieve our plates, halted in the doorway when she saw the disarray and subjected her polished floorboards to close scrutiny – taking a great swerving path round by the window to do so – in case we had dragged the furniture and left score-marks, but she said nothing.

'We don't expect coffee, my dear Miss Clatchie,' Alec said heartily. 'Tea will be fine.' Miss Clatchie boggled; it was quite obvious she had not been about to offer either but could not bring herself to argue with such ringing tones. 'After that we'll need nothing else until cocoa at bedtime,' Alec swept on.

'Cocoa!' Miss Clatchie said, sounding like a calling bird.

'Or Ovaltine,' I said. She swung and glared.

'I have neither thing in my house and I've never seen them in the shop either,' she said.

'Well, then more tea, quite weak, with milk and plenty sugar,' Alec said. 'You are very kind.'

Miss Clatchie, outwitted and undone, left without the plates and we could hear a pump being worked somewhere in the bowels of the kitchens as she filled the kettle.

'That's the trick,' Alec said. 'Don't ask for anything and give her the chance to turn you down. Just tell her and tell her loud.'

'She's terrified of you,' I said. 'Her knees were buckling.'

'She's right to be,' said Alec grimly. 'And so, Dandy, where do we start? What do we do when we set out to do it bright and early tomorrow morning?'

4

We had a plan, slightly 'of sorts' although more of a plan and less of sorts than sometimes. In brief, we were going to pass ourselves off as scholars. A pair of folklorists, anthropologists one might almost say, or even *philologists*, here to document the speech, songs and ways of the fisherfolk, like butterfly catchers with our nets, except that we would preserve specimens in notebooks and not on cork with long pins.

'I wish we had a phonograph machine,' Alec said. 'That would lend us no end of authenticity.'

'If we had also had time to learn to use it,' I replied. 'Not very authentic to be bumbling about, shattering the cylinders. Perhaps it's best for us to make cryptic notes and nod sagely. Anyway, hush now.'

We were nearing the kitchen door, planning to fetch Bunty and take her for her morning airing. Breakfast had been the inevitable porridge and two slices of nasty dark toast made from health bread, along with another two pats of butter and the tiniest pot of marmalade I had ever seen. If the rinds had been cut as thick as Mrs Tilling cuts ours at Gilverton, I am not sure one slice would have fitted inside it.

Bunty took some shifting. The kitchen range was the only warm spot in the house – I tried not to shoot black looks at Miss Clatchie's chair pulled up close to it – and outside the weather was unappealing: that same pewter tray, tinged with purple this morning, and a few enormous flakes of snow drifting down in spirals to alight on the iron-cold ground like dandelion seeds. I had seen an Italian greyhound in London in the summer wearing little mackintoshed bootees during a downpour – 'Look at that poor whippet!' Hugh had said. 'Some people have no right to a dog.' – and I wished now that I had accosted its owner and asked her where she had got them, for something similar would have been a boon to poor Bunty.

Instead, she set out whimpering as the warm pads of her paws suddenly met the shock of the cold cobbles. Alec and I, in contrast, set out wearing almost everything we had, like Heidi climbing her mountain: jerseys, woollen stockings, a felt hat with a scarf around it for me, a scarf crossed over under a mackintosh for Alec and fur-lined gloves for both. I was mourning my fur coat, or even my fox-fur collar, but Alec had persuaded me that a scholar with an interest in fishing folk would not wear such a thing and I had left it behind. Bitterly did I regret it now, thinking that I could have passed myself off as an eccentric (I should probably have no option, truth be told, for my scholarly ways were hardly likely to echo any earlier examples in the eyes of someone who might have come across scholars before).

It really was the most grindingly, achingly cold day and I was mean enough to feel glad that Alec's cheeks turned white and his nose pink as he rounded the corner and got the full blast coming off the sea. He pulled his coat collar up and buttoned it over, plunged his hands into his pockets and set off down a winding stairway.

It was more than just the weather, I thought as I joined him a few minutes later at Bunty's pace. That heavy purple sky and the first few grudged flakes of lazy snow always did have a pent-up kind of feeling about them but there was something else going on in the little town of Gardenstown that day.

A great deal of furious sweeping was underway, for one thing. Despite the chill, cottage doors all up and down the laddered brae were thrown open and women in shawls and aprons were busy with brooms. Others were standing on chairs set on the cobbles, polishing the windows furiously. Still more stood pegging out washings on the ropes which were strung cottage to cottage or lamppost to chimney or anywhere that a line could be secured. At first I thought it was sails they were drying, but closer inspection revealed the billowing, cracking expanses of white to be sheets. Blankets too. It seemed an odd sort of day, with snow in the air, for housewives suddenly to tackle such sizable washings. It seemed an odd sort of day, if I were honest, all over. The school term appeared to be over, and gangs of long-legged girls in short pinafores and short-legged toddlers in long ones were racing around, singing and laughing and every so often hopping up onto walls or outhouse roofs to gaze out to sea. Where were all the boys, I wondered. Then I emerged from the mouth of the lane and saw them. They were lined up two and three deep at the harbour wall, in conscious imitation I am sure of the old men who waited there too. The elders smoked and spat and conversed with one another in the low tones of old acquaintance with nothing to say but a long habit of speech to continue. The boys spat less expertly but with equal gusto, sparked their boot nails on the cobbles and tried, by hooking thumbs in their braces, plunging hands in their pockets and lobbing endless stones into the harbour, to look as though they did not mind at all being too young to smoke.

I had thought it might be easy to strike up an opening chat with the local people. To be sure, once we started to ask the more searching questions we might find ourselves faced with oysters – and Scotch oysters at that; no small matter since the most loquacious of Scots could join a monastery and never notice the difference – but I had expected the appearance of two strangers in such an isolated spot to stir up enough interest at least for a how-do-you-do. Besides, a large spotty dog is usually of note amongst the children and so it was rather surprising to find ourselves of no interest whatsoever to Gardenstownites of any age. We had no way of knowing that it would have taken more than two strangers and a Dalmatian to distract the locals that day.

Chastened, we took our wounded pride for a stroll along the shore road. It was flat, as shore roads and promenades inevitably must be, and fairly smooth underfoot, being paved with great slabs of the local stone and so drenched in salt twice a day that not a single snowflake had a chance there. On the other hand it was not so much a road, or even a lane, as a mere ledge, just a little wider than a cart, with the gable-ends of the bottom-most cottages abutting the one side and a sheer drop of ten feet to the seaweed and rocks of the beach at the other. The locals were clearly inured, for we watched a grocer's boy on his bicycle swing wide to pass a housewife with her basket of washing and neither one of them paid the smallest attention to the edge of the shelf. Alec and I could think of nothing else. He is something of a martyr to his fear of heights and has gradually infected me with a sympathetic case of the same trouble over the years, so that this morning we walked in single file hugging the cottage walls and keeping away from the precipice. Bunty made three, in her case because the opportunities for useful sniffing are always to be found at the base of walls and not out in the open. We must have been an odd sight altogether, as our little procession made its way.

'Bloody acrophobia,' Alec said. 'Would it kill them to put a bit of wire up? There are those hulking great things to hang it from.'

'Those are washing poles, I think, though,' I said, eyeing one of the stout posts set at the outside of the lane as we passed it. 'Odd that they're bare, mind you.'

'We'd get our heads in our handies if we strung a washing up on the shore side the day,' said a voice from just behind us. I looked back. We had passed the dark opening of a narrow

34

lane – it could not have been three feet wide and the overhang of the cottages' upper storeys on either side shrank it to half that before the roof tiles began. The woman who emerged from it almost filled it. She was not tall and was not exactly fat either – the shawl stretched tight across her bosom and tied behind was there for warmth and not extra corsetry – but she was just as solid, from the scarf which bound her head like a bandage to the hem of her wool skirt which hung to the ground like a bell, as though she were made from the same granite blocks that formed the cottages around her.

She beamed at me and then at Alec, one huge smile for each, apparently from an overstock of them she must spread around for sheer relief, and Mrs Tiggywinkle suddenly popped into my mind, making it impossible not to beam back.

'They're coming home,' she said. Then she added, with an air of explaining everything: 'Quines on the Ellen and loons by the Dear's grace.' Her accent, the Doric as it is grandly named, was as stiff as a bundle of twigs, as different from the Perthshire burr as Cornish from Cockney. One could hardly believe we were but half a day's drive away.

'Now, I wonder,' I said, whipping out a little notebook and a propelling pencil, 'whether you would have a minute just to recap for me, Mrs . . .?'

'Mason,' she said. 'Greta Mason, madam. Fit's thon?' She was staring at the pencil with some mistrust and to be fair it did look a little like a medical syringe, especially given my far from adept stab at deploying it. Alec did not snort but I imagined there was a snort gathering inside him; he is always scathing about my notebooks and the propelling pencil had afforded him considerable entertainment when I had unveiled it for the first time.

'*Mrs Mason*,' I wrote on a fresh page. 'Fisherman's wife?' I asked.

'Widow,' she said, 'and my family was quines all three, but

this time next week, if I'm spared, I'll have menfolk to call my own again.'

'And could you just repeat what that was you said, Mrs Mason? About . . . Ellens and loons?' I asked her, ignoring the second helping of mystification. 'I'm terribly interested in the local tongue, don't you know.'

'They're coming home,' she said, taking care to speak slowly. 'The lasses are on the LNER special service and the men are on the herring boats.'

'By God's grace,' I finished.

Mrs Mason's beaming face clouded for a moment.

'Course they are, and my lasses'll be here to meet them or not long ahint,' she said. 'So I'll need to get myself sorted.'

'I shan't keep you,' I said, clicking and pushing until my pencil lead was gone. She bobbed, then bustled back up the little snicket where the shadows swallowed her.

I drew breath to translate the exchange but Alec had pulled ahead of me.

'The fleet is coming home,' he said, 'and so the view of the sea is not to be obstructed with washing. And the girls are on a train. Is there a station here?'

'Macduff, I imagine,' I said. 'Did you catch the second bit?'

'A widow with daughters,' said Alec. 'But next week . . . no, not really.'

We were passing another gable end, this one with a bench set against it, in the middle of which, despite the weather, an elderly man in carpet slippers was sitting to enjoy his pipe.

'Aye, Greta Mason has not had her troubles to seek,' he said. 'Does my heart glad to see her birling and gockat.'

'Birling,' I repeated, propelling pencil busy once more. 'Gockat. My goodness but there is linguistic treasure to be had in these parts for philologists such as we. Now, sir,' I sat down on the end of the bench, causing the old gentleman to raise his eyebrows and straighten somewhat from his lolling.

36

'How would one gloss those splendid terms in English, if you don't mind me asking?'

'Eh?' said the man.

'Take pity on us poor southerners,' Alec said, sitting down at the other end, 'without a scrap of Scots in our heads. What did you say there?'

'English, eh?' said the man. 'Well, we've all got our troubles. Like I was just saying about Greta Mason – her man dead at fifty and no sons, then lost a lassie. But the tide's turning. Her two lasses she's got left are promised to good men, fine laddies the both of them, and a double wedding come Saturday.'

'How marvellous!' I said. 'Small wonder then that she's . . .'

'Birling,' said the man.

'And gockat too,' said Alec.

'Aye, I've no time for daft old nonsense,' said the man. Then he dismissed us with a nod, and turned his gaze back to the sea.

'A village wedding is a stroke of luck,' I said, as we went on our way. 'If we can infiltrate it, tongues will be loose and guards will be down. We'll hear every story and piece of gossip Gamrie has to offer.'

'Only five days to wangle an invitation, though,' said Alec doubtfully, causing me to shout with laughter.

'A ceilidh, Alec dear,' I said. 'They won't be ringing up the printers and begging for another engraved card. And if you manage to keep that bottle of whisky intact until then, even better.'

'I thought you said Gamrie was dry.'

'Officially. But round the back of the village hall at a wedding is something else again.'

'I shall take your word for it and hold you responsible if I'm thrown in jail,' Alec said. 'Now, what's the polite way to encourage Bunty into her morning ablutions so that we can turn to more pressing affairs?'

Past the end of the low road the rocks gave way to a small sandy beach at the foot of some cliffs. It was not precisely a picnic spot, facing due north as it did with a stone church lowering down from the cliff edge (as only Scotch churches can), great heaps of rotting seaweed littering the little patch of sand like slumbering elephants, and the sea itself, the relentless, irascible North Sea, battered away at the land as though fixed on obliteration. Even Bunty simply sat down on the ash path and stared up at me.

Besides, if we turned our eyes out across the waves, into the wind, and squinted against the dark – remarkable darkness for this time of day – we could just see, in the distance, the first sighting of what the men and boys were waiting for, what the women were scrubbing and cleaning for, what those long-legged girls and short-legged tots were leaping up onto walls and searching for.

Far out against the horizon, the smudged line where grey-black sea met grey-black sky had turned jagged. As we watched, the shapes grew distinct and spread apart from one another, and the first faint scraps of colour began to show – a yellow flag, a patch of green paint, the tiny dot of a red bucket – then suddenly, seemingly on the swell of one wave, there were masts and funnels and cabin doors and even, impossibly tiny, hands lifted in greeting and faces turned to peer back as we peered at them. The boats were coming home.

Alec and I trotted back along the shore road as fast as Bunty's gait would allow and got there just as the cottages of Gamrie began to empty and every villager not in a cradle or a bath chair joined the throng pouring out and down the lanes to line the harbour walls. Soon the whole place was a packed mass of cheering, beaming, weeping humanity, as though the harbour itself, its two arms open, had come to life to welcome back its men.

Soon handkerchiefs were waving madly from every wife

and mother on the land and caps were waving just as madly back from the men aboard, hair whipping up into the wind or bald heads showing pale against the dark sky, and all around us we could hear their whispered names – 'Wullie! Oh my Wullie. Robert, Robert, thank the Dear. Daddy! Look, girls! Daddy's home.'

Then, just as the excitement reached such a pitch that one would hardly have been amazed if some of the women had launched themselves from the harbour walls and taken to swimming, behind us, up on the hill, came shouts and whoops and the tooting of horns, and down that treacherous dog-leg brae came three carts and a motor van – still tooting – and, jammed onto every seat, packed into the backs of the carts, hanging from every side of the van, laughing and waving and shouting and whistling, came the girls. The herring quines, in their long skirts and thick boots, their jersey sleeves rolled to the elbows and their necks bare and red below the head-squares that kept their hair scraped up out of their way, not a scarf nor a coat amongst them, as though it were a gentle day in spring instead of the bitterest that December could send us.

They jumped down and in pairs grappled with their luggage until the carts and the van were emptied. None of the old men made a move to help and although I saw Alec stir at the prospect of fair maidens lifting such weights unaided, he soon fell back when he saw the first of them, their forearms corded with muscle and their feet planted wide and sure, hoist the trunks and set them down as though the girls were dockers or the trunks flower baskets. All the time they were talking, not chattering exactly, for their voices were deep and rough, salt-soaked and stone-washed, but one could not mistake the high emotion as they cried out their joy.

'Aye, we're back.'

'Aye, good time. The Ellen was birling.'

'Aye, home again like bent pins and we've betten they loons again.'

When the boats were close and had fallen into formation to enter the harbour one at a time, the herring lasses turned to their trunks and worked at the straps, loosening them to remove long oilskin aprons. They put these on and then, extracting strips of cloth from little cotton bags, they embarked on a curious enterprise at whose nature and purpose I could not guess. I stepped closer to watch them, but could not catch anyone's eye to ask, for the quines had their gaze fixed upon the approaching boats. When the men were close enough, the girls began to add jeers and catcalls to the greetings and whispered prayers, shouting their triumph at beating the boats home.

'Nah, nah, we'll wait. Don't you make yourselves dizzy hurrying!'

'I've knitted a jersey, waiting. Here, try it on!'

'We've stopped off in Dundee for a picnic. Fit kept ye?'

Then, like nothing so much as the village wedding scene which tops off many a ballet, there was a great orchestrated surge of movement. The girls in their aprons flitted over to an open-sided shed just as the first boat drew into the lee of the harbour wall and the crew threw ropes to waiting men. The fishermen leapt ashore and began relaying crates of fish along a line of villagers – old men, women and the larger children – passing them like fire buckets to the waiting girls. Before the last of these had arrived at the shed the second boat was moored and another line joined the first. Then a third, and by now the herring girls were at work with their knives, their mothers with their creels, until it seemed that everyone in the village, from the tiniest child who could drag an emptied crate to the swaggering fishermen themselves, leaping from boat to shore and hefting impossible weights on their necks like stevedores – everyone except Alec and me – was in the dance and thrilling at it.

I could not speak for Alec, but I was completely caught up in the spectacle. Despite the low light of a December morning the herring sparkled, each one a little silver plate upon which pink and blue and gold jewels winked and twinkled with every movement, and as boat after boat entered the harbour and family after family welcomed their menfolk home, the gutting quines worked harder and faster until their hands were flashing, quick red darts amongst the churning silver of the herring, as the crates were spilled into the table-troughs and the gutted fish were flicked with a snap of a wrist and a spark of light into the waiting tubs.

The tubs themselves, it had to be said, were unlikely ever to feature in the wedding scene of a ballet, no matter how odd and modern interpretations might become in these outlandish days, and it was while watching a pair of lasses guddle, elbow deep, in the pinkish water, rinsing the blood out of the fillets, that a thought began to trouble me. The girls lifted the fish out of the tub in a kind of colander and shook it until the drops of reddened water had stopped, then they tipped the load into a creel and bent over double to pack it. When a creel was full, one of the older women would lift it onto her back and stump away across the harbour head and up the lane. I followed one of them with my eyes, aware that I was frowning but still not quite sure what was worrying me. When the woman disappeared around a corner I turned to find Alec staring at me. He was frowning too.

'They do it right here on the harbour side for everyone to see,' he said. 'How could somebody possibly have done the thing we know they did without everyone knowing? Without the collusion of . . .' he pointed to an aged crone with a creel on her back. 'And . . .' He pointed to a child of about four in leggings and mittens who was emptying small buckets of guts into larger buckets for his older brothers to haul away.

'I never thought of that,' I said.

'Why?' said Alec. 'What's troubling *you*?'

'It's December,' I said. 'What was Birchfield talking about? It's December instead of July and it's herring at Gamrie as far as the eye can see!'

One of the herring lasses had stepped away from the trough-table in the open-sided shed to take a break in the fresh air and I turned to address her.

'I suppose you know Mr Birchfield?' I began. The woman laughed.

'All of Gamrie's arled to Birchfield's,' she said. 'Fine and well do we know the man that gives us every penny we have to our name.'

'Ah, yes, the arling,' said Alec, knowledgably.

'He's a fair man, Mr Birchfield,' she continued. 'Not the best price but a fair man if the storms or the markets go agin us. I'd rather have a steady arling any day than be at the mercy of the herring.'

She grinned again and knuckled her back and it was then I noticed the unmistakable swell under her oilskin apron. She saw me looking and chuckled.

'I've been on the gutting tables since I was wee bit of a lassie,' she said, 'and I've never minded the smell of a herring till this while. But now I'm sick to my gills and glad to be nearly done with it.' Even still, as she spoke she turned back and was at her station again before I could stop her. Instead, I followed. Stepping very carefully – the girls were neat workers but inevitably the ground around their feet was beginning to bear the marks of the hundreds of tumbling herring, not to mention the flashing knives – I tried to breathe through my mouth, imagining that the sharp stink of fish could be avoided that way, but if anything the slight taste of oil and slighter iron tang of blood was stronger in my mouth than in my nose and, to the delight of the herring lasses, I had to rummage for a handkerchief and press it to my face before I could speak to them.

'It's an unexpected pleasure,' I began, trying not to look

too closely at the nearest girl, who had the job of stripping the guts out of the slit-open herring and scraping them into a bucket before the fish itself was tossed into the rinsing tub. 'An unexpected pleasure actually to see you all at work. We are folklorists, my brother and I, and we were led to believe that the fish only visited these waters in the summer. We never dreamed of seeing you all in action, as it were, at Christmastime.'

'Aye, that's right,' said the girl I had followed over. 'This is not a catch. This here's just the scrag end the men have got on their road home.'

'But still,' I persisted, 'there are a few barrels of herring every December. The scrag end, as you say.'

The girls laughed and shook their heads at that, nudging each other, until one took pity on me and spoke up, being very careful to talk slowly and clearly as though I were an idiot; which, in this case, I suppose I was. She was so like the first girl I had spoken to that I concluded they must be sisters. And I was interested to note that her condition was even more advanced, her oilskin apron jutting out over her middle like an army tent.

'Nah, missus,' she said. 'These here are not for the barrels. Our mothers are away round the farms with these to sell fresh. Mr Birchfield wouldn't fash himself with these few wee spents here.'

'I see,' I said. 'I see now. This last catch is . . . under the . . . off the . . . independent?'

'A few pennies for the weddings,' said a third girl. 'Hurting nobody.'

'I thoroughly agree,' I said and, fishing in my bag, I found a few pennies more to add to the kitty. A few shillings, actually, which I set down on the edge of the trough before taking my leave.

'All's well,' I told Alec, as I rejoined him. 'This catch is sold in its fresh state.'

43

'It still doesn't account for the fact that herring is gutted and packed with a hundred witnesses,' Alec said.

'That might work in our favour though, you know,' I said. 'If we can truffle out a report of some gutting crew last July trying to cloak themselves in secrecy – moving operations to someone's cottage scullery, or under cover of darkness or something – well then, we might have found our culprits.'

'I think it would make more sense to find out who the dead man was,' Alec said. 'That should lead us to his killers.'

'If he was killed.'

'Indeed. If he was killed. In any case, his curers.'

'Either way,' I said, 'I vote that for now we leave them all to their reunions. No one is going to want to talk to philologists today.'

'Yes, it does niff a bit, doesn't it?' said Alec, seeing right through me. 'But let's watch this one particular reunion first, eh?' He nodded to where Mrs Mason was barrelling along the harbour side with an empty creel on her back, making for the gutting shed. I watched with interest to see her greet her girls and then with growing horror as it became borne upon me to which section of the shed she was bound and which two of the gutting quines were hers.

'Oh, dear Lord, Alec,' I said. 'I think there might be trouble in store.'

Mrs Mason had said to us not an hour since that her girls were betrothed to fishermen and that their weddings were planned for that very week. I could not imagine what she would think, say and do when she saw the state of those daughters and discovered how very thoroughly they had jumped the matrimonial gun.

She had spotted them and was waving madly, the light creel jumping around on her back with the movement.

'Peggie Ness!' she cried. 'Nellie Marr!'

'Mammy!' the girls chorused back. The three of them joined

44

hands as though about to sing ring-a-roses and all stood beaming.

'Now, look at the bonny size of you, my quines!' said Mrs Mason. 'Oh, but this is a blessing from above. Our tide has turned, chookies. Our tide has turned and the Dear is smiling down.'

'Huh,' I said. 'Well.'

'Quite,' said Alec. 'We seem to have come across a little patch of Bohemia, Dandy. Quite a surprise, eh?'

5

The explanation was not long in coming and it made perfect sense, in its own way. Nevertheless, from that moment on Gardenstown and its fisherfolk held an extra pinch of curiosity for me. I would not, I thought, have to feign interest in their ways as I set out with my propelling pencil the next day.

For the moment though, we contented ourselves with a visit to Gamrie's other curiosity, where innards were long gone and the smells of death banished for ever. The walk was beyond Bunty, who took up her post at Miss Clatchie's fireside with the greatest of enthusiasm and barely glanced at Alec and me as we set off without her.

'There's a road round, of course,' Miss Clatchie said. 'Up out of the village and then onto the dead man's way at the next turn. Carry on past the church.'

'Dead man's way?' said Alec.

'But it's easier to take the footpath from the end of the beach unless the weather is against you,' she went on, ignoring him. 'You cannot miss it from the churchyard.'

'The footpath it is,' I said. 'We'd never get my motorcar through the crowds at the harbour anyway.'

Miss Clatchie's face clouded briefly.

'We've seen the last of peace for this week,' she said. 'Five weddings to come. Five! Can you imagine anything worse?'

I could think of nothing to say in immediate response to this and Alec only managed to stretch his lips in the kind of grin one makes when swallowing medicine.

'Will you have a lot of extra guests?' I asked at last, trying to account for her distress. This notion seemed to startle her more than anything I had said yet. Her eyes did their golf ball trick again and her lip trembled.

'I wouldn't have fisherfolk in the Three Kings,' she said faintly. 'Even if they asked me.'

It was an interesting stance to adopt with respect to paying guests, but one which would serve us well, since when looking for someone, the smaller the crowd the better.

'What a misery-guts,' Alec began, when we had pulled the front door closed behind us and were choosing a route through the paths and steps down to the shore.

'Well, Scottish village weddings can get a little raucous,' I said. 'Even in Perthshire.'

'Have you been reading up on them,' said Alec, 'or have you attended?'

'I've stopped in at the village hall with a banknote,' I said.

'And can you share pearls about the dead man's way too?'

'It's not as sinister as it sounds,' I said, pointing as we arrived at the shore side again. 'This way – along to the beach and up a footpath – is the quickest route to church for the villagers each Sunday morning. They only go up out of the village and round by the road if they're taking a funeral bier with them.'

'Well, I'm all for the shortest route today,' said Alec, as a particularly biting blast of wind sliced into us. 'I think sauntering round the dead man's way might just kill me.'

There was still plenty of life to be seen on the shore road; the fishermen's ganseys and oilskins had been slung over the washing ropes – no restrictions on their use now that the boats were home – and wives and children were setting about them with soapy brushes and pails of water. The men themselves were busy with their nets, whether spreading them out on the foreshore and squatting to knot up holes, or dragging them, once mended, up to their cottages where it appeared that they were taken inside to dry. I tried and failed to imagine the smell of a herring net at the end of a long season, drying out in a house with such tiny windows as these cottages had, and those windows tight shut to keep the fresh air out and the peat smoke and cooking smells in.

'Interesting architecture,' Alec said, squinting up one of the narrow closes. 'One would hardly believe there was space for a single room here, never mind a house this size. But those back windows look out onto solid rock. Must be like living in a cave.'

'A very welcome cave when the storms pick up,' I said. 'As one might well be about to now.' Out in the bay the sky was roiling with banks of black and indigo clouds and we could see sheets of rain lashing down into the sea. Here on shore it was still snowflakes which fell, sparse and reluctant like salt from a damp shaker, but I shivered to think what might happen if the land-chill and the sea storm met over our heads.

At the far end of the beach the footpath rose fairly broad and fairly smooth, following a small burn into a fold in the hills, before crossing, doubling back on itself and skirting the cliff face up towards the church we had seen squatting there. It was ash underfoot and the bracken to either side had been kept in check by the passage of worshippers every week, so the going was not too alarming. Still, I was glad the wind was buffeting us back against the cliff face for had it been whipping around us from the landward side it might easily have blown us off into the void. Even at that I was happier when we turned a final corner and found ourselves on a plateau of sheep-nibbled grass with the wall of the churchyard ahead. The gravedigger's cottage sat by the side of a road leading back into the trees – the dead man's way, one presumed. At the other edge of the clearing were two stone gateposts, topped by creatures I could not identify at this distance; beyond them, a drive led onward into another, denser wood, swallowed within a few feet by the perfect blackness of close-planted pine trees.

I had stopped for a moment, to knock ash out of my insteps and catch my breath before starting up again, when Alec exclaimed loudly beside me.

'Good God,' he said. I turned to where he was pointing. High up in the end wall of the church, where stained glass windows might be found in southern parts, there were three niches set into the stone, and in each of these rested what looked horribly like real human skulls.

'They might be carvings,' I said, doubtfully. Scotch gravestones often had carvings of skulls, and crossbones too, not to mention the gargoyles and grotesques known as green men.

'They might be,' Alec said, just as doubtfully, for there was in honesty no mistaking that yellowed gleam and the way the grey teeth were lodged into the jawbones, with a dark line of old dirt along the join.

We both took a step back as a scrabbling behind the churchyard wall startled us. First two hands in rough mittens appeared, and then a capped head with a bearded face below. The figure wriggled itself into better footing on the wall and addressed us.

'Warrior kings,' he said. 'Danes. Defeated at the Battle of the Bloody Pits.' And his face split into a leer, showing teeth just as grey and a ridge of old dirt just as dark. 'I can give you a penny tour if you wait a minute till I'm finished here.'

'Finished doing what?' Alec said. It was a good question and my mind briefly boggled over the answer.

'I'm Chalmers, the gravedigger,' said the man and I felt a flush of shame, for what else would someone be doing in a churchyard really? If this place had been in an English suburb I should not have entertained the ghoulish thoughts which had just overtaken me. But then if this place had been in an English suburb the skulls of defeated Danish kings would not have been worked into the church walls as decoration.

49

'No, you'd better just carry on,' Alec said, stepping forward and giving the man a coin for the offer, regardless. 'If there's a need for a grave it must be dug.'

'Ocht, I'm just getting ahead of myself while I can,' said the man. 'We'll be needing a few I daresay when the cold weather sets in and they're easier dug the now.'

Had I not been recently made aware of the trouble with the herring barrels, this might have been the most monstrous thing I had ever heard. Digging graves on spec when one had time on one's hands and then waiting for the corpses to fill them stood against every scruple I knew. I wondered if the minister was aware that his sexton had implemented such an unfeeling brand of efficiency.

Alec, in contrast to me, either did not care or managed to hide his concern. He only nodded sagely with his lips pushed out in that thoughtful way that all gentlemen use to consider important matters, whether they be the age of whisky or the management of pheasant chicks.

'I suppose you must get a fair idea of how many will die every winter,' he said. 'It *is* mostly winter, I suppose.'

'Like clockwork,' said the sexton. He had settled himself quite comfortably, with his arms draped over the copestones of the wall and his chin resting on it. He was rather like a gargoyle himself, or perhaps a scarecrow, with the way his hair stuck out straight from under his cap.

'What do you do all summer?' Alec said. 'If there are no graves to dig.'

'I wouldn't say none,' said the man. 'And I cut the grass and keep the place tidy.'

'And is cremation making a dent in your trade?' Alec continued. I could see where he was headed but it was horrible nevertheless. Standing there in the chill and gloom of a dark December day, conversing on death and its manners with this leering head.

'Heathenish habit, that, sir,' said the sexton. 'You'll not

get Gamrie folk taking up with that. If a buddy dies in this parish he's mine.'

Even Alec faltered then, for there was something miserly and gloating about the way the man spoke and one does hear tales of gravediggers tugging off wedding rings and knocking out gold teeth, the age-old tradition of keeping vigil until the coffin lid is nailed notwithstanding. At least, though, one could be sure that a sexton as keen on his work as this fellow would hardly let one of the blameless dead of Gardenstown end up in half a dozen herring barrels instead of one tidy grave. We bid him farewell and resumed our journey.

'So our corpse can't have been a local,' Alec said. 'At least not one who died in his bed. If there's as neat a tally between dead villagers and filled graves as the sexton suggests, we must look elsewhere.'

We were passing between the gateposts now and I noticed that the headers were not lions or griffins or even eagles as might be expected. It was just another nasty little detail to add to this day's growing total that on the left hand gatepost a marble crow, ten times life-size, was pulling hard on the cast-iron figure of a worm, as though trying to free it from the stone of the gatepost. On the right, a marble owl, equally large, was holding down an iron rat with its claws and pecking at it, its beak drilling into the unfortunate creature's side.

'I know we're rather passing time until the homecoming is over,' I said, 'but actually this place is the only obvious draw for strangers. Hugh had heard of it after all.'

'Is it a proper museum?' Alec said. 'Volunteers from the SWRI and shilling tickets?'

'I've no idea,' I replied. 'If so, I hope it's open. Christmas week, it might well not be.'

As we rounded the corner of the drive and got our first glimpse of Lump House, though, sitting there framed by the black pines on the edge of the cliff with the endless dark sea and sky just beyond, all thoughts vanished of lady volunteers and shilling tickets torn from a roll.

It was a Georgian house, bigger than a manse, smaller than a mansion. A manor house it would have been called in Northamptonshire, where gentlemen's residences of just this size abound. It had the moderately run-down look of many houses these days, when gardeners are in short supply and owners try to get another winter out of their paint and rooftiles, but it was far from decrepit: the windows were sparkling clean, the gutters and downpipes free from rust and water stains, and the gravel only slightly mossy and not beset with dandelions, which spoke to someone's vigilance if not his purse.

Besides, one hardly noticed the house itself and might have overlooked much more in the way of neglect and disrepair, for on the gravel sweep was a remarkable sight. The carnivals of Buenos Aires, the *processiones* of Italian mountain towns and the circuses of jolly old England had been stirred together, dumped in front of Lump House and left there.

There were Brobdingnagian figures cut of out thin planks of wood, painted every colour in the paint box with more gusto than care and propped up on buttresses, to peel and fade in the Scotch weather as they had clearly been doing for years now.

There were dragons which might have been dinosaurs, if anyone is really clear about the distinction; enormous birds of unlikely hue which might have been dragons, for the painting on their sides was as unlike scales as it was feathers; and, largest and most fearsome of all, sea creatures which might well have been demons for they were fiery red and pulsing instead of the cool blue and green one expects on the ocean floor.

Finally, amongst the creatures and painted with the same slapdash hand were signs galore: Welcome to Searle's Circus of Wonders. Enter Our Realm of Wondrous Bounty. Marvel at Gifts of Loving Abundance. And in just as vivid a hand: Ring Bell and Wait.

We rang and could make out the muffled clank of a cracked bell deep in the innards of the house but after a full minute, which is quite long enough on an Aberdeenshire doorstep, nothing more. Alec took a couple of steps back and scanned the front of the house in the way that people do when a door remains unanswered, as though he were about to scale the walls and gain admittance through a bedroom window.

'We could try round the back,' I said, but he held up a finger and leaned in and, as I joined him, at last we heard footsteps pattering towards us.

I arranged my face, glad that the sea-monsters and dragons were behind me, for every time I glanced at them I could feel a frown begin to form on my brow, and waited to be greeted by the maid; those footsteps did not sound like a butler or footman.

When the door opened, the individual who stood there was no butler nor footman indeed, but was certainly not a maid either; in fact, he was only moderately less outlandish than the painted giants on the drive.

He was very small and a little crooked, not precisely hunch-backed – one thought of Rumpelstiltskin rather than King Richard – but certainly far from hale. He was dressed in a kilt of sombre dark tartan and a bed jacket of pale blue wool, which he wore like a coat, that is to say on top of a checked flannel shirt, waistcoat with watch-chain and what looked at first glance like a regimental tie in a Windsor knot. On his spindly little legs were black woollen long-stockings and evening slippers of ancient pedigree, cracked patent boat-like things, twelve inches long and as pointed as witches' hats which he held onto his little feet by passing more of the striped silk I had taken for regimental honours under his instep, and tying it in a bow on top. On his head was a velvet smoking cap with a tassel which clattered against his spectacle frames as he bowed to us. Upon looking closely I was arrested to find that in fact it was the claw of a bird, wizened and black with age, bound onto the tassel-rope of his cap with a cord the way that straws are bound to a broomstick.

'Durban Searle welcomes you to Searle's Realm of Bounteous Wonder,' he said. 'Welcome, welcome, welcome.' Then he stood back and swept one of his surprisingly long arms in a gracious gesture, finishing with a flourish. Alec and I, trying not to look at one another, trotted inside and I made a promise to myself that I should give Hugh credit at long last for steering me towards true diversion after a lifetime of worthy dullness.

'Are you open, Mr Searle?' Alec said.

'We are never closed,' said the little man. 'The wonder of taxidermis is in no small part the way that our friends never tire. They are always ready to delight you.'

'Your friends?' I said. Mr Searle gave another enormous sweep, this time with both arms, and finished with his head bowed like a conductor at the end of a symphony. That smoking cap had to be held on with pins for it did not budge an inch as his chin snapped down to rest on his chest. I dragged my eyes away from him and looked around.

Gilverton is, as are many of the houses of my friends, fairly well-off for stuffed corpses. Even at home in my childhood there were foxes in the dining-room, icicle-toothed and button-eyed, but Scotch houses are in a class of their own. Hugh had stags a-plenty, not to mention Sir Gilver, the salmon of his life, but neither my house nor any I had ever seen could hold a candle to what had been wrought here on this cliff top.

There were the requisite stags, does and fawns on the walls, as well as a tiger-skin on the floor and a polar bear standing to attention at the bottom of the stairs. This much was unremarkable in any house where the gentleman had gone on a grand tour in his hey-day. There were also two lions on the landing and a table with elephant's legs, suggesting that someone in the family was either a fairly good shot or had parted with cash to a native. Then matters got a little strange. There was an eagle clinging to the chandelier above us with its wings spread and, all around the cornicing, a parade of rats and squirrels were frozen in their capers. A badger with two cubs was scuttling along, close to the wall opposite the door as though it were a hedgerow, and on the mantelpiece seven hedgehogs had been arranged in a kind of tableau of poses from one rolled in a ball at one end to another standing on its little hind legs with its forepaws in the air at the other.

'Remarkable,' said Alec.

'Come this way,' said Mr Searle and pattered off along the side of the staircase. Alec and I hurried after him, glancing into the rooms as we passed and seeing a confusing jumble of images: horses at a billiards table, pigs in evening clothes dining on wax food served by liveried sheep. I was looking over my shoulder at the astonishing sight of an octopus hanging in mid-air from invisible threads when I all but fell over little Mr Searle, who had stopped walking.

'Searle's Realm of Bounteous Wonder,' he repeated and stood holding the handles of a pair of double doors.

'What was all that then?' said Alec.

'Oh, that,' said Mr Searle. 'That's just our bit of fun. *This* is our life's work.' He cocked his head. 'And here comes my brother now. We shall show you round together.'

'Durban?' said a voice.

'Guests, Warwick,' said our host. We waited and in a moment, around the bend in the passageway, came the other brother Searle. He was as far from being the second one in a matching pair as could fairly be imagined. Although he shared his brother's colouring, with pale blue eyes and the purplish-pink cheeks got either from weather or whisky, this new brother Searle was tall, straight-backed despite his age, and dressed impeccably in those orange-green hairy tweeds of which Hugh had a limitless supply and which even Alec took up once he moved to Perthshire for good. The one odd note in the costume was the thick linen apron in which Warwick Searle was swathed from neck to knee, but it went along with the tray he carried, which was also swathed in linen, to hide whatever it bore. Since this man was a taxidermist, I turned my mind resolutely away from the contents of the tray and from whatever the linen apron might be keeping off his tweeds too.

'Here to see the exhibits?' said this new Mr Searle, casting a suspicious eye over all three of us.

'We are indeed,' I said. 'My husband sent us, saying they were not to be missed. He was here as a boy and never forgot it.'

'Ah, we've been busy since then,' said little Durban Searle. 'It would be well worth a second trip. And when we've finished what we're working on now, a third!'

'Sherry in the library afterwards?' said the new arrival. Temperance did not extend along the beach and up the cliff-path it seemed. 'I shall meet you there once I'm finished with these.'

He nodded to the tray and swept off.

'Searle's Realm of Bounteous Wonder,' said Durban for the third time and this time he unlatched the handles and swung the doors wide. We were both holding our breath but at first it seemed not half as bad as dining pigs served by sheep. There was a kind of ante-room, or broad passageway lined with small exhibits arranged on stands. A kitten orchestra, a courtroom of finches and sparrows, a squirrels' cricket match; they were rather grisly, but anyone who suffered through a Victorian childhood has seen worse.

At the end of this corridor, however, where evidently a wall had been knocked out to join the original house onto a new wing, we entered Searle's Circus of Wonders proper and it was beyond remarkable. For one thing, it was huge, not so much a wing as a warehouse, and thinking back to how close the cliff edge was I wondered if we were now standing on some kind of cantilever arrangement built out over thin air. I clenched every muscle, trying to weigh less, in case we were.

The size of the undertaking was not the only or even the greatest surprise, however. As one penetrated deeper and deeper into the Searles' kingdom one could feel a shriek gathering inside and it was never quite possible to know whether it was a shriek of laughter or terror, or some lunatic mixture of the two. The banner across the first doorway, painted in the same manner as the advertisements on the drive, proclaimed in letters two feet high: The Garden of Bounteous Wonder. Inside was no more and no less than the same. It was Eden. There were the fish of the sea and the winged fowl of the air and every creeping thing that creepeth upon the earth. And in the midst of it all, coiling around every inch of the place – which had to be quite twenty feet deep and forty feet long – was a serpent; an endless, undulating serpent. Alec stepped closer and studied it, tiptoeing along its length and scrutinising it.

'Seventeen,' said Durban. 'And you can't see the joins. Not one!'

'Your work?' said Alec, looking rather sick. The serpent *was* disgusting somehow. It was far worse than the musical kittens, to think of seventeen serpents joined head to tail.

'My brother,' said Durban. 'I did the tree.' He gestured proudly to another flat wooden puppet of a thing like the monsters in the driveway. 'And this.'

'What?' said Alec, for Durban appeared to be pointing at an undistinguished bit of the backcloth

'It's before the Fall, you see,' he said, busying himself with a little cleat set into in the wall. 'No fig leaves.' After a minute's work, he had unwound a string from the cleat and began to pull it. Up rose a curtain disguised by being painted in the

57

same pattern of leaves and flowers as the backdrop around it. 'But we've been rather clever and preserved all the decencies.'

Behind the curtain were two wooden figures, painted a shade of bright pink as though they had just stepped out of hot baths, and with faces picked out in such crude daubs of colour that they looked like circus clowns at the end of a long day, smeared black eyes and smeared red mouths. Indecent, I should have said, to the point of blasphemy. On the other hand, Eve's upper body *was* covered by luxuriant tresses of hair and, in front of both figures, lower down, there *were* two artfully placed coils of the endless serpent.

I heard Alec make a snuffling noise followed by a whinnying noise and I knew that there was no help to be had from him.

'Very impressive,' I said, as I fought to regain my composure.

'And if you'll follow me,' said Durban, 'across the way is the Ship of Bounteous Mercy. Two of everything. Absolutely everything. And there is no need to fear, dear lady, for Noah and his wife and Shem, Ham and Japheth are all in robes.'

By the time we had gained the library and the tray of sherry Warwick Searle brought to us there, I was in dire need of a glassful. The library, thankfully, was not too dreadful, with only some rather tame Victorian songbirds under domes of glass. Although it pierced one's heart a little to see the very tiniest of them, the wrens and linnets, they were a world away from the seventeen serpents in one, and the horror of the ark where the Searles had decided to increase the charm of the display by choosing not just pairs of animals but pairs of baby animals: soft-eyed little elephants and downy little bear cubs.

'Aren't they sweet?' Durban had asked.

'Adorable,' Alec had replied with no laughter in his voice at all.

'Now, you must just imagine that I am a parlourmaid,' said Warwick as he set the tray down and poured three glasses. His brother was to have milk in a mug. 'Since our dear Helen is having an afternoon free. I trust you enjoyed the Realm?'

It was odd to imagine that they ran this great tomb of a place with just one girl, dear or no, but when I thought of what my housemaids would make of dusting rats and combing the coats of dead kittens, I supposed they were lucky to have even her.

'It's quite remarkable,' I replied, unable to find another word. 'You are the taxidermist, your brother told us.'

'Durban is too modest,' said Warwick. 'We work together in the initial stages. I do most of the finishing. I do not have Durban's way with a paint brush so it makes sense to arrange matters that way.'

He was either tremendously loyal or completely blind and since he could not, presumably, stuff those pairs of infant hippos and alligators and the rest of it we had just seen without a keen visual flair, I concluded that he loved his brother and put up with the daubing. Alec's interest, naturally, had been caught by quite another part of the speech.

'The initial stages,' he said. 'I've never seen anyone stuff anything. I don't suppose your workshop is open as well as your tableaux?'

Warwick Searle smiled gently and just as gently shook his head.

'I'm afraid not, Mr Osborne,' he said. 'We have in the past allowed spectators but it's not a pretty sight and guests fainting can be rather a distraction.'

'I got used to putrefaction in the trenches,' Alec said.

'Oh, there's no putrefaction,' said Warwick. 'We don't let anything of that sort happen.'

I wondered how they could help it, for the carcass of a zebra, say, could surely not arrive in Aberdeenshire all that quickly after the animal dying in its native land. Perhaps they waited for zoos to supply them but could any competent zoo have two babies of every species conveniently dying together? One would imagine not.

'What is it you're working on now?' I asked. A great draught of their excellent sherry had revived me.

'We haven't decided what to call it yet,' said Durban, beaming behind the moustache of milk he wore after draining his glass.

'Durban names the exhibits,' said Warwick with a smile.

I smiled back at him. There was not so much of a flicker of irritation. If I were a taxidermist and my skill – macabre as it might be – was made a mockery of by garish signs and ridiculous titles, I would be hard-pressed not to sigh, but Warwick Searle merely leaned forward and handed his brother a handkerchief to wipe the milk away, saying nothing.

'It's an out-of-the-way spot here,' Alec said.

'And yet you found us,' said Warwick.

'We are here on other business,' I said. 'Collecting folklore from the fisherfolk.'

'Do you have many visitors besides them?' Alec persisted.

Warwick laughed.

'The locals leave us very severely alone,' he said. 'They're a strait-laced bunch, these Grampian fishermen. Bounteous wonder leaves them quite cold.'

'I expected them to be so, certainly,' I said. 'And yet we witnessed something odd today, didn't we Alec? Now, how can I put this without causing blushes all round?'

I did not have to go too far in my explanation before Warwick Searle stopped me.

'Handfasting,' he said. Alec and I waited politely to hear more. 'I'm surprised you haven't come across it before, Mrs Gilver.' I had told him of my long sojourn in northern parts. 'Perhaps it doesn't reach as far south as Perthshire. Yes, handfasting – it's an ancient tradition. A man and woman are betrothed one to the other and if, at the end of a year, things look fair to be fruitful they marry. If, in contrast, there is no sign of . . .' here he waved a delicate hand '. . . then the knot is cut and each is free to try again.'

'Fair to be fruitful,' Alec repeated. 'I see.'

'And this chugs along hand-in-hand with the Presbyterian Church, does it?' I said. I was astonished, truth be told.

'Oh, quite amicably,' said Warwick Searle. 'Needs must. A fisherman relies on his sons and it would be a disaster to be bound to a woman who could not provide them.' I felt myself bristle a little and Warwick Searle must have noticed it too. 'In their eyes, my dear Mrs Gilver. In their simple view of the world.'

'Very practical,' Alec said. 'And very surprising. I thought fisherfolk were quite the most superstitious sorts ever born. Luck and fate and portents as far as the eye could see. It's an eye-opener to hear of them being so down-to-earth about something.'

'They are, as a rule,' Warwick said. He bestowed a smile on Alec and then on me. 'As you must know only too well being scholars of folklore. What an odd thing that your studies never introduced the handfast to you, eh?'

'We are philologists properly,' I said with an attempt at haughty grandeur.

'And yet,' said Warwick, 'it's such a wonderful old expression too.'

6

'Do you think he's onto us?' asked Alec, when we had left the Searles and were walking back down the drive towards the church.

'Possibly,' I said. 'But we needn't see him again.'

'Agreed,' Alec said. 'I don't think he's germane. Him or his brother.'

'Except in that they're peculiar and anything peculiar, anything out of the ordinary at all, is of interest to us.'

'And shouldn't be hard to winkle out,' Alec said. 'In such a settled place as this.'

We were back at the churchyard wall again and could tell from the scraping and huffing that the sexton was still at work on its other side.

'Hallo there,' I called. 'Hard at it yet?' I had learned quite an array of such remarks to lob at working men, tramping around Gilverton with Hugh in the early days.

This time the head which popped up was that of a child, wild-haired and dark-eyed. She pulled herself up until she was sitting astride the copestones, which must have been terribly chilly despite her thick stockings. I winced to see it.

'It's yourselves again,' said the sexton's head, joining who I presumed was his daughter.

'It's us,' Alec agreed. 'I don't suppose you'll see more strangers than us in a day or even a week, eh?'

'Aye, it's a quiet place right enough,' the sexton said, looking around at the graves and chuckling.

'An odd place to have a museum for that very reason,' said

Alec. 'We wouldn't know about it at all had not a friend of mine come in the summer and then told us about it.'

The gravedigger smiled politely but did not, unsurprisingly, manage to find a reply.

'Perhaps you remember him,' I said, taking over the baton.

'Aye?' said the sexton. 'Fit like was he, like?' I struggled for a translation and then thought about it briefly. When we had first heard of him he had been starting to disintegrate from immersion in salt.

'Average-ish,' Alec said. 'But how many strangers do you see?'

'This summer past there?' said the gravedigger. 'That summer just by?' Then he and his little daughter exchanged a look.

'We had strange men coming out our ears this last summer by, did we not, Nesta?'

'Aye, tons,' said the wild-haired child in a lusty tone. It appeared that Warwick Searle had been too modest about the number of pilgrims who came to view the Bounteous Wonder.

'All together in a crowd?' I asked. 'I think you said your friend was alone, Alec, didn't you?'

'Nah,' said little Nesta. 'One after the other. All summer long. A right queer lot they were, eh Daddy?' I believed that they might be. 'But they're all away home now.'

'Jolly good,' I said, wondering two things: whether one of the queer lot had not made it home at all, and what it would take for the child of this fellow to find a person queer.

'Well, we shall leave you to your labours,' Alec said.

The onshore wind had, as I had feared, brought the squalling rain in from the bay to lash the land. As we left the cover of the trees and struck out across the clearing the wind plastered my hat against my head, my hair against my face and my coat against my legs, while the rain ran in streams down my stockings until my feet squelched in my shoes. Alec made the trip down the cliff path with one hand clamping his hat onto his head, making me grateful for the secure anchoring of my cloche even if it left my face and fringe open to ruination. When at last we were in the scant shelter of the overhang, our feet back on the gritty sand, he finally let go and shook his arm, grimacing.

'I've got a pint of water up my sleeve,' he said. 'What a day!'

It seemed indeed as though we were the only ones still abroad in it. As we walked along the shore road – the seatown road as the locals called it – close to the cottage walls to avoiding the slippery edge ten feet away, we could see inside the houses lit lamps, families gathered around the returned men, pipes being smoked, broth being stirred, all in the hazy glow of condensation over the windows.

Alec stopped and peered in at one place, cupping his eyes.

'They look a friendly lot to me,' he said. 'I'll bet we could crash the party without anyone turning a hair.'

'I'm not ready,' I said. 'I need an evening's preparation and so do you.'

He sighed but stepped away from the vision of warmth and comfort and began trudging again.

'And look,' I said. 'We're not the only ones out and about after all.' Ahead of us a door had slammed and a figure, hunched into an overcoat and with his hat pulled down even harder than Alec's, began to walk briskly towards us.

'Miserable day,' I said as we met. It was another useful phrase I had picked up from Hugh.

'Hallo!' said the figure, tipping his head to look at us from under his hat brim. When he transferred his leather Gladstone bag from his right to his left hand to allow him to greet Alec I realised we had come upon the doctor.

'You must be the strangers who're asking all the questions,' he said. His tone was affable enough, but his words might have been picked especially to unsettle us. We had hardly started and if this was the consensus already, we might be doomed.

'We're folklorists,' said Alec. 'Alec Osborne, and this is my sister, Mrs Gilver.'

'Dr Trewithian,' replied the doctor. 'Folklorists, you say?'

'Philologists,' I added, with relish. I did so enjoy that word.

'You're surely a long way from home,' said Alec, 'with that name.' It added a wonderful Henry Higgins-ish touch to our *bona fides*, I thought, although he ruined it a bit by adding: 'I'm a Dorset man myself.'

'All the way from Dorset for the Banffshire folklore?' said Dr Trewithian. 'Had enough of ashen faggots and bound beating, eh?'

'Well, indeed,' said Alec, nodding vehemently.

'Not much chance of a Filly-loo in these parts.'

'Hah!' said Alec.

The doctor stepped closer, looked hard at Alec and then at me.

'*I wander in the ways of men, alike unknowing and unknown*,' he said. Then he stepped back and smiled. 'None of my business what you're up to, I suppose.' Alec swallowed, leaving it to me to try to regain some of our standing.

'We thought this place seemed perfect for our purposes,' I declared. 'So very settled and so very intermarried. Just the spot to find all manner of survivals. But we've only been here a day and all we hear of is visiting strangers. It's worse than the wireless when strangers come and dilute the splendid old dialect, you know.'

'Strangers?' said the doctor.

'I daresay you've spread the odd bit of Cornish yourself,' I went on.

'I?' said the doctor, surprised enough to unhunch his shoulders and let a squall of rain in at his neck. He shook himself before he went on. 'I'm the last one who'd want outsiders descending,' he said. 'It's that bally minister you want to speak to about strangers, dear lady. Not me. You'll forgive me if I don't raise my hat in leave-taking, won't you? Such a filthy day.'

With that, he stepped to the side and disappeared into the shadows of one of the lanes as quickly and completely as a mouse into its hole.

'Gone like a rat up a pipe,' said Alec, even more prosaically. 'What an unnerving individual!'

'He didn't think much of our story,' I said. 'What was all that about faggots and beating?'

Alec shrugged. 'I didn't expect to have to display a working knowledge of the south-west this far up in the north-east. If we run into him again I'll say my interest developed after I'd left and I've never been back.'

'And what about me?' I said. 'If I'm your sister then I'm from Dorset too and presumably I stayed put there until my wedding?'

'You could be a graduate, Dandy,' said Alec. 'You could pass yourself off as a blue-stocking.'

'I wouldn't dare pass myself off as anything around Dr T,' I said. 'I think we should stay away from him, don't you?'

We had at last reached one of the lane-ends which led, albeit by a meandering route, to the Three Kings and it was with great thankfulness that we left the shore road and the endless buffeting wind behind.

'He said an interesting thing, though,' Alec pointed out, stopping to wipe his face with his handkerchief and resettle his hat at a less extreme angle, the better to see where he was going. 'That we need to speak to the minister about strangers.'

'Oh, that,' I said. 'Well, yes. That's certainly what he *wanted* us to think about, I daresay. But it was what he let slip about outsiders that interests me.'

Alec pondered for a minute and then let out a low whistle. 'You're right,' he said. 'Why wouldn't a country doctor

66

want "outsiders descending"? You'd think he'd welcome a bit of novelty.'

'And why would any doctor not from these parts choose to come here in the first place? Did he marry a local?' I said, shivering as we emerged onto the Main Street and stepped over a gushing rill of rainwater which was coursing along the dip in the cobbles. Alec did not answer. He grabbed my arm and pulled me into the shadow of the baker's shop doorway.

'Look,' he breathed and pointed along the road to the Three Kings, where the front door had just opened to allow the exit of a tall dark figure. Just as the tweeds, cloak and Gladstone bag had proclaimed Trewithian to be a doctor, the black garb of this individual, from the shallow-brimmed hat to the narrow shining shoes, as well as the spindly umbrella he was just opening, shouted to the world that this was a man of the cloth.

'It's the bally minister,' Alec breathed. 'That's a piece of luck.' He strode forward hailing the man. I followed him.

'Dreadful day to be out and about,' Alec said. 'I don't suppose your umbrella will be of much use, sir, when you get down to the shore road.'

'Thankfully,' said the minister, 'I am bound for home.' He pointed his half-rolled umbrella away from the sea at an angle of forty-five degrees. Following it, we saw, high above the jumble of cottages and lanes, a stark grey manse on top of the hill.

'I'm glad to hear it,' I said. 'Poor you, having to stir at all.'

'Whenever my flock needs me,' said the minister.

'I trust Miss Clatchie is well,' I said. 'Oh! Do excuse me. Of course you can't say a thing.'

'Miss Clatchie is quite fine,' said the man. 'She is her usual self.' This seemed a contradiction but I simply smiled and held out my hand.

'Mrs Gilver,' I said. 'And this is my brother, Mr Osborne.'

'Oh yes,' said the minister. 'I've heard all about you.

Reverend Lamont, at your service. But you'll be Anglicans, I suppose.'

'We've just been hearing about you too,' said Alec. 'And if your sermons draw crowds to this lonely spot, then I shall look forward to hearing you.'

'Crowds?' said the reverend. 'Who's this that's been saying that?'

'Well, not to say crowds, exactly,' I put in, 'but we heard that you bring strangers to town, Reverend Lamont.'

'You've been misinformed, I'm afraid,' said the minister and he shook his umbrella. I am sure his purpose was simply to emphasise his point but he made no apology for the other consequence: the showering of Alec and me with large drops of cold water. 'It's my "opposite number" who brings the strangers.'

'I see,' I said. It was a precursor to a question I had not quite formed but I did not get to ask it, for the minister carried on, stepping quite close to us and speaking softly.

'Strangers,' he said again. *'We do hear them speak in our tongues the wonderful works of God.* Good day.'

Alec and I, despite the rain, stood for quite a few moments looking after him. Alec was the first to speak.

'What?' he said.

'Do you suppose his opposite number is a Catholic priest? Is there such a creature here?'

'He might mean the doctor,' said Alec. 'That's how my mother always referred to the medic and the parson in the village. "That pair," she used to say.'

'So did mine,' I replied. Then with a laugh: 'So do I! Neither of them likes it. Let's get inside, Alec, before we're washed away.'

'Let's,' Alec said. 'And I've thought of something to do when we get there.'

'Oh?'

'We've been chumps, Dandy. The obvious place to look for strangers is right here at the town's only hotel.'

'Of course,' I said. 'A register.'

We knocked, waited, heard hurried footsteps descending and eventually gained entrance to the fortress of the Three Kings ready to prostrate ourselves about our wet clothes and grovel to be allowed further than the doormat; but Miss Clatchie surprised us.

'Fine, fine, sort yourselves however,' she said and then beetled off upstairs again. We heard a door bang and then there was silence.

'Odd,' I said, glancing at my wristwatch. 'Perhaps she has a wireless up there and is engrossed.'

'Let's make the most of her inattention,' said Alec, and stepped over to the hall table, where indeed there was a long slim book inside a leatherette cover. He swiped it up and slipped it into his inside coat pocket.

'I only hope Miss Clatchie doesn't show us the door for borrowing it,' I said.

'It'll be back before she knows it's gone,' Alec said. 'Besides, it's worth taking the risk for the treasure within. Any single men last summer shall be subjected to the closest scrutiny.'

'How exactly shall we scrutinise them?' I asked him. 'We're here, and if they stayed in the hotel they're clearly from somewhere else.' Alec thought for a moment and then grinned.

'Grant,' he said. 'I'll set Grant on them.'

I could not help but grin back. Grant, my lady's maid, had taken to detecting with abandon the previous year on a case in the Borders and since then had become more and more Gilver and Osborne's factotum and less and less Mrs Gilver's maid. Everyone was the winner in the arrangement. We had a secretary; Grant had more interesting work; and I had respite from her attentions in matters of wardrobe and hair arrangement, just when the simplicity of modern fashions had begun to make a lady's maid a nonsense and Grant's assiduous nature a burden to me. Her assiduity would be welcome here for if anyone could devise a way of ringing up strangers and asking if members of their family had headed north on holiday and never been heard of again, Grant could.

We parted to change into dry clothes and then Alec rejoined me, although he hesitated on the threshold of my room, nonplussed I suppose by the acres of linoleum and the singular lack of armchairs.

'I don't suppose that door leads to a sitting room,' he said, nodding at it, entertaining just the hopes that I had.

'Afraid not. I think it's Miss Clatchie's room,' I said, 'judging by how startled she was when I tried the door.'

'Should we keep our voices down?' said Alec.

I shook my head.

'She doesn't seem to spend much time in there,' I said. 'Maybe it's a shrine to her dear dead mother or something.'

Alec threw himself down on the counterpane and cracked the slim leatherette spine with a sigh of deep contentment.

'Jot down these addresses, Dandy, will you? Grant is more used to your handwriting than mine so it makes sense for you to be the amanuensis.'

I said nothing, but only thought my private thoughts about how often it made sense for me to do whatever task Alec did not fancy.

'Mr and Mrs Thos Hood,' Alec began. 'A week last July. The Misses Ernespie – no, scratch them, no men with them. Good Lord!'

He sat bolt upright, making the headboard bang against the wall. I sat bolt upright too and broke off the lead of my propelling pencil. There had been the most unearthly and mystifying noise on the other side of the locked door: a squealing, groaning shriek, somewhere between young pigs and bagpipes.

'What in the name of God was that?' cried Alec.

'Certainly not a wireless,' I said.

We waited, eyes wide, to see if it would sound again,

wishing at least on my part that the notion of a departed Mrs Clatchie had not been aired. The silence went on and on, and eventually Alec sat back, I clicked out more lead and we resumed.

'So scratch the Misses Ernespie,' he said again, and turned a page. 'The Rev. Murray, Mrs Murray, Miss Murray and Master Murray. Nasty to think of a clergyman ending—'

He was interrupted by a peremptory knock on the door. There was not a moment to say come in or go away, much less to swing legs off Miss Clatchie's good bed and get shoes off Miss Clatchie's good linens, before the door opened and she stood there.

'Is that my book?' she breathed in a kind of strangled yelp.

'Forgive us, Miss Clatchie,' Alec said. 'We—'

I would have been very interested to know what excuse he might come up with, for I had drawn a blank. There was not a single respectable reason I could imagine to have purloined a hotel register and be copying down names and addresses from it. Unfortunately, Miss Clatchie interrupted.

'I only ask for guests to register if I want to keep in touch,' she said, putting us right in our place. 'For Christmas cards and to exchange letters about valued visitors coming back.' The implication was that when she shut her door behind us and all our traps she would be glad never to lay eyes on us again.

'And what can I do for you, Miss Clatchie?' I asked in my grandest voice. Alec might be using her bedclothes ill, but she had only seen him because she barged into my bedroom and I was not pleased about it.

'A telephone message for you, Mrs Gilver,' she said.

'Oh, do you have a phone?' said Alec, flicking a glance at the register and planning, no doubt, to dispense with Grant's services and do the sleuthing himself.

'A telephone message brought over by Mr Muir from the Post Office,' Miss Clatchie said.

'I didn't hear him knock,' I said, still endeavouring to put her in her place.

'He came while you were out,' said Miss Clatchie. 'This is the first chance I've had to pass the message on. If you'd let me.' Her glare told me that I had failed.

'Ah, yes,' I said. 'You've been busy in the room next door, haven't you?' I was partially gratified and partially ashamed to see a flush, almost purple against her very fair skin, rise up from her collar and spread all the way to the start of her wispy hair.

'It's a message from a Mr Silvermeadow,' she said. 'I'm sure that was the name. "Your mutual friend can stand on his own two feet."'

'Is that it?' I said. 'Mr Silvermeadow? What friend?'

'That's all I'm privy to,' said Miss Clatchie. She really did have a talent for disapproval.

'Right. Well. Thanks,' I said. She took the register out of Alec's hands, swept the room with a look as if checking for cigarette burns or bottles of rum and then scuttled out.

'Did that make any sense to you?' I asked, but Alec shushed me. He was writing something on a scrap of paper.

'Thos. Hood, Hill Street, Inverness,' he said. 'And Murray of Banchory. Grant should be able to find them without too much trouble.' He looked up. 'What were you saying?'

'Why couldn't she give us the message when she let us in?'

'Presumably because she had to rush off and do whatever made that god-awful noise,' Alec said.

'Yes, but what was it? Did you see the way she blushed? This place is beginning to give me the creeps,' I said. 'Between Reverend Lamont, Dr Trewithian and Miss Clatchie, not to mention those Searles!'

'They are all a little odd,' said Alec, 'but at least the telephone message is clear.'

'Is it?'

'Of course. It made perfect sense.'

'Well, our mutual friend must be Mr Birchfield,' I said. 'Is this Silvermeadows chap warning us off? Should we ring Mr Birchfield up and tell him?'

'Oh Dandy,' said Alec in his kind voice; the one which makes me want to kick him. 'Silvermeadow *is* Birchfield. It was a code. Mr Birchfield couldn't use his real name in Gamrie where everyone is in his employ.'

'Well, how very Boy's Own Adventures-ish,' I said crossly, ashamed of not having seen through the ruse. 'What did the message mean?'

'Our mutual friend is obvious enough,' Alec said. 'And now he's got two feet to stand on. The second-to-last barrel has evidently turned up. Well, well, well. One to go.'

7

If I had been given free rein to order up a day for snooping, I could not have dreamt a better one than the Tuesday before a Banffshire fisherfolk's wedding. On this day the men had it rather easy, only required to visit the barber, pay the minister, and stand on the harbour side gazing out to sea and smoking, but the women of the village, the brides-to-be, their mothers, aunts and elder married sisters, had important work to do.

We heard of it first in the Post Office, as soon as it opened at nine o'clock the following morning. Alec had composed a letter of instruction to Grant and was keen to send it off, worried that the gathering storm might close the roads and disrupt His Majesty's mail.

'Aye, it could come to that one way or another,' said Mr Muir, the postmaster, when Alec voiced his concerns. He craned forward from his little cubicle and peered out of the ten square inches of his shop window not obscured by notices and bills. He was a dapper little man who had, accidentally or by design, affected exactly the same ogee curve in his moustaches and in the two wings on either side of the central parting in his hair. His rounded celluloid collar made a third the same. 'Thon brae's no gift when it snows, but the floods on the top road are just as bad when the rain comes hard.'

'It's hard to know which to hope for then,' I said.

'Aye, you're right. But it's the wind'll take your roof off and bash a boat to chips whether it throws snow or rain when it blows.'

'Perhaps we should take the car up to the top and find somewhere to stash it, Dandy,' Alec said.

'Not a bad idea,' said Mr Muir. 'You can always get up on foot, for there's rails and ropes and all sorts, but if we get a good frost the bairns'll have the brae like a sheet of glass with their sliding.'

'Monkeys,' I said. 'I'm surprised they're allowed to.'

'Ocht, wedding week,' said Mr Muir. 'Nobody's going anywhere. Nobody'll be in or out to next Monday now.'

'We'll not have time!' All three of us jumped, upon discovering that we had been joined by a fourth. It was one of the gutting quines from the harbour side the day before, a magnificent figure, tall and broad with such a short neck that her bosom seemed to swell from under her chin. Without her apron today, she had her jersey sleeves rolled down and was wearing a skirt of navy serge instead of the shapeless bell of heavy sacking. 'I'm just running out to draw my erlin the day and that'll be the last of me out away fa my ma and aunties to Sunday! Are they in, Mr Muir?'

'Aye, they're here, Janet,' said the postmaster. He closed his ledger of stamps and pulled from a shelf below the counter a strong box which he proceeded to open with a key on his watch-chain.

Alec and I edged away politely, understanding that money was about to change hands, but the young woman did not have the reticence of a music hall turn. She took the banknotes Mr Muir handed over, spread them into a cox-comb and used them to fan herself.

'Ach, that's the memory of that Shetland boat away already,' she said and she sprang over to the door, throwing it wide, ignoring the gusts of sleety wind which blew in around the Post Office and the protest from Mr Muir as he tried to hold down half a dozen piles of official papers with just two hands.

'Our erlins are in!' she shouted out into the street. 'Billy! Jackie! Netta! Our erlins are here!'

The news brought a stampede of men and girls through which Alec, I and its instigator fought our way out onto the street.

'I'm sure you worked hard for every penny,' I said, as Janet tucked the sheaf of notes into the neck of her jersey.

'Aye, fine and I did,' she said. 'And now it'll be spent before it's had time to warm me. I'm away to Fordyce's. It's filling the tick the day.'

Alec looked mystified. I took pity on him.

'Tick is credit,' I said. 'Now that it's pay-day and the arlings have been collected, everyone must settle up.'

At that Janet threw back her head and laughed as though she might burst.

'My mammy would have me over her knee, all five foot eight of me,' she said. 'Credit! She'd kill me. Fordyce's is the drapers yon and I'm away to get my doings. If you want to find out all about tick-filling, you come with me.'

'Well, it's odd you should say that,' I put in, scrabbling to re-establish some dignity even as I felt my cheeks flush. 'I certainly would like to spend some time talking to you.'

'Aye, I know,' she said. 'Peggie Ness's mammy telt me you were they "philly-oolies".'

'Philologists,' I said, although her version had a ring to it. '*Who* told you?'

'Mrs Mason.'

'Ah yes,' I said. 'And Peggie is one of her girls.'

'But what is it you want to talk to us about?' said Janet.

'Nothing,' I told her. 'I want to *listen*.'

'Aye well, there's plenty to hear filling the tick,' said Janet. 'Your ears'll be stinging by tea-time, mind. Don't say I never warned you.'

'What about you, Alec?' I said. 'I take it tick-filling is a female endeavour?' Janet snorted.

'I'm going to talk to the coopers,' said Alec. 'Fascinating business, coopering. There's plenty I want to know.' I nodded and said nothing. What he wanted to know was whether barrels were ever filled in private, whether Gamrie barrels were ever sold elsewhere, whether – he had regaled me with this theory over breakfast and was greatly enamoured of it – the work of Gamrie coopers, so distinctive that Mr Birchfield would know it anywhere, could be further categorised into the work of particular families or even (would not this be grand?) individual men. I wished him luck, and my teeth were hardly gritted at all, for I could see what a step forward it would be in the case if we could say that seven barrels made by one Jock McTavish were those whose contents had rattled poor Mr Birchfield so.

It was on account of such wished-for discoveries and not at all to steal Alec's thunder that I broached a similar point with Janet as we climbed a set of steps to the next street where, I presumed, the drapers lay.

'I'm thrilled to be here,' I began. She cocked an eyebrow, since I daresay Gardenstown in December was not thrilling to any of its native sons. 'Such riches. I've only scratched the surface so far – "arling" and "birling" and so on.'

Janet laughed her hearty laugh again and I supposed the demotic phrases must sound rather comical in my voice, which had not a trace of an accent to go along with them.

'My brother will no doubt hear a great many cooper's terms,' I persisted, 'but you must have just as many, you "gutting quines".'

'For barrels?' said Janet. We had arrived at the drapers, which was still in darkness, with paper blinds drawn down inside the display window and the outside door tight shut, milk on the step. 'Jeannie Fordyce is not a lark,' Janet said, pounding hard on the wood, 'but she'll aye open up if you give her a good dunt and keep at it.' Her fist thundered again and she raised her voice to be heard over it. 'We've no special names for barrels.'

'No, no,' I said 'But perhaps for your tools – the knives and so on, and for methods.'

77

'Methods?'

'Patterns of herrings?'

She looked blankly at me.

'Are there different arrangements perhaps?' I said. 'Spirals? Starbursts? These must surely have names?'

'Starbursts of herring?' said Janet. 'Here she's coming now.' I had not heard any movement inside but I took her assurances and was glad of them. Even on that narrow street protected by roofs all around, it was bitingly cold.

'Or do you just lay them in any old how?' I said, beginning to wish I had not begun.

'In the barrel?' she said. 'Aye, we just pack them in, like. There's no spirals or ocht.'

'Perhaps I was thinking of quilts,' I said lamely. 'Herringbones, you know. Or fair isle jerseys. It's rather confusing.'

'Ocht, well, quilts,' said Janet. At last the door was opening. I could hear locks turning and chains rattling. A bleary face looked around the edge of it.

'It's yourself, Janet Guthrie,' said a voice after a throat-clearing cough. 'Away you come in then. That's it started, eh?'

It certainly did seem so; before the double doors were opened and we were invited inside by Miss Fordyce in her hair curlers and tartan dressing gown, another batch of herring lasses had appeared at the top of the steps, clutching their arle money and jostling to enter the draper's and spend it "before it had warmed them".

At the back of the little crowd was, however, an unexpected figure: Warwick Searle, looking almost as outlandish as his brother had the day before, in a lambskin coat of ancient vintage and a deerstalker hat. The lasses who entered with him fell back, all in agreement that such a grand individual should go straight to the front of the queue.

'Did my order come in, Miss Fordyce?' he asked, sweeping back the skirts of his coat and rummaging in a pocket for his wallet.

'It did that, Mr Searle,' said Miss Fordyce. She seemed unperturbed by a member of the county – an unconventional member, but county unmistakably – catching her in her dressing gown, but perhaps she knew that Durban Searle spent his days in a blue knitted bed jacket – perhaps she had even sold him the wool. In any case, it was wool she was selling his brother today. She took a handful of white balls from where she had set them aside and began to make a parcel of them, not so much as patting at her hair curlers in the way that self-consciousness causes us to do.

'Now do you have fine pins, Mr Searle?' she enquired. 'This is three-ply and it needs a gey skinny pin to knit it up into ocht but a fish-net.'

Warwick Searle paused and considered the point.

'Best throw in a pair,' he said, and drew a ten-shilling note out of his wallet. 'I'll call in after I've been to the baker. Let's not keep these young people waiting.' As he swept them with a look, he noticed me for the first time and blinked.

'Good for you, doing the shopping, Mr Searle,' I said. Ordinarily I would not comment as openly on a person's domestic arrangements as I seemed to be doing, but here in Gamrie where the draper went about in hairpins, the usual requirements of politeness need not apply.

He gave me a calm look, not the slightest tug of a frown at his brows, and yet I knew I had displeased him.

'Very wise,' I added hurriedly. 'It's getting harder and harder to hang onto staff and it's a dreadful day.'

He tipped his hat and left the shop. The herring lasses, to give them their due, managed to wait until the door was closed behind him before they started laughing.

'A right queer pair of buddies them.'

'Are they knitting now? Aye, well I'd not put it past them.'

'They've never got a maid to stay in thon place with all they beasties?'

'I'd run a mile!'

79

'You've seen it then?' I said. 'I stopped in yesterday.'

'And fit did you make of it?' This was the bold Janet.

'Words fail me,' I said, which was met with further gales of laughter and, in boisterous spirits, the lasses fell to their choosing and measuring and counting out of payment again.

I was completely caught up in the fun and fifteen minutes later I found myself carrying a large brown-paper parcel back down to the shore road again to Janet's mother's house, where her aunts and elder sisters were waiting with a kettle on the range and the kitchen table cleared and scrubbed.

'This is Mrs Gilver, Mammy,' Janet said. She showed me to the rocking chair by the fireside, just visible in the gloom of a typical Highland kitchen, where the windows are always so very tiny it is a wonder the masons bother with them at all. The one which provided air and light for the Guthries was perhaps ten inches square and set into a wall ten inches thick. Gas lamps above the range threw a little light down on the dark oilcloth floor and the dark distempered walls, and when Janet untied her parcels and threw the bolts of cloth over the table, I saw that the garish stripes and checks I had found so offensively loud in Miss Fordyce's well-lit little shop with its electric lamps, were rendered mute here in the sort of cottage they were to call home.

'Good day to you, Mrs Gilver,' said Mrs Guthrie, politely enough but with a hint of query in her voice. She was a shrewd-eyed woman, as tall as her daughter but built on different lines, as firm and flat as a board. I surmised that Janet's brawny frame came from her father's side.

'Mrs Gilver's one of they philly-oolies that are here to study us.'

'Oh, you've missed it by fifty years, my doo,' said Mrs Guthrie. 'The old ways are fallen away most sore these modern days, with the newsreels and the railway.' Then she loosed a string of utterly unintelligible speech, no doubt intended to illustrate how cosmopolitan and unexceptional

Gamrie had become. Since I did not understand a word of its structure and could not hazard the foggiest guess as to its content, though, it only reinforced my growing conviction that Gamrie, even amongst Scottish villages, was tacked by a long rope to the very back of beyond.

'I shall make the best of it, Mrs Guthrie,' I said. 'I shall sit here and write everything down and only trouble you for translations when I absolutely have to.'

This seemed to satisfy everyone and the tick-filling began. I had begun to guess at its nature in the drapers' shop and soon saw that I was right. They were making a mattress and some pillows and bolsters, these women; stitching and filling, and indulging as they did so every last bit of bawdiness that such an operation might be expected to spawn.

'I'm stuffing it good and tight this side, Janet,' said one of the aunts. 'Bobby's a fair size of a man and could flatten a skinny mattress before the week's out.'

'It's Janet's side you're needing to stuff harder, Mammy,' said one of the young girls. 'It's her side'll have the most weight gin long, eh?'

Janet laughed and rubbed her middle.

'Aye, I'll be as fat as a June tick before he's home for Easter,' she said.

There had been more handfasting in the Guthrie household, I concluded, and Janet and Bobby 'looked fair to be fruitful'.

'So you're not going back out on the boat then?' I asked.

'Nah, following the herring's not a wife's do,' said Mrs Guthrie. 'Janet'll stay here with the weans now and gin they're up a wee and can help their daddy, Bobby'll not be trailing round neither.'

It took some work to establish the meaning of this, but after five minutes of further questioning I thought I had it. The young men shared boats with their brothers until one of them had a wife and enough children of sufficient age to pick bait and load lines and take his catch to market; then he stayed at home, the brother next in line became the skipper of the herring boat and the next again waited his turn. By the time the youngest brother was allowed to marry and start his own little band of workers the eldest son of the eldest brother was ready to take to the seas in the herring trade and the family's fortunes rolled along in waves. Children, and plenty of them, were the thing.

'Hence the handfasting,' I said, wondering if I were being too bold.

'Aye, true enough, true enough,' said one of Mrs Guthrie's many sisters. 'There's no sense in a quine and a loon joined for life if they're not to be . . . "smiled upon".'

'And the Dear smiles where the Dear will,' said another of the aunts.

There was a silence after she spoke and I took the chance to shift the conversation a little nearer where I needed it to go.

'Absolutely fascinating,' I said. 'Such a wealth of material on weddings. I cannot tell you how interesting it is to me. And . . . ah . . . I suppose that birth and death are just as richly set about with old expressions and ancient ways?'

'We don't care to talk about a birth before the babby's here,' said old Mrs Guthrie. I saw Janet touch her middle again and I nodded, filled with understanding.

'And death?' I asked. 'I suppose when your men folk do such dangerous work, it might not be the done thing to discuss funeral ways either?'

'In the midst of life we are in death,' said Janet's elder sister. 'There's no harm talking it over for you cannot escape it.'

'If you're sure then,' I said. 'If it wouldn't be too morbid to talk of death at such a happy time. What is the tradition in these parts for a funeral?'

'All depends,' said Janet. A better answer could not have been mine.

'Well, let's take an example,' I said. 'Something far enough back for mourning to be over but recent enough for memories to be fresh.' Now I had come to the moment of greatest portent. Now I wanted to sound as casual as ever I had in my life. 'Did anyone die in the village . . . this summer, for instance?'

'This summer when we were all back?' said Janet. 'Nah. Nah.'

'Old Mrs Minty was awfy not well for a bit but she rallied.'

'What about Ina Balloch?' said Mrs Guthrie. I drew breath to make clear I was asking after men, but then stopped myself. For one thing, how could I explain such a restriction on my interest and for another . . . had Mr Birchfield actually said it was a man? He had said it was a corpse and that the larger portions of it were terribly corrupted. He had said that he had looked closely at the extremities. Perhaps we had fallen prey to that habit, as inexplicable as it was offensive, of assuming that everyone was a man until one heard better. I would rather die than ask Mr Birchfield; that much I *did* know.

Before my thoughts had entirely caught up with themselves, Mrs Guthrie was speaking again.

'But she was the year before, wasn't she? I mind her funeral, out on the hill with the seagulls crying. It was beautiful just. But wee Maggie was lapped up in a shawl, not even walking, so it cannot have been the summer just there.'

'So no deaths in the village for more than a year,' I said. 'That's a splendid run of luck.'

The silence which spread after my words was as deep and thick as the mattress the women were stuffing. At first I thought it was the word 'luck' which had done it, for although fisherfolk have more charms and superstitions and sources of luck, ill or fair, about them than the rest of Scottish peasantry combined they might not like to be reminded of it, good God-fearing, church-going, sin-shunning people as they are.

'Aye, well,' said one of the aunties. She pushed away the portion of mattress upon which she was working, rose and came over to the range to pull forward the kettle for tea.

'It wasn't in the village exactly, Mrs Gilver,' she said, softly. She flicked a glance behind her and lowered her voice further. 'One of our youngsters was taken by the sea in the spring there, don't you know.'

'One of your sons?' I said, aghast at myself for having blundered into such a thing.

'Nah, nah, a village lad,' said the woman. 'The laddie Gow. Poor soul. But nothing to do with us.'

This was a different kettle of fish from Ina Balloch and old Mrs Minty who rallied, for these women, laughing and joking and making bedclothes for a wedding night, all had husbands, sons and brothers who set out each morning on the tide with nothing but the grace of God to bring them home again. Naturally the death of one of the fishermen would be a blow to everyone in Gamrie.

'Aye, He moves in mysterious ways,' said one of the nearest women, who had been listening.

Janet Guthrie raised her chin and looked down the length of her nose at us on the other side of the table, like an archer sighting prey along an arrow shaft.

'Will you haud yer wheesht about John Gow?' There was a collective rise and fluttering fall as everyone resettled to their task with greater concentration and with their wheeshts held. I, with nothing to occupy my hands, was the only one left staring back at her, unblinking.

'I was fasted to John Gow three year back but it did not keep,' Janet said. 'And if it had I'd be a widow woman now.'

'That's what I'm saying, Janet,' huffed her aunt. 'It's an ill wind.'

'It's all she's saying, Janet,' said Mrs Guthrie. 'I would not be in Greta Mason's shoes for all the silver in Aberdeen.'

'Mammy, don't!' said Janet Guthrie. 'Have a care.'

'Ach, the meen's nane the waur fur a dug's bark,' said the eldest of the ladies gathered around the table. I had taken her to be Janet's grandmother and the way that her words appeared to settle all discussion confirmed it for me.

'What a wonderful old phrase,' I said, grasping my notebook. 'I wonder if you could explain its meaning to me.'

But this was met with such stony silence that, gobbling over my words in my haste to get them out of me, I tried again.

'Or actually what would be best of all, what we're really supposed to encourage you to do – for proper study, you know – is to tell stories. One falls most easily into one's mother tongue in all of its flowering when one tells a tale.'

'Fit aboot?' said the aunt who had now filled the teapot and was distributing cups and saucers around the waiting women.

'Well,' I said. 'What about . . . a stranger who came to town? Would that give you any ideas? You spend such a lot of time away from home! But tell me a tale of a stranger who came to town when you were last here to see him.'

'Last July that would be,' said Janet.

'Really,' I said, with admirable lack of concern. 'Very well, then. On you go.'

'Aye, there was strangers over the summer for sure,' Mrs Guthrie said. She took a sharp breath and then let it out as a deep chuckle. 'Mind on him as went pestering Phemie Clatchie at the Kings? Oh, he was a tale in himself, was he not?'

My ears pricked up on hearing this and with my notebook balanced on my knee and my teacup abandoned (no sacrifice, for the tea was as thick and dark as Windsor soup) I urged them into as much detail as they could supply, only cursing that I had to blow away a great deal of chaff to glean my little bits of wheat, but I could hardly ask them to talk the King's English while pretending to collect dialectal folklore.

★　　★　　★

85

It was luncheon time, or noon at least, before I left them. I ventured out into the weather again to find that, just as on the previous day, the rain coming inland was winning out against the snow blowing down from the high ground and was showing off more than ever as it did so. I pulled my hat down and turned my coat collar up but was soon soaked through regardless. It did not help that I got hopelessly lost, trotting up and down odd little sets of steps and into blind corners before backing out again, and all the while squelching through the streams of water which coursed down the paths and along their edges. Soon I saw that downwards was the only answer for me too, down to the harbour to get my bearings, despite knowing that the Three Kings was on a higher level than the Guthries' cottage and I should only have to haul myself back up again. I turned resolutely and, like the gathering rivulets and gushing spouts, made my way to the sea.

Out on the harbour side, suddenly, the wind took me quite by surprise and would have blown me off my feet had not an elderly village man gripped me firmly by one arm and kept me upright.

'Thank you,' I cried over the din of the rain, the wind and the high tide booming in the harbour and crashing over its wall. 'Gosh, what a day.'

'Thank the Dear our laddies are home,' said the old man.

I nodded but wet tails of hair in my mouth stopped me giving any more answer before he was on his way again. For a moment I stood there, pressed into the lee of a cottage wall, staring at the heaving boats and beyond them to the swell and crash of the charcoal-coloured sea and the smear of rain which hid the horizon. I am as fanciful as the next woman and as beset by idle dreams – as much the heroine of my own foolish imaginings as anyone who ever watched a steeplechase and felt the horse move under her, watched a ballet and felt her toes crunch against the blocks in her shoes, watched a newsreel of war and felt the cold steel of her rifle as she whooped and charged – but I could not imagine with, even the furthest corner of my fancy, getting into one of those little boats and putting out into that endless stretch of emptiness. Not for a pot of gold and certainly not for herring.

Reluctantly, I left my scrap of shelter and scurried crab-like along the harbour head until I reached the bottom of a lane I recognised from coming down it the day before at Bunty's pace. Even better, looking up from under my hat brim and blowing the water away from my eyes, I saw Alec just half a flight of steps ahead of me, huddled into his overcoat, but bareheaded for some reason, and I hied him to wait for me and show me the way.

'My hat blew off,' he said, ten minutes later. We were in Miss Clatchie's front room in dry clothes and carpet slippers, Alec towelling his head with one of her embroidered hand-towels and I pressing my hair gingerly with another trying to blot the water without fatally compromising my shingle. Grant had set it like toffee on an apple, the way she always does if I venture from home without her. 'I'll be lucky not to catch pneumonia, but it caused a good bit of jollity amongst the men and served as my introduction.'

'An ill wind,' I said.

'But I shall have to buy another. Either take a trip into Macduff in hopes of a gentleman's outfitter or get a toorie bunnet from Ingram's here in town.'

'A toorie bunnet!' I said, laughing. 'Golly, you have been paying attention.'

Alec laughed too.

'I'm sure they're putting it on because they think it's what we want,' he said. 'No one could really speak such nonsense all day every day. I've had to shovel through cartloads of muck to get any sense out of anyone.'

'But having shovelled?'

'Ah, yes. A stranger,' Alec said. 'Last July. Everyone saw him arrive and no one saw him leave. Which is not to say he didn't, of course. But not much gets missed around here and the men did remark upon it.'

'I heard about him too,' I said. 'What did the coopers have to say?' I was confident that my clutch of ladies would have furnished me with more than a group of men, but Alec had been soaked and chilled and deserved the first crack.

'In his seventies, long grey beard, dressed very rough, but paid his passage round from Aberdeen with cash. Dandy, why is your mouth hanging open? It's not pretty.'

'His passage round from Aberdeen on a boat?' I said.

'A few of the men take it in turns to offer excursions to tourists if the fishing is slow,' Alec said. 'The Brothers Gow picked up this old chap on a one-way trip apparently. Dropped him off at the harbour steps and my informants this morning never saw him again. But if you heard tell of him from village women then *someone* must have.'

'Not him,' I said. 'Mine came on the bus from Macduff along with some of Janet Guthrie's aunts who'd been to market. He was in his fifties, a fine figure of a man by all accounts and caused no small outbreak of interest when he got off here in Gamrie. The ladies had him filed away as a suitor to one of the herring lasses – an islander, they reckoned, from his swarthy colouring. And again, as you said, no one witnessed him leaving.'

'Where did he go when he got off the bus?'

'Hah!' I said. 'Now this was interesting. He asked for directions to a rooming house and they sent him here.'

'A single man?' Alec said, his eyes dancing.

'And something happened,' I said. 'Miss Clatchie managed to choke out some of the details in the grocer's shop the next day. But the Guthrie women couldn't tell me this morning for laughing.'

At that moment, we heard the unmistakable sound of Miss Clatchie herself and her luncheon tray approaching. We had learned the day before not to lick our lips with any anticipation and when she appeared in the doorway, it was with a tureen of the same lentil broth as the previous day and the two thin slices of bread with two miniature pats of butter we were beginning to know so well.

I did not catch on immediately to Alec's motives when he leapt to his feet and took the tray out of her hands.

'Thank you, Miss Clatchie,' he said, setting it down on the card table. 'This will be most welcome after our soaking this morning.'

Her eyes flared as she saw the two hand towels.

'I'll take these and press them in the kitchen,' she said, as though we had used a precious item roughly and ill.

'I'm trying to find the best words to tell you something,' Alec said. 'I wouldn't want to alarm you.' Too late, of course. She was alarmed to her core. 'It's just that we've been hearing this morning of that dreadful time you had in the summer.' I was almost sure I heard her eyelids squeak as she opened her eyes wider than she ever had before.

'The . . . the men?' she said.

'One man, anyway,' Alec said. 'The dark-haired gentleman.'

'Dark-*haired*?' said Miss Clatchie and she forgot herself so far as to sink into a chair and leave the two sacred hand-towels crumpled up in a ball on its back rest. 'He was dark-*skinned*, Mr Osborne. He was . . .' she worked her mouth frenziedly as she searched for adequate words. 'He was . . . not from Aberdeenshire.' I might have been able to keep my composure had it not been for the way Alec stretched out a comforting hand and nodded solemnly. As it was, I uttered a shriek and clapped both hands to my mouth. Miss Clatchie only pursed her lips and nodded, taking my cry for shock to match her own.

'He asked for a room,' she said. '*For one night.*' One was

perhaps to take it that a room for one night was practically as bad as those *hôtels de passe* in Paris where they go by the hour. 'Of course, I sent him on his way. And I let John Robb at the police house know he was about.'

'A sensible precaution,' said Alec. 'Did Constable Robb catch up with him?'

'He did not,' declared Miss Clatchie. 'The man vanished. Up to no good, you see.'

'So much for him,' said Alec. 'But you said there were two of them?'

'Not that day, thank the Lord,' Miss Clatchie said. 'It was a week or two later when the next one arrived. He was a Scot, right enough, although Glasgow and with a very rough voice.'

'And . . .' Alec said, which was plenty.

'He asked for a bath!' said Miss Clatchie. I bit my cheeks and even Alec had to pull his face into very severe puckers to keep it under control.

'Every night?' Alec said. 'Or when the hotel was full of guests?'

'No, my dear Mr Osborne,' Miss Clatchie said. I did not miss the epithet. It had taken Alec longer than usual to become 'dear Mr Osborne' to this goose-like female but he had got there in the end. 'You misunderstand me,' she went on. 'He wasn't staying here. He knocked on the door and said he'd heard it was a . . .' she dropped into a whisper '. . . rooming house and he'd heard there were no public baths in the town, so would I, for a shilling, let him have my bathroom for half an hour and grant him the use of a towel!' She snapped her head round at the end of this speech, remembering the two lost lambs she had been distracted from gathering back into her fold. She snatched them up, shook them out, refolded them and hugged them to her. Just as well, because it took all of that time for Alec and I to be sure of mastering our faces and voices.

I ventured to speak. It was my turn.

'How awful,' I said. 'What a cheek! One would think he'd know better how to behave by his age.'

'What age?' said Miss Clatchie.

'Wasn't he an elderly chap with a long grey beard?' I said. Miss Clatchie held the handtowels even tighter.

'A long grey *beard*?' she echoed, almost retching at the thought of it. 'I didn't see *him*, thank the Lord. The one who accosted me about my bathroom – right out there on the front step too! – was a youngster. A *model*.'

'A model what?' said Alec.

'I mean to say, a mannequin,' said Miss Clatchie. 'An artist's mannequin. He said he wanted to be clean from head to toe before he went to his job!' She squeaked and buried her face in the hand-towel then squeaked again – perhaps she smelled Alec's hair tonic – and then sat staring at us out of stricken eyes, breathing as though she had run up a flight of stairs.

'How awful,' I said again. 'An artist's model, standing on the doorstep saying he had to wash before he . . . and asking to use your bath?'

'And my towels,' said Miss Clatchie.

'And is there an artist hereabouts, who paints n— who paints the human form?' asked Alec.

'There are artists,' said Miss Clatchie, much in voice of one reporting that there were maggots. 'There's two of them along at Crovie who live there all year round and there's plenty here as well in the summer. But they paint the sea and the boats mostly.'

I nodded, for it made sense. Why would one make the pilgrimage to this rain-lashed northern shore except if one were a landscape painter? The bathing youth notwithstanding, I imagined it would be easier to find a life model almost anywhere else in the world. So it seemed a safe conclusion that anyone summoning a model here must live in the vicinity.

We pressed Miss Clatchie for directions to the artists of Crovie and then let her go.

'I'd almost be ready to believe she killed him herself and chopped him into pieces,' Alec said. 'Except she'd have had to let him in. And touch him.'

'Poor Miss Clatchie,' I said. 'I do sympathise. A woman alone with strange men knocking at one's door. I shouldn't like it.'

'I suppose not,' said Alec, reluctantly.

'And speaking of a woman alone, Alec,' I went on, rather dreading to, 'something occurred to me. Are we entirely sure that the body in the barrel was a man?'

'What?' said Alec, spluttering. 'Of course we are.'

'Yes, but should we be?' I asked. 'Have we jumped to conclusions?'

Alec was shaking his head. 'I think Mr Birchfield would probably have mentioned it, don't you?'

'If he noticed,' I insisted. 'If he looked closely.' I could feel a blush begin to spread over my cheeks. 'He did say he only looked at the extremities with any real care.'

'The size apart from anything else,' Alec said.

'But some of these gutting quines are quite strapping,' I argued.

'Telephone to him,' said Alec. 'And ask.'

'Or you could,' I said. Alec gave me a look of infuriating smugness.

'I don't need to,' he said. 'I'm perfectly satisfied without checking. But you feel free.'

'Let's return to our strangers for now,' I said.

'Let's for God's sake,' said Alec. 'I suspected little Nesta Chalmers of making up stories yesterday, but the evidence is mounting.'

'Indeed,' I said. 'And then there were three.'

8

Miss Clatchie's lentil broth had the makings of a sustaining meal on this, its second day. If it had been accompanied by warm rolls, copious butter, and a jug of cocoa and served in front of a roaring fire it would have set us up very well for the afternoon to follow. Thin slices of day-old bread, a scrape of cold butter with which to tear it, two glasses of water and possibly as many as seven small pieces of coal hissing sulkily in the grate, however, failed to make the notion of venturing out again a pleasant one.

Our coats, in addition, were still sopping wet from the morning (I made a mental note to ask Grant to send sou'westers when we spoke to her) but at least this afternoon we were not battling into the teeth of the wind. Our journey took us in the other direction from the shore road, the beach and the path to the church, and the rain soaked our backs instead of our faces as we crossed the harbour head and entered into a maze of boatyards crowded onto the flat patch of ground there. The yards were a perfect hive of busyness; every shed had its double doors thrown open and men bent over tables, looking surprisingly like their womenfolk filling the tick.

'Hard at it!' Alec called to a pair of young men who were scrubbing nets with wire brushes, scarves up over their faces against the dirt.

'We need to get this by before we start stitching,' said one, plucking the covering down from over his mouth.

'Stitching what?' Alec asked.

'Flags for the weddings,' he replied.

'Aren't you cold working outside today?' I asked. I do seem at times to be turning into an out-and-out matron.

'Ocht, we'd only be under the quines' feets in the house,' said a man I took to be his brother.

'Well, I'm glad to have run into you,' Alec said. 'Perhaps you can direct us to the Gow brothers' boatshed if they're about today. Do they have a wedding to stitch a flag for?'

Both of the men frowned quickly and one even scuffed his foot in the dust, staring hard at the pattern he was making. The other took a moment and then answered.

'Aye, John Gow's boathouse is just over b'yon,' he said pointing. 'And the doors is open.'

We looked towards where he pointed and, through the smirr of rain which was falling in a heavy curtain here in the lee of the hill without the wind to whip it around, we saw another shed and another pair of men busy inside it.

'I thought – pardon me for speaking of so sad a tale,' I said, 'but I thought John Gow had died.'

Now the brother who had spoken dropped his head too and we could not get another word out of either of them. It was with trepidation, then, that we scuttled over to the Gows.

'Mr Osborne,' said one of the men, politely, when we had hailed them. He put down the net hook he was holding and wiped his hand on his trousers.

'Mr Gow,' said Alec. 'This is my associate, Mrs Gilver.'

'Sister,' I murmured, but Alec was busy with his introductions. 'Dandy, this is Robert and his brother William, to whom I was speaking this morning.'

'And what is it you're doing, if you don't mind us asking?' I said. 'We're simply drowning in fascinating new material here.' Just too late I realised what I had said and put a hand up to my mouth. Alec was staring at me, aghast. The Gow brothers, however, did not turn a hair.

'Aye, we're just getting a wee bitty primpit up before we

94

fly the flags on Friday,' said Robert. 'The nets is fair heelster gowdy fa the trail home.'

I tried not to let my shoulders slump but the effort of translating these endless clods of impenetrable Doric was beginning to wear me down.

'So there's a wedding in the family,' I said. 'Who am I to congratulate?'

'Both of us,' said William. 'We're both of us getting wed Saturday coming.'

'That's unusual, isn't it?' I said. 'Two brothers at the same time?'

'Aye, it is that,' said Robert. 'It's strange days for the Gows, Missus, this year past. Two weddings is the least of it.'

'I did hear about your brother,' I said. 'I'm so very sorry.'

'Oh?' said William. 'And who was taking John's name then?'

'I wouldn't say that,' I protested. 'It was the ladies of the Guthrie family who touched on the sad news.'

'Aye, sure and they did,' said William drily. Then he said again what old Mrs Guthrie had pronounced – 'The meen's nane the waur fur a dug's bark.' But before I could request a translation, Alec had changed the subject.

'Now, lads,' he began. I glanced at him. He is normally scrupulously civil to the working people we go amongst and I had never heard him use such chummy language to men his age. Then I thought again. From their complexions, I had imagined them to be north of forty but probably the wind and salt and occasional bursts of sunshine were to blame for their leathery cheeks, that same salt and rain and rough ropes for their cracked and swollen hands. Given their straight backs and dark hair, though, they were probably young enough to be my sons and easily young enough to be 'lads' to Alec. Besides, they had found no cause for grievance in being addressed that way. They looked with friendly interest to see what he was about to say.

'About this passenger service in the summer,' he went on.

'About this old chap with the long grey beard. We'd really like to find him, Mrs Gilver and I.'

'Why?' said William, which was a fair question.

'Because if he's been here for six months he'll be a very valuable informant for us. He'll be a sort of halfway house between you Gardenstownites who know every last word of your native tongue and we poor students who know none at all.'

This was a stroke of absolute genius. I wondered when Alec had dreamed it up even as I was falling over myself to echo him.

'Indeed,' I said. 'A newcomer of six months' standing would be a great boon to our enterprise. Where is he now?'

'He did not stay,' said Robert. 'He got off the boat there and tramped away along the shore and that was the last of him.'

'You're sure?' I said. Both brothers nodded. 'And did you see the other chap? A foreigner, apparently. Miss Clatchie spoke about him.'

Now they chuckled.

'Oh, aye, him!' they said. 'Nah, he didn't hang about either. He went away fa Phemie Clatchie's with a flea in his ear and spent the night lying out.'

'Sorry, he what?' said Alec.

'He dossed down on the beach just,' said Robert. 'It was a fine night and no trial. Wee Elsie Dickson saw him when she was down getting bait the next day.'

'Aye, he gave her a right fright,' said William, 'rearing up as black as Auld Clootie. But he was away the next night and he's never been back.'

I repeated the name Elsie Dickson to myself, lest I forgot, and Alec and I took our leave, letting the brothers Gow return to their toil.

'I'm stumped on Greybeard and absolutely stumped on the artist's model,' I said as soon as we were underway, 'but I'm beginning to see a glimmer about this dark stranger.

96

Perhaps someone took badly to the idea of a foreigner sleeping rough on the beach.'

'Wouldn't Birchfield have said if Mr Pickle was dark-skinned?'

'It depends what they mean by swarthy,' I said. 'One wouldn't need to be very dark to be darker than the average Scot, after all.'

'Hmm,' said Alec. 'And actually Birchfield did mention discolouration, didn't he? I wonder if he's sure that it was a white man.'

'You could ring him up and ask him,' I said. 'And while you're at it . . .'

'Oh no,' said Alec. 'I am not asking your questions. If you want to make Mr Birchfield confirm that it's male, you do so.' I glared at him but then relented.

'Well, if it was the dark stranger,' I said, 'at least there's a trace of a motive – if Mr Dickson didn't like his little Elsie being frightened.'

'Or if the chap was here to claim the hand of a Gardenstown maiden, perhaps *her* father took against him.'

'The Gows don't seem to have heard any rumours to that effect,' I said. 'They laughed without a care in the world when we brought him up. No, it was the talk of the Guthries that bothered them.'

'Well, if their brother was betrothed to Janet Guthrie and she spurned him . . .'

'And yet when I opened my accursed mouth and said "drowning in material" – I could have kicked myself! – they didn't blink.'

'Let's see what we can hear about the young chap,' Alec said. 'If we find the artists at home. Perhaps we'll even discover that all three of the strangers were models. Just because only one of them mentioned it, there's no reason to think the other two couldn't have come for the same reason. Now where is the start of this path?'

I should not have called it a path. It was barely that around the jutting cliff-foot and on the beach beyond it disappeared completely and we had to clamber over boulders for a stretch. They were boulders slick with seaweed too and it occurred to me that when the tide came in we would be stuck in Crovie.

At least the rain had stopped. When we rounded the headland there was even a minute or two of oppressive cloud one could almost call grey again, lighter by far than any we had seen since we had arrived and, in that moment, we caught our first glimpse of Crovie, seeing instantly what would bring artists there. It was no more than a single row of cottages, gable-end to the sea as usual, crammed onto the tiniest little lip at the foot of a steep drop, with an even narrower lane than the Gamrie shore road separating the cottages from the beach below.

The roofs were red-tiled, the walls harled in a soft grey or painted white and the doors and windows were every colour under the sun. In July it would have been charming. Even in December, we were spurred on by the sight of it, as well as by the renewed lashing of another shower of rain on our backs.

Right at the end, the last cottage of all was 'Northern Light', which proclaimed itself to be an artist's dwelling by the peculiar shade of mustard yellow chosen for the paintwork and the way the windows were scoured and bare, without lace, net or velvet, and with nothing on the windowsill to block the precious stuff from entering. I peered in as we passed on our way to the front door and saw one of the artists herself sitting at an easel with a palette on her lap. She was not painting, but was slumped, staring at the canvas, her cigarette glowing as she sucked on it.

Alec lifted a lion's head knocker, rather cloudy from lack of polish, and rapped at the door.

'Thank God,' said a woman's voice from within. 'Deliverance.'

I thanked God along with her, because the words had been spoken in the King's English with not a trace of Doric about them. At last, I should be able to ask questions and understand what was said to me in reply, for between the garbled tongues of the fisherfolk and the strangulating effect of Miss Clatchie's propriety I was beginning to dread every conversation which came along.

A moment later the door opened to reveal the smoking woman. Her eyebrows rose and then she stepped back to let us enter.

'You poor sodden things,' she said. 'Harry! Visitors.'

'Hurrah,' said a man's voice, English again, from the room on the other side of the front door and he appeared, grinning and wiping his hand on a rag.

'Good grief, you're wet!' he said. 'Did you walk from the top road? Where are your sou'westers and oilskins?'

'Round the beach from Gamrie and we have none,' Alec said. 'Alec Osborne and this is my . . . sister, Mrs Gilver.'

'You can borrow some of ours for your journey back,' said the woman. 'Lydia Bennet. Yes, I know. I tell Harry it proves my love as nothing else could. Now come in and get warm.'

She led us into the room from which her husband had appeared, talking all the while.

'Harry likes a nice muddle – a habble they call it in these parts – so there are chairs and whatnot in here. I must have space around me so there's nothing in my room at all. I can't begin to tell you how good it is to see you. Even if you've decided already you don't care for our work, please stay and look at it all, or just stay and don't look.' She was lifting newspapers and sketchpads out of the armchairs in the room as she spoke and she waved around the walls where large paintings, stretched but unframed, were hanging.

'These are rather fine,' Alec said, looking about. The paintings on the walls were of figures, as we had been hoping, but would not help us. They were clearly of local people, close-up studies of quines' hands, gutting herrings, packing barrels, winding those cloth strips around their swollen fingers.

'Mrs Gilver and Mr Osborne?' said Harry.

'Is it too early for a glass of something?' said his wife.

'Gilver and Osborne,' said her husband again, in a musing sort of way.

'Now, what are those cloth ribbon things?' I asked hastily.

'What makes you so glad of the interruption?' put in Alec at the same time.

'The cloots,' said Mr Bennet to me. 'The quines bind their fingers to save them from being cut.'

'Darkest gloom,' said Mrs Bennet, answering Alec. 'Harry thought these would sell like hotcakes but they're too avant for tourists and not avant enough for anyone else so we're rather stuck with them and we've gone back to . . . .' She waved another hand at the easel which sat amongst the jumble of furniture. Upon it was a painting of almost complete blackness, touched here and there with the deepest purple.

'Seascapes,' said her husband. 'December in Banffshire. This one is perhaps too literal.'

Alec laughed and I had to smile too. He sounded, in his dejection, just like Donald and Teddy when they had been told to expect cough mixture.

'We couldn't afford to fly south for the winter this year,' said Lydia. 'Aren't times *grim*? And so we gave ourselves the gift of solitude and reflection to do great work. If you hadn't turned up we might have hanged ourselves before tea-time.' She had been rummaging in a small cupboard and had produced a bottle of whisky. She poured four glasses and handed them round.

'Cheers,' she said.

'Gilver and Osborne,' said her husband again.

'Cheers,' said Alec and took a good glug of the stuff. I raised my glass to them, touched it to my lips and then set it down.

'Do you ever draw whole figures?' I asked. Both Bennets

began thinking furiously, clearly trying to remember something – anything – they could sell.

'We could,' said Harry at last.

'No, we're trying to find out if a certain life model who
fetched up here was on his way to you,' I said.

'Oh,' said Lydia and her shoulders slumped again as they
had in front of her easel. 'You're painters too.'

'Is *that* why your names seem familiar?' said Harry.

'Let's give it up, Alec,' I said. 'He'll get there in the end.'

'We're not painters,' Alec said. 'We're just trying to track
down this particular chap and we've lost the scent.'

Harry sat straight up in his chair with his eyes wide, as
though he had been poked in the ribs suddenly.

'Gilver and *Osborne*!' he said. 'You're the detectives, aren't
you?'

'How thrilling!' said Lydia. 'And what has this life model
done? Strangled a painter when he saw the results? I modelled
in college and I wouldn't cast judgement on him.'

'He hasn't done anything,' I said. 'Except disappear. Actually,
three men have disappeared. And here is the last place any of
them was seen.' I had been lamenting to myself that there were
three strange men to track down (or rather two to track down,
leaving one who must be Mr Birchfield's pickled friend) but
now I was glad. We could not let the Bennets or anyone else
hear a whisper of the herring barrel end of things, and three
missing men was a nice innocent diversion.

'Here?' said Harry, looking around.

'Well, Gardenstown,' said Alec.

'And where are they originally from?' said Lydia. Alec's
smile disappeared.

'What are their names?' said Harry. Alec's eyes flashed at
me in panic.

I could not think of a single thing to say. How could it
come about that we were engaged to find three men if we
did not know their names or where they belonged?

'Our client,' Alec said and I could tell that he had recovered his composure. He had that undertaker's assistant tone in his voice again. 'Our client has issued the strictest instructions that we are not to divulge those pieces of information.'

'Gosh,' said Lydia, awestruck.

'Won't that make it the very devil to find them?' said her husband.

'They're quite distinctive,' I said. 'One is an old chap with a long grey beard; one is a dark-skinned gentleman, very tall and broad; the last is a young man with a Glasgow accent who touts himself as an artist's mannequin.'

'Are you sure?' said Harry. 'Those three would stick out in Gamrie. How could they possibly disappear here?'

'What sort of accent do the other two have?' said Lydia.

Again Alec and I had to work not to catch one another's eye.

'Our client didn't say,' I plumped for at last.

'Can you ask him?' she said.

'No,' said Alec, spinning the word out long and slow while he thought of more. 'No, unfortunately not. Our client is dead.'

'Ah,' said Harry. 'Inheritance.'

'But if he's dead he can hardly rebuke you for sharing information,' said Lydia. 'So do tell.'

'Our bond of confidentiality is not broken by death,' said Alec in his funereal voice again. I saw the Bennets wiggle eyebrows at one another but they were polite enough not to snort.

'Well, I'm sorry we can't help you,' Harry said. 'Not least because if we could and you solved the case you might tell us all the dark secrets. I shan't sleep tonight for trying to work it out.'

'If we promise to tell you everything as soon as we can,' Alec said, 'will you help us out now by not telling anyone who we are? We're incognito as far as Gamrie at large is concerned.'

'Doesn't that make it rather awkward to investigate?' said Lydia.

'Not at all,' I said. And with some pride we related all the arcanery of our scholarship, our philology, our stock requests for tales of unusual incidents and strangers who came to town. We even showed them the copious notes we had amassed, our jotters rather soft and limp from being battered in the rain, and, joy of joys, they translated some of the knottiest of our findings.

'The moon's none the worse for a dog's bark,' said Lydia. 'I've heard that one a lot. I think it means that you can gossip all you like about me, without causing me any harm.'

'The exact opposite of "Aye some watter far the stirkie droons",' her husband added. Alec and I scribbled madly. 'Roughly no smoke without fire.'

'Amongst the crows or you'd not have been shot,' said Lydia. 'I always liked that one.'

'They certainly go in for a lot of gossiping and stone-casting,' I said. 'They are well-served for sayings in that area. Which makes it particularly odd, if you think about it Alec, that no one we've asked about the strangers has been anything except amused. Well, Miss Clatchie aside.'

'But where did you hear the moon's no worse?' said Lydia.

'Oh, that was another matter entirely,' I told her. 'We are kicking up a fair amount of chaff as we go. I offended the Guthries and Gows by asking about the Gow brother who died and was betrothed to the Guthrie girl.'

'Ah, yes,' Harry said. 'Well, that's a different thing from grey-bearded strangers. A man overboard from a fishing boat is the blackest luck in the world. No one will want to talk about that to you.'

'But I didn't think it was a Guthrie he was fasted to,' said Lydia. 'I know those Guthries – they are Amazonian. Can you remember, Harry?'

Harry laughed.

'Hardly. It's worse than musical chairs the way they fast

and break, fast and break. And it doesn't help that they all have the same names.'

'No more than anywhere else surely,' I said.

'Don't be fooled,' said Mrs Bennet. 'They disguise themselves.'

'The Masons, for instance,' said her husband. 'Greta is no doubt a Margaret. Peggie Ness is a Margaret and the Marr of Nellie Marr is Margaret too.

'The Agneses are worse,' she continued. 'There are battalions of them, Nessies and Nans and Nancies and Nettas. Janet Guthrie is probably Jean Agnes really.'

'I met a Nesta too,' I said. 'That's another Agnes, isn't it?'

'The sexton!' Alec said. We all turned to look at him. 'Excuse me,' he went on. 'I was trying to remember who *wasn't* sanguine about the strangers. It was the sexton, if you remember, Dandy. Or at least his little girl.'

'Hmm,' I said. 'And the Gows did say that one of the men had frightened another little girl, didn't they? Elsie Dickson.'

'Don't think for a minute that Elsie is short for Elizabeth,' said Mrs Bennet, 'because I'll bet she's a Helen Agnes.' Her husband had done with names, however.

'You sound as though you think these chaps might have come to harm,' he said. His eyes were alive with interest and it occurred to me that, pleasant as it was to have a pair of allies whose speech we could understand without straining, we would have to be more guarded if we were to spend any time with them. 'And how did you come to meet the sexton, if I might ask?'

'He was digging graves,' said Alec in such dark tones that all four of us laughed.

'Ah, you went to see the church?' said Lydia. 'Isn't it horrid? Did you see the gateposts to Lump House too?'

'Not just the gateposts!' I exclaimed. 'We introduced ourselves to the Searles and went on a tour of the exhibits.' To my surprise, both the Bennets shuddered.

'We try to forget it's up there,' Harry said. 'Dreadful,

dreadful place. A friend who came to stay with us said they have hedgehogs and kittens!'

'Not to mention a seventeen—' Alec began. At my glare, he swerved mid-word and finished '—strong rabbit ballet. It's pretty vile.'

'We're vegetarians, you see.' said Lydia, 'and anti-vivisectionists.'

'Although out of sheer desperation since moving here we have been eating some herring,' said Harry.

Over Alec's face there spread the innocent look worn by small boys who are planning to put a spider in their governess's tooth mug. I knew exactly what he was hoping: that we would one day have the chance to reveal Birchfield's secret recipe for pickled herring.

'Now,' said Lydia, looking at her watch and standing. 'We usually have high tea and turn in early when it's as filthy as this. Can we persuade you to stay?'

There was not much in it, between Miss Clatchie's boiled mutton and a dish prepared by a slap-dash vegetarian with her mind on her art, but at least Miss Clatchie did not converse upon anti-vivisectionism. We thanked the Bennets, promised to return, donned their loaned oilskins with relief – for the weather was blacker than ever and the sun had gone down too – and left them.

'That was no help at all,' said Alec. 'Although a relief to have English spoken.'

'Eliminating possibilities is a kind of advancement,' I said. Then I stopped, turned back and looked to where the squares of yellow light were shining out of the Bennets' uncurtained windows. 'We've missed something,' I said.

'Undoubtedly,' said Alec. 'It's what we do.'

9

No more was accomplished that day, if indeed anything had been. Despite what I had claimed, we had made not an inch of true progress in our quest to identify the three mysterious strangers and even a prolonged pow-wow at Miss Clatchie's fireside in the evening had borne no fruit.

'We shall have to think of reasons to keep mentioning the strangers as we go about our business tomorrow,' I concluded. 'Someone must have seen them. It's a tiny place and the means of transport out of it are one road, one bus and a boat crewed by local lads. I'll bet even the station master at Macduff doesn't see too many people he doesn't recognise.'

'If only we knew something about them,' Alec said, and not for the first time. 'Or perhaps we can think it out, Dandy. Why would single men – young, old, and middle-aged – flock to Gamrie? If we can call three a flock.'

'"Flock" brings us back to the minister, who *was* accused by the doctor,' I said.

'And thence to the doctor accused by the minister. If "opposite number" means what we think it does.'

'But accused of what?' I sighed.

'Since we don't know,' said Alec, 'let's go back to the question of why the men would come here.'

'To visit relations,' I said, 'in which case everyone would know who they were, where they stayed and when they left. To work: ditto. To paint the boats in the harbour and the sunset over the sea?'

'In which case they would have been seen with easels and

paint boxes on the harbour. And I think you're only being drawn to the idea of painting because Miss Clatchie said one was a model and because of the Bennets, really.'

'You might be right,' I kicked off my shoes and stretched out towards the fire. Miss Clatchie seemed to have achieved a kind of scientific miracle: even with my feet practically in the grate, I felt not a whisper of warmth from the coal although the flames leaped brightly upwards towards the chimney. 'Well, then they must simply have been tourists.'

'Here for . . .?'

'Searle's so-called Circus is the only thing that springs to mind.'

'I suppose so,' said Alec doubtfully. 'Only they didn't sound much like tourists. They sounded more like tramps.'

'Who didn't ask anyone for a single cup of tea. Let's ask the Searles if *they* have a visitors' book.' Alec groaned at this. 'I'll go alone if you can't face it,' I went on, guessing the cause of the groan. He denied it.

'Doctors, ministers and taxidermists are beside the point,' he said. 'The chap turned up in herring barrels. It must be the fisherfolk who know who he was and why his grisly fate befell him.'

'But actually if anyone is going to nip up to Lump House in the name of completeness, you'll have more time for it.'

'How did you arrive at that conclusion?'

'Well, you can just drift over to a boatshed, remark upon the weather and get down to it,' I said. 'I have to drink tea and listen to all the marriage news and baby news and admire bolsters.'

Alec did not even try to hide his grin and I realised much too late that I had let myself in for all manner of lofty condescension.

'Yes, men don't have the same propensity to piffle on about nothing as women do,' he said. 'It's a rare thing to hear a woman confirm it, mind you.'

'Well, there you are then,' I said, wresting the glory back again. 'If you go to the Searles, the three of you together will make short work of their visitors' book. Who knows how long I might "piffle on" if it's left to me.' I gave him my sweetest smile and he could not say what he wanted to because at that moment Miss Clatchie appeared with the evening cocoa. She was still smarting from the enormity of having to provide it and entered the room with a hunted look on her face.

'We met Reverend Lamont and Dr Trewithian today, Miss Clatchie,' I said, and just like that her brow smoothed and she drew near to smiling. She did not actually smile, but her mouth bunched up like a little rosebud and unless she were about to whistle it must have been pleasure that caused it.

'How lovely!' she said. 'We are very lucky here at Gamrie.'

'But is it my imagination that the two gentlemen don't get along?'

'I know nothing of that,' she said, crisply. 'If you've heard gossip I'd rather you didn't share it with me.'

She put the cocoa down on such a far-away table that we would have to leave our chairs to fetch it and then she was gone.

'How inadvertently revealing,' I said, and then since I was going to have to move anyway I began to gather my notes and cigarette case to retire for the evening. Even Miss Clatchie could not stop a bottle filled with boiling water from warming a bed, no matter what magic she had worked on these coals.

The first order of business in the morning was to find a quiet telephone kiosk and see what luck Grant had had with the Hoods and Murrays, assuming that my letter had arrived and that Pallister, the butler, had not nobbled her. Pallister is displeased about Grant's new sideline and he has a particular talent for displeasure. If he knew that her stipend as detective's assistant brings her total income up to within hailing distance of his he would probably pack his traps and leave. So we box a little shy, the pair of us, and try not to upset him.

'Good news,' Grant said when the exchange had put us through. Alec and I huddled a little closer together on either side of the earpiece. We were in a rather horribly exposed spot, about three-quarters of the way up the brae leading out of town to the high road, where a telephone kiosk was plonked down on the grass without so much as a tree for shade and privacy. On the other hand, if reports were true that the villagers were too busy with wedding preparations to go to Macduff this week then, bald as the kiosk was, we had more privacy here than in the Post Office on the Main Street, our only other option.

'Oh?' I said, egging her on. Grant is as efficient an assistant detective as she is a maid, but she does tend to the dramatic in both: peacock prints and eye-black in my bedroom and dramatic pauses like this one when reporting over the telephone.

'Yes, Mr Pallister is away to his bed with a chesty cough so I managed to get all the phoning done just lovely.'

'And?' said Alec, rolling his eyes at me.

'Yes, well Mr and Mrs Hood were both at home,' said Grant. 'They said they'd had a very enjoyable week in Gardenstown. Mrs Hood painted the sun going down behind the church and the picture won second prize in the Inverness Amateur Watercolourists' Autumn Show and Mr Hood went out mackerel fishing every day and caught so much he sold it to a wifie with a creel who took it into Macduff to the market. And a lobster.'

'Excellent,' I said. 'What about the Murrays?'

'Ah, yes, now the Murrays are a different matter altogether.' There was another long pause filled with portentous crackles on the line. 'The Reverend Murray has been taking his seaside week at Gardenstown since he was a boy.'

'Has been,' I repeated. 'He's not dead then.' I felt a heel

for deflating her as soon as I had said it, but it was extremely draughty in this kiosk, despite the rather brighter day and the three jerseys I was wearing under Lydia Bennet's oilskin.

'He's not,' said Grant. 'Him and his wife and their children came home safe and sound. But I did learn something from Mrs Murray that I think will be right up your street.'

'Excellent,' said Alec. 'Do tell.'

'Well, the Reverend Murray is an awful one for taking God's gifts and flinging them back in His face, it seems,' said Grant. 'He won't let her bring flowers into the house and he won't agree to tea in the rose garden where they can see them and smell them either.'

'What does that have to do with our case?' I asked.

'I'm setting the scene,' said Grant. 'The only thing he'll let his wife and their daughters do with the half-acre of rose garden that the last minister planted at the manse is pick them and make posies for the hospital. They give the whole boiling away all summer and don't get to keep a single one.'

'Grant,' I said, 'I don't know what sort of weather Gilverton is enjoying today, but it's filthy in Banffshire. Bunty declined a walk. It's that sort of day.'

'Same here,' said Grant.

'Yes, but where are you speaking from?'

'I'm in your sitting room,' she said. 'Madam.'

'And we're in a draughty telephone kiosk on a windy hillside with our teeth chattering so would you please get on with it?'

'And as well as the roses,' said Grant, not noticeably faster, 'the only way the old misery-guts will consent to taking a summer holiday is if they spend it doing good works. So they do good works in Gardenstown for two weeks every July. And the good works they do is handing out tea and bannocks to the needy and selling them for tuppence to everyone else at the Seamen's Rescue to raise money for the lifeboat and stop the Murray women from having a single day in the year to call their own.'

'Ah,' I said. 'Well, now this is getting very promising, Grant. Do go on.'

'And last July when they were on their way they saw a tramp on the road. Now, there was already the five of them in the motorcar and it won't be a big one on a minister's stipend, will it? But nothing would do but Reverend Murray pulled off the road and asked the tramp where he was bound and he said Gamrie – the tramp, this is – and it ended up they all had to squash up and lay some of their bags over their knees and give him a lift. And Mrs Murray said he didn't smell too pleasant and I believed her.'

'Did you get a description?' said Alec.

'Just unwashed clothes and tobacco probably.'

'Not of the smell!' I said. 'Of the tramp. Beard? Complexion? Age?'

'I got a very full description,' Grant said. 'The Murrays had a five-mile journey on a bad road to sit and look at him. They'll not soon forget. But that's not the interesting news, madam. Far from it.' After a longer pause than ever she went on. 'This is. Reverend Murray told the chap all about the tea and bannocks and said they'd be serving as soon as they'd unpacked their traps and boiled up the first urnful of water. They'd brought a batch of baking with them from home. And the tramp was glad to hear it, as you can imagine, and said he'd be there before the end of the afternoon, he just had to sort out his accommodation first. And then they let him out of the motorcar and he headed off and guess what?'

'They never saw him again,' said Alec and I in chorus.

'They never saw him again,' said Grant. 'Not a whisker.'

'That is very interesting, Grant,' I said. 'Well done. Where did they let him off and what was he in Gamrie for and where was he going to stay? Do you know?'

'He had come to do a job,' said Grant. '"I've come up from

Glasgow on a promise of work," he said. But Mrs Murray didn't believe him, for he didn't seem like a working man. He didn't say where he was going to be living. But you know, madam, being a tramp, he maybe just planned to find a haystack and doss down. And as for where they let him off – well, that was what made the Reverend Murray keep such a close eye out for him and that's what makes him so sure that the chap disappeared completely. They didn't take him right down into the village itself. They dropped him off at the church. He asked to be put down there most particularly.'

'Was that where he was supposedly working?' I said.

'Mrs Murray didn't know,' said Grant.

'Never mind that, Dandy,' said Alec. 'Which one of them was he? The dark one, the young one or the one with the long grey beard?'

'He wasn't bearded,' said Grant. 'And he wasn't young. Mrs Murray said he was in his fifties.'

'So he must have been the swarthy one,' Alec said.

'He wasn't swarthy,' said Grant. 'I asked Mrs Murray about his height, hair, eyes, complexion and distinguishing marks – he had a black thumbnail, by the way – and she said he was pale and a bit blue with the cold, because it was a nasty windy day and he'd slept out the night before and hadn't warmed up yet.'

'A black thumbnail isn't much to go on,' I said.

'And his head was shaved and painted with iodine for the ringworm,' said Grant. 'He had a cap on but she could see the purple around the edges. Imagine! In a closed motorcar with her and her children. Ringworm.'

Just then the operator chipped in and asked if we wanted another three minutes. I declined, told Grant to send a written report and thanked her again. Alec replaced the earpiece and stood staring at me.

'Miss Clatchie would have mentioned ringworm,' I said.

'Of course she would,' said Alec. 'So this is number four.'

'It looks disgustingly like it.'

'Poor chap,' said Alec. 'Thin and pale and blue with the cold and painted purple for ringworm and his last journey spent with the toffee-nosed Murray women glaring at him.'

'But the promise of work and bannocks too,' I said. 'Although presumably he never got either of them.'

'Ringworm, mannequin, swarthy, greybeard,' said Alec. 'It's getting ridiculous.'

'But at least one thing is cleared up,' I pointed out. '"Opposite number" isn't Dr Trewithian or the Catholic priest, whoever he is. It's this Murray chap.'

'But if Mr Ringworm was going to the church wouldn't that mean he had a rendezvous with the Reverend Lamont? Murray might get to take over the seaman's relief but he wouldn't get near the pews and organ.'

'Unless it was the poorbox full of cash that was the draw,' said Alec. 'Could any tramp be brazen enough to ask a minister to let him off there for that reason?'

We stood there mulling it all over in the scant shelter of the telephone kiosk for a moment or two and could have stayed there a good while longer, at least until we had had a cigarette and readied ourselves for the cold winds outside, but when we heard the sound of a motor engine approaching all of a sudden it struck us – more or less at the same moment – that two people in a kiosk, not using the telephone, were rather conspicuous. We had just stepped out and begun the walk down the hill when Dr Trewithian was upon us, slowing down and hanging out of the open window of his little motorcar.

'Trouble ahead,' he said.

Alec and I both looked downhill where he was facing, but the doctor smiled.

'You mistake me,' he said. 'The imminent trouble is behind if anything! I mean there's trouble in store. The weather, dear lady. *The mercury sinks in the mouth of the dying day*. Shouldn't be surprised if there's a Bellowsnow for the weddings.'

'A Bellowsnow being . . .?' said Alec, sounding weary. It was bad enough to be bombarded with arcane dialect from the villagers, his tone seemed to say, without the likes of a Cornish doctor chipping in.

'A snowstorm with thunder and lightning,' said Dr Trewithian. 'Quite a remarkable sight but the locals don't care for it. They'll make more fuss about a half hour's bang and flash than they would about the much greater bother of the road being closed. Which it will be, no doubt, quite soon.'

I tried not to look quizzical but it was hard to see why a spot of rain and a bit of a breeze should close a road.

'I hope not, Dr Trewithian,' I said. 'With your patients at the foot of the hill and you at the top. The fisherfolk are your patients, aren't they?'

'To a loon,' he said. 'To a quine. I am their doctor and the keeper of all their— Well, *secrets are edged tools, and must be kept from children and from fools.* Toodle-oo.'

'What was that all about?' said Alec once the doctor had puttered off down the hill.

'There is definitely something very fishy about that man,' I said. Alec rolled his eyes and I apologised. 'And a doctor would certainly know how to dismember a corpse.'

I had to raise my voice towards the end of this for the sound of a second engine, much louder than the first, was beginning to draw near. We half-turned to watch for it and before long a lorry came around the bend and passed us.

'Oh, my good God,' I said, putting both gloved hands over my face like a mask but still feeling my gorge rise.

'Hell's bells,' said Alec, turning green. 'What in the name of everything holy *is* that?'

The lorry was rocking along at a fair clip, considering the dreadful road and the patches of ice in the shady places on corners and, as it went, out of the back doors a dark liquid was dripping and splashing onto the ground.

'This must be the trouble coming along behind,' I said. 'The abattoir's man on his rounds?'

'No knackers' van in the world on the hottest day of summer ever smelled that bad,' said Alec. 'That's worse than gangrene.'

'Please, Alec,' I said.

'Because gangrene isn't . . . fishy.'

'Alec, please!' I said again. The fug was beginning to clear but the drops of liquid on the road under our feet were not a joyous sight. I took a deep breath and bent over to look closely at a particularly large puddle. There was nothing to be learned. It was rusty and slightly viscous, thickened here and there by nameless scraps of matter. Perhaps Sherlock Holmes could have named its components and he too might have scraped some of it up into a snuff-box and put it away for a rainy day. He is a better man than I. I stood up straight again very sharply and tried not to look down again nor think about where I was putting my feet while not looking.

It was Mr Muir at the post office who revealed all. As we passed he was just opening his doors and Alec glanced at his pocket watch.

'Rather late, aren't you?' he said.

'No, just that the gutter's been by,' said Mr Muir. 'I shut my doors and shutters down for a minute there.'

'Fish guts,' said Alec, greening again.

'Aye, it's not so bad when the sea's for sailing,' said Mr Muir. 'Ninety-nine tides out of a hundred the guts go round to Peterhead by boat and it sits nice and far out and nobody's the worse. But sometimes on the springs and here the now at Christmastime the sea's just too rough and they send the lorry. If you want to see the streets of Gamrie emptied like the *Mary Celeste*, come by on a Wednesday morning when the water's high and the guts are going by van.'

'But why on earth don't they just toss them into the sea for the gulls?' I said. That is what Hugh and the boys always did with heads and tails and nameless innards when fishing for sea-trout.

'Away!' said Mr Muir. 'There's money in guts, Missus. The factory in Peterhead makes the best muck your garden could want. Grows tatties like turnips and turnips like pumpkins. Grand rhubarb too.'

I felt like Marie Antoinette, suggesting that the peasants throw the cake away because it was a little stale.

'And how long until he passes again the other way?' I asked.

'Ten minutes,' said Mr Muir. A customer was hurrying along the street with a parcel in her hands.

'I'll be in and out and let you get closed over, Mr Muir,' she said. 'Dearie me, but you forget, don't you? It's been the boat since March there and it never gets any better, sure and it doesn't.' Then Mr Muir and she disappeared into the post office and closed the door.

'Ten minutes?' said Alec, checking his pocket watch again. 'Well, then Dandy, I think I'll slip along this way and take the back lanes down to the shore road then go up to the Searles, as we agreed. Just to dot the 'i's and cross the 't's. After that we'll concentrate on the herring folk.'

'If you see the sexton,' I said, 'or perhaps you could even knock at his cottage door and ask him if you can think of a way to bring it off without it seeming strange, you could try to find out if he saw Mr Ringworm and also what the dark man did to make himself notable to his little girl.'

Alec stared at me and worked his jaw. I had thrown down the gauntlet with a smack, right at his feet, for if he did not approach the sexton now I would sympathise that he could not think of a way to do it. I smiled at him but he smiled back and I knew he had thought of a move to escape from check.

'Come with me that far,' he said. 'It makes more sense for you to interview both his child and Elsie Dickson, to see if their stories tally.'

And so it was I who opened the garden gate twenty minutes later and rapped on the gravedigger's cottage door as Alec strolled off towards the Searles' whistling and looking as pleased with himself as anyone dressed in sou'wester and oilskins can look in the driving rain. The day's weather had deteriorated rapidly from its bright opening and as I stood there the thunder clouds began rolling in, just starting to rumble far out towards the horizon, and I could see the few fishing boats which had put out as far as the inshore waters that morning already starting to make for home.

The sea they sailed on was a deep bottle green viewed from up here, heaving and swelling as though monstrous creatures were turning over just below the surface, and for some reason there being no breakers – not so much a rim of white – made it all the worse, for if the waves break there is relief. This bulging, darkening sea was pure menace with no relief anywhere. I turned away thankfully from the prospect as the door opened behind me.

The woman who stood there, with her neat brown bun and her paisley apron crossed over her front and tied with pink tape, was as cheerful and everyday as her husband – I supposed – had been leering and strange.

'Away you come in whoever you are,' she said. 'It's no kind of a day.'

'Mrs Gilver,' I replied. 'I'm a philological scholar doing a little study in the village at the moment and I met your . . . daughter and her daddy the other day.'

'A . . . what are you?' she said, not without reason.

'A studier of language,' I said. 'I wonder if I might ask your little one a few more questions. Odd questions they might seem – the aim is to get her talking; it doesn't really matter what about – and then I write down the words she uses and the way she pronounces them.'

'She's only wee,' said the woman. She had led me into the living room of the cottage, a cosy little place with crocheted cushions on every chair and sparkling brasses hanging around the fire. 'She's not half the Doric her daddy and me have and we're watered down fa her granda.'

'Exactly,' I said, extemporising madly. 'It's so important to get a clear view of how the language is changing what with the pictures and the wireless. And your daughter was particularly chatty. Some of the fisherfolk's children are quite tongue-tied in the presence of strangers.'

'Ocht, they're a queer lot,' said the sexton's wife. 'They've their own ways and no mistake.' She opened a door which evidently led into the kitchen and spoke in a gentle voice. 'Nesta? Here's a nice lady come to ask you questions, come away in here and tell her what she wants to know.' She ushered little Nesta in.

'Nesta,' I said as the child – much less bumptious inside the house in her mother's domain than she was out in the churchyard with her father – sidled in and sat opposite me with her hands tucked under her legs, 'that's a very unusual name.'

'It's ma teename,' she said. 'Nesta Pillie. I'm named fa my granny, Margaret Agnes.'

'I'm Nesta too,' said her mother. 'Nesta Soothie is my teename. Margaret Agnes Chalmers is my married name.'

'Mine's Dandy,' I said. 'If teename means pet name, as I think it must.'

'Not really, Missus,' said Mrs Chalmers. 'More like to mark you off fa all the others named the same.' I nodded; this confirmed what Lydia Bennet had told me. 'We need it in a place like Gamrie.'

'Ah,' I replied. 'Well, in that case perhaps not. I'm Dandelion Dahlia officially, and there aren't too many of *them*.'

The child giggled and I knew what was amusing her. In Scotland the dandelion has a reputation as a diuretic and a common name – unrepeatable – which thence arose.

'Nesta,' said Mrs Chalmers warningly and then she smiled.

'I'll put the kettle on. And there's a batch of rowies nearly ready. You make yourself at home.' With that she disappeared and shut the door, whether to keep the smell of cooking out of her living room or to stop the kitchen drafts getting in I could not say; but getting to speak to the child alone, without parental chaperone, was an unlooked-for bit of luck and I did not waste a minute of it.

'Now then, Nesta,' I said, 'the other day you were telling me about the queer strangers who were around over the summer and I'd like to hear more.'

Nesta simply stared at me out of her round eyes.

'What did they look like?' I said. I did not imagine that a child would notice a fringe of iodine around the edge of a cap but a long grey beard and dark skin might stick in her memory.

'Men,' she said, unhelpfully.

'But not nice men,' I prompted. 'You didn't care for them.'

'Nah,' said Nesta.

'Why not?'

'They were funny.' I suppressed a sigh.

'What was funny about them?'

'The beasties,' Nesta said.

Now, in Scots, a beastie can be anything from a flea – which would certainly render a person unwelcome – to a dog, which might frighten a small child, to an elephant, which would cause comment in London, let alone Gamrie. I wondered if ringworm would count as beasties and urged her to go on.

'Tell me about these beasties, please.'

'Well,' said Nesta, 'some was just like cows but with great big horns – muckle big horns! And some was just wee tiny horsies but there was one man brought a horrible big ugly lumping beastie like a monster. I ran in under the table and stayed there.'

I managed to keep nodding and did not let my mouth drop open.

'Beasties,' I said. 'I see. And these men brought the "beasties" here to the church?'

She nodded. 'Down the lane in wagons and then led them up the drive,' she said. I sat back and almost laughed.

'I see,' I said. 'I really do see. The Searles had animals delivered to them. Yes, I see.' Then I saw a little more and stopped laughing completely. Warwick Searle's adamant claim that his materials were fresh made sense now, for it seemed that the animals were delivered on the hoof.

'It's all right, Missus,' said Nesta, evidently reading my expression and being moved to offer comfort. 'There's na beasties at all to fret you now.'

Her mother at that point edged open the door with her hip and came in carrying a tea tray. She laughed too.

'Ocht, Nesta, you're not still on about they beasts for the Searles, are you?' She set the tray down and explained to me. 'The Searles always used to go and pick their beasts up fa Macduff station. Sometimes they even went away on trips and brought them back their own selves. But they've started having deliveries now. Well, they're no as young as they were. I don't think they've stirred from their door all year, except down the street for their messages.'

'You know them quite well then,' I said. 'Has little Nesta seen the museum?'

The woman flashed me a look.

'No,' she said very slowly and firmly. 'She knows that the animals are still being *trained*.'

'I understand,' I said.

'She was bad enough when she saw thon pretendy things at the front door,' her mother went on, serving me a cup of tea and splitting open a steaming pastry to slip a pat of butter into its interior. My mouth watered and I was reminded of the Murrays' bannocks and the purple-headed man.

'I wonder what the smallest animals were which the Searles had delivered during the summer,' I said. 'If perhaps some of their latest collection came in boxes and jars. I was hearing about a chap who got a lift to the end of this road and I'd like to speak to him. I don't know if he was a local or one of these animal breeders Nesta's been describing.'

'What did he look like?' said Nesta's mother.

'Thin, pale, rather unkempt by all accounts. Sometime early last July.'

She shook her head.

'We don't see folk just walking,' she said, 'for we needn't open the gate to them – there's a wee slip-through at the side. It's only if a buddy's got a cart or leading a cow or ocht that we'd know they were passing.'

'It must be very quiet,' I said.

'Except for a Sunday or weddings or funerals, aye.'

'Or ghosties,' said Nesta. I inhaled a crumb and had to cough a little before I could reply.

'I expect so,' I said. 'Here if anywhere.' I was paying close attention to both of them, trying to decide whether Nesta was in earnest and trying to gauge what her mother made of her claim.

'Not fa the graves,' said her mother. 'Not after a good kirk burying. But the three kings don't rest easy.'

'The three . . .' I said, somewhat mystified, thinking of Miss Clatchie's establishment and only then wondering for the first time why it had such a biblical name.

'The Danish chieftains,' she said. It was a measure of how very packed with incident, new terminology and outright puzzles the last two days had been that I had quite forgotten about the skulls of battle chieftains in the church walls.

'Aye, they loup about a bit,' said Nesta, 'but they cannot catch you.'

'Oh?' I said.

'Their heads are stuck in the kirk,' she explained. 'So even if they chase you, you're fine.'

'My mother had the sight,' said Mrs Chalmers, filling a

silence. 'She never sat in an empty room but somebody came to see her. It's skipped me like it does but wee Nesta's fair shaping up.'

'And are there more ghosties here than just the Danes?' I said. I was reeling a moderate amount. Not as much as I should have been before the beginning of my detective career for, during my many journeys into quiet corners of Scotland, I had encountered a fair handful of outwardly normal people who calmly regaled me with tall tales of every kind.

'Aye, tons,' said Nesta, she took a lusty bite out of her pastry and chewed it thoroughly before washing it down with a draught of milk and continuing. 'There's the poor fishermen lost at sea. I cannot really see them right fa up here – they're just like lights, like lanterns. But if I'm down the seatown road and the tide's coming in, I can see their faces.'

'How terrifying,' I said. I meant it. The thought of glowing ghosts of drowned sailors being borne into shore on that swelling tide was enough to make my hair stand on end.

Nesta frowned at me.

'They're just coming to see their pals and their mammies,' she said. 'They're not scaredy.'

'You are a very brave and remarkable little girl,' I said.

'It's not everybody either,' said Nesta. 'And they don't stay long. They just need to come a wee few times and see everybody's doing away.'

I turned my eyes to the living-room window and peered out to the cliff and the sea beyond.

'There's none the now,' she said and I am ashamed to admit I was relieved to hear it.

'So,' I said 'Headless chieftains and drowned fishermen. I have to say Mrs Chalmers, I'm very glad I came to visit. This is wonderful material that Nesta is providing.'

'I thought you said it didn't matter what she said as long as she said it in the Doric,' said Mrs Chalmers.

'I'm delighted to hear the Doric, of course,' I said. 'But

the traditions and tales and myths and folklore are wonderful too.'

'It's not tales, Mammy,' said Nesta. 'It's true. It's not . . . they things she said.'

'Less of your cheek!' said Mrs Chalmers.

'And the slow lady,' Nesta said stoutly. 'She's not a tale!'

'Right ye are there, my doo,' said Mrs Chalmers. 'I was forgetting the slow lady. Even I've seen her.'

'She's not been here that long,' Nesta added. 'And she doesn't come that close. She just walks about in the woods.'

'Slowly,' I said.

'Aye, slower and slower,' Nesta said. 'One day she'll just stop and maybe she'll just stick there. Like a statue. Like they angels in the kirkyard at the other kirk.'

I blinked but Mrs Chalmers laughed.

'We have no more than a plain stone here in the parish kirk, but there's a chapel in Macduff with all sorts. Nesta was right taken with the angels.'

Nesta, in my opinion, was a little ghoul, between the glowing fishermen, the headless chieftains, the slow lady, and her interest in gravestones. I had finished my pastry, I did not think the Chalmers had seen our Mr Ringworm and so, thanking them, I took my leave.

It was perfect timing, since I met Alec outside the graveyard wall more or less where we had parted company half an hour before.

'They've got a visitors' book,' he said, without any greeting at all. 'They showed it to me without hesitation and there are no single men in it. I asked if all their guests sign it – since we didn't, you know – and they assured me that the oversight has been troubling Durban greatly and he won't be happy until you've gone back and recorded your thoughts.'

'He wouldn't be at all happy if I recorded my thoughts,' I said. 'Oh, Alec, let's hurry.'

We had rounded the corner of the cliff to begin our descent

of the path and the rain now seemed to be falling upwards, if such a thing is possible, getting right in under the peaks of our hats and numbing our cheeks.

'Yes, the entries I read were masterpieces of ambiguity,' Alec said, raising his voice above the wind. 'Remarkable. Speechless. Never seen anything quite like it before. That sort of thing. How did you get on?'

'Lots of local colour,' I said. 'Mainly a ghostly grey.'

'What?' he shouted. I was walking ahead of him and my words could not carry back to him. I turned.

'Nothing much of use,' I said. 'Ghost stories. And the strange men she spoke of – it turns out – were delivering animals. It was the animals that startled Nesta, actually. Not the men.'

'And so we're finished with all of that,' said Alec.

'The ministers, taxidermists and doctors?' I said.

'And artists, gravediggers and hoteliers too. It's the herring folk from here on in, Dandy.'

It must have sounded wonderful; it certainly felt purposeful enough to say it. We were done with extraneous matters and were about to set about the case, instead, like surgeons with scalpels. Little did we know that the chaos into which we would pitch ourselves during the days to come would make us feel as though we had tumbled over a cliff in a barrel and were helplessly being borne out to sea.

10

For the time being, we managed to cling to the ash path down the side of the cliff, although with a few unnerving moments on the way.

'Warwick Searle told me that the ladies will be busy plenishing today. That sounds like something two scholars of folklore would want to witness, doesn't it?' said Alec as we began to pick our way.

'And the men?'

'Should have been fishing for the Thursday market in Banff if the sea let them.' He raised his head briefly and let the stinging rain spatter his cheeks. 'More flag-making in the boatsheds as it stands.'

'Well, you wouldn't want to miss that,' I said. 'Oh, good Lord, surely there will be some shelter in the lanes. Let's get down off this godforsaken hill before we're washed away.'

In the end, however, the filthy weather worked in our favour. We were trudging along the shore road – the seatown road as the locals appeared to call it – when little Mrs Mason, still in a jersey and crossed scarf although she had consented to put a man's cap over her head, opened her door and peered out.

'It's yourselves!' she cried. 'I heard the feets and thought it was my sister. We're plenishing the day.'

'I heard,' I said, licking my lips to stop the raindrops spraying as I spoke. 'Although I'm not sure what it means, actually.'

'Filling the presses, just,' she said. 'You'll have a plenishing set to go to, have you?'

I shook my head and more droplets scattered from my hat brim and the tip of my nose.

'Come away in and study ours then,' she said. 'Come away. You'll not want to miss the plenishing if you're set on Gamrie ways.' I hesitated. I had already quizzed the Mason girls rather closely and my plan had been to latch onto a fresh family of potential witnesses. 'I've got a rare pot of broth just boiling,' said Mrs Mason. I gave Alec a guilty look. Surely Mrs Mason's broth would be an improvement on Miss Clatchie's which Alec, if I deserted him, would have to face alone. And he had not shared the buttery delights of Mrs Chalmers' rowies, of which I had gobbled up two. 'Aye, my sister's got a hard afternoon ahead of her with my two as well as the Dickson lot. She'll need a good plate of broth and a slice of warm gingerbread before she gets started, but we've plenty.'

'Dickson?' I said.

'Eldest auntie,' said Mrs Mason. 'My sister married Rab Dickson so she's all that lot's eldest auntie too. Away you come in and I'll tell you.'

'I'll just go to the hotel then,' said Alec. He was a picture of dejection standing there with his sou'wester drooping all around his head and the rain streaming in sheets from the bottom hem of his oilskin to course across the cobbles to the sea. 'And then tramp the boatyards until tea.'

'I'm awful sorry, mister,' said Mrs Mason. 'But plenishing's just the women. It's flags for you today.'

Mrs Mason's kitchen was the twin of Mrs Guthrie's from the day before. The same pair of gas lamps with china bellies stood on either side of the same high mantelpiece with the same brass clock between them. There was another scrubbed table, a hooked rug, a copper kettle put-putting out steam like a little train and the only difference was that the pillows and bolsters were not spread around in all their half-made glory – the Masons' finished 'ticks' were tidily piled on the box bed in two neat heaps – and instead the table-top was groaning with bags of sugar and flour, canisters of tea, sacks of oats and potatoes, and cakes of soap. Two of everything.

'Ye'll just find a wee corner there, Mrs Gilver,' said Mrs Mason, 'and get putting your plate down.' She had lifted the lid from a black cooking pot on the stove and slid a heaped ladleful of broth into a shallow bowl. One could not say she poured it, for the broth was thicker than many a southern stew, but I have been blessed with a marvellous constitution when it comes to barley and can consume pints of the most viscous and solid concoctions that even a Scotch kitchen could muster. If only I had the same aptitude for porridge and whisky I might have passed for a native and saved endless mortification.

'How delicious,' I said, edging the plate onto a tiny corner of the table. 'I've just got enough room here. Thank Heavens you don't have more than two daughters, eh?'

Almost as soon as I had said it I knew I had committed a grave blunder. Mrs Mason stilled and stood frozen with her back to me.

'My dear Mrs Mason,' I said, 'I'm so very sorry. How dreadfully thoughtless of me. And what's worse is that I think one of your neighbours mentioned it and I had forgotten.'

She gave a determined sniff and turned round again with her own plate of broth. Her eyes were shining.

'Ocht, away!' she said. 'You'd never think to worry about a lassie. I mean, twixt the lads on the boats and the lads at the war, we're aye hearing about a son that's lost. But who'd think on a lassie.'

'How old was she?' I said, imagining a cradle and a fever.

'Twenty-two,' she said. 'It was just this year's end past and she's not died. She's just away. I don't know where she is in the world.'

'Oh my,' I said. 'I can't imagine if that's worse or better. What happened? If it's not too painful to revisit it.'

'It'll do me a sight of good,' said Mrs Mason. 'For when

the quines get home and my sister lands I'll need to have a smile on my face for the rest of the day.' She took a handkerchief out of her skirt pocket and from the way she gazed at it before she blew her nose I guessed that it was her daughter's, kept close and treasured.

'She was handfasted to the Gow lad that drowned,' she said. 'And after he died, last year's end this was, she took off.'

'Oh my,' I said again, remembering all the awkward silences and averted eyes when the Gow boy was mentioned at the Guthries'. 'Oh dear.'

'Aye,' said Mrs Mason, with her head down. My broth was cooling and I was hungry and cold but it did not seem polite to tuck in. I waited and eventually she spoke again. 'I don't know if she flang herself in the sea or ran away to some big city and I don't know why she'd do either. She was a young lass with her life ahead and her friends and family round her.'

'Was it a love match?' I asked. 'Was she heartbroken?'

Mrs Mason lifted her head and gave me a look of mingled puzzlement and pain.

'No, none of that,' she said. 'I cannot account for it at all. Ocht, they were fasted and if the Dear had smiled they'd have been as happy together as anybody else is.' She checked herself. 'I sound hard-hearted, I know . . .'

'Not to me, Mrs Mason,' I said. 'I'm married and I know that life is not the way the pictures tell it.'

'Pictures!' she said and, in her exasperation she found her appetite, picked up her horn spoon and set about the broth. I joined her. 'They turn quines' heads! We've none here, but when they're off at Dundee or Grimsby or any they rackety places, Dear knows what they're seeing.'

It was a novel view of Dundee and Grimsby but compared with Gardenstown I supposed it was true.

'So this double wedding of your daughters to the other two Gow brothers will be bittersweet,' I said. 'Especially falling

on the anniversary of the death and your daughter's disappearance.'

'Nah, it wasn't the year's turn,' said Mrs Mason. 'It was the
year's end – end of the herring season. March it was when
John Gow was drownded and it was after that that Nancy
Nell took off wherever she's off to.'

I could only stare at her as my mind, instantly, froze. Nancy
had disappeared sometime after the spring? Alec, I knew, did
not agree but we had to ask Mr Birchfield, once and for all,
if he was sure the body was male. Now that we had a female
possibility, we simply had to. But for the moment I must
think of something to say to poor Mrs Mason and not just
sit there gaping at her any longer.

'Perhaps she'll come back,' I said. 'For her sisters' weddings.
Did she know they were planned?'

'She knew,' said Mrs Mason, rather grimly. 'My lassies
came home at the end of the season with all the news together.
John Gow was drownded and they were handfasted to Wullie
and Robert. 'Twas done and no undoing. And all the time
Nancy was mourning they were walking out. Her on her
own. It broke my heart to see her.'

'But would you really have undone the handfastings and
upset your other daughters?' I asked. The diplomatic niceties
of the fisherfolk's life were beyond me.

'I'd fain have died myself than let Peggie and Nellie get
tied to the Gows! My lasses fasted to the brothers of a
drownded man! Right there on the boat with them! But there.
Here we are.'

Indeed. I felt even more as though I were trying to decipher
the politics of some jungle race whose sensitivities were utterly
beyond me.

'To change to happier topics, then,' I said. My bowl was
empty and I took my notebook out of my pocket and opened
it on my knee. 'What more can you tell me about a
plenishing?'

Before she could answer, the front door opened and on a gust of cold wind with a good lashing of rain at its back, both Mason girls, a woman I took to be their aunt and a gaggle of little girls all burst in, laughing and shaking themselves.

'What a day!'

'It better not be hammering down like this for the procession on Saturday.'

'I mind of the bad rains of twenty-three when we had boat sails held out over the lassies' heads like tents to keep the sleet off them.'

'Oh, sister!' said Mrs Mason, joining in. 'Thon was a right cullieshangie! All they quines with their new rig-outs up to the cuits in glaur for the shaimit-reel!'

'A fine old muddle,' Mrs Gilver,' said Peggie Mason, taking pity on my confusion. 'Girls in new outfits up to their ankles in mud when we did the wedding dance down the street there.'

'Thank you!' I said.

'Ach, it was a rare laugh,' said the woman I took to be Aunt Dickson. 'I love a wedding and I feared the day'd never come.'

It was hardly a tactful remark and it did produce a short silence but, within a minute, the boisterous Mason girls were laughing again, each of them proudly holding a hand under her blooming middle and seeming almost to wink as they looked into one another's eyes.

'Mrs Gilver was asking about the plenishing there,' said Mrs Mason.

'Ach it's easy understood,' said Aunt Dickson. 'It's no more nor no less than just filling the presses in the bride's house with everything she needs in her kitchen.' She ran a loving hand over the packets of salt and boxes of mustard which, being the smallest items, were close to the front and near at hand. 'And what a grand plenishing this it too. Your mother's good to you, quines.'

'Just as well,' said Peggie, looking out of the tiny kitchen window. 'There'll be no extra silver this week, with the boats not getting out.'

'Aye, true, a catch or two more for the market would have been grand,' said Nellie. 'Ocht, well.'

'Now, this is something I think I do understand,' I said 'They catch fresh fish at will when the seas are calm, but all the herring belongs to Mr Birchfield. Because of the farling.'

All the women and the little children too let out gales of laughter.

'Cos of the *arling*, Mrs Gilver,' said Mrs Dickson. 'The farling's the big table trough where the gutting gets done. It's the arling that says the fish goes to Birchfield's by barrel and no to market in a creel. Ach, but you're nearly right. They're not out of arle to March, to the year end.'

'Speaking of gutting,' said Peggie. 'Did you smell thon cart gutter this forenoon? What a stink to it.'

'That man's saving himself time and trouble never cleaning out that lorry fa one year's turn to the next,' said Mrs Mason. 'He's a clarty so and so.'

'Is he a local man?' I asked. There was more laughter.

'Dear save us, he is not,' said Peggie. 'Can you think on him coming home to your door at night? The gutting's bad enough with it fresh every day.'

'A stranger then,' I said, driving the conversation like a pair of oxen.

'Peterhead,' said Mrs Dickson. 'Strange enough.'

'And is there a Doric word for stranger?' I said. 'What would you call a traveller who was passing through? The people who come to the Murrays' tea stand every summer, for instance.'

'I'd call that Murray a—'

'Don't you speak ill words fa a minister,' said Mrs Mason, quelling her daughter with a glare.

131

'Because he attracts tramps, serving up tea and buns that way?' I asked innocently.

'Ocht, there's no harm to a walking mannie,' said Mrs Dickson. Then she shouted with laughter and nudged the eldest of her girls. 'Mind how Elsie waked up thon mannie on the shore summer there?' I tried not to look too overly interested but readied myself.

'Tell Mrs Gilver, Elsie.'

One of the older children turned to me.

'I fell over him, when he was sleeping on a rock!' she exclaimed. 'I was just having a wee caper and I near jamp on him, seeing he was all bunnelt up and dark like the stones!' She did not seem the least little bit perturbed by her ordeal. She giggled and demonstrated the capering and the shock of finding a rock to be a man.

'Were you frightened?' I said.

'Nah,' said Elsie. 'He was just a mannie.'

'I heard he was very swarthy and strange,' I said. 'Miss Clatchie at the hotel said so.'

'Fit's swarthy?' said Elsie, giving up on me and my peculiar speech and turning to her mother for elucidation.

'Dark,' said Mrs Dickson. 'Black in his face.'

'Oh aye, he was right "swarthy",' said Elsie, making everyone chuckle. 'Like Tinker Jimmy. But not with gold in his ears like Tinker Jimmy, though.' When set against Euphemia Clatchie, she was quite the cosmopolitan.

'And did he speak to you?' I asked. 'What did he say?'

'He didna say ocht,' said Elsie. 'I just said sorry I jamp on your belly, mister, and he just said, "Ach you're fine hen," and then he got up and stretched himself and went away to where he was going.'

'He called you "hen"?' I said. 'Hmm. Possibly Glasgow, then, wouldn't you say?'

The Masons and Dicksons shrugged politely but they clearly did not share my interest in varieties of Scots tongue.

I decided to let the matter drop at that and closed my note-book, winking at Elsie.

'He didn't call you cushie-doo!' This set them off laughing again and teasing me gently about the hilarious fun of a good Doric word in my unworthy mouth. Elsie and her sisters even tried an imitation and their giggles grew higher and faster until they threatened hysterics.

By this time, Mrs Dickson had finished packing the first of the plenishings into a capacious old pram and Mrs Mason peered out around the front door, looking to the sea and to any hopes of a break in the rain. I gave both girls my blessing and a ten-shilling note to share between them and left them.

There were gaggles of women on the move all over the town: aunts, proud mothers, married sisters, little girls and the betrothed maidens themselves (less maidenly though they might be than in parts where handfasting was unknown) were all cramming themselves into the narrow lanes to oversee the stocking of cupboards in the gloomy bottom-back kitchens.

'It's hard to believe there are so many houses tucked in there,' I said to a very old woman who stopped beside me, watching. Her working days were done, I surmised from the snowy white apron she wore over her long canvas skirt and the short shawl, just as white, pinned over her jersey where the fisher wives might have a crossed scarf to cushion them against the creel straps.

'Aye, it's a wee squeeze, right enough,' she said.

'Four separate families in each building, isn't it?' I asked.

'Not separate, my doo,' she said. 'All the same. And there's only three hoosies to a roof.'

I stared at the building. There was a front and back house on the bottom and so surely there was a front and back house on the top, unless the top house under the eaves was a kind of penthouse, twice the size.

'Are you needing to know for your learning?' the woman asked, with an air of respect which shamed me. I nodded.

'Well, this front bottom hoosie is the best one,' she said, pointing a gnarled finger. I noticed that only the first two fingers could be straightened at all and that the other were curled tight against her palm. 'And then . . . Ocht, come in and I'll show you. Tis easier far that way.'

We entered the cottage and I followed her through a kitchen, parlour and bedroom to a door which opened into the back house. 'This is the youngest son's,' she said, 'being as black as night and wee bitty damp like. Or the granny's if there's no two lads in the family.' A couple, elderly, though not by many years as my guide, were sitting by the fireside and did not bat an eyelid either at her frank description of their home or our sudden presence in it.

'Never mind on us,' my guide said to them. 'I'm just showing the philly-oolie fit like the hoosies are.'

'Aye, you're fine there, Annie Mhor,' said the husband of the pair, sucking at his pipe and rocking in his chair without the slightest break in the rhythm of either.

In the corner of the kitchen, Annie opened a door and began to pull herself up a steep set of steps, almost a ladder. 'Come away, come away,' she said, until I began to follow her. 'Up here' – she opened a door – 'is the second-best house for when the first son gets married and through the front there is the net loft.' We doubled back on ourselves and entered what I had taken to be a fourth set of rooms. It was instead one large attic open to the sarking, strung about with drying nets. The old woman crossed it and opened a kind of hayloft door in the gable-end, revealing a sheer drop of fifteen feet to the stone slabs of the shore road.

'But why on earth not make this a house and store the nets at the back downstairs?' I said. She looked at me as though I were an imbecile.

'The nets would never dry down there in all that wet,' she said. 'They'd rot away. And now, I'll have to get on,' she added, dismissing me. She gave a wistful look out of it as she was closing the hayloft door.

'Time was I'd be down out of here on a rope with my petticoats flying up,' she said 'But old age gets us all. Last time I came in through a net door was twenty-three in thon storm where the boats was right up to the walls here and the tide was going up they closes like spouts.' She gave me a wide smile. 'I'd not be surprised if we saw another like it this wee while coming,' she said. 'Thon sky's got trouble for us if my old bones are worth heeding.'

I sympathised with her, for rheumatism can be the very devil, but secretly hoped she was wrong. Gamrie was comfortless enough in the rain and snow we had seen so far. I did not relish the prospect of the sea submerging the road and washing up the lanes. On the other hand, I thanked Providence that we were in Gardenstown and not Crovie, for surely one good storm could wash that little clutch of perching cottages clean away.

'Great riches,' I told Alec when we convened in my bedroom an hour later. I had filled two of Miss Clatchie's enamel buckets with piping hot water from the bath taps and we sat side by side on my bed, stockings off, trouser-legs rolled, soaking some life back into our feet.

'She'll kill us if she finds us,' Alec had said.

'She won't have to try hard unless I warm up somehow,' I replied.

'Huh,' said Alec. 'How was *your* broth? Mine was a new batch – mostly cabbage and water.'

'Well, yes the broth was one of the jewels,' I admitted, 'if you care for barley. But not by any means the only one. I found out that Elsie Dickson and the dark stranger parted friends. There's no reason to think that her father would have gone after them with a jigger.'

'With a what?' said Alec, but not crossly. The hot water

was clearly doing him some good. He had relaxed enough to fill his pipe and had even grown roses in his cheeks.

'A gutting knife,' I said. 'I learned a great deal of herring fishing vocabulary today; quite sorted the arling from the farling and the crans from the creels.'

'Are you making words up?'

'No, I'm perfectly serious. A cran is the number of herring that fit in a barrel. The farling is the gutting table, not the arrangement with Birchfield's that runs from one year's end to the next. A year's end being March, mind you, not December. December is the year's turn. And on that note, I must warn you that I'm returning to an unwelcome topic, Alec. Because I also found out that someone did indeed disappear from Gardenstown.'

'Hallelujah,' said Alec. 'Who *was* the man?'

I drew a deep breath. 'It was a woman.'

'Dandy, give it up, for Pete's—'

'Nancy Mason disappeared,' I said, cutting him short. 'And she is the first of our expanding list of vanishing strangers who wasn't a stranger and who actually vanished. Instead of just perhaps moving on or going home. She was handfasted to the eldest Gow who drowned and she disappeared from home sometime after the end of the season. In other words, in late spring or early summer.'

'Sounds more likely that she killed herself,' Alec said. 'If her lover died.'

'If her *lover* had died, yes,' I countered. 'But John Gow was only a prospect, I think. The eldest son of a family with a good boat and a bit of cash behind them. Her mother is absolutely mystified. As am I.'

'She's right about the good boat,' Alec said. 'The Gows have a paraffin engine.' I had no comment to make on that. 'Most of the Gamrie boats are still stream drifters, with five of a crew, but a paraffin boat can get by with three. Splitting the same money. So John Gow, the skipper, was a fair prospect and no mistake. But,' he concluded, 'it was a man in July. Not a girl in April.'

'Ask Mr Birchfield,' I said. 'He'll swallow his tongue if I ask him. It would be better coming from you.' There was a silence. 'What else did you get today?'

Alec was thoroughly thawed now. He loosened his tie and his collar and even went so far as to lift his feet out of the water and wave them about a bit to cool them off.

'I can't be sure,' he said. 'I think the men were pulling my leg with some of what they claimed was Doric Scots today.'

'Oh, I'm sure they weren't. It does seem quite outlandish and unnecessary, I grant you, but I think it's genuine.'

'Hmm,' said Alec. 'I'd like to hide behind a barrel by the farling and see if they don't speak perfectly normally to one another when there aren't gullible linguists in view.'

'Besides,' I went on, 'you can cross-check the words with what I've been hearing.'

'Ah yes, but I wasn't treated to any fine manly fishing terms,' Alec said. 'I was regaled with the language of cooking.' I raised my eyebrows slightly, waiting for the punchline, but it appeared that he meant what he said. With a sigh, for I was heartily sick of the endeavour, I reached for the notebook which I had laid on my bedside table.

'Glashicks,' he said, 'are what you and I would call sweets. And if there's not enough "bree" in one's rations one might end up "keekit".'

'What does that mean?' I said.

'Gravy,' said Alec. 'And choked by dry food. But I couldn't pin them down on what an "oaty earl" might be. Some kind of posh biscuit perhaps, although it doesn't seem that likely. Or a "barkit sloppy".'

'I can't help with the earl,' I said, 'but a barked sloppy is nothing to do with food. It's what they call the ganseys the fishermen wear. Someone mentioned it yesterday.'

'You say "gansey" as if it's the King's English, Dan,' Alec

said. 'You're turning into one of them. And I assure you it was mostly food. Even recipes, if you can believe that. There was a great deal of joshing and joking about someone who "slicked an oaty".'

'Slicked?'

'Slicked.'

I added it to the list of terms, wondering about the spelling and telling myself I would ask the Bennets when we saw them next, but Alec's words about my going native had stung and I determined to guard against becoming so immersed in our philological disguise that I forgot our true purpose.

'But in amongst all of that endless chaff,' said Alec, reading my mind as he often did, 'I heard about another candidate for the role of Mr Pickle. I did begin to wonder if they were drunk at this point but I think they were merely in high spirits. Looking forward to the weddings, and whatnot. Anyway, they told me about a Viking.' I looked up from my notebook. 'Well, a large red-haired stranger with elaborate moustaches and a chest like a warrior.'

'Are you sure?'

'I am. They joked that had he been around at this time of year instead of the summer he would have been much in demand as the worst man . . .'

'The worst man?' I said, and shook my head. 'That's another new one too. Are you sure they didn't say 'first man'? First foot? I know the first foot over the door at New Year is supposed to be dark-haired, specifically to be sure it's *not* a Viking, which would be dreadful luck. And with their 'fit's and 'fa's instead of 'what's and 'who's it might have been either.'

Alec heaved a sigh.

'I can't imagine actually being one of those philly-oolies, can you Dan? It would drive me stark staring mad.'

I nodded. The warm water was beginning to make me feel sleepy. I set the notebook down and rubbed the bridge of my nose. Then I picked it up again.

'I know we said we'd concentrate on the herring folk but . . . Damn it, Alec. Who *are* they all? Greybeard, Swarthy, Ringworm, Viking, Mannequin. What on earth were all that many strangers *doing* here?'

'And it's not even the fact that no one seems to know who they were so much as the fact that no one seems to be at all perturbed by them,' Alec said. 'No one is hiding anything. No one heard any gossip or saw anything suspicious. If they were looking for work on a farm they'd go to a farm. If they were looking for fishing or coopering work all the fisherfolk would know they were. If they were visiting family they would be related to half the village.'

'So who are they?' I said. 'What would bring someone to Gamrie?'

'Searle's Circus of Wonders.' Alec held up a hand as I sighed.

'We've been round that already,' I said, 'and we vowed not to go round again.'

'We've been round the question of *visitors* to the place,' said Alec. 'Have we thoroughly dismissed the question of men delivering animals? They might have come down into the village after dropping off their charges.'

'Not the young one the Murrays gave a lift to.'

'He might have had a dormouse in his coat.' This time my groan had some laughter in it too.

'If we're really abandoning our good intentions to stick to the fisherfolk, we should simply go back to the Searles and ask,' I said. '*They* didn't put him in a barrel, whoever he is. They shouldn't mind telling.'

'While the ones who should mind telling do nothing but chuckle,' I said.

'But we'd still need some kind of excuse for such blatant nosiness.'

We both thought about it for a moment.

'We can come at via the ghosties,' I said at last. 'Ask them about this slow lady and the glowing fishermen – they'd have a good view from Lump House – then surmise that young Nesta might be mistaken, fanciful child that she is. From there it's only a step to the way she was startled by the animal handlers, since no one in the village seemed to find them remarkable etc etc.'

'I tell you what's remarkable,' said Alec. 'Your sleight of hand with the truth, Dandy.'

I nodded then sat still just looking at him.

'What is it?' Alec said

'I don't know,' I replied. 'Something you said. Or I said. It was bothering me earlier when we touched on how they speak, these villagers. Or something about the dates. I keep thinking we've missed something very obvious, Alec. I just can't say where.'

'How they speak?' Alec said 'Worst man? First man? Dates? Midsummer? Midwinter? Year's turn? Year's end? Something about that?'

'Don't,' I said. 'Don't badger me. I'll ask the Bennets about all of it if we can get along there tomorrow. Or maybe it'll come to me on its own. But don't go truffling or I'll never remember what it is to my dying day.'

I I

When I awoke the next morning, I kept my eyes screwed shut and wished with every fibre of my being that I was at home. If, by magic, I could have transported myself out from under Miss Clatchie's meagre blankets and placed myself instead in the cocoon of eiderdowns in my bedroom at Gilverton, with a maid lighting a fire and another bringing a tea-tray, I would happily have left Gamrie behind for ever. Bunty, who had got round Miss Clatchie and gained bedroom privileges, was pressed hard up against me down one side. That side of me, in consequence, was almost warm, but every other part, my nose and Buntyless shoulder and both my feet, were aching with a chill which must have taken all night to settle into me. I could hardly believe I had slept through it at all and I resolved to speak in the strongest terms to Miss Clatchie until either she lit the bedroom fire or produced a paraffin heater or in some way made this comfortless chamber worth what it was costing Mr Birchfield to keep me there.

The curtains shushed as a particularly strong draft rattled the window and I got up to see if I could turn the catch a little more. It was so dark outside that I was surprised to catch a glimpse of a figure slipping along the street and opening the door of Baird's the Grocer's, and even more surprised to see the light spill out before the door shut again. If the shops were open it had to be at least eight in the morning. I craned and looked up at the sky – as black as midnight – then turned away, lit my lamp and hurriedly dressed myself. I had recognised that figure and wanted to catch him.

Alec was finishing off the teapot in the front room when I clattered downstairs and Miss Clatchie was just coming through from the kitchen to the front of the house with a tray to clear the breakfast things. She glared at me.

'I was beginning to wonder if you were ill,' she said.

'No, I'm fine,' I told her. 'I just slept in.'

'I suppose it's a compliment,' she replied, most grudgingly, 'to the warmth and comfort of my accommodations, but I can't provide you with another breakfast, I'm afraid, so you'll just have to— Where is it?'

She was staring down at the card-table which, apart from a few crumbs and a smear of marmalade, was stripped bare.

'I was rather hungry,' Alec said.

'You ate two breakfasts?' said Miss Clatchie. 'Two whole breakfasts?'

'Two helpings of porridge and two slices of toast,' said Alec, correcting her, but she could not be shifted from her state of scandalised amazement.

'Sorry, Dan,' Alec said. 'I was starving.'

'After that lovely dinner I put on last night? How could you be?' said Miss Clatchie.

'I went out for a walk,' Alec said. 'Up to the telephone kiosk.' He gave me a hard stare. I raised my eyebrows, asking silently what Mr Birchfield had told him. He rolled his eyes at me, answering silently that Mr Birchfield had confirmed what Alec knew and that I had been wrong.

'I'll go over to Baird's and buy some biscuits,' I said.

Miss Clatchie only stared, caught between letting herself be mollified and allowing herself still to be outraged, but Alec recognised the note in my voice. He knew that I had more than biscuits in view. He was standing and dabbing his lips, asking me to wait while he fetched his coat, as I let myself out of the front door onto the street.

A gust of wind straight from the Arctic almost blew me off my feet as I stepped out from the lee of the building and my stockings, below the hem of the oilskin, were immediately drenched as the wind whipped up a little tidal wave out of a puddle and lashed it over me. I knew I would have itchy legs now for the rest of the day.

'Godforsaken, miserable corner of Hades,' I muttered. 'Freezing cold outside and in and starving too!'

Then I was at Baird's door, gathered myself and entered. 'Why, Mr Searle!' I said. 'Good morning.'

Warwick Searle paused in the transaction he was negotiating with the grocer and turned to greet me with a bow.

'Mrs Gilver,' he said. 'What an unexpected pleasure.' He stepped aside and ushered me forward to the counter. 'Please, go ahead of me. I don't want to take up your time.'

'Nonsense,' I said. 'You were here before me. I can wait.' From inside me I could feel a loud growl which would suggest I could not wait a moment, but I trusted that my layers of tweed and oilskin, not to mention the howling of the wind and the drilling of the rain on the windows, would muffle the worst of it.

'I was just asking Mr Baird if he thought his van might get up the hill today,' Mr Searle said, raising his voice over an even louder thump of wind which set the roof slates creaking and made the glass scrape in the window frames.

'And I was just saying that I can't see my way,' said Mr Baird. 'That brae's like a spout already and the top road'll be a sea of mud.'

'I shall take my provisions in two baskets then,' said Mr Searle, 'if you can spare a barked sack to top them.' The shop bell tinkled again and Alec joined us. He nodded to Warwick Searle and shot me a quizzical look.

'I can't let you have two baskets today, Mr Searle,' said the grocer. 'Everybody's laying in for the wedding feasts and I'll need them all.'

'Well, what's to do?' said Searle. He was getting rather flustered. He pointed at the list in the grocer's hand and spoke quite frenziedly. 'We need these things, Mr Baird, and it might not – it almost certainly will not, be at all suitable for me to come down again.'

'I think you're wrong there,' said Mr Baird. 'I think you and your brother should come down and stay put, Mr Searle. There's a storm coming. The doctor and the minister will be down off the high road and you should be too.'

'That bad?' I asked.

'A house on a cliff edge with old trees all round?' Mr Baird said. 'You'd no catch me staying up there.'

'We shall be fine,' said Mr Searle, far from convincingly. His thin cheeks were flushed with circles of pink and his hand, so languid when he had been entertaining us in his drawing room the other day, shook as he drew his wallet out of his pocket.

'Have you had a mutiny?' I said, in a light voice to defuse some of the tension which crackled in the air.

'What's that?'

'Won't your maid stir in this filthy weather?'

Warwick Searle looked astonished and even Alec gave me a bit of a glance. I had thought the servant problem was a safe topic with anyone these days, and the Searles' maid who did not answer the door nor serve the tea nor do the shopping sounded like the worst kind of problem servant.

'I like to be out and about,' he said with very little effort to sound convincing.

'Well, let *us* help out anyway,' I said. 'We'll walk up with you and then bring the baskets back to Mr Baird in time for the rush. What is it today anyway? More plenishing? Tick-filling? We are very lucky to have got here at just this most interesting of times.'

'Washing and mucking and dishes today,' said Mr Baird. 'But not till after dinnertime.'

'Plenty time for us to walk to Lump House and back then,' I said.

'Dandy,' said Alec. 'A word if you please. Excuse us, chaps.' He drew me outside where I was horrified to see Bunty sitting in the scant overhang of the entryway.

'Alec, what on earth?' I said 'She must be freezing.'

'She came downstairs after you rushed out and Miss Clatchie wouldn't let her take up her place in the kitchen until she'd been, well, "exercised" was the polite term she used. But I didn't want Searle to see her.'

'I should think not,' I said. 'His eyes would light up.'

'Anyway, what's this nonsense about carrying his shopping home? Rather suspicious, isn't it?'

'Needs must,' I said. 'It would be a great deal more suspicious to slog up there for no reason at all and saunter in saying we felt like a stroll in the driving sleet. Anyway, I feel sorry for them. This maid they speak of is clearly imaginary. They're shifting for themselves. So I don't mind helping.'

'Well, Bunty can't walk up that path in this weather,' Alec said. We looked down at her and then both moved in a little closer to protect her from the rain. 'So you take her off and I'll tackle Searle.'

'Oh, no,' I said. 'You got your crack at him yesterday. It's my turn today.'

'You think he's going to reveal all, don't you?' Alec said.

'One can dream. He might say a red-haired chap delivered a . . . giraffe and then never appeared back at the pet shop.'

'Very well,' said Alec. 'I think I shall investigate the brae. Do we really want to be stuck here if the weather worsens and the roads close?'

'We'll discuss it later,' I said. 'Get Bunty away before he sees her.' I rested my hand on her briefly and rubbed her between the ears, but her tail did not even twitch. She simply looked up at me with her forehead drawn up into a peak. If she could have magicked herself out of Gamrie and back to my sitting room and a blanket on my pale blue chair she, like me, would be off like a shot. 'And thank you, Alec dear. For the telephone call.'

'Quite the most uncomfortable I've ever made,' said Alec. 'And I expect poor Birchfield had to go for a lie down.'

'Mr Osborne has had to go to take care of some other business,' I said, as Warwick Searle came out of the shop a moment later.

'There's really no need for you to go to so much discomfort and trouble,' he began. I wrested one of the enormous baskets out of his hands, surprised at the weight of it, and shushed him.

'I wanted to speak to you anyway,' I said, 'so let's kill two birds with one stone.' I hoisted the basket higher onto my arm, pulled my sou'wester down with my free hand and started the long, uncomfortable and probably pointless trudge along the shore, up the path, and through the trees. From the corner of my eye I saw Alec peering around the corner of the Three Kings, waiting for us to get on our way before he slipped inside out of the rain. I could not be sure but I suspected that he was smiling.

'I've been hearing about your ghost,' I said to Warwick as we entered a lane cut crossways into the hill and the wind died down for a moment.

'My ghost or Gamrie's ghost?' he asked.

'The slow lady,' I said. 'I don't suppose she's yours exactly, but she haunts the hilltop, or so I hear.'

'Indeed,' said Warwick. 'I'm not a fanciful man, Mrs Gilver.'

I supposed not. How could he do what he did if he were?

'Have you not seen the glowing spectres of drowned fishermen out at sea?'

'I regret to say I have missed that entertainment.'

'Well, there are none at the moment anyway,' I said. I supposed John Gow had finished his goodbyes or did not care to wash into shore and see his brothers and his betrothed's sisters enjoying what he would never know. 'It was little Nesta Chalmers the gravedigger's daughter who told us about them,' I said. 'She has a flair for finding the dramatic possibilities in life.'

'Oh?' said Warwick, but we were at the corner of the lane and our respite was over. As we turned into the teeth of the wind, surely close to a gale now, all conversation became impossible. I felt a stab of pity to see such an elderly gentleman as Mr Searle put his head down and battle his way along with stinging cheeks and smarting eyes. Could the budget of the two brothers really be beyond a single servant? Or could they simply find no local girl who would consent to live in the ghoulish place Lump House had become under the Searles' peculiar stewardship?

It was not until we turned off the beach into the fold in the cliff that we could talk again. The bellowing of the wind stopped as though someone had turned off a gramophone and although the rain still fell, it came down in sheets without the wind to blow it around. I raised my head and let my neck straighten.

'Your animals upset her,' I said. Warwick stopped dead in his tracks and stared at me, his mouth working silently.

'Nesta Chalmers,' I said. 'The gravedigger's girl.'

'Oh,' said Warwick and he shook his head. 'I had forgotten, forgive me.' Then he started walking again. 'I wasn't aware she had ever visited us.'

'Oh, she hasn't seen the . . .'

'Exhibits,' said Searle.

'It was your brother's creations on the drive. And then she saw some being delivered and was startled for some reason.'

'Oh?' said Warwick again. 'What in particular frightened her?'

'The unfamiliar,' I said, 'which is all that ever really frightens anyone, isn't it? She said "a monster". Which could be anything more outlandish than a sheep, cow or chicken to a Banffshire child.'

Warwick nodded distractedly. We had worked our way to the back of the crevasse and now we crossed the burn on the footbridge and began to wind around the front of the opposite cliff. Once again we had lost our shelter and we fell into silence.

At the top of the path, even after the gust of wind which had unbalanced me on the Main Street that morning, I was astonished to feel just how determined this storm was becoming and for the first time I was glad of the heavy basket making my arms ache, for at least it served as ballast. I stood at the edge of the clearing looking into the trees beyond the gateposts, watching their crowns whipping and thrashing and listening to the groans and creaks as their roots clutched the meagre soil and their trunks bent and threatened to snap.

'Mr Baird might be right,' I said. 'Wouldn't it be a better idea to come down to the Three Kings for a few nights until this blows itself out?'

'We'll be perfectly comfortable at home,' Warwick replied, which was more than could be said of any of Miss Clatchie's guests, to be sure, and so I did not argue any more.

As we trudged into the woods, however, I was sure that Warwick quickened his pace, as though he, like me, did not want to spend a minute longer than he had to with the creaks and cracks promising disaster. Indeed after a particularly loud report just ahead of us, I watched a large limb fall ten feet before it got stuck in the branches all around. I hesitated and looked to see if there was another way we might go. It was then that I realised we were not alone.

I did not see her clearly, for one could not see anything all that clearly on the north slope of a hill in the north of Scotland in December under trees and through a film of rain, but if I had to describe her I should have done so in just the words little Nesta had used: a slow lady. She was drifting between the trees, her head covered with a shawl and her body a shapeless mass of cloak and skirts. I opened my mouth to alert Mr Searle but as I did so the vision grew even less distinct as the shadows darkened, then we turned a corner in the drive and she was gone.

I was not looking forward to a second viewing of Durban's painted figures on the drive and was not sorry that Warwick peeled off onto a pathway before we reached them and took us, splashing on an ill-kept brick walkway, around the back of the house. From here it was easy to see the extra wing where the Garden and Ship of Wondrous Bounty had been installed; it was an enormous warehouse-like structure of very work-a-day pink brick, quite at odds with the old stone of Lump House proper. The roof, I was surprised to see, was made of tarmacadam rolled over the eaves in sheets and nailed down. It creaked alarmingly as we passed by and I saw Warwick give it a wary glance.

'Miss Clatchie has plenty of rooms,' I said. 'Although some of them are reserved for ladies, it's true.'

He did not answer but only opened the kitchen door to enter. I followed him in.

I know that I am blessed with Mrs Tilling; she bakes unstoppably in that rather grim Scotch way, with very little chocolate and a lot of sultanas, and especially in the winter months she tends towards the rib-sticking and comforting rather than the delicious exactly, but she runs a very tight ship. Pallister, in turn, keeps the silver and wine and all of the maids ship-shape and as for Grant, it is almost like having Nanny Palmer back again to be in her care. So all in all I felt very sorry for the Searles and their imaginary maid when I saw the mess two men trying to look after themselves had made of the kitchen. There were a great many pots and pans steeping in water in the sinks and hardly any left on the dresser shelves. There was a loaf of bread, a packet of butter and a pot of jam, each with a knife sticking out of it, on the table and enough crumbs and smears around to draw rats like the piper of Hamlyn.

'I'll just empty all this out,' Warwick said, beginning to unpack one of Mr Baird's baskets, 'and let's go to the drawing room for some sherry. Durban likes to put the provisions away.'

I glanced at the bottles and jars of this-and-that proprietary concoction which littered the sides of the stove and hinted at Durban's cooking, and thought to myself that he seemed to prefer leaving them lying around.

'I'd welcome one,' I said. 'Miss Clatchie does not run to sherry and while I should never have admitted it, I have been missing a glass of something to punctuate the day.'

I unpacked the last of the wrapped packages – one I rather thought from its shape and soft weightiness was either bacon or tongue, certainly something for a cold larder immediately, but I did not want to interfere.

In the drawing room, under the suspended octopus, trying not to look at a family of small monkeys which cavorted on top of the piano, I returned to the point where our conversation had been overtaken by the elements outside.

'We're studying folklore, Mr Searle,' I began, 'as you know. And while all the stuff about the fishing boats and the wedding plans is marvellous I think we might have stumbled on something even more intriguing.'

He inclined his head with gentle interest and waited for me to go on.

'There are so very many peculiar stories of mysterious fleeting strangers,' I said. 'I came across the tales having plucked a topic quite at random just to get them talking, you know. I certainly didn't expect to hear of so many. At least five of them. I was almost beginning to wonder if it was some kind of elaborate tease, something they say to outsiders for fun, but Miss Clatchie at the hotel has confirmed sightings of two of them and fun is not Miss Clatchie's way.'

'*That* was why your brother asked about our visitors' book!'

said Warwick. He had drained his glass and he refilled it now. 'Why didn't he say so? I was puzzled about that yesterday.'

'He didn't want to seem suspicious, I expect,' I said. 'These people are your friends and neighbours. He didn't want to appear mistrustful of them.'

'But yet he told you he didn't believe our protests of innocence and you returned to try again?' said Warwick. He spoke in an airy, off-hand way, but there was a rebuke in there somewhere. I should have to tread carefully.

'It was what Nesta said about the animals that made me think of a possible answer to the puzzle,' I said.

'Does she watch out for them?' said Warwick. His glass was empty.

'I think when they have to open the gate, you know.' I could speak as airily as he could any day. 'She liked the cows and horses.'

'Horses?'

'I'm sure she said "wee horsies". . . . perhaps not . . . but she was alarmed by something she didn't recognise. So if you had a kangaroo or a rhinoceros this last year . . . Anyway, that's beside the point, forgive me. But it did occur to me that if you had animals delivered, the men who brought them might well stop off in Gardenstown for a bite to eat.'

'They might well do,' said Warwick.

'So I wondered if you remembered any of them.'

'My eyes are for the stock, not the delivery boy,' he said. 'Even from trusted suppliers one is always slightly on edge until one sees the beast in all its glory.'

'But these were memorable men,' I said. 'There was a dark man and a red-haired man of very sturdy build, who put the villagers in mind of a Viking. An old Glaswegian with a long grey beard and some poor soul with a case of ringworm! Also a rather beautiful young man, but actually he can't have been anything to do with your animals because he said specifically that he was an artist's model. We asked the only resident artists about him but he didn't ring any bells there.'

'The only resident artists,' said Warwick and there was an amused glint in his eye. 'You do not consider what my brother and I are doing an art, then?'

'Oh,' I said, fearing that I had begun to colour. 'I do apologise. Why of course it is! How rude of me.'

'I'm teasing you, Mrs Gilver,' Warwick said. 'The fisherfolk aren't the only ones to want a little fun.'

I laughed sheepishly, but stopped when Warwick held up a finger.

'Here comes Durban,' he said. 'Now, he takes things very seriously. And I know you wouldn't want to upset him.'

Durban Searle was without his cap this morning and wore a cloth turban instead. He had his bedjacket on but it looked stretched and mangled as though he had wrung it out hard and then put it on when it was damp.

'Have you been outside?' his brother said, leaping up and drawing the little man forward to the fire.

'A stroll,' said Durban. 'A little very gentle exercise. So important, you know. Fresh air too.' He rubbed his hands and held them out to the blaze.

'It's not much of a day for it,' I said. Durban turned his magnified eyes in their spectacles until he was gazing at me with a rapt expression on his face, all the more striking because he was shivering, presumably from the cold but added to his stare and his solemn voice one could not escape the sensation that he was trembling from excitement.

'It's a wonderful, wonderful day, dear lady,' he said.

'Durban,' said his brother.

'We are so very busy and so very nearly finished,' he said. 'Our life's work! Our magnum opus! Our legacy!'

'What is it?' I asked, reasonably enough, but he shook his head and put a finger to his lips. 'And is that why you're so dead set against coming down out of the storm?' I asked

Warwick. 'But wouldn't you be taking a little holiday for Christmas anyway?'

Durban's eyes were dancing.

'A Christmas holiday!' he said. 'That's the last thing on our minds, isn't it Warrie?'

'Durban,' said his brother again, 'why don't you go to the kitchen and put the shopping away. There's a good chap. Open the door of the range and let the warmth dry your coat.'

Durban immediately trotted towards the door.

'Did you get everything we need?' he asked. 'Is everything ready?'

Warwick nodded patiently and his brother pattered out. It was only as I watched him leave that I noted the wet footprints his carpet slippers had left on the dusty boards. He had not even put boots on to go out in the rain.

'Would it surprise you to know that my brother has a degree in chemistry from the University of Oxford, Mrs Gilver?' said Warwick once he was gone. 'He's a brilliant man. Far cleverer than I.'

'So is the taxidermy *your* profession?' I said. 'Did your brother join you when he retired from his work as a chemist?'

'Oh, he never worked,' said Warwick. 'He didn't hold a position. Why, he could no more do a job than he could fly.'

'He's a very pleasant gentleman,' I said. 'And taking care of him this way as you do? Well, that's hardly the work of a rotter either.'

I left him shortly afterwards, setting out from the front door, past the dripping monsters, swinging one of Mr Mason's baskets in each hand.

It was only as I was passing the gravedigger's cottage that I realised Warwick Searle had managed not to tell me what outlandish creatures had been added to their menagerie in the summer. Nor had he given a definite answer to the question of remembering the delivery men. He had even wriggled out of saying how he came to taxidermy and embarked on these gardens and ships and whatever this last one was of bounteous wonder.

All in all, it was a long cold wet trip for just about nothing.

Or it would have been if I had retraced my steps down the cliff path. Instead, I decided to walk the dead man's way, stopping off at the doctor's and the minister's house, which should not be hard to find. Both men still puzzled me somewhat, as did Miss Clatchie's view of them, and I had the perfect excuse to go and pester them today; I would pretend – though I would not need to try too hard – that the warnings of storms and maroonings had frightened me.

Halfway along the dead man's way I began to change my mind, but since I was probably about as far from the good ash cliff path as I was from the main road I pressed on, 'over my cuits in glaur' as Mrs Mason had said, but telling myself I was five minutes from the Chalmers' cottage and no more than ten from all of Gardenstown and so it was silly to be worried about getting lost or washed away in a mudslide, or indeed about the slow lady. I told myself it had been a trick of the light, or Durban Searle rearranging mannequins, or Mrs Chalmers out collecting mushrooms. I did not believe what I told myself, but the telling passed the time and, in any case, I reached the road without the spectre troubling me.

It was a relief too, to be out from under the trees. The planting was less dense on the glebe land than in the grounds of Lump House and the soil was deeper too away from the rocky edge of the cliff so that there were fewer alarming noises overhead the further I went, but still the thrashing branches made the storm sound worse than it could possibly be and far from providing shelter, the canopy seemed merely to gather the raindrops into larger servings. All in all I was happy to be on the road, bowling along with the wind behind me, ignoring my stinging cold fingers and toes and planning another assault on Miss Clatchie's hot water. Probably the large glass of sherry after missing breakfast was insulating me a little too.

A manse is never hard to spot and I knew that Reverend Lamont's house was square and grey and stood on the hilltop facing the Three Kings directly, so when I saw a square, grey house on the road, midway between the Lump House lane end and the Gamrie turn-off, I unlatched the gate and walked confidently up the weedy path to knock at the door. The paint was faded and the brass tarnished and it seemed to have exactly the look of a place where a busy minister's wife tried to keep Boy Scouts, Girl Guides, parishioners and dirt at bay with no money for decent staff to help her. When the door was opened, however, it was not this harried wife, nor her unsatisfactory maid who answered; it was Dr Trewithian, in his tweeds but with his stethoscope around his neck.

'Mrs Osborne,' he said. 'Have you come to the surgery? How can I help you?'

'Gilver,' I reminded him. 'You've got us mixed up.'

'I beg your pardon,' said the doctor. 'Miss Osborne as was. Well, it's easy to mix up a brother and sister if the family resemblance is strong.'

I faltered, my guilty conscience lending portent to what was surely just empty chit-chat, and then as the sky above us seemed to gather a breath and redouble its efforts at driving needles of rain down to wash the world away, Dr Trewithian shook himself and stepped back to usher me in.

'I won't come further than the mat,' I said, eyeing the parquet floor of his hall. It was dusty but it was finely worked and I feared for it if I were to cross it, dripping like a gripped sponge. 'Actually, *I'm* in rather a muddle too. It was Reverend Lamont I was looking for.'

'Ah,' said the doctor. '*Nothing the body suffers that the soul may not profit by.*' Then he went on in his ordinary voice. It's the next barracks along. This is Blyth House. You want Blackscares Manse for the minister.'

I could not suppress a titter. 'Blyth House and Blackscares Manse?' I said. 'Really?'

'Quite a flavour of the Pilgrims' Progress, I've always thought.'

'Actually,' I said. 'You'd do just as well as the minister. I only wanted to ask Reverend Lamont if this dreaded storm is really going to be as bad as the village thinks.'

'The village!' said Dr Trewithian. 'Most odd to hear you, of all people, refer to it en masse that way.'

This was true enough: a scholar of peasant traditions should find endless variety and nuance in the people of Gamrie and not view them as one great dollop, as normal people do.

'If so, we need to decide whether to leave now,' I said, ignoring him. 'Or at least bring the motorcar up the road to save being stranded there.'

'You are quite welcome to park here,' said the doctor. 'But I don't think the storm will hit until Christmas Eve or even Christmas Day at the earliest.' He waited. I said nothing. 'You're not thinking of staying on over Christmas, are you?' he said. 'That's a great deal of dedication to show to folklore.'

'But observing the local Christmas traditions is a rich seam,' I countered. 'And besides, it's the wedding week. It's the high spot of the year for folklore.'

'And such a wedding week!' said Dr Trewithian. 'Five of them. Your husband doesn't mind your staying?'

It was a charge I had often had laid, sometimes in the form of a question as now, but more usually framed as a declaration, from middle-class matrons who believed that their seniority entitled them to harangue me. The doctor was a bit of a departure then, but his effrontery summoned the same response as the effrontery of all the matrons down the years. I stared hard and then turned away from the subject as one would from a dead dog in the gutter.

'Thank you for the offer, Dr Trewithian. We shall see. Now,

I wonder if you could tell me something, since I'm here.' I paused. He said nothing. 'It's about the "strangers". I think we mentioned the stories of strangers?'

'I think you did,' said Dr Trewithian.

'I don't suppose you saw any yourself?' I said. 'Only I'm beginning to suspect that the villagers are pulling our legs.' Of course, I suspected no such thing. 'It's not uncommon,' I went on, 'to tease interlopers with such tales. I believe that the natives of Borneo have managed to convince many an explorer that there are cannibals in the next village. Always the next village, you see.'

'I've heard of no such thing here,' said Dr Trewithian. 'But I've had no strangers in my waiting room either. If they exist at all, they're a healthy lot. And unless a man falls ill or injures himself, I'm none the wiser about the comings and goings below.'

'They are all men, as it happens,' I said. 'Well, good day, Dr Trewithian, and thank you again for your advice and your kind offer.' I turned to go, then half-turned back again.

'Are the brides or grooms ill?' I said. He frowned. 'Only I'm wondering how you know that there are five weddings, "below"?'

'Oh, I take a keen interest in anything of that sort,' said the doctor, utterly contradicting himself.

Anything of *what* sort, I wondered to myself as I went on my way. He was a most peculiar individual. Then I turned my thoughts to the next one.

The manse was plainly visible just a little ways further along the road and I made for it determinedly, ignoring the squelch underfoot, a triple squelch from my saturated stockings, sodden shoes and the waterlogged ground at the edge of the road, three parts moss to one part grass if that. It looked as though I was to be denied the shelter, coffee and shortbread for which I had begun to hope, however, for as I arrived it was to see the Reverend Lamont letting himself out of the front door and a woman dressed in the same severe black, going as far as a little scrap of black lace on her head, seeing him off.

'Mrs Gilver?' said Reverend Lamont. 'Mrs Gilver and her brother are those sociologists I was telling you about,' he said to the woman beside him. 'This is my wife, Mrs Gilver.' I was recovering from the surprise of my promotion – sociologist! – but managed to smile.

'I shan't shake hands, Mrs Lamont,' I said. 'Your hands are dry and my gloves are soaked.'

'Dreadful day,' she murmured.

'That's what brings me,' I said. 'I'm wondering about all these warnings. Are we really in for it, Reverend?'

'In for it?' said the minister.

'A bad storm,' I said. 'Ought my brother and I at least to drive the motorcar up here to the top road in case we're cut off down there?'

'*Praise the Lord upon the earth*,' said Reverend Lamont. '*Ye dragons and all deeps; fire and hail; snow and vapours: wind and storm fulfilling his word.*'

'Exactly,' I said.

'Oh, Douglas!' said his wife and, without another word, she slammed the door shut on both of us and turned the key. Or perhaps the wind caught the door just as she was shutting it politely, but she certainly locked it.

'My wife is a worrier,' said Reverend Lamont, unperturbed by the scene. He lifted his hat, unrolled his umbrella and began his journey, back the way I had come towards the church. In short, he left me standing there.

I stood there for quite a few minutes too, dripping, shivering, staggering a little to keep my footing as the wind threatened to topple me. Shortbread! I thought to myself. Some hope. Then I turned and squinted towards the village. I had seen something. I cupped my eyes and squinted harder and there it was again: a flash of light somewhere in the endless stretch of greyness in front of me. It was too far to be in the field, I thought, and too near to be out at sea. If I had to hazard a guess, I should have said it was just about where the huddle of Gardenstown itself separated the two.

It was not until I was almost back at the Three Kings that I realised where the light must have come from, if not after all from a boat out in the bay or a farmworker's lantern. I was actually standing on the Main Street at Miss Clatchie's front door when it occurred to me. Reverend Lamont had pointed his umbrella up the hill and shown us his home. I looked again now. It was a mere coincidence that, as the jumble of cottages had been squashed in, each on top of the last, a series of lanes and steps had happened to line up so that from here, halfway along Main Street, one had a view all the way to the high road and Blackscares. And if looking up from Miss Clatchie's one saw the manse then the reverse was true, if looking down. Was Miss Clatchie sending signals? What about? And to whom?

It was Alec who answered my knock. He was probably slightly chilly and rather peckish, as was the resting position at the Three Kings, but he looked to my eyes replete with warmth and comfort and I must have been a sorry sight in his because he drew me inside very tenderly and urged me to the front room while he went to scare up some tea for me.

'I heard that noise again,' he said when he returned. 'The banshee wail. It definitely comes from that room next door to yours.'

'Could it be something mechanical?' I asked. 'Perhaps a lantern of some kind? I saw a flashing light when I was outside the manse and thought perhaps she was sending signals.'

'To the minister?'

'Or the doctor,' I said. 'He said something rather odd about his knowledge of "comings and goings below" – meaning here in the village. And he contradicted himself.'

'Oh?' said Alec. 'Contradictions are always welcome. People only make mistakes if they're lying. What did he get wrong then?'

'Nothing very definite, just that he said he didn't concern himself with village life but then he mentioned that he took a "keen interest" in the weddings, for instance. A wedding is surely village life of the first order.'

'Interesting,' said Alec.

'He called the weddings "*that* sort" of thing.'

'What sort?'

'Precisely,' I said. 'I loathe hinters. And he was definitely hinting at something. Gloating almost. Most unpleasant man. I'm sorry I ran into him.'

'Who?' said Miss Clatchie. Alec had left the front room door unlatched and she had nudged it open silently to come in with her tray. 'Who's an unpleasant man?'

I assumed the only thing one could assume: that Miss Clatchie, like the scared little rabbit she so closely resembled, feared the advent of another uncouth foreigner in our midst. And so it was on this point that I reassured her.

'Don't worry, Miss Clatchie,' I said. 'There are no more queer strangers in Gamrie as far as I know.'

'So it's a local man who has displeased you?' she said. And she did not sound like a scared rabbit at all now. She had pink spots on her cheeks and her voice thrilled with emotion. 'I told you the fisherfolk were a rough lot.'

'They are simple people,' said Alec. 'But they've treated us with perfect courtesy.'

'Well, who else is there?' demanded Miss Clatchie. 'Mr Muir is as nice a man as you'll ever meet. Mr Baird too.'

'Indeed they are,' I said. 'And Reverend Lamont.'

'A saint amongst men,' she said. 'He hasn't an easy life but you'd never hear him complaining.'

'And then of course, there's Doctor Trewithian,' said Alec.

Miss Clatchie sniffed.

'You'd be hard pressed to find anyone who calls *him* a saint,' she said. 'We're not as green as we're cabbage-looking.'

'How tantalising,' said Alec, once she had left us again. I was concentrating on the luncheon tray, having eaten not a morsel all morning, and so I let him carry on instead of guessing. 'Dandy, I think you might be onto something with your flashing lantern theory. Miss Clatchie might well be communing with the saintly Lamont. Or, even more interestingly, to Trewithian, about whom she has just protested a little too much.'

'What would she be communing about?

'Strangers,' said Alec sepulchrally. 'Fresh meat for Dr Trewithian's underground laboratory. They come to Miss Clatchie's hotel and are never heard of again.'

Of course he was joking but his smile did not last to the end of the speech and mine faded on my lips too.

'A couple of them *did* come here after all,' I said. 'And we *did* wonder what a Cornish doctor was doing in Banffshire.'

'Dandy,' said Alec in his patient voice. 'We heard an odd noise and you saw a flash of light. We don't even know if they are connected. Perhaps the light was out at sea and Miss Clatchie keeps a . . . thing that makes that noise in the locked room.'

'What thing?' I demanded, caught between relief that the dreadful idea had gone again as quickly as it had come, and chagrin that my theory, its origin, was dismissed in its wake.

'I don't know,' Alec said. 'An inefficiently serviced set of bellows. Or a sea-monster in a tank. I'll pay closer attention if I hear it shrieking again.'

12

looking.'

And the day was not even half done. I was determined to
track down another of the five brides, besides the two Mason
girls and Janet Guthrie. It did not take me long to do so.
Clambering down one of the lanes from the Three Kings,
beginning to think I recognised it and if given six months
with nothing to do but wander might eventually make a map
of Gamrie, I was surprised to see on a bare patch of rough
grass six feet square a huddle of women, about eight or nine
of them, all facing the other way, looking as though they were
waiting for something. Had they been at a bus stop in a town,
one would not have given them a glance, but they were in a
dead-end corner halfway up a lane in a tiny village at the
beginning of a renewed bout of rain. This had all the mark-
ings of a piece of Gamrie tradition that a philly-oolie should
not miss. As I slowed and watched, one of their number
suddenly sprang to life.

'That's us,' she said. One of the women shuffled forward
and began strenuously working at something I could not
see.

'Hello, ladies,' I called out. A couple of them turned.

'Ocht, it's yourself, Mrs Gilver,' said one.

'What are you doing?' I said. I edged forward until I had
a clear view of the woman at the head of the queue. At the
back of the empty patch of ground was an iron pump with
a stone basin below and the first woman in line was filling a
bucket. All of them, I could see now, had buckets with them
and that should have been the end of my interest except that

amongst their number was Mrs Guthrie and I distinctly remembered Mrs Guthrie drawing water for tea out of a tap in her kitchen.

'It's feet washing today,' said the woman nearest to where I was standing. 'I'd be very pleased if you'd come and see my Cissie getting done.'

'I would love to, Mrs . . .?' Her name was Walker, she told me. 'I should be honoured. I wonder if I could start my pestilential questions now, in fact. Why are you out in this terrible weather to get water from the pump?'

'Ocht, thon kitchen water's not right for washing the quines' feets,' she said. 'We had our feets washed in this good water, and our mothers and our grannies. Twould be bad luck to use that kitchen water.'

I nodded, as though in understanding; perhaps I did understand at least partly. For how was it different from the way my own mother used to have milk and vegetables sent from Northamptonshire on the train every day when she opened her London house for the season? I could understand asparagus and melons being carted the hundred miles, but even the onions and potatoes of Covent Garden market were spurned in favour of those which had the good soil of home still clinging about them.

'And might I just ask,' I said, 'why you did not fetch the water when the rain was off? Oh well, I suppose you've been awfully busy.'

'We couldn't wash the quines' feets with old water that had been lying,' said Mrs Walker and there was a murmur of assent from her friends. 'We waited until the clocks struck noon for there's bad luck you cannot escape in this life but there's bad luck you bring on yourselves.' This earned an even stronger murmur and some headshaking and tooth-sucking too.

Then a voice piped up.

'All the more queer not to see Mrs Mason here, eh?'

I pricked up my ears.

'Aye, I'd be making sure I didn't catch Auld Clootie's eye.'

'I think Auld Clootie's forgot about the Masons,' said a third voice. 'Maybe she's right not to help him remember.'

Mrs Walker had got to the front and was filling her bucket. Her head was slightly bent and her expression innocent but there was the smallest curling smile on her lips and I took a guess that she enjoyed a gossip. My heart, accordingly, leapt.

'Now, Old Clootie,' I said. 'Would I be right in thinking he's the chap I'd know as . . .' but I could not go on for every one of the words I brought to mind – Satan, Beelzebub, Lucifer – was the most shocking taboo to any Scotch villager, I knew.

'Old Harry, my English auntie calls him,' said one of the women.

'That's him,' I agreed. 'And I'd be honoured to watch you outwit him.'

'Welcome you are, Mrs Gilver,' Mrs Walker said.

'I need to take these baskets back to the grocer but I'll be straight along, if you tell me where to come to.'

'We're at 74 Seatown,' she said, which meant that while it would be easy to find, not tucked into the maze of lanes, I would receive another buffeting and another soaking on my way. I was beginning to run out of dry clothes and did not relish the prospect of storming Miss Clatchie's kitchen and demanding my share of the dolly.

Mrs Walker was boiling the water from the pump when I arrived, the bucket set right on top of the range. As I seated myself at the scrubbed table in the lea of a high mantelpiece with its pair of lamps and the inevitable wooden clock between them, I could not help my nose wrinkling

'Aye it's good strong water,' she said, wiping her brow. She had been hanging over the pail watching the proceedings and her face was shining with heat, her thick wavy hair beaded with moisture. 'Just take a sniff of it. That's no peelie-wallie kitchen water! Greta Mason should get herself up there and fill every pail in the house. Auld Clootie misses nocht.'

'Is Mrs Mason particularly in need of good luck?' I said. 'I know about her daughter.'

'Her, they quines, they laddies, old Gow too. It's not right, Mrs Gilver, It's just not.'

'The double wedding?' I said, making a very hazy guess. Annie Mhor, showing me round the cottage, had said that an eldest son married first, so I could see that both Gow boys marrying together might be unusual. But these were financial considerations surely, and nothing to do with luck. Or was it, I wondered, a question of two brothers marrying two sisters? Was there perhaps a whiff of something nasty about *that* to the fisherfolk? But surely that could not be. These families were intertwined and intermarried like a thicket of vines, hence the need for teenames to tell which Nelly or Nesta or Norah had married which Jimmy or Johnny or Jock.

'Two brothers and two sisters and John Gow a drownded man,' said Mrs Walker. 'I'd no more let my Cissie marry to a boat with a drownded man that I'd let her marry a chimney sweep up the town there.'

Mrs Mason had been about to say something similar, before she caught herself and stopped it, and at last, it began to make a glimmer of sense to me. At least I thought I could see the sense it made to others, for of course the reason that fisherfolk from the tip of Shetland down to the Scilly isles were so very closely concerned with luck, the reason for this foot-washing and plenishing and eldest aunts and flag hanging and the whole rigmarole, was that if bad luck came along what it came along and did was wash a man overboard and carry him to the bottom of the sea. A woman on a boat, a minister on a boat, a black cat, a pig or a white hen glimpsed at the harbour – all of these things were dreadful luck. But a drowning was by many measures the worst of all. Now I understood Janet Guthrie's sickly relief that her handfasting to John Gow was over with by the time he died, and her mother's rather unseemly satisfaction (disguised as pity) for poor Mrs Mason whose girl had snagged the Gow boy after Mrs Guthrie's own girl had failed to keep him. I understood too why the double wedding was felt by all around to be tempting the devil far beyond what he would bear.

'It is rather surprising,' I said mildly and then I could not continue since at that moment the rest of the party arrived in the shape of the bride, young Cissie Walker, in high good-humour, and her elder sister, whose condition was beyond that even of the older Mason girl. She moved at a lumbering waddle and looked from every angle like Humpty-Dumpty just before his fall. Behind her was a further Walker woman, either a much older sister or a young aunt; and finally there came my acquaintance, Annie Mhor, from the day before, stumping along with that same determined stride which had taken her up ladders and got her within a whisker of launching herself from an upstairs doorway on a rope, as in her youth.

'Here's Granny Annie!' said the waddling girl.

'Come away, Annie Mhor,' said Mrs Walker. 'And we'll not keep you.' She turned to me. 'Annie Mhor here – Agnes Baird, she is – is the oldest wifie in Gamrie parish. She'll be busy enough today!'

'I've got five quines' feets to see tae,' said old Mrs Baird, hugging herself. 'Five! Aye, it's a happy day.'

'So you're doing the Mason lassies?' said Cissie Walker. Now all the women shuffled a little and cleared their throats, shooting little glances between themselves, Mrs Baird and me.

'I am,' said Mrs Baird. 'There's no ill luck can come to me fa it, only good fa me to them and Dear knows they need it.'

'But you've not been there yet,' said Mrs Walker. 'You've not come here fa their door?'

Now even old Mrs Baird looked a little shifty.

'I haven't, no. I thought to myself I'd maybe get round the rest and then finish at the Masons last of all.' There was a rush of air as all gathered let out their held breath. Mrs Walker reached down an enamel basin from a shelf behind the range, and I took out my notebook, twisted up a good inch of my propelling pencil and readied myself to record the ritual.

To be honest, I was almost interested. There was such a biblical flavour about it along with an undeniable tenderness. As the bride took off her stockings and sat in the best chair and her sister, puffing and laughing, managed to settle her bulk onto a low stool, I could not help but look upon them kindly.

'When is your baby due?' I asked her.

'Any day!' she said, with a shout of laughter. 'Just like the thing if I get to wash Cissie's feet but miss the dancing!'

'Heavens,' I said. 'That's rather unfortunate timing.'

'Aye, tis the way,' said Mrs Baird. 'The lads is home in April at the year's end so the babbies aye come in at the year's turn. Then they're back at the year's turn too like now when the seas are too high for the fishing so it'll be the same come September. And the babbies that are started in July in the season will be here to meet their daddies come next April again when it closes.'

'Gosh,' I said, almost dumbstruck by the strong whiff of an agricultural almanac that arose from these very definite timings.

'Grannie Annie, you've made Mrs Gilver turn red!' said Cissie.

'Fit?' said the old woman, throwing me a look of disdain. 'You're a married woman yourself, are ye not?' I nodded. 'With cradles filled?'

'Two sons,' I said faintly.

'Well, then,' said Mrs Baird, an argument which could not be faulted.

'Mrs Gilver, since you've brought it up,' said Mrs Walker. She cleared her throat and I gave her an encouraging smile. I had no idea what subject she was circling.

'You're a married woman, as you say,' she went on. 'And interested in our ways.' I smiled again. 'You'd no be wanting to hold back the luck you could bring.'

And so it was that I found myself, in my turn, crouched on the low stool with a towel spread over my lap, gently washing the feet of young Cissie Walker while the women of her family looked fondly on. Of all the unexpected tasks my detecting career had bestowed thus far, it was certainly one of note.

Grannie Annie, Annie Mhor, Agnes Baird had gone off to her next appointment by then and as soon as she had left, the Walkers began, softly but determinedly, to pick over the morsel of gossip she had left them. 'I never thought she'd do it,' said the fat sister in a low voice.

'Though she's right enough there's no harm to her fa it,' said the young aunt. 'Different story come the procession. I wonder fit they'll do.'

'They never asked somebody!' said Mrs Walker. 'Never!'

'Asked what?' I said, looking up from my task. They ignored me.

'Not that I've heard,' said Cissie. 'Poor souls.' She gazed down into the water and wriggled her feet, which were beginning to shrivel up from the lengthy immersion. 'I warned Nancy Mason. I told her not to fast to John Gow. But you ken Nancy! There was never telling her anything. She was the same fa she was a bairn.'

'Headstrong,' said her mother. 'Flighty as a town quine.'

'That *was* a mystery wasn't it?' I said. 'I mean, if the handfasting could be dissolved and no harm done, one does wonder why she ran off.'

'Ran off?' said Mrs Walker. I looked up to see them all staring at me.

'Who telt you she ran off?' said Cissie.

'Her mother,' I said. 'That is, she assumes . . .'

'She might be telling herself that to ease her pain,' said the young aunt. 'But a quine fasted to a drownded man? Auld Clootie came for Nancy and took her. Stands to reason.'

'I don't follow you,' I said. Nancy Mason still troubled me; possibly only because she had led me into error and given Alec a reason to scoff at me.

'There's her sisters and the Gow brothers fasted two and two,' the young aunt went on. 'Should be the blackest ill luck in the world and yet the Dear has smiled on them both already. I'm telling you, Auld Clootie has taken what's his before now. Nancy paid the price of a drownded man or her sisters would not be flourishing.'

Even though my hands were immersed in hot water almost to the elbow, I shivered. In the low light of the cottage, as near windowless as made no difference and black as night as the sky lowered and rumbled outside, the faces of the Walker women gleamed like orbs, the only parts of them visible against their dark clothes and with their dark hair.

'But if the debt is paid already,' I said, 'and I do hope for the sake of poor Nancy that you are wrong, then why the concern about the bad luck of the Masons spreading?'

'Ah, you never can tell,' said Mrs Walker. 'You can't take too much care with they things.'

'Aye well, I warned her,' Cissie said again. 'If she'd listened to me she'd still be here the day.'

I had left them and was on my way to the boatyards to look for Alec before it occurred to me to wonder about Cissie's warning. If the bad luck of the Gows and Masons came from 'a drownded man' then what was there to warn a girl about when that man was still alive and walking around?

Out in the streets, the wedding preparations were in full swing. I caught sight of old Mrs Baird trailing a coterie of youngsters in her wake on her way from her second engagement to her third and then, as I turned a corner, there was *another* procession, another band of women, elders to the fore, youngsters at the back, and somewhere in the middle that special category one had come to expect in Gamrie: the blooming bride.

'Aha!' I said. 'This makes the full set of five. What wedding is this then?' There was laughter all round and the bride, spoke up shyly. 'I'm Maggie Dowie,' she said. 'Fasted to Iain Dorbie.'

'Well, all the very best Miss Dowie, or Mrs Dorbie, should I say?'

The laughter grew so raucous at that that I was given greatly to wonder whether the drouth of Gamrie had been relaxed two days before the dancing and the barrels behind the village hall. Other heads poked out of the cottages all around and my little speech was repeated to gales of hilarity. 'Mrs Dorbie! Miss Dowie, is she!' Illumination broke over me before too long.

'What a silly mistake for a so-called scholar!' I said, rolling my eyes and joining in. 'Maggie Dowie and Iain Dorbie are your teenames, are they not?'

'Aye, that's right,' said a woman nearby. 'It's Margaret Wilson by rights and her mammy Margaret Wilson and thon's my mammy Margareta Wilson. Maggie was dowie when she was a bairn in a shawl – never thrived and never thrived – but look at her now!'

'Indeed,' I said, surmising the meaning of 'dowie' like the scholar I pretended to be. All the Wilsons were fine figures of women, but Maggie was positively plump and not only in the way that all Gamrie brides were plump, she was as bonny and round as a baby, with a baby's sweet face and dimpled chin. 'And what is it that you're doing?'

'Carrying the dishes!' came a chorus in reply. Maggie Dowie's mother pointed to a woman with a basket in her arms.

'That's ma sister-in-law, Peggie Man – Margaret Wilson, she is, in the parish book – and she's carrying Iain and Maggie's dishes to the new hoosie.' I peered over the rim of the basket on tiptoe, thinking that it was easy to see how Peggie Man had got her teename; for she was a towering figure of a woman even amongst the run of the Gamrie fisherfolk who did not err towards daintiness as a rule. Inside the basket was a service of good white china with a thin gold rim, the china I had seen on the high shelves of every kitchen in the town. The milk jug and sugar bowl were balanced on top and in them were stuffed silver coins, buffed shiny, and ten-shilling-notes which looked as though they might have been ironed before they were rolled up and added to the treasure.

'Dear me,' I said. 'Yes, now, let me just see.' I opened my bag and my purse and, managing not to hesitate at all, although I quailed inside rather, I extracted a pound note, which was all I had, rolled it and threaded it into the milk jug amongst the silver coins.

The gathered Wilsons stopped laughing at that, and the eldest Mrs Wilson drew me aside and put a hand on my arm.

'You cannot start that, Mrs Gilver,' she said. 'There's five brides in this town – or even if you're thinking on three just – and there's still the procession to go. It would be black ill luck to put more in the dishes than you give at the procession and you'll rook yourself if you keep this up.'

I agreed. A pound in the milk jug and more on Saturday times five weddings in all would make quite a dent in my purse, especially considering that Alec was probably pouring the contents of his wallet into the pockets of the bridegrooms elsewhere in the town.

'If you've a shiny shilling bit, you'd be a true friend,' said Mrs Wilson, taking the note back out and handing it to me. 'We're not moochen or poochen, you know.'

'Of course not!' I said, matching her severity, although I

had not the faintest notion what she was talking about. 'Mooching and pooching are the last thing I should suspect of you.' I had found a shilling.

'With my very best wishes,' I said. '*Mrs Dorbie*.' Allowing them to laugh at me once again was, I felt, a fair exchange for nineteen shillings saved and I waved them on their way.

'"Five brides or even if you're thinking on three just",' I repeated to myself as I made my way to the voices of the men I could hear down beyond the harbour. 'In other words, even if the Mason girls were to be discounted completely.' The Wilson clan obviously shared the common view of the Mason-Gow alliance and I was beginning to agree with Mrs Guthrie: I would not be in Greta Mason's shoes for all the silver in Aberdeen.

The sight that awaited me at the boatyard was striking enough momentarily to drive all thoughts of the unlucky Masons, poor drowned John Gow, even Mr Pickle and the five mysterious strangers, quite out of my head. It seemed that every man in the town had gathered there and in the middle of the great crowd of them, a handful of men – quickly I counted five heads – were staggering around as though intoxicated. At three in the afternoon in a town like this, however, that could not be.

As the crowd nearest to me parted and I caught a glimpse of one of the figures, top to toe, and matters became clearer in one sense although no less mystifying in another. They were staggering because they were barefoot and attempting to walk through a slick of harbour mud and seaweed, clutching at one another, wobbling and skidding, all to the great entertainment of the watchers. As one of them finally overbalanced altogether and went walloping down, taking another with him, an enormous cheer went up from everyone around.

'Poor blighters,' said Alec, appearing beside me.

'What's going on?'

'Foot mucking,' he said. 'While the brides have theirs

washed the grooms have theirs greased and muddied and tarred and – I'm sorry to say but – I rather fear there might even have been some animal droppings. It's barbaric. Savages with bones through their noses could not have dreamed up anything less civilised in their jungles.'

'You sound positively gleeful,' I said.

'Of course,' said Alec. 'It's the funniest thing I've ever seen. Whoops! There goes another one.' This time the unfortunate bridegroom fell flat on his back and pin-wheeled around, tripping up a second who landed on top of him.

'I think I shall leave you to it,' I said. As the mother of sons, I had long ago passed beyond being amused at mud and grease and tar, not to mention the last ingredient Alec suspected in the current concoction.

'There is something I want to ask you, Dandy,' Alec said.

'I'll wait for you back at the hotel,' I replied and was turning to leave when I saw an elderly gentleman advancing.

'Mr Osborne, is it?' the man said. 'I'm John Gow.' His voice was doleful and his face was cadaverous and just for a moment the dark day and the talk of the devil and the shrieks and howls of the men all around reached into me, shook my reason and left me with the fleeting notion that a ghost stood before us. He cleared his throat and put his pipe in his mouth and the notion was gone.

'My laddies have told me of your offer,' he said. 'It's right couthie of you.'

'Um,' said Alec.

'It means kind,' I said.

'And you're a couthie buddy yourself too, missus,' said Mr Gow.

'This is what I was meaning to tell you, Dandy,' Alec said. He had the airy tone he gets in his voice when he has made some sweeping decision without me and hopes to get it past at a trot and without inspection.

'Thank you, Mr Gow,' I said. 'I hardly know whether to

congratulate you on your sons' upcoming marriages or give you my condolences on your dreadful loss this year. You must be quite at sea with so many reversals of fortune and causes for joy and sorrow.'

'At sea,' said the old man. I gulped. 'Nah, don't say sorry, my quine! That's just the word for it. I'm at sea. But I've found calmer waters than I hoped to, thanks to you.' He tipped his hat, turned up his coat collar and went stumping off into the gloaming. I watched him until his figure was swallowed up by the darkness and the sheets of rain and then turned to Alec.

'Every wedding needs a best man and a best maid,' he said. 'No one can argue with that.'

'No one is trying to,' I said. 'Alec, what have you done?'

'I've helped,' Alec said. 'I've inveigled us both right into the heart of the village on the most important day of all.'

'Have you volunteered me to be some kind of matron of honour to the Mason girls on their wedding day?' I said.

'Absolutely not,' Alec said. 'You couldn't be more wrong.'

'Good.'

'Peggie and Nellie are going to be one another's best maids, which is rather sweet. And Robert and William Gow are going to be one another's best mans.'

'Men.'

'Quite.'

'I daresay they always would have done so, no matter what had happened or not happened. But do you happen to know why we have best men and maids at weddings, Dandy? They are there to confuse the evil spirits. To draw bad luck away from the happy pair.'

'I didn't know that,' I said. 'That's actually rather interesting. I must say, if it weren't for the impenetrable vocabulary I'd be getting genuinely diverted by some of these quaint traditions.'

'I'm very glad to hear it,' Alec said. 'Because that's only

half the story. As well as the best man and best maid, the quaint tradition here in Gamrie is to have a worst one too. A sort of double bluff. Keep the wicked spirits on their toes. It's like a Shakespeare comedy, in a way, lots of mix-ups.'

'Go on,' I said.

'And obviously, the worst maid and man dress in a particular way, differently from the other members of the party. And so, just as obviously, the Gow boys and the Mason girls can't do both jobs. And because of the drowning – which is the most appalling bad luck for fisherfolk – they were having the devil of a time finding anyone else who'd volunteer.'

'Oh, Alec!'

'But for rational people such as ourselves there can't be the slightest worry.'

'Of course not,' I said. 'But . . .'

'But what?' Alec was scowling at me. 'I've pulled a masterstroke, Dandy, and you know it. We're going to be smack in the middle of things on the wedding day, able to talk to anyone and watch everyone. I should rather think congratulations and thanks were in order instead of complaining.'

'What about these "different clothes"?' I said. 'We're going to be guyed up, aren't we?'

'Well, yes, frankly,' said Alec. 'Yes, we are. Old clothes and blacked faces. But—'

'And what if the investigation leads us elsewhere?' I asked. 'How can we track down leads at Lump House, for instance, if we're cavorting around the village in rags all day?'

'One day,' said Alec. 'And it'll put us in better stead than ever with the locals for all the investigating that comes after.'

'Only with the Gows and Masons,' I retorted. 'Serve us right if everyone else in Gamrie slams the door in our face once we're full to the brim with bad luck!'

'How did you get on with the Searles, by the way?' he said. 'I meant to ask you earlier but Miss Clatchie's mysterious noise distracted me.'

'You're changing the subject,'

'Back to the investigation, where it belongs.'

I sighed. 'Warwick Searle is a slippery customer, I've decided. He told me nothing.'

'Do you think he knows anything?' said Alec.

'Not really,' I said. 'The Searles clearly can't have put someone where Mr Birchfield found him. So . . . I suppose you're right. At the very least, the townspeople will believe in us all the more if we blacken ourselves in the name of research.'

'The blackening is tomorrow, actually,' said Alec. 'And not to be missed, I'd say.'

'I'm glad there's nothing else on the docket for today,' I said. I was chilled to the bone and wanted nothing except to hug Bunty, huddle over Miss Clatchie's three pieces of coal and sip at a small cup of her lukewarm tea.

There was, as it transpired, one more encounter before I could do so. As I regained the Main Street I saw the Bennets enter Baird's the grocers with baskets over their arms even larger than the one I had lugged all the way to Lump House for nothing. I could not even remember what it was I wanted to ask them, only that there was something somewhere in my notebook and so, hoping that I would either find it or remember, I hurried after them.

Inside Baird's a paraffin heater was going at full blast, turning the air thick and delicious.

'Oh,' I said. 'That's the first time I've felt properly warm all day.'

'Mrs Gilver!' said Mrs Bennet. She pushed her sou'wester back and unwrapped the scarf she had wound around her head inside.

'I haven't come to return your things!' I warned her. 'They've saved me from pneumonia so far and unless the forecast is for a change . . .'

'Far from it,' said her husband, turning from where he and

Mr Baird were poring over a list together, 'and that's what brings us here. We're stocking up and battening hatches.'

'Aye, we're in for a bad one,' Mr Baird said. 'And what we get here Crovie gets twice it.'

'Wouldn't you be better to stay put in town?' I asked.

'Oh, we'll be fine,' said Mrs Bennet. 'It's rather fun to shutter the house and sit tight, so long as we can keep the range lit.'

'Well, I don't want to keep you,' I said. It was the sort of thing Scotch housewives said all the time and it usually signified 'I've had enough of you, be off,' but in this instance I meant it plainly. I could not imagine slogging back along that beach path to Crovie in the dark with the tide coming in and a storm on its way. 'But,' I went on, 'there was something I wanted to ask. Some particularly puzzling bit of Doric that we came across. Now what was it?' I was leafing gingerly through my notes, trying not to tear the damp paper.

'Mooching and pooching!' I said. 'That wasn't the one I meant but I'd love a translation if you have one.'

'Hmm,' said Harry Bennet. 'They both mean more or less the same thing, don't they Mr Baird? Trying to take something you've no right to have . . . not stealing exactly, but in that general area.'

'Moochen is wheedling a favour,' said Mr Baird. 'Poochen is poochen like poochen anywhere, be it salmon or rabbits or anything.'

'Poaching!' said both Bennets and I together, then all four of us laughed.

'And I remember now the item that gave Alec all the trouble,' I said. 'It came back to me when you said salmon and rabbits, Mr Baird. It's some sort of recipe. What might someone have done if they said they had "slicked an oaty".'

'Slicked?' said Mrs Bennet.

'Slicked,' I said.

'An oaty what?'

'That was the entire phrase, as far as I know,' I told her.

'Slicked doesn't sound like Doric, does it Harry? "Slickit", might it be? "A slickit oaty" might be some kind of buttered biscuit. Mr Baird?'

Mr Baird was busying himself packing the Bennets' basket, but he looked up with a blank expression and shook his head.

'That's a new one on me,' he said. 'I can't help you there.'

I did not miss the fact that he held himself rather stiffly until the Bennets and I began our leave-taking. Not until it was clear we had no more questions did he unhunch his shoulders and let his breath go.

13

Dr Trewithian had sounded very certain that the storm would not be upon us until Christmas Day but I lay in bed on the night before Christmas Eve, wide awake from four o'clock onwards as the wind howled and banged around outside, whistled and groaned inside, and set the roof timbers creaking like the rigging of a sailing ship. In the moments when it dropped I could hear the sea walloping harder than ever, booming and crashing, and occasionally too there were shouts, even as early as this, long before dawn, and I imagined the fisherfolk retying ropes, battening, tightening, taking to safety all of those barrels and lobster pots which had until now been stowed in the lee of the breakwater wall. I hugged Bunty harder, huddled deeper under the covers, and told myself that the silver lining to sleep's being banished was the chance to review all that Alec and I had learned. Five strangers. Five strangers in this tiny town, with no tea-room, no public house, no reason for strangers to be there at all. And only that one, the young chap who called himself an artist's model, with the slightest hint of a purpose in coming. Warwick Searle had shown no sign of remembering a swarthy face, a long beard or red hair and, when I thought it over calmly, what sense did it make for a deliverer of exotic animals – or even of horned cows and wee horsies – to be murdered by the fisherfolk and hacked to bits? Where was the motive?

And if one of the strangers had been so murdered and hacked, surely someone in the town would be unnerved by Alec and me turning up asking about them. Alec, however, had been right on the score. The strangers had made no impression for good or ill. No one wondered about them; no one cared about them. Certainly no one appeared to be unwilling to talk about them. Or about anything else at all. Granted, Mr Baird had been reluctant to talk of poaching but a grocer in a fishing village might well be. Or was it the 'slickit oaty' which discomfited him?

By and large, the 'drownded' man and the bad luck he brought were the only topics which turned the fisherfolk silent and that at least was easy to understand; perhaps there was some guilt mixed in. Perhaps no one had cared much for poor John Gow and so they all felt uncomfortable now. After all, *something* had caused Cissie Walker to issue her warning. Unless she were prescient it could not have been his future drowning.

I turned again, causing Bunty to groan and open one eye to look balefully at me. I really had to forget all the distractions. If I humanly could I had to forget about the endless esoteric rituals of handfasting and weddings. Someone last July had died or been killed and been put in seven herring barrels, right here in this little town. The fishermen, Gows or whoever, who caught the herring might not know a thing, just as the coopers who made the fateful barrels could not be blamed. It was one of those lasses who held the key. The herring lasses packed the barrels; they had knives which flashed as quick as the silver shoals themselves. Sharp enough knives to butcher a corpse? They worked quickly. Quickly enough for the deed to be done there at the farling with dozens of people around?

I flinched as the wind gave an extra roar and a slate slithered down the roof to smash on the cobbles. Immediately the drafts inside the house grew stronger still and the whistling through my bedroom keyhole rose in pitch until, simply to escape from it, I threw back my bedclothes, felt for dressing gown and slippers and got up to claim the bathroom and begin the day.

I met Alec in the front room half an hour later, unsurprised to see him looking haggard.

'Not a bloody wink,' he said. 'Even before the roof started blowing off above my head. I'm going to insist that she shift me downstairs tonight, Dan.'

'Poor thing,' I said. 'I'll loan you Bunty if I can get an extra eiderdown in her place.'

'But at least it gave me some thinking time,' Alec said. 'We've got to stop letting ourselves be distracted.'

'I agree,' I said, but it did not cause him to temper his rather belligerent tone.

'The weddings are beside the point,' he said. 'We've been in danger of letting our disguise mislead our investigation. There are scores of people in Gamrie who have no son or daughter marrying this week, and we've been neglecting them. I think we should make a systematic survey of the town and try to compile a list of herring gutters, then make sure we talk to all of them.'

'I agree,' I said again.

'So you take care of that,' said Alec. He saw my mouth drop open but he sailed on. 'And meanwhile I shall be doing a census. If Mr Pickle wasn't a stranger he must have been a local man. I'll bet you a fiver that some household in Gamrie has reduced by one since this time last year – some chap who said he was leaving to seek his fortune in the south and never actually got away. I bet you a fiver that somewhere in this town is a mother or a sister who is waiting for a letter that never comes and who'll be only too glad to speak of her loved one to me. So. A census.'

'Very seasonal,' I said. 'You do realise it's Christmas Eve, don't you? It's odd to be in a place where Christmas is so stringently neglected.'

'Are you homesick?'

'Not a bit of it. Hugh and the boys will be as happy as can be in Norfolk. They'd eat their goose between slices of bread in the stable yard if Aunt Elizabeth Gilver would let them.'

'Aren't you even a little sad?' said Alec. 'Not to be with them when Father Christmas comes?'

'I cannot begin to explain the dreary misery of this house party I'm missing, Alec,' I said. 'And even if I were at home: the servants' party; visiting the tenants with their Christmas boxes; wretched charades; Boxing Day drinks with God-alone-knows-who.'

'Me, usually,' said Alec.

'Well, since you are here, I'm glad I am too,' I said, smiling. Then we both ducked instinctively as an enormous clap of wind hit the house. 'Or I will be unless the roof blows off and we're sucked out to sea.'

Miss Clatchie, entering with the breakfast tray, overheard this and deepened the frown she had already been wearing.

'My roof is well-made and in excellent repair,' she said. Then she coughed. 'You might need to move to one of the back rooms Mr Osborne, away from where the slate got a wee tate dislodged.'

'Dislodged?' said Alec. 'It blew clean off and crashed to the ground, Miss Clatchie. I shall be moving downstairs today. I'll take the room adjoining my sister's.'

'I can't allow that, I'm afraid,' Miss Clatchie said. 'Reverend Lamont and his family are moving down into the village this afternoon and I'm expecting the Searle brothers too, in all likelihood – they usually come down when it gets bad. So I won't have room on the first floor.'

'Do you mean to tell me that the Searle brothers and the Lamont family are to be lodged in the large comfortable rooms which were forbidden me on account of my sex?' said Alec. The word shrivelled Miss Clatchie like salt on a snail, but even still she managed, faintly, to reply.

'The Searles are elderly gentlemen and Reverend Lamont is a *minister*.' She banged the tray down and without even pausing to unpack it, leaving us to shift for ourselves in fact, she turned to go. 'None of them would subject me to rough talk in my own front room,' she threw over her shoulder from the door.

'I wonder how she fares with the Bible if that's rough talk,' said Alec once she had gone. He unloaded the plates of porridge and cupped his hands around his own for warmth. 'And she's wrong about the Searles. They told me they were staying put no matter what theatrics the weather laid on for them. So as soon as she gets a room prepared for them, I'm moving in. And if they crack and come down after all they can have the attic. It won't kill them.'

'If they come at all,' I said. 'But returning to herring quines, if you're doing a census, you don't think you could just ask about occupations while you're at it and leave me free to pursue other matters?'

Alec shook his head.

'We'll rattle through it twice as fast if we split it,' he said. 'And if we don't get sidetracked with a lot of nonsense about strangers and mattresses and the like. Tomorrow, when we're at the weddings themselves, we can reap the rewards of a day spent in preparation.'

He spoke so stoutly that I found myself nodding. It was fairly typical, then, that in fact we spent the day up to our necks in yet more wedding rituals, discovered yet more mysterious strangers and even got in a third visit to Lump House, which we had just agreed had nothing to do with the case at all. Thank goodness for all three of our failures too, for a list of herring gutters as long as the wedding processions themselves and a census that Caesar Augustus would envy would not have helped us one jot as we cast off into the coming stormy days.

To kill two birds with one stone I decided to start with the Masons. Old Mr Gow had seemed pretty sure that the girls would welcome my offer, but it seemed to me like the worst cheek to barge into their wedding party without at least a semblance of waiting to be asked. As soon as old Mrs Mason clapped eyes on me, however, as she opened her door the merest crack to see who was out and about on this wild morning, I could be in no doubt of what favour I had conferred.

'Hold they shutters, Peggie,' she shouted over her shoulder. 'Nellie! Shut over the range door lest the fire blow out.' When she was satisfied, she opened the door and pulled me in but, even in that short space of time, the wind bludgeoned in with me, wrenching the door almost out of Mrs Mason's grip and setting the china rattling and the clothes on the dolly waving. Together she and I hauled the door over and she fastened it tight, wedging a blanket roll along the bottom to stop the draft whistling across the stone floor.

'Fit a day, fit a day!' she said. 'Dear grant that it blows out tonight and lets us have our procession and dance tomorrow.'

Peggie and Nellie were standing on either side of the hearth, looking strangely shy, for they were towards the cocky end of Gamrie womanhood and none of the herring quines would have made a deb. They smirked and looked at the floor and pushed one another forward for quite a minute before their mother lost patience and appointed Peggie the spokesman.

'Come on, cushie,' she said. 'You're showing me up.'

'Old John Gow said you and the mannie were going to help us out,' said Peggie. 'And we're right grateful. We'd not like to get wed without a worst maid, would we, Nell?'

'Aye, we're much obliged, Mrs Gilver,' said Nellie. 'I hope it's not rain, sleet or snow when you're walking with us. Sure and I do.'

'I'm tremendously pleased to be asked,' I lied. 'Such fun to embed oneself right into the very heart of the celebration. Alec and I shall get a journal paper out of the experience unless I'm mistaken.'

Mrs Mason turned from the stove where she was busy with the kettle and cast me a sharp look.

'You're going to talk to the papers about us?' she said. Peggie and Nellie had stilled.

'Not a newspaper,' I said. 'A scholarly journal and all anonymous.'

'But if you tell our tale,' said Peggie – 'Two sisters wedding brothers in Banffshire, everyone'll know it's us just the same.'

'We shan't mention the double wedding,' I said, kicking myself for mentioning the entirely fictitious journal. 'We shall simply say that we served as worst maid and man for a—'

'But everyone'll know,' said Nellie. 'They'll know it was the wedding that couldn't get a worst maid and had to settle for—'

'Here!' said Mrs Mason. 'Less of your cheek.'

'Let's talk of other things,' I said, making a valiant effort not to be outraged by their ingratitude. 'My brother and I have gathered all sorts of wonderful material in the last few days, but rather unsystematically. If you really would like to show your appreciation you might answer a few questions for me now.'

The tea was ready and as it was poured and drunk I coaxed them into telling me more than anyone – folklorist or fish-monger – could ever want to know about herring.

I learned that whereas there were three, four or five men to a boat, according to their skill or the type of engine, no matter what, there were always three lasses in a gutting crew: two to ply the knives and one, the tallest, who could bend over and reach to the bottom of the barrel without toppling, to pack the gutted fish.

'Nancy was our packer,' said Peggie with a glance at her mother, 'Till last year's turn.'

I nodded unthinkingly and then her words struck me.

'The year's turn?' I said. 'Not the year's end? You mean she didn't go back after Christmas?'

'She had other work,' said Mrs Mason. 'And I'd not been well. She wanted to stay at home with me.' Then she sighed, took her handkerchief out of her sleeve and wiped an eye.

'I thought it was a rare treat to have one of my lasses stay behind with me for the season,' she said. 'If only she'd gone she'd be here now. And John Gow too, I daresay.'

'Mammy?' said Peggy.

'If Nancy had been there on the boat, he'd have been thinking on her,' said Mrs Mason, 'and not hammering himself for that one last catch. He'd have been sitting safe and tight, talking on the nonsense folk talk on when they're fasted and he'd still be here the day.'

'Aye, you might be right,' said Nellie, turning fearful eyes on her sister. It was the first inkling of guilt or discomfort I had seen from either of them. It got short shrift from Peggie, though.

'Ocht, John Gow would na mair have left his nets bunnelt when he was oot ae erle than he would jump aff a cliff,' she said, her accent thickening with her scorn. 'Catch him sitting wenching if there was herring in the sea! He cared for silver and nocht else, did John.'

I concluded that the custom not to speak ill of the dead was not amongst Gamrie's collection.

'So . . . what wedding preparations are in store today?' I asked hastily. 'Does the worst maid have any duties?'

'Nah, you're fine til tomorrow,' said Peggie. 'We're blackening the brides and hanging the flags this afternoon and then when the sun goes down there's the beds to make and you're not the one for that!' Now all three of the women put their hands up to their mouths and tittered.

'Aye, Rita Mitchell's going to be busy tonight!' said Mrs Mason. 'As busy as Grannie Annie was yesterday.'

'And she's coming, Mammy, eh?' said Nellie, with an anxious look.

'Aye, she's coming,' said Mrs Mason. 'I seen her yesterday and she said she'd be here by nine.'

'We're last again then,' said Peggie, frowning.

'About this blackening and hanging,' I said. 'Where does all of that go on?'

'Harbour head after dinner,' said Peggie.

'I shall look forward to it,' I said, then thanked her mother for the tea, refastened my coat, tied the string of my hat more securely under my chin and prepared to go out once again. The Wilsons were the ones for me. They had been moderately forthcoming about Granny Annie yesterday and I felt sure they could be coaxed into a little more gossip now.

The Rita Mitchell question was easily got out of the way.

'The bride's bed must be made by a woman with milk in her bosom,' said Mrs Wilson. She was busy at her kitchen table, mixing ingredients in an enormous pan. She had poured in a whole tin of treacle and was now grating mutton fat on top of it.

'Ah,' I said. 'Well then, I understand the hilarity when I offered to help.'

Mrs Wilson, although she shared the plump and youthful visage of her daughter, was still able to skewer me with a look.

'Cannot see why,' she said. 'You're a young enough woman still to give your man more sons should he want them.'

I opened and shut my mouth a time or two before going on, and when I did I was careful to start up from quite another area of inquiry.

'I've been very interested to hear more details of the lasses in the gutting teams,' I said. 'They stay together for the whole season, do they not?'

'Sometimes for years,' said Mrs Wilson.

'And sometimes not,' I put in. 'It was odd that Nancy Mason left the trio when the other two were her sisters and they were working with such excellent fishermen.'

'Excellent fishermen with a paraffin engine,' said Mrs Wilson. 'Doubtless she had her reasons, mind,' she went

187

on. 'Her mammy had no been well and she had work at Crovie.'

'And who took over?' I said. 'Who was the third girl in that team for the end of the season?'

'Janet Guthrie,' said Mrs Wilson. 'She's a fine big lass and a quick packer and she was suited fine to get a part season's arlings off the Gow boat. Cissie Walker would have done it too. Her that let John Gow slip out of her grip.'

I coughed as a mouthful of tea went down the wrong way, then carefully set my cup down.

'Let him slip?' I said. 'Do you mean to say that when John was washed overboard, Cissie Walker tried and failed to save him?'

Mrs Wilson stared at me aghast, then she bit her cheeks to keep from laughing as she began to crack eggs into the mixture in her pan.

'She wasn't on the boat home! Neither of them were. It wouldn't be right for a quine fasted and broke from the skipper. They both came home on the Ellen. I meant to say she'd have been happy enough to take the good wages off the Gows' boat even if she didn't manage to keep herself fasted to John and get wed.'

'Cissie Walker was fasted to John Gow?' I said. 'As well as Janet Guthrie?'

'Aye and then Nancy,' said Mrs Wilson.

'Cissie Walker,' I said again. 'She told me she warned Nancy not to fast to him. She spoke from experience, didn't she?'

'Ach, it's the way these clackety times,' said Mrs Wilson. 'In my day a quine would fast to a good clutch of loons before it took and no harm in it. All this lovey-dovey nonsense is ruining the old ways.' She took a wooden spoon and began to beat the mixture she had made. I wrinkled my nose; it seemed that at least one of those eggs was past its best.

'Mrs Wilson,' I asked, 'what exactly are you making?'

'Mixture,' she said, unhelpfully. 'For the blackening. Come down to the harbour head at two o'clock and you'll see.'

Then we both turned to the front of the cottage as a wave swept so far up and over the pathway that we felt the foam spatter against the windows before it ran away.

'Such a shame if the weather spoils the weddings,' I said.

'Ach, a wet dress and a short dance,' said Mrs Wilson. 'The weather can please itself when the boats are home and the loons are safe.'

'They wouldn't go out fishing in this, if the herring were in season, would they?' I said. I was dreading a walk along the street and up the lane; to put out beyond the harbour mouth in one of those rickety little steam drifters was unthinkable.

'Not in arle,' said Mrs Wilson. 'Not with Mr Birchfield, the fair man he is. After the year's end with money tight, who knows what they'd do for an ooty they can sell at the market.'

'An ooty?' I said.

'An out-of-arle catch, I should say,' said Mrs Mason.

'An Ooty!' I cried. 'It's our oaty earl.' Mrs Wilson put down her wooden spoon, put her hands on her hips and laughed merrily until the tears ran in her eyes.

'I know it's funny to you, Mrs Wilson, but that phrase has been driving me batty.'

'Aye, Mrs Gilver,' she said, 'you're a tonic.'

It was high praise from a Scotch housewife and I took it graciously.

'One last question, though.' Truth be told the combination of treacle, mutton and stale eggs was tipping the scales in favour of a wild wet walk as nothing else could. 'What does "slickit oaty" mean? Is it the same oaty as the earl?'

Mrs Wilson laughed louder than ever.

'Slichtin' an oaty?' she said. 'For shame! The Gamrie fisherfolk would never do such a thing. Who told you that, eh?'

And no matter how much I badgered her, she refused to be drawn. It was a puzzle. One might almost have said it was a secret. But the merry laughter and the dancing eyes convinced me that the secret was an innocent one and nothing to do with our concerns. Indeed, one of the first lessons I learned in my detecting life was that everyone is hiding not *something*, but a hundred things, and of a hundred people hiding a hundred things each perhaps two of the ten thousand little facts are pertinent. So, laughing off questions and refusing to answer them rings no alarm bells at all. More, in this case, is the pity.

My next stop was the Walkers' where I hoped to learn more from young Cissie about her doomed betrothal to John Gow and her warning to Nancy Mason, where I *should* have been asking for the names of gutting crews I had yet to meet, compiling the list to match Alec's census. When I got there though, strangers were the order of the day once more.

'It's yourself, Mrs Gilver,' said Mrs Walker. 'Come away in. I was expecting Rita Mitchell but come away, do, and have a nice cuppy with me. The kettle's just on boiling.'

I was awash with tea already but one cannot be rude and so I accepted a third cup and was sipping at it when Cissie and her sister appeared. The elder girl was walking with the slow rolling gait of extreme gravidity today and I could not help but cast an appraising eye over her, for all the world like another of the village women. She saw me looking and laughed as she eased herself into a chair and put her swollen ankles up on the low stool.

'You're right enough, Mrs Gilver,' she said. 'I'm losing hope of seeing Cissie wed. This bairn'll never hold to Sunday.'

'Ocht, we'll just have to bring the long reel through the hoosie and see you that way,' said Cissie.

'Twouldn't be the first time,' said Mrs Walker. 'At my own wedding to your daddy, my Auntie Nessie Dooker was bedded and not kirked yet and the reel went through. Do you know about our kirking, Mrs Gilver?'

I nodded. Truth be told, the Scotch habit of churching women when they rose from their childbed was just about the most outlandish of the outlandish goings-on I had come to know, but years at Gilverton had inured me.

'Aye, well she was,' said Mrs Walker, 'and there she'd flang my blackening not two days before.'

'Oh, Mammy! Not the blackening!' said Cissie. She swallowed hard and pressed a hand to her mouth. 'I'm that sick with the bairn coming, Mrs Gilver. If my best maid flang mutton fat and cabbage water over me I'd disgrace myself.'

'I think I saw Mrs Wilson preparing it a moment ago,' I said. 'There were rotten eggs too.' Cissie gulped. 'And we throw it at the bride, do we?'

'For luck,' said Mrs Wilson. 'So's Auld Clootie wouldn't touch them with a pole.'

'Oh, Mammy,' said Cissie again. 'I'll be sick, I know I will.'

'I've put a wee tate of flour and a wee tate of fresh milk in a bottle of ginger wine left over fa last year,' her mother said. 'It's as sweet as sweet and it'll not turn your peuch.'

'But if it's sweet and nice will it work and bring luck, Mammy?' Cissie said.

'You're not needing to be chasing luck,' said her sister. 'You've got a fine man in Jimmy Drew and you've got a baby well started and a good house. Treacle and eggs is neither here nor there.'

'What do you think, Mrs Gilver?' said Cissie.

'I think ginger wine is extremely sticky stuff and with milk and flour added, you'll be as repugnant to Old Clootie as anyone in Gamrie.'

It was quite the strangest reassurance I had ever given, but it worked on Cissie Walker. She sat back, smiling. Then she turned to her sister and frowned.

'Different story when it's not you, Jenny,' she said. 'Mrs

Gilver, my sister saw a mannie in the summer there the day before she knew for sure this one was on its way,' she pointed rudely to her sister's bulging middle, 'and then we knew all about chasing luck.'

'That's different,' her sister said. 'You cannot be too careful with they things.'

'Which things?' I asked.

They all shifted a little and none of them spoke.

'I'm interested in anything at all,' I said, coaxing. 'I'm interested in your names, for one thing. How do you come to be Jennifer and Christine and not need teenames?'

That got them laughing again. All three of them repeated the names, exotic in Gamrie, over and over.

'I'm Jane Helen, by rights,' said the older sister. 'I got Jean Nell when I was wee and it turned to Jenny. Cissie is Agnes Margaret after our granny.'

'I have a lot to learn,' I said. 'I do wish you would tell me the story you alluded to.'

Jenny sighed, caught her mother's eye, nodded and began.

'I was coming from Rosehearty on the bus,' she said, 'and there was a mannie sitting next to me that I didn't know.'

'A stranger,' I said.

'A stranger and a funny one,' said Jenny. Her sister rolled her eyes and clucked her tongue but Jenny ignored her. And even Mrs Wilson frowned and shushed.

'Nobody's wiser than us all, Cissie,' she said. 'You need to be careful with the ways of the other one.'

'What happened?' I asked.

'I fell asleep,' said Jenny. 'It was a hot day – it was hot all through last July – and while I was asleep this mannie was in my dream and when I woke up I had my head on his shoulder and he was asleep too.'

'I see,' I lied, not seeing at all where the devil fitted into this harmless tale. 'How embarrassing for you. I hope he didn't make a pest of himself.'

'That's not really what was worrying me,' said Jenny. 'It was later that day. I quickened, you see, Mrs Gilver. This one,' she patted her stomach, 'quickened and I felt it. And everyone knows about dreaming together. If that strange mannie had been dreaming of me while I was dreaming of him . . .'

'I see,' I said again and this time it was true. I had come across this sort of notion before. That to see a stranger as your child first moves in your womb is to invite the looks and the luck of the one into the life of the other. It makes no more sense than the tales of women who are mauled by dancing bears and nine months later give birth to furry children, but I knew better than to dismiss it.

'What did you do?' I said. 'Is there any way to circumvent the trouble? Head it off,' I added, at their blank looks.

'Aye, there surely is,' said Jenny. 'Give the stranger some wee thing – anything at all – that belongs to the baby's father and the curse is broken. So I came home and I got one of Gordie's hankies that I'd been keeping and I went to look for the mannie.'

'But he had vanished off of the face of this earth,' said Cissie. 'We searched every street and close and yard in the town and all the farms and both the churches and we could not find him anywhere. Him nor his pal neither.'

'His pal?' I said.

'There was two of them right enough, but they weren't pals, Cissie,' said Jenny. 'They didn't know each other at all. They were just on the same bus.'

I tried to hide my excitement, but this was news indeed. I had not heard before that two of the strangers had arrived in town on the same day.

'Now, Jenny,' I said, 'What did the stranger look like?'

'Oh, Mrs Gilver, no!' she said, real distress in her eyes. 'I couldn't find him. I couldn't break it. If this bairn comes out like that . . .'

'Like what?' I asked her. It took all of my self-control not to prompt her. I knew it was not the ringworm chap for he had come in the Murrays' car, but it could be the swarthy man, the model, the greybeard or the Viking. 'What did he look like, Jenny?'

'Chinese!'

I blinked.

'Are you sure?'

'He was Chinese, or Japanese or one of them. Black, black hair like a hank of silk and a face as pale as a seasick bairn and as round and flat as a plate and he had a wee black moustache that hung down.'

'A Chinaman on the bus from Macduff?' I said, absolutely unable to make the idea enter my brain and stay there.

'Not Macduff,' said Cissie. 'The other bus that comes fa the east. Fa Fraserburgh.'

'And there were two of them?'

'Not two Chinese,' said Jenny. 'Two strangers. The other one was like us except for his long hair. He'd long hair like a picture out of Sunday School.'

I smiled. I was familiar with those highly romantic and highly coloured Victorian renderings of Bible scenes.

'But it was the Chinaman that I sat beside and dreamed about and if he dreamed about me . . .'

'So you searched for him?'

'Until the sun went down,' said Jenny. 'And he was just nowhere. He was on that bus when I got off at the top of the road – I was mortified and I jamp off as soon as I wakened, you know – but he vanished into thin air like a magic show.'

'But,' I began. I took a breath and organised my response into something more conciliatory. 'But he might not have got off the bus in Gamrie at all,' I said. 'He might have carried on to Macduff or even Banff itself. They both might.'

'I went to the kiosk and phoned the bus station as soon as I came and told my mammy,' Jenny said. 'And the wifie there said there was no strangers at all ¡on the bus by the time it got to Macduff. No Chinese and no one with long hair. Two farmers and the minister's wife got off and that was all.'

'Were the boats out that day?' I asked. I knew she would not understand why I was asking but I had to know. 'If it was July, I imagine that all the lads and the lasses and coopers were here at home, weren't they?' All three of the women were frowning at me. 'Only if the boats were in the harbour they might have left that way. Gone for a trip round the coast. I'm just trying to imagine how two men could vanish.'

'The boats were all busy that day,' said Mrs Wilson, very definitely.

'So if you had to set to and start gutting and packing as soon as they came back,' I said, 'the chaps might have been here and then taken off again in the time you were busy.'

'I . . . I . . . I,' said Jenny. 'We . . .'

'Ocht, Jenny, 'said her sister. 'Don't be such a fearty wee rabbit. Mrs Gilver doesn't work for Mr Birchfield, does she?'

I think I managed not to let my astonishment show.

'The boats *was* out that day,' said Jenny. 'It was a fine day and a good wind, but they weren't herring fishing. They were setting lobster pots. One day a year, two if you're lucky, you get a right good wheen of lobster round by here and if any man can take a day off of the herring and he's got some pots to set he can make himself a good bit extra.'

'Well, I certainly don't feel the need to go running to Mr Birchfield with that shocking news,' I said, twinkling at them.

'Aye, that day's lobsters have got me my rig out for tomorrow,' said Cissie. 'A right good blue costume I can wear to church for years as long as I get ma figure back nice after the bairn's been.' Her sister's face clouded again as she remembered the worry which was pressing down on her. We sat in silence for a minute then all three of us started at a rap on the window. The Wilsons had drunk their cups of tea and came to no harm. I, unable to absorb any more after my first two visits, had been nursing mine and it splashed down my front and soaked me.

'It's Gordie and Jim,' said Mrs Wilson. She went to the door and admitted, along with a blast of wind and a flurry of wet snow, two laughing young men, flushed and dishevelled from the weather and in boisterous high spirits.

'Think ye were sitting at a wake!' said the chap I took to be Cissie's betrothed since he came and stood behind her chair. He grasped the back and rocked it. 'How are ye feeling, my lass? Still as sick as you were?'

'See if you break my good chair, Jimmy Peltie!' said Mrs Wilson.

'And what's wrong with *your* face?' said the other man to Jenny. 'It's months since you felt peelie-wallie.'

'I'm fretting and you know why or you should,' said Jenny. She tried to look stern but there was a smile curling at her mouth; his good humour was impossible to resist.

'Ocht, not the wee mannie on the bus again!' said Gordie. 'Here, it's Mrs Gilver, is it not? You're English Alec's sister, aren't you?' I smiled. Alec had got himself a teename. 'What do you think? Will my first son have a pigtail cos Jenny fell asleep on the bus?'

'Of course not,' I said. 'I'm terribly interested in all your ways and find them charming but when it comes to disturbing your peace of mind at a time like this, my dear, I say "phooey".'

'There you go,' said Gordie.

Jenny scowled at him.

'You'll just have been getting Cissie's flag ready, have ye not?'

'That's different,' said Gordie. 'That's a bit of fun and harms nobody. And that's what we came to tell you. The rain's kind o' stopped and the snow's no quite started yet so, if there's to be a blackening and a hanging in Gamrie today, we better get on with it.'

'A blackening and a hanging,' I echoed, as Cissie took herself off into a back room to prepare for it. 'I never dreamed of such entertainments, I must say.'

'Just as well you like it,' said Jimmy, 'for you'll not get up out of Gamrie now. Not by road nor by sea, so you might as well enjoy it. Bellowsnow and all.'

'Jimmy, don't,' said Cissie. 'If we get that on our wedding day, Auld Clootie'll have us.'

'Is the Bellowsnow really so bad?' I asked.

All of them looked around, waiting for someone else to speak first. Eventually Gordie answered.

'You'll know it if it comes,' he said. 'Seeing you're staying put like we all are.'

I tried to smile, but in truth I felt a cold dread steal over me. We had been warned and we had decided to stay, but it was different somehow knowing that we were trapped here. Jimmy's voice echoed in my thoughts as I made my way to the harbour head. 'Not by road, nor by sea. You'll not get up out of Gamrie now.'

14

Most of the citizenry of the town appeared to have gathered at the harbour head. The women were bareheaded, without coats, some of them in the wooden clogs they wore inside the house in place of carpet slippers; and amongst them the brides were prominent in shapeless sacking dresses, with their hair undone and wild in the wind. There was great hilarity – cat-calling, whoops and cackles of laughter – as the women holding the muck pans swung them and advanced on the cowering girls.

'Absolutely barbaric,' said Alec, strolling up to my side and joining me. 'Chivalry from the men and barbary from the women. It's a rum old place this, Dandy.'

He made a good point about the chivalry. In threes and fives – in crews, I supposed – the young men were processing along the breakwaters carrying rolled bolts of cloth across their shoulders. They slipped down the stone steps with the ease of long practice and made their way across the packed harbour, hopping from deck to deck, mountain goats in their sure-footedness despite the way the boats reared and plunged on the swell. When each crew had reached its own boat, the men busied themselves with the rigging and, within minutes all five colourful flags were being hoisted high, snapping and cracking in the wind, straining hard against their fastenings.

'Nailing their colours to the mast,' Alec said. 'There's nothing for it now. The church service is just paperwork. This is the moment when the handfasting binds you for life.'

'How very interesting,' I said, but before I could go on a huge cheer arose behind us. We turned to see that the first of the brides, Janet Guthrie, had been doused from head to toe in a noxious drench of oil, treacle, eggs and milk. It dripped from the ends of her hair and soaked the sacking dress until it clung to her. Out on the boat, her betrothed pulled the foghorn and gave three deafening blasts and the village burst into more cheers and a storm of clapping.

'I think the idea is that the devil would be interested in a new bride,' Alec said, 'so at the salient moment, her friends make sure she's not an attractive prospect. It's quite easy to understand.' I raised my eyebrows. 'If one adopts the necessary, rather insane, point of view.'

Then the crowd whooped again as Cissie Walker underwent her own deluge of ginger wine, treacle and flour and out in the harbour Jimmy pulled the foghorn. I was glad to see that she was laughing and capering and that the mess dripping down her face and front had not sickened her.

'How goes your census?' I asked Alec.

'Splendidly well in the most unhelpful way,' he replied. 'The first door I knocked on offered up the village gossip who told me in great detail about everyone who lives here and anyone who has left and where they went and why and whether they're gone for good and the upshot is that no one disappeared in the summer.' He sighed. 'So we're back to the five strangers.'

'Ah,' I said. 'Except now it's seven.' And as the three remaining brides were blackened and the three remaining grooms blew foghorns I told him about the two men Jenny Wilson had seen on the bus.

'A Chinaman,' Alec said as wonderingly as had I. 'And the dark man and the Viking. Each alone would be out of place. In succession . . .'

'I know,' I said. 'And do you know who it makes me think

of? Dr Trewithian and his "anything of *that* sort" in reference to the weddings.'

'What are you talking about, Dandy?'

'It's rather hazy. More of a hunch than a theory. But it's about Dr Trewithian's presence in a place as settled as Gamrie, with all the women here – except the gutting quines – and all the men gone on the boats, and suddenly there are these strangers. And the way everyone goes on and on about having sons. Breaking and fasting, marrying and breeding. I know you were joking about a laboratory, but still.'

'He's unappealing,' said Alec with a look of great distaste, 'but not as bad as all that surely.'

'I didn't say I liked the idea,' I retorted. 'Only that it had occurred to me. Anyway, there's a problem with the notion that the Chinaman or the long-haired fellow is Mr Pickle. The day they came wasn't a herring day.'

'Was it a lobster day?' Alec said. 'I heard about them this morning too. And do you know what they're called?' I shook my head. 'Slick-ting the oaty.' He made a valiant attempt at the pronunciation, rumbling in his throat as though he had swallowed a fly.

'Are you sure?' I said. Alec glared. 'Only the oaty is the last catch in March, so it's hard to see where summer lobsters come in.' Then I relented. 'But I suppose a windfall of lobsters is illicit enough to explain why people giggle and say nothing when the subject comes up. Still, though, it bothers me.'

'I tell you what bothers me,' Alec said, deftly changing the subject as an elderly man stumped up to stand beside us. I rather thought we had taken his reserved position. Alec took his pipe out of his mouth and pointed to sea. 'Those clouds,' he said. 'I got a weather forecast from some of the lads this morning.'

'It's certainly getting very cold,' I agreed. I shifted my feet on the wet cobbles and was sure that I could feel the crackle of frost under my shoe soles.

'Aye, we're for it,' said the old man. I was beginning to recognise the Gardenstown countenance and this chap had a great deal of it. There was certainly Wilson blood about him somewhere. 'I've felt it turn like this many's a time,' he said. 'Doctor's coming down the hill, minister too and Chalmers the sexton'll be next.'

'I wish the Searles would reconsider,' I said. I turned and looked up at the headland through a sudden swirl of snow. The trees which hid Lump House from view were bent back like stalks of corn and I shuddered to think of the way they had thrashed and cracked all around the house. I faced the old man again.

'When do you think the storm will hit?' I asked. 'Mr Baird said tomorrow night.'

'That's right,' he said, after sniffing the air. 'They'll get the weddings done but there won't be much dancing this Christmastide.'

'Oh, Alec,' I said. 'Christmas too! We can't let those two poor things spend Christmas up there all alone with trees falling on the roof and windows blowing in. If we could get round in the motorcar to pick them up do you think they'd come?'

'No chance of that,' Alec said. 'The top road's flooded, Robert Gow told me this morning.'

'They Searles have themselves a pony and trap,' said the old man. 'Good big wheels and high off the road. If they think on coming down they'll get through the flood just fine.' He nodded. 'So long as they don't wait till it freezes. No pony and trap'll get down that brae if it's icy.'

'Well, that's decided me,' I said. 'This afternoon before the weather gets any worse, I'm going to go and persuade them down to Miss Clatchie's. I shall walk up the path and then come round with them in their trap. In fact, if I time it nicely and get there just as the sun goes down, they might feel obliged to come, just to bring me with them.'

'You can't go alone,' said Alec.

'The chivalry would work better if I did.'

'*Their* chivalry,' said Alec. 'But mine demands I go with you.'

'Wouldn't you rather stay at the hotel and guard your stake in a downstairs bedroom?' He looked so wistful that I had to bite my cheek to keep from laughing.

'I couldn't possibly,' he said, unconvincingly.

'I shall be fine,' I declared. 'I've walked the path three times and it'll be easier with a bit of snow on the ground. Reflected light, you know.'

Besides, I thought to myself as I set off an hour later, it was hardly as though there was any detecting to be done. Unlikely as it seemed, I was truly beginning to believe that a man had come from nowhere, been missed by no one, and been chopped into pieces and stowed in barrels without anyone seeing it done. Except that was impossible. But life out in the open at the harbour was everyone's alibi. Only on a Sunday morning when they were at church, or in the night when they were all asleep, could any nefarious work be carried out. I stopped. There was one other time the streets of Gamrie were deserted. I had seen it myself. I looked around and caught sight of a woman in a nearby cottage yard; she was stirring a barrel with a stick. I unlatched the gate and walked up to her.

'It's yourself, Mrs Gilver,' she said. 'I'm Rita Mitchell's auntie. Nessie Shavie was telling me about you.'

'Shavie?' I said. 'A teename?'

'Aye, aye, Agnes Walker, I mean, by rights. I'm Agnes Walker too – Nandie Toshie, you can call me if you need to make sure the constable gets the right buddy!' She laughed again and then took a firm grip on her stick and hauled a load up out of the barrel. 'Blooming frying oil,' she said. 'Nessie said she put ginger wine and treacle just in Cissie's blackening. How could Rita not help *her* home!'

'Oh! You're washing the blackening clothes,' I said. 'What are you using?' The water in the barrel was fizzing rather alarmingly.

'Ocht, just a wee tate soap and some lye,' said Mrs Walker.

'Well, I wonder if I can pester you,' I said. 'I have a question about the gutter's van.'

'That thing,' said Mrs Walker. 'Fit aboot it?'

'It only comes when the sea is too rough for the boat,' I said, checking. She nodded. 'Was it here in the summer at all? Was there a bad storm any time then?'

'In the summer . . .' she said, giving it serious thought. 'I don't think so, Mrs Gilver, why do you ask?'

'Oh, we ask all sorts of odd questions,' I said.

'So I hear,' said Mrs Walker. 'You and that brother of yours. Only I thought it was our ways you fancied.'

'That's right,' I said, but I was beginning to feel very uncomfortable.

'But all these questions you've been asking, you and your brother, about this summer . . . Our ways were the same this summer as every other summer and winter too.'

'Of course, of course,' I said. 'Anything to get people talking. It's the talk that matters. Not whatever's talked of.'

'Is that right?' said Mrs Walker. She was dressed in the livery of the Gamrie housewife – a long skirt and a jersey with rolled sleeves, a scarf crossed over her front and an apron on, but standing there stirring her barrel I could not help thinking of a cauldron and a broomstick and could not help seeing the piercing look she gave me as cause for alarm.

'You wouldn't be working for Mr Birchfield, would ye?' she said. I stared at her. Finally, *finally*, I had come across someone who had some information!

'Because I always thought he was a good fair trusting man that knew when to be strict and when to let leave.'

I was turned to stone. She could not possibly be insinuating that Mr Pickle was something a fair man would 'let leave', but on the other hand she certainly did seem, alone of all her tribe, to know something.

'I think we might be at cross purposes, Mrs Walker,' I said. 'What on earth has given someone the idea that Mr Osborne and I were . . .'

'Spies?' she said. I blinked. She went on. 'You've been very keen to hear about slichtin' the oaty, have ye not?'

'We've been very keen to hear all the wonderful rich linguistic . . .' I began, but I ran out of steam before I could get to the end of it. 'Mrs Walker,' I said. 'I can assure you that Mr Osborne and I could not care less about a day's lobster fishing. It's of no interest to us whatsoever.'

'You're not spying for Mr Birchfield?' she said. 'On your honour?'

I hesitated for a mere second before answering.

'On my honour,' I said. 'We are not Mr Birchfield's spies.'

It was true. We were detecting a crime, not spying on the fisherfolk for possible breach of contract.

When I went on my way, however, I was conscious of needing to think resolutely of other matters lest I be consumed by shame. Almost I could feel the spirit of Nanny Palmer hovering above me, looking at me over the tops of her spectacles and calling me 'Dandelion'. I ignored her.

And to be frank my attention was drawn away elsewhere quite easily. Even my short talk with Mrs Walker had taken up valuable time and the light was low when I arrived at the beach. It was bitterly cold, too, and the wind was an icy knife, stabbing me through four layers of thick clothes. As I turned into the teeth of it, I let out a whimper and pulled my scarf onto my face. It was hard to know what to call the objects which were striking me. They were not raindrops, nor were they anything as gentle as snowflakes, but I did not think that hailstones could be so sharp, hitting my face like needles and stinging my skin. I huddled further under my hat, pulled my scarf higher still and with only the narrowest slit to see out of, like a knight in armour, I scurried on.

I was only minutes from the Chalmers' cottage; it made no sense to be afraid. But the white swirl was growing faster and faster all the time, blinding me and mesmerising me, reminding me that one false step would send me stumbling down the cliff face to the rocks below. I tried to press myself into the shelter of the hill as I went along, until I was scrabbling like a crab, but all that came of that was that I stumbled over the rough inner edge of the path and put myself in more danger of falling than ever.

'Good heavens, Dandy,' I said to myself. 'It's a path that people walk every Sunday to church. You are not Scott of the Antarctic.' Then because of the unhappy associations that name evoked, I told myself even louder: 'You are not Shackleton.' I set my shoulders back, ignoring the numbing cold on my face and telling myself I was over halfway there, and pressed on.

All was quiet and dark at the sexton's cottage when I reached the clearing and I surmised that they had packed their traps and gone already down to the village to take refuge. I would tell the Searles that as part of my persuasion, I decided.

Under the trees the day was a different beast altogether. The wind still walloped about in the canopy and, far below, the tide still boomed, but perhaps I was becoming used to both; certainly with the woods all around me filtering a stinging spray that was not rain nor snow but worse than both, and with the slight increase in warmth that came from their shelter, I began to feel less sure that the Searles would listen to me. It was a worry that lasted until I reached the drive and rounded the house to knock at the kitchen door. There I felt the full force of the storm for the first time. Without the sheltering cliff, the whip of the wind made my eyes water. Here it was definitely snow, great splinters of icy snow which hit the walls of the house and skittered across the yard. I stood and watched for a moment. If that continued to fall and the wind stayed in the same quarter, the doors would be useless by morning. I started forward again and banged loudly with the edge of my fist. It was a large house and if it was as draughty as Miss Clatchie's the wind could have set up a Wagnerian overture in there.

After a minute, I knocked again.

If I had missed them and was forced to battle my way back down that path, freezing half to death, only to find both Searles in Miss Clatchie's front room with a pot of tea I would feel like the world's premier chump, but if I left the house without making sure I would be the world's most heartless wretch. I tried the handle and it opened so, spreading the enquiring grin of nosy neighbours everywhere over my face, I entered.

'Yoo-hoo,' I called. 'Mr Searle? Misters Searle? It's Mrs Gilver. I've come to take a firm line with you.'

I had got to the kitchen, where I knocked again and then put my head round the door.

'Mr Searle?' I said. There was a scuffling on the far side of the room beyond the range and I thought I saw the door move as though it had been pulled closed behind someone.

I stepped inside and looked around. They were still in residence; that much was clear. The range was lit and someone had been washing laundry; the soft damp air wafting through from the scullery smelled of soap and there were towels and sheets drying over the dolly far above. I crossed the kitchen and opened the passageway door.

'Mr Searle?' I called. 'It's Mrs Gilver. I've come to persuade you down to the village with me.'

The door at the other end of the passageway opened and a figure, very slightly backlit and shadowy, stood there. It was neither of the Searle brothers, that much I knew right away.

'Hallo,' I said. The figure moved and something about its formless outline and the way it shifted triggered a memory and made all the hair on the back of my neck stand on end. It was the slow lady. Here in the house. I stepped back and let the door fall shut. I was halfway across the kitchen to the outside door again before I managed to catch hold of myself and turn around.

When I tried again the figure was halfway along the kitchen corridor towards me. And it was not a ghost, of course. It was a woman. A girl, I rather thought as she came closer. It was, I decided, the Searles' fabled maid. Real after all and not just a figment of Warwick's prideful reluctance to admit that they were without one.

'I was looking for the Mr Searles,' I said. 'You must be . . .'

'The maid,' she said. 'Aye, I am.'

'I wanted to scold them into coming down to the village for the night,' I said. 'There's a dreadful storm coming and everyone in Gamrie seems to be agreed that Lump House isn't safe in this sort of gale.'

We were back in the kitchen now and I got a good look at her. A slovenly sort of person, with greasy hair caught up in a ribbon and a shapeless dress, something like those brides had worn for the blackening. I could not decide if it was a nightgown or the foundation layer of some very rustic maid's uniform which was missing its apron and cuffs. Either way, I could understand the Searles answering their own door and even making their own tea. This girl had the dazed look of a simpleton.

'You've missed them,' she said. 'They're away.'

'To the village?' I said.

'Aye, they put the pony in the shafts and went away on the dead man's path half an hour ago.'

'Leaving you here?' She looked to be no more than twenty-five.

'I said I'd stay,' she told me. 'If it gets too wild I'll go down to the Chalmers.'

'The Chalmers have gone,' I told her. 'My goodness, I think it's a bit rich of the Searles to take themselves to safety and leave a member of the household behind.'

'I'm not complaining,' she said. 'I've seen worse storms than this and I'll get a good bonus when they come back up if I keep the range lit.'

She spoke in a kind of weary drawl and all of a sudden I wondered if, as well as taking off her apron and letting her hair down when her masters had gone, she had helped herself to a glass of sherry or two. Indeed, as I studied her, she blinked lazily and sat down at one of the kitchen chairs as if her strength had run out.

'I'm fine, madam,' she said. 'I really am. You should get back down to the village before it's full dark if you're going on the Sunday path.'

'But it's Christmas Eve,' I said. 'Surely you don't want to spend Christmas Day here all alone in a storm.'

'Christmas Eve!' she said, opening her eyes wide. She looked down and curled her fingers, counting. 'Aye so it is, right enough. Ach, but we're no over much for Christmas in these parts, madam. Hogmanay, it's a different story.' She shifted in her chair and raised a hand to shove a strand of hair back from her forehead.

'Well, it still seems very strange to me,' I said, 'and I shall give Mr Searle a piece of my mind when I see him.'

She merely nodded. I was almost sure the creature *was* drunk. Perhaps if I told the Searles that the maid they had left to hold the fort was swigging the sherry they would make a trip back up here to collect her. In any case, there was no more I could do and I turned to leave. As I gave a last look over my shoulder she was on the move again, trailing across the room with the shuffling steps of an old woman. I tutted before I could help myself. An imaginary maid would not be materially less use than this creature, I thought to myself, and I let myself out into the storm again.

It really was a storm by this time too. Darkness had almost fallen and it was colder still, with a crunch underfoot and that endless, dizzying spiral of snow all around, spinning and swirling and leading me out of my way so that I found myself at the stable wall instead of the path to the driveway. I should, I thought, have asked to borrow a lantern, but if I hurried I would be on the path before the last of the twilight was quite gone and would be down on the shore road again in minutes.

Before I could move though, there was a crackle and suddenly the whole of the yard was illuminated, just for a second, and just a second later an enormous thunderclap resounded overhead. It was the Bellowsnow, just as Dr Trewithian had warned and I did not blame the villagers for fearing it, because there was something ungodly about the dazzling white snow suddenly blaring in one's eyes as the thunder boomed in one's ears. Blinded by the spinning snowflakes, I felt a very primitive kind of terror start to grow in my breast, the terror of being unable to see or hear what monsters were lurking close enough to catch me. I hurried on, through a second sheet of light, ducking as another enormous rumble and crack resounded above me. This one set up an urgent whinnying and knocking of hooves on wood from inside one of the stable stalls.

'Poor thing,' I thought, finding a cure for my fears in hearing another creature's greater terror. If the Searles had taken one of their ponies with the cart and left another on its own in all of this, it would be petrified. I only hoped the slovenly maid had enough compassion and sobriety to go out and calm the poor beast if this most theatrical storm carried on for long.

It certainly had shown no signs of letting up by the time I was trotting along the seatown road. There had been four more sheets of lightning and four more claps of thunder, each one illuminating a world of blind whiteness, snow building up in banks wherever the wind could blow it no further. Already the cottage yards were inches deep when I started looking for the turn to Miss Clatchie's; it was harder than ever to tell which lane was which.

'Dandy!' Alec was standing at the top of some steps in front of me, another shapeless form in his oilskins with the wind ballooning it out around him.

'Oh, Alec,' I said 'I've—'

'I've been worried sick,' he said. 'The doctor didn't see you on the top road and nobody saw you on the shore road.'

'Are the Searles here yet?' I asked.

'Not the last time I checked in at the Three Kings looking for you. For heaven's sake, let's get inside for the night. This is giving me the willies.'

'It's rather odd, isn't it?' I said as another thunderclap rattled the very walls around us and we clutched one another.

'But it's an ill wind,' said Alec. 'The minister and his family have scared a decent scuttleful of coal out of our Euphemia and the doctor, who after all can make all sorts of medicinal claims, has brought with him a bottle of excellent port he's intent on sharing.'

15

It was a different world in the Three Kings with Dr Trewithian and his bottle of port.

'Do you think you'll be here long?' Alec asked him in a hopeful voice, after dinner, when the Lamonts had gone to settle their sons in their quarters and the three of us were alone. I knew why he was asking: we had seen bales upon bales of cardboard files all tied up with Treasury tape, stacked on the stairs until Dr Trewithian gave the Lamont boys half a crown to shift them.

'A night or two,' the doctor said.

'And yet you've brought all of your patients' medical records,' I put in, not quite asking.

'No, no,' said Trewithian. 'Not the records. My work. My real work.'

'We did wonder,' said Alec. The doctor arched an eyebrow.

'You're not just a country doctor,' I said.

'And you're not philologists,' said Trewithian.

'Well,' Alec said with an admirable laugh, 'not good ones.'

'Perhaps I can help you with what you're doing,' said the doctor.

'Perhaps we can help you,' said Alec.

'My work is confidential,' he replied.

'And so is ours,' I put in. 'But we give our word of honour that it's nothing to do with yours.' Again the doctor gave us a look of sly suspicion, almost winking. Thankfully, before anyone could speak again, Reverend and Mrs Lamont rejoined us.

'Padre!' said Dr Trewithian. I had always disliked to hear a Protestant minister hailed that way. At least – I caught myself short. I am sure that when I first moved to northern parts it would not have troubled me a jot. It was Hugh's stern dislike and I had contracted it from him.

'Care to fortify yourself against your hard day's toil tomorrow?' Trewithian went on, waving the port bottle at the minister in the most provocative way.

'I'm for my bed,' said Lamont, 'and have no need of stimulants. *By night on my bed I sought him whom my soul loveth.*'

'Ah,' said the doctor. '*Surely slumber is more sweet than toil.*'

Alec groaned, but quite quietly so that only I could hear him. If there was anything worse than a minister with a good memory for Biblical snippets it was an admirer of English poets with the same; both of them together were a severe trial.

'Rather apposite, actually,' Trewithian added. 'Doesn't it go on: *the shore more sweet than labour in the deep mid-ocean, wind and wave and oar*?'

Mrs Lamont made an inarticulate noise and then put her hand to her mouth, staring over it at the doctor.

'Don't upset yourself, my dear,' said Lamont.

'Oh, Douglas!' she exclaimed and, as she had once before, she turned on her heel and left, slamming the door behind her.

There was a ghastly silence. As I had been brought up to do, though, I filled it.

'It's a big day indeed, Reverend Lamont,' I said. 'The feast of Christmas and five couples to wed.'

'Hmph,' said the minister. 'Well, as to Christmas. I believe Jesus Christ is the same yesterday and today and for ever.'

'Of course,' I said hurriedly. 'As do I.'

'And yet the Bible tells us,' said Trewithian, '*this is the day which the Lord hath made; we will rejoice and be glad in it.*'

'Nonsense,' said Lamont, making Alec choke a little on his latest mouthful of port. 'That's the Book of Common Prayer.'

'But it's certainly the Bible which tells us to rejoice with them that do rejoice and weep with them that weep,' I said. 'Goodnight, gentlemen.'

Alec downed the rest of his port and followed me out into the hall. We could hear Miss Clatchie along the passageway, however, clearly enough to suggest that she had the kitchen door open and so I did not speak until we were on the landing.

'We've been misled,' I said. 'By portentous words and dramatic tones. I don't think that pair know anything or are hinting at anything. They're just a couple of stags clashing their antlers! No wonder Mrs Lamont is sick of him.'

'I'm not so sure, Dandy,' Alec said. 'It was the stuff about wind and wave and oar which upset her. And the doctor's up to something. Something connected to his medical knowledge, something connected to the villagers and something that makes him inimical to the idea of strangers too.'

We stood staring at one another for a moment, each hoping that inspiration would strike us. Then Alec let his breath go in a huge puff.

'Let's turn in,' he said. 'Wait till you see my new billet.'

He showed me the room he had bagged on the first floor, across the landing from mine. It had two narrow beds, one narrow window and one of those tiny bedroom fireplaces set across the corner, but to see his dancing eyes it might have been the honeymoon suite at the Ritz.

'No luck with the one joined on to me then?' I said, stepping over the landing and trying the door. 'It's probably bigger.'

'The door remains locked and the beast sleeps,' Alec said. 'I haven't heard a thing since that last time, have you? But I have a ceiling with plaster and am very content. It's only a shame I have to shut my eyes all night and miss it.'

The next morning, whether from devotion to the church, snobbish pandering to the doctor or some faint recognition in her niggardly soul that Christmas was a feast – albeit a southern, popish, almost heathen one – Miss Clatchie produced bacon and egg along with the solid porridge and misjudged the tea to the lavish extent that every other guest got almost a whole second cup. So what with that, the extra warmth that six more bodies brought to the front room, and the presents which were exchanged, there was something closer to a festival atmosphere than Miss Clatchie's establishment had, I daresay, ever seen before.

The Lamont boys were given books by their father, mittens by their mother, and envelopes containing postal orders by absent but generous godparents, judging by the way their eyes danced as they read the numbers. Mrs Lamont had knitted her husband a curious garment, something like the neck portion of a jersey, which could be tucked into a coat to take the place of a scarf. It seemed an odd affectation for Aberdeenshire, serving to make the wearer look more cosy than he could possibly be and, besides, it was not much of a testament to married bliss to knit one's mate rather less than a quarter of a nice warm jersey. But then Hugh's present to me, handed over before we parted although opened only now, was yet another item of his mother's hideous jewellery, which he has been doling out for birthdays and Christmas every year since she died, and which show no signs of running out. This latest was an evening cuff of opals and garnets set in dull gold and I wished yet again upon seeing it that he had had sisters.

Alec gave me scent – a good big bottle of Worth – and I gave him cigars, chosen by Pallister without my revealing for whom he was choosing them.

The one dull note in all the jollity was that the Searle brothers had failed to appear. Alec, naturally, was unconcerned to the point of sheer delight. He had spent the night in their room and would be sorry to see them at all.

'Stop fretting, Dandy,' he said as I turned yet again to the window at the sound of footsteps in the street outside. 'They must have turned back when they saw how bad the road was.'

'Two old men in a pony cart in that weather!' I said.

'I daresay the maid knew they wouldn't get through and that's why she stayed behind in the warm instead of going out with them and getting chilled and wet for nothing.'

'Lump House, is this?' said the doctor. 'I'd not like to be up there in a storm like this one. That planting was done in the old colonel's time and the soil's no more than a spit thick. The trees'll come down like spillikins one day. Maybe not today.' He added the last point hastily in answer to a mewing from Mrs Lamont and a gulp from me.

'*God is our hope and our strength*,' intoned Reverend Lamont. '*Though the earth be moved and though the hills be carried into the midst of the sea.*'

I was sure that one of his sons sighed. It must be tiresome in the extreme to have a parent deliver quelling little remarks all the time, shutting down discussions and gossip with knockout blows about God's will.

'Perhaps the storm will blow itself out with no damage done,' I said

'*He maketh the storm to cease so that the waves thereof are still*,' said Lamont, inevitably. Even his wife looked rather wearied at that.

'Not a chance,' said the doctor. If he had a bedside manner he evidently saved it for actual bedsides. 'A Bellowsnow is just the beginning. It only happens when the warm air from the landward side mixes with a cold north blast from the sea and whips the rain and snow and ice up into a kind of incendiary cocktail. It can be quite thrilling. If the boats are in. And everyone's down from the high land. Wouldn't care to be at Crovie, mind you.'

'Will the Crovie people come along?' I asked.

'If they can get here,' said the doctor. He was slapping marmalade on a final slice of toast and could not have looked or sounded more delighted with life for a pension. 'Most of them will have come last night to make sure they don't miss the weddings. The rest might try the top road while it's light today.'

I exchanged a worried glance with Alec.

'The Bennets were buying provisions yesterday,' I said. 'That rather suggests they'll sit it out.'

'Were the Bennets here in twenty-three?' said the minister's wife. 'Do you think they know how bad the storms can be?'

'*Poor naked wretches, wheresoever you are,*' sang the doctor, '*that bide the pelting of this pitiless storm.*' I decided that tiresome as they both were, the doctor had it for smug heartlessness. For did not that bit of the play carry on to ask 'how shall houseless heads and hungry flanks and raggedness defend against such seasons?' Although the Bennets had oilskins to spare and a stout little cottage in the shelter of the cliff, not to mention their baskets of provisions, the Searles might as well be naked in the pitiless storm, unless they had indeed turned back and made it home again.

We got no news of them during the morning. Alec set off for the Gows and I for the Masons to be inducted into the ways of the worst man and maid, and while we slogged along the seatown road, bent at forty-five degrees into the wind, we passed a band of refugees, a father, mother, two children and a perambulator on their way to take succour at 'an auntie's'.

'It's raging bad at Crovie,' said the man by way of a greeting. I lifted my chin to look at him. He was dark wool and serge coloured all down his front and solid white all down his back.

We, heading in the other direction, were coated with white down our fronts and still in the colours of the clothes we had chosen down our backs. I shook myself and stamped a couple of times but it was a dreadfully sticking kind of snow.

'Did you just get to town?' I asked them. The man's wife was busily tucking a blanket over the opening of the perambulator hood to stop the whole thing turning into a bucketful of snow.

'Aye, we got the bairns up early and walked the top road,' said the man. 'The shore path's away.'

'Away?' said Alec. 'What do you mean?'

'The tide's shifted big stones and the path's covered,' said the man. 'Next tide'll do worse, doubtless.'

'Do you know if the Bennets, the artists at the far end of the village, have come along?'

'The man and the woman one?' The pair shared a look and then shook their heads. 'Never seen them, but they'd be mad to stay with what's coming.'

'Did you see anyone coming the *other* way?' I asked. 'On the top road?'

'Nah, lass,' he said. 'Thon dip in the road to the Macduff side is full of snow. It's ayeways the first to fill.'

'So no sign of a cart?' I said.

'Only a bloody fool would have a cart out in this,' said the man. His wife hissed a reproach for his shocking language but their children giggled so infectiously that in the end she smiled too.

And so the mood was lightened just a little as we arrived chez Gow, where old Mr Gow had been watching for us and opened the door as we arrived. Alec started to shake and stamp but Mr Gow pulled him inside, scolding.

'You're on a hiding to nowhere, son,' he said. 'The snow's coming down faster than you can brush it off so in you come and we'll take a mop after you.'

'But Alec,' I said, as he was disappearing, 'we haven't—'

The door was closing and there was nothing for it but to follow him. I jostled in and stood on the paper Mr Gow had spread at the entrance.

'Come in, come in, missus,' he said. 'Are you here to see the bed?'

'I . . .' I said. 'Alec, we haven't decided when and where to meet or what to do.'

'What to do?' said Alec. 'Surely the brides and grooms will tell us.'

I cursed his unhelpfulness. What was undecided was any kind of plan to use this wedding day to our advantage. We would see everyone and between the processions, the services, the dancing and the long wedding reel, we would have the best chance yet of uncovering cracks in the smooth surface of village life, for everyone loves a gossip at a wedding, that much we knew, but the advent of the minister and the doctor had robbed us of our morning meeting and our struggle along the seatown road had hardly been the kind of stroll during which one can usefully talk things over.

'Come away and see the bed, while you're here,' said Mr Gow. He drew me across the kitchen and through a door into a parlour where the curtains of a box bed were open.

'There she is,' said Mr Gow. 'Marriage bed, all ready and waiting.'

I was stumped, could not have come up with a comment if my life had depended on it.

'And there's the brides' part all nice and ready and waiting,' he said. On the snowy bosom of the counterpane, beautifully made by Rita Mitchell, with not a wrinkle or tuck anywhere, there rested a bottle of whisky and two small packages wrapped in waxed paper.

'And what, if it's the sort of information one can share, is in the parcels?' I asked.

'Cake and cheese,' said Mr Gow. 'They'll have plenty to

keep them going.' I could hear Alec, in the kitchen, making the noise he believes covers a desire to laugh.

'Will we go up the stair and see Robert and Nellie's?' said Mr Gow.

'I'd best be getting along,' I told him. 'It's fascinating, but I'm abandoning my scholarly duties rather today, to make sure I'm a good worst maid. I haven't the faintest idea what constitutes success in that endeavour.'

'Ocht, it's just our way,' said Mr Gow. 'Dear knows what any of it is all about.'

'Luck, isn't it?' I said. 'Drawing good luck and banishing bad.'

He gave me a look then which was so naked that I had to work not to step back, simply to remove myself from the pain of it.

'When you've been through what we've been through,' he said, 'the blackest illest bad luck that affronted Providence can send down on your head, you don't think so much on these things any more.'

'But I thought you *wanted* a worst man for your sons,' I said.

'I didn't want them shamed in folk's eyes,' he said. 'But as for luck! I've tried to understand. I've listened.' I waited in silence, not even looking him square in the face, in hopes that he would go on. At last he did. 'I never heard the like of it before,' he said. 'Time was a drownded man would scatter a crew to the four winds.' I glanced to the side and saw that Alec had joined us. He, like me, was moving as though trying to coax a wild animal out of hiding. 'But there's they two quines fasting to my lads, all four of them still together, four times the black luck, and you'd think they'd never known a fisherman in their born days for they couldn't care tuppence about it.'

'It's really so very unusual, Mr Gow?' Alec said.

'What?' cried the old man. 'As soon as they told me, as

soon as I'd said my wee prayer, I was thinking on where would I get the brass for a new boat, for my two laddies would never put to sea again together in the same hull. Never! I was thinking on selling the new boat and getting two steam drifters for the price of her. I was thinking on buying a cooper's apprenticeship for Robert or sending Wullie to crew for another man, if a man would take him with such a thing hanging over his head. I thought they Mason quines would scatter too. For sure I thought they'd be getting the Ellen around and maybe not going to the islands, for who would take them?'

'But they managed to put all of it in the past,' I said. He stared at me again out of those naked, anguished eyes.

'Aye, all except Nancy Nell,' he said. 'I'll never know if it was John dying or her sisters and his brothers doing such an unaccountable thing that sent her off her mind and sent her packing.'

'Just like Mrs Mason,' I said. 'She doesn't say much but she's as bewildered as you are.'

'Bewildered,' he said, 'is just the word. Aye, well. Cats is all grey at even. And maybe poor Nancy drew the luck off with her when she went.'

'If you believe in luck,' I said, smiling, teasing him a little, trying to lighten things.

'Ach, who am I trying to fool?' he said. 'I'm as bad as the rest. When you see my wedding gift to them you'll ken I'm worse than any.' He looked sorrowfully down at the bed, fresh-made by a new mother, laid with drink and cake and cheese, over a mattress filled by the Mason women, here in a house with cupboards plenished by eldest aunties and dishes carried by Grannie Annie while everyone watched, feet washed and mucked, flags hung, brides blackened, everything done that could be done to cheat Old Nick of his spoils and bring good fortune, and all for two couples who had broken what seemed to be the golden rule and yet were flourishing.

'I don't understand it,' said Mr Gow, reading my thoughts.

'Not at all. It's like they know better than the rest of us. Like they know something we don't.'

I looked directly at him, and Alec did too, and all three of us were thinking the same thought: that the thing everyone 'knew' was that John Gow had drowned and if the four who had been aboard with him 'knew' something different there was only one possible thing it could be. Possible, but unthinkable.

'I'd best be getting along, Mr Gow,' I said.

'Aye, fine, cushie,' he said. 'I'll take English Alec here and show him his rig-out.'

But as I made my way back to the door Alec dodged away and came to me. He gripped my arm and whispered fiercely. Not only had he thought the unthinkable but he was willing to say it too.

'John Gow didn't go overboard,' he said.

'Ssssh!' I hissed. 'He'll hear you.' I shook him off, called out a goodbye to the old man and hurried away.

Back out in the wild of the gale I almost whimpered, unequal to another bout of it. The sea roared and surged, dark green as a bottle of blood, seething and shattering endlessly against the rocks and making my head throb with the din. Or was it the cold that sent knives of pain through me? The battering cold, stinging my face and clawing up my legs from the iron ground. But it was not just the cold either, it was the iron bands of tradition locked tight around the place, everyone doing the same things on the same day, trying so hard to outwit the great slumbering beast of misfortune they all believed was waiting for them out there in the black sea.

I could not bear to believe what Alec had said. If those four had come back to Gamrie and told old Gow that his son was dead, lying, they were the coldest-hearted villains I had ever met.

The theory did have its merits, though. If John Gow ran

away and sent for Nancy Mason to join him, then at least *her* disappearance was explained. If, later, John Gow came back and tried to take over the boat again, tried to take back his rights as eldest brother, then perhaps at that moment, in July, the darkest deed was done. Again I whimpered. All I wanted to do was escape, from the wind and the tide and all the whispers and secrets, to find a way up that brae and through the drifts and keep going until I was at home, or perhaps at Barcelona.

I settled for the Masons' cottage and turned into the yard out of the worst of the gale. Mrs Mason answered the door and greeted me with a bright smile on her face, brave and heart-breaking.

'The lasses is getting dressed,' she said. 'On you go up. I've got the kettle started.'

I opened the door of the box stair and climbed up to the little bedroom at the top of the house. Peggie and Nellie were in their petticoats, best stockings and Sunday shoes, working at their curlers, with their two dresses laid out on one of the beds.

'Good morning!' I cried out as brightly as I could. 'But what a morning!'

'It's good luck to get soaked on your wedding day,' Nellie told me.

'Of course it is,' I said. Both girls moved slightly out of the way so that I could sit down on the low stool in front of the dressing table, the only seat in the room, even though they both had to peer round me to finish taking out their curlpapers.

'I hope that you both have all the luck in the world,' I said, and began to take off my gloves; it is so much easier to talk without looking a person in the eye sometimes. 'You won't be going back out next season, I don't suppose.'

'Nah,' said Peggie. 'When we get home fa the west in April that's us done with the gutting.'

'And Robert and Willie will be off without you,' I said.

'Aye, them and Bobby Guthrie. He's the third of the crew now.'

'Ah, they got a third crewman,' I said. 'That's splendid. Jolly good.'

'Oh, aye, it's a braw boat and the Gows are good fishers,' said Nellie. 'There's a grand living to be made.'

'Good for you,' I said, swallowing. Their insouciance, after old Mr Gow's sorrow, was far from appealing. I tried to find some generosity within me; after all, it was their wedding day. 'Now, where are my glad rags?' I asked and was gratified to see the Mason girls both laughing again.

My glad rags were quite something: a battered bowler hat, ancient and faded and rather dark around the inner brim. I subjected it to closer inspection and sniffed it too before I agreed to put it anywhere near me. There was also an extraordinary garment which I turned round and round and studied for many angles before I gave up looking for armholes and decided it was a cape; a coachman's cape from the turn of the century, with braid and flaps and silver buttons.

'Where did this come from?' I asked the girls. Their hair was finished now, closely curled and shining like elfin caps against their heads, so that they almost looked shingled from the front. When they turned, though, one could see the great knot of hair held in a bun on the napes of their necks; they could ape the London fashions on this special day but were not fast enough to join the modern age permanently. I pitied Cissie Walker with her luxuriant tresses if she were busy right now trying to attempt the same.

'The old doctor gave it,' said Peggie. 'Him that retired when Dr Trewithian came. He gave us a load of funny stuff out of his attic when he was moving.'

'At least I'll be nice and warm.'

'Oh aye and there's gloves and a scarf too,' said Nellie, opening a drawer. 'You'll not catch a chill, so you'll not.' The gloves were knitted mittens in red-and-pink stripes and the scarf was bright sunburst orange. 'And, eh . . .' she cleared her throat and held out a pair of bright green stockings, thickly knitted and the colour of a lime.

'All good fun,' I said through teeth hardly gritted at all. 'But I'm afraid my shoes won't fit on over them. I might have to be the worst maid from head to knee and let the rest go hang.'

'Well, aye but there's boots,' said Peggie. She nodded towards the corner where, tidily on a sheet of paper, were a pair of working men's boots, terribly turned up in the toes and with nails in their heels and soles.

When I emerged from the box stair ten minutes later, Mrs Mason, who was standing in front of the over-mantel mirror, fastening her own best hat onto her curls, stopped what she was doing and let out peal after peal of laughter.

'Oh, Mrs Gilver,' she said. 'Oh, you're a tear! Look at you.'

For I had decided to go the whole hog and had ruffled my hair up out of its set until it stood out all around the bowler brim like a sweep's brush.

'I'm actually very comfortable,' I said. 'Nice and warm and with nothing digging in or pinching. Much more comfortable than I ever was as a bridesmaid, much less on my own wedding day.'

'What did you wear?' said Peggie.

'A very tight and very scratchy dress with a hundred buttons up the back so I couldn't turn my neck and looked like a pouter pigeon,' I said.

'And what about your brother?' said Nellie.

'At his or at mine?' I asked. 'Well, it was regimental colours at both.'

'I thought he wasn't married yet,' said Peggie. 'That's what Robert and Wullie told us.'

I stammered a little covering my mistake.

'I assumed you meant my older brother. My younger

brother wasn't actually at my wedding – he was in India – which is what confused me.'

'But he told Robert and Wullie that he tied cans to a motorcar,' said Nellie. 'He was telling them about weddings down in London and he said he tied cans to your motor when you were going away.'

'Oh no, he meant our other sister, Mavis,' I said. 'He was very naughty at Mavis's wedding, it's true.'

The girls were preoccupied and gave me ready enough grins, satisfied at the explanation, but I did not miss the way Mrs Mason, facing the mirror again to skewer her hat with a long pin, looked hard at my reflection and did not look away for as long as I could hold her gaze.

I had thought that the villagers' blithe talk of a procession was wishful thinking and that plans would have to be amended on account of the storm but when, ten minutes later, the three Masons and I, along with Uncle Bobby Tosh who was to give the girls away, stepped out of the cottage and down to the shore road, it was into an eerie moment of calm. Granted, it was still bitterly cold and the snow lay thick enough for footprints and had drifted up against the cottage walls, but the wind had dropped and the sea, at full high tide, was slopping sulkily against the breakwaters without sending up any spray.

'Look at that!' said Mrs Mason. 'And here's the Wilsons coming.'

From the beach end of town a crowd advanced and at its front were all the Margaret Wilsons, four generations, with a father, grandfather or uncle proudly holding the arm of the bride and dragging her along at a fair clip. It was only when I saw them that a thought struck me.

'Aren't they going the wrong way?' I said. 'And actually, aren't we going to be rather struggling to get up to the church?'

'We're not for trying,' said Mrs Mason. 'We've the chapel of ease just at the brae's turn in the town here. Many's a time we cannot get to the church and not only for December weddings.'

The Wilsons reached us. Their worst maid was traipsing along just behind the matron of honour and was dressed easily as outlandishly as me with a battered top-hat and a soldier's dress tunic, long tattered petticoats trailing below. One had to smile at the sight of her. In fact, it seemed that in the high spirits of a wedding day, the suspicion and disapproval of the Masons and the Gows had been set aside and the calls and greetings which rung out were clear and cheerful.

'Look at this!' said one of the oldest Wilson aunts. 'Look at Providence smiling upon us!'

It was an admirable attitude. The clouds were purplish grey, thick and low, there was not a blink of sunshine, and had it been my wedding day I should have felt cursed by Thor, but these Gamrie brides were dimpling and twinkling as though they walked through a bower of blossom in May. Who was I to argue?

By the time we had arrived at the church halfway up the brae, a very plain sort of parish hall affair with none of the romance of the cliff top (but with no skulls either, one had to say), I had become quite used to my appearance, helped no end by the fact that no one laughed or pointed. Not a single villager, down to the tiniest child tripping along in its bonnet, paid me the slightest attention at all. Only Alec, who spotted me when all five bridal parties arrived at the church door and began to mingle with the five sets of men, found my outfit too much to bear. He bit his cheeks, pulled his brows down hard and tucked his chin into his collar. I met his appearance with sanguinity, or so it must have seemed. In fact, I could not bring myself to laugh for, in his tattered frock coat and striped trousers, he was nothing like as well protected from the chill as was I in my cloak and he looked pale in the complexion and blue about the lips and was shivering.

At least inside the chapel we found the more welcome of two possible options. Scotch churches are often colder than the weather outside, colder indeed than the very grave, with one smoky oil heater at the front which does nothing more than make the minister cough during his sermon. Sometimes, however, they are threaded through with hot pipes between every set of pews, too hot to put anything but the thickest boots against and producing a sleepy fug in which no sermon ever devised can make the slightest dent, no matter how much hell and damnation the minister promises one nor how loudly he delivers the promise to the flock. The chapel of ease at Gardenstown was fugging up nicely and, as I slid into a pew and tested the hot pipes with my borrowed boots, I felt sure that even five lots of wedding vows would not stop me from drowsing.

Not that the spectacle of this clutch of weddings was quite without its charms. The minister's habit of quoting the Bible was not half so annoying when he was standing in front of a congregation as it was at other times, even if he did ignore the gospels' Christmas tidings and even the cleaving to wives in Genesis and choose instead from the writings of that old killjoy St Paul (surely the most grudging of all the Apostles) passages about unbelieving husbands and unclean children, making it all the harder to forget that every bride was already on the way to her first confinement, and that therefore there was something very odd about the shy way the five couples joined hands and gathered at the altar for their church's blessings.

I had no idea how the batting order was decided, but this time the Masons were not left until last lest their bad luck infect whoever followed them. Janet Guthrie was married to a Robert Wilkie first and then sat down patiently to wait while the minister turned to Peggie Mason and Robert Gow,

Cissie Walker and Jimmy, Nellie Mason and Willie, finishing up with Margaret Wilson and Gordon Wise, before we delivered an unaccompanied but heartfelt singing of 'Peril on the Sea'. I imagined it was pretty much the favourite in Gamrie, as in many a fishing village. There was then a stern, thundering sort of blessing, which I took to be aimed at the men who might desert the tea urns in the village hall and go around the back for something stronger, and with that the five couples came marching down the aisle again, the brides beaming and the grooms smirking as the villagers stood to follow them.

'Here, Mrs Gilver,' said the newly minted Peggie Gow, as she passed my pew. 'Come on out behind us and see the scatter.' Alec and I joined arms, as others of the worst maids and men were doing, and felt rather jolly.

The small children were busy jostling themselves to favourable positions around the bridegrooms outside.

'Scatter?' said Alec.

'Just watch,' I replied.

I knew what was coming. Jimmy Peltie was the first to reach into an inside pocket and take out a small cloth bag. He loosened the drawstring and poured out into his hand a heap of copper with the odd glint of silver too. The children locked their eyes on the mound in his hand and bent their knees like runners awaiting the starter's gun, then Jimmy threw the shining handful high into the air and ducked away as it showered down to where the children were already scrambling.

It was like nothing so much as watching a shoal of little fish devouring a meal of scraps. Within half a minute every penny was gone and it was the turn of the second groom, Robert Wilkie. His handful was studded with more silver than the first and a gasp of awe broke out from the children when they saw it. Even some of the grown-ups eyed the glinting heap with desire in their eyes.

'That's a rare scatter, Bobby Tosh,' called out one of the worst men, his grin showing bright in his blackened face. 'Did you slicht another oaty or sell your granny's teeth?'

There was a roar of laughter at his words but I felt Alec stiffen and I murmured my agreement under my breath to him. We were both circling the same thought. Not near it yet, but drawing just a little closer with every journey around.

'We've been asking the wrong question,' he murmured to me. 'It might mean a day off to catch lucrative lobster, but the point is not what it *means*. The point is . . .'

'The etymology,' I said. 'Etymology is the word you're searching for. It's rather a hobby of Hugh's. And look!' I added, interrupting myself. 'Look, Alec. It's not my imagination, is it?'

Robert Gow had stepped forward to cast his handful of coins up into the air and, while there were numerous little children who dropped to their knees and scrambled as hard as ever, I could not miss the fact that a few of the womenfolk held their sons – especially their sons – by the scruff of the neck until the Gows' tainted money was gone. William Gow saw it happen and his expression was one I could not decipher. He was not angry, not hurt. He caught his brother's eye and they exchanged a look which, had I been pressed, I should have called satisfaction.

'Very interesting,' Alec said, even more quietly. 'Very interesting indeed. Watch again, Dandy, when Willie Gow throws his bag of coins. Watch who holds their little ones back and who lets theirs snatch.'

Gordon Wise went next and all the children did their best to gather the treasure. Their pockets were bulging by this time and the grown-ups were starting to joke that they would be richer than their daddies before the scatters were done.

Then, finally, there was Willie Gow. I watched the crowd and not the coins this time. Most children carried on but some little boys squirmed and wriggled, unable to escape the grip of whatever aunt or grandmother was holding them. I could make no sense at all of who was whom.

'I don't know what I was supposed to see,' I said to Alec.

'I've spent more time amongst the men and boys than you,' he replied. 'Don't you find it odd that the Guthries and Walkers – two families very intimately connected with the Gows, whose daughters were fasted to John Gow and then found wanting – are not concerned about catching bad luck from their silver?'

We had to leave it there for the moment, though, for Nellie Mason, the other new Mrs Gow, was making her way towards us and beckoning.

'The procession,' she said. She cast an eye over the rooftops of the lower cottages, out across the sea. 'There's just time, we're thinking, before the weather hits us.' Sure enough when I turned to look, not only there was no horizon, but the blurred line where it should be was closer than ever.

'Lead on,' I said, linking arms with Alec again and in no time at all, the entire village, crones and worthies, mothers and fathers, quines and loons, lads and lasses, children and tots were arranged in pairs and tramping up the brae to the mouth of the nearest lane. The brides and grooms, and best and worst maids and men, were at the head of the party.

As we doubled back on ourselves down a dog-leg lane I passed Cissie Walker.

'Congratulations, Mrs Peltie,' I said. Both she and her new husband chortled.

'I sound like my granny!' she said 'She was a Peltie too. I'll stick with Cissie Nandie.'

'Does your teename stay the same or do you take the teename of your husband's family?' I said

'No, I'm Cissie Nandie till I die,' she said, laughing again.

'And is your sister here?' I said. 'Did she make it?'

Again Cissie shouted with laughter.

'She did not! She's in her bed the now. The bairn started

at first light and as soon as ma mammy's finished here she'll be away to Jenny's to see what's doing.'

'Such a shame!' I said. I was having to call out now, because the bottle-neck had passed and the crocodile was moving again.

'Och, tis the way of it,' Cissie called out. 'The bairns aye come in wee clumps in Gamrie. When they come at all.'

I stood staring after her until the people behind me jostled forward.

'Dandy?' said Alec. 'What's wrong?'

'Nothing,' I said. 'Nothing I could put my finger on anyway. Look out, Alec! My goodness, they must be mad to want to traipse about all of these lanes and steps with so much ice upon them.'

But traipse we did. I do not think that a single snicket or dead-end yard in the whole town of Gardenstown missed out on the procession and, by the time we arrived at the village hall down on the shore road by the boatyards, the low clouds which had blurred the sky and sea were rolling over the harbour on a fresh burst of keen cold wind and beginning to fire enormous raindrops at us like a hail of arrows.

16

Laughing and shivering, shaking themselves and enjoying every minute of it, the villagers hustled inside and threw off their hats and coats ready to start celebrating in earnest. At the far end of the hall there were heaped plates of pies and pastries, snowy pyramids of sandwiches and huge bowls of jelly trifle. In pride of place, five iced cakes stood on stands and already an army of women with their sleeves rolled past the elbows were beginning to set out cups and fill milk-jugs ready for the tea.

'Now, you must excuse me, Dandy,' said Alec. 'I've come across these meat pies and those crumbly things before.'

'Sausage rolls,' I said.

'And I cannot for the life of me understand why they are not served in the Savoy grill and the members' tent at Ascot. I mean to eat my fill and line my pockets for later. Miss Clatchie will have no hold over me tonight with her thin soup and her floury potatoes.'

'Potatoes plural, Alec?' I said. 'If only!'

I do not share either Alec's appetite nor his enthusiasm for the peasant foods of our land, but the tea – once I had convinced the guardian of the teapot that it would be strong enough for me and did not need another ten minutes 'mashing' – was hot and fragrant and the fish paste sandwiches were fresh and savoury, so I made a perfectly adequate luncheon and while eating it made what I hoped would be more than adequate plans.

I had questions to ask in the course of the dancing. I

wanted to ask Cissie Walker about her warning, and I wanted to ask a woman who held her sons away from the Gows' coins why she did so (although I suspected the answers would be the usual appeal to 'bad luck'). I would also have liked to ask the Guthries and Walkers why they, in contrast, let their children join in, but could not think of a way to broach the question which did not show my hand. And then there were questions so vague and yet so outrageous that I could not quite articulate them to myself, never mind to one of these villagers before me. I let my gaze drift over the assembled company, deciding who to approach.

'Are you up for a wee dance, Mrs Gilver, or are ye taking notes just?' It was old Mr Gow. He had a cup of tea in one hand and a plate of trifle in the other but was jigging from foot to foot in anticipation of the band.

'I only know the very simplest of reels,' I said. 'Nothing much more fancy than the Grand Old Duke of York or I shall cause havoc.'

'Aye well, you'll get plenty to write in your wee book before the night's old,' he replied. 'Mind and not miss the long reel and the bedding. Don't go home early and miss that.'

I gave him a rather sickly grin. Viewing the prepared bed had been bad enough but was not the worst of it: at the end of the night's dancing apparently the whole party formed one long line of couples and danced their way to the house of every new bridegroom, there to shut the newlyweds up in the box bed with the whisky, cake and cheese and stand guard outside until morning. I supposed that a folklorist would want to see it, but I could not honestly say that I was keen.

'And mind and write down the wedding gifts,' he said. 'I'll wager the gift I'm giving Robert and Wullie'll not see the like in Gamrie today.'

'What is it?' I asked, but he shook his head and grinned.

'Nah, nah,' he said. 'It's bad luck to tell. But they'll be tickled pink, that I can say.'

233

At that moment the fiddle band began to tune up and all conversation was lost for a while between the wail of the violins, the cheers from the villagers and the scrape of chairs as they cleared the floor.

I watched for a polite interval, tapping my foot in its heavy boot and patting my hand against my knee, then I spotted one of the women I wanted to speak to on the far side of the room, slipping out of the hall into the little scullery. I followed her.

She turned with a scowl on her face as I entered, but then blushed when she saw me.

'I thought it was one of the men,' she said, looking at my feet and laughing. 'You'll be tired out clumping round in they things all night.'

I laughed along with her.

'I didn't think to put a pair of shoes in one of my enormous pockets,' I said. 'I suppose I could walk up to the hotel and back but to be honest it gives me an excuse not to dance and make a spectacle of myself.'

'Aye, I see your brother out there,' she went on. She was draining an urn of stewed tea, still chuckling. 'He's doing a good turn to the Gows, capering on like that as a worst man should. And you too.'

'I should be dancing?' I asked, but she shushed me.

'Ocht, no,' she said. 'Men's made for nonsense. You're fine. I meant you did them a kindness, when nobody would risk the ill luck.'

'I saw you not risking ill luck earlier, outside the church,' I said. She set the urn down and busied herself unrolling a packet of tea and digging into it for a fresh brewing. It was a few moments before she spoke again.

'I telt myself not to be daft,' she said. 'But my lad's ten and he'll be at sea soon enough. When it came to the bit I just couldn't. I couldn't.'

'I understand,' I told her. 'I have two sons of my own.'

'Aye but you'll never have to see them off on a steam drifter, doubtless,' she said.

'No indeed,' I said. 'They hunt – I hate to think of them jumping ditches in foul weather – and I'll be very lucky to keep them both out of the army, but no.'

'You keep them as safe as you can,' she said. 'I cannot understand they Mason lasses,' she said. 'They're thumbing their noses at Providence, so they are. It's like they've . . .'

'What?'

'I don't know how to say it. I'm not a clever woman.'

'Try, please, Mrs . . .'

'Mason!' she said, and her ready laugh was back. 'I'm Netta Toshie, married onto Nellie Gyka's man's cousin fa the Shavie side.'

It was all I could do not to put my head in my hands and groan.

'I know the teenames are supposed to help,' I said, 'but in all honesty they just confuse me even more.'

She laughed again.

'Aye but there's Masons and Walkers an Wilsons all over Gamrie and Crovie. And you aye cry your first-born son after the father's father and the first-born daughter after the mother's mother. Then the next two are the other way on. And if there's a third it's the father and mother themselves, but if they were called for their granny then it's all the same names.'

'No more,' I begged.

'So the teenames help,' she said. 'Agnes I am, and Toshie for my Granda Tosh Wilkie. Nellie Gyka is Helen Margaret and she's Greta Mason's niece. Without the teenames, where would we be?'

'Granted,' I said. 'If every Nessie and Nandie was known as Agnes.'

'And not just they two,' she said. 'Sometimes I think every woman in the parish is called Agnes. If this here's a lass,' she rubbed her middle, 'she's getting Linda and I don't care what anybody says.'

'Linda!' I said, astonished. 'It's very pretty. You might start a fashion.'

'I might at that and to hang with luck.' She had forgotten our earlier conversation completely. Now was the time to pounce and jolt her into speaking.

'So, back to the Mason girls who married today,' I said. 'Try again. It's like they've . . .'

'Got a chitty,' she said. Then she clapped a hand over her mouth. 'I'm sorry, Mrs Gilver,' she said. 'It's not like me to speak ill words.'

'A chitty,' I repeated. 'A free pass, you mean? I don't think those are ill words, Mrs Mason. I agree. They should be worried and they're not. They should be scared of how badly they're tempting fate and they're not. As if they know something that no one else knows and are not doing a very good job of hiding it?'

'Dear save us,' whispered the woman. 'That's it exactly. What do they know?'

I was not about to tell her, but it was clearer and clearer in my mind. They knew that John Gow had not drowned at sea, that they had no bad luck to fear and that their marriages were not doomed.

I tried very hard not to get ahead of myself. John Gow had not drowned in March. That did not mean he had died in July in the town of his birth and been disposed of there. He might be nothing to do with Mr Birchfield's problem at all. On the other hand, two herring lasses who knew more than they should about a man who had disappeared, fasted to their sister who had disappeared too? Of course it was all of a piece. It had to be. John Gow gone, Nancy Mason gone, a body in a herring barrel and four fisherfolk mysteriously lacking the sense of misfortune they should have if the drowning at sea were true.

236

I went to search for Alec. He was not dancing now. In fact the dance floor was suspiciously short of men altogether and I surmised that the beer barrel and whisky bottle had been breached, out there in the cold and the rain. Well, he was welcome to both. Besides, the women dancing did not seem to miss menfolk in the slightest, having just as much fun making reels of their own. As I watched, Cissie Walker spun round several times very fast in the middle of a web of her female relations, then she broke out of the circle, fanning herself, and went over to sit down. I joined her.

'Oh my, but dancing a reel's as bad as getting mucked,' she said. 'I'm that dizzy and sick-feeling!'

'Can I fetch you a cup of tea?' I asked and she nodded faintly.

'Right weak with a tate of sugar and no milk,' she said. It was just how I drank my tea in the early months too.

When I rejoined her she was looking rather better and she sipped at the tea with enjoyment.

'Might I ask you a question?' I said. 'It's probably not at all the thing to be speaking of today, but I'd love to know.'

'Aye, go on,' said Cissie. 'It's awful good to be an expert in something!'

'It's not a scholarly question,' I said. 'It's nosiness.' Cissie laughed.

'Aye, aye,' she said. 'A college degree and a wee notebook and papers in they journals but you're still a woman.'

'I am,' I said, laughing along with her. 'I most certainly am.'

'Well, then?' she said.

'It's about Nancy Mason,' I said. 'And John Gow.'

'Poor souls,' said Cissie.

'Your sympathy does you credit,' I said. 'And you tried to help, didn't you?'

'I tried to help Nancy,' said Cissie. 'Not *him*.'

'By warning her,' I said. She nodded. 'About "him"?' She

nodded again. 'What about him?' This time she shook her head. 'Was he cruel to you?' I persisted. 'Was he brutish?'

'He was nothing to me,' said Cissie. 'I tried to tell Nancy she was wasting her time.'

'But she *wasn't* wasting her time,' I insisted. 'They hand-fasted, didn't they?'

Cissie was staring straight ahead with her jaw set. I wondered if perhaps she was fighting nausea but when her eyes flashed I realised that it was anger she was suppressing.

'Aye, they did,' she said. 'Just like him and me and him and Janet.'

'Did you think him high-handed?' I said. 'Is that it? Granny Annie Mhor said there was no shame in fasting a few times until one took. Why did you warn her, Cissie?'

She opened her mouth to answer and then she sat up straighter in her chair and put her feet, which she had been resting, flat on the floor.

'Here's my Auntie Lena,' she said. 'Fit's the news?'

A red-faced woman, bare-headed and soaked to the skin, came trotting up.

'A boy,' she said. 'You've a nephew, Cissie, and he's a fine big dumpling of a laddie.'

'And Jenny?'

'Jenny's having a cup of tea and asking for wedding cake!' said Auntie Lena. The band had stopped and most of the party of villagers had drawn close to hear.

'Will she let the reel through?' called a voice to general laughter.

'She said Dear save you if you dare,' said Lena. 'But she'll be up to get kirked with the brides the morn's morn.'

'Churched, do you mean?' I said, startled out of embarrassment at last. 'Isn't tomorrow rather soon?'

'Aye, well it's a hard life at the herring,' said Auntie Lena. 'A Gamrie wife cannot lie in her bed ten days before she's kirked and up again.'

238

'Well, that's just grand,' said Cissie. Her husband had appeared, also rather bedraggled but rosy-cheeked from whisky.

'Fit are you at, sitting out?' he said 'Come on away and have a wee bit dancing. I'll no birl ye.'

He pulled Cissie to her feet and as they skipped off together, she gave me a look it would take me a week to unpick and sort into its component parts. Triumph was there, and pity and sorrow, and there was just a little yearning too. She would tell me if she could, her eyes seemed to say, but she begged me not to ask her.

Alec had come back in too, his hair dark and slicked back in rat's tails and the shoulders of his borrowed coat showing spreading patches of damp.

'It's getting pretty wild out there,' he said, 'but at least the rain is melting the snow. If they really mean to dance through the town at the end of the party, it's better this way.'

'And while you're carousing,' I said, 'I'm working hard and uncovering all manner of things.'

'Such as?' said Alec. He shrugged off his coat and then pulled me onto the dance floor. 'I've no idea what the villagers are doing but this sounds like perfectly acceptable foxtrot time to me.'

'We'll be thrown out for lewd behaviour,' I said.

'A blameless foxtrot between brother and sister?' said Alec. 'Now, what have you been finding out?'

I told him, surprised to discover that it sounded rather paltry. The conclusions I drew from the few threadbare facts, on the other hand, were anything but. 'So I think Cissie Walker knew something to the detriment of John Gow, and she told Nancy. It's connected with his disappearance – he did not drown, I'm sure of it – and it beggars belief to think that a man disappeared and a body turned up and they are not one and the same.'

'But then where was he from March to July?' said Alec.

'I don't know.'

'And do you think Nancy killed him? And that's why she disappeared?'

'I don't know that either. Perhaps.'

'For what motive?'

'Because of whatever he did that Cissie warned her about,' I said. 'I don't know what *that* is either, but if I can get Cissie alone again, I'll try harder to make her tell me.'

'I think I know,' Alec said. 'And I think I know how to check, too.'

We had drifted rather too close to another group of dancers and had to be quiet for a moment but when we had a patch of floor to ourselves again he went on. 'Ask Janet Guthrie,' he said. 'She was handfasted to John Gow and then all three Gow brothers, the two Mason sisters and Janet were together in that last stretch of the season, weren't they? While Nancy was here at home.'

'That's right,' I said. 'But what are you getting at?'

'The two Masons and Janet were together all day every day, gutting and packing. And gossiping. I think Janet Guthrie told them what Cissie Walker told Nancy. And I think the Mason sisters told the Gow brothers. Or maybe all six of them had it out together. But somehow, through Janet, those two brothers and those two sisters came into a piece of knowledge that changed everything.'

'But what was it?'

'Ask Janet Guthrie,' said Alec again. 'She doesn't believe John Gow drowned. None of the Guthries avoided the Gows' scatters. They don't think the Gows have the bad luck of a "drownded" man.'

'Why won't you just tell me what it is?' I said.

'I'll tell you why after you've spoken to Janet.' The song ended and Alec swung me round with a flourish and then released me. When I stopped spinning, I was staring right at Janet Guthrie who clapped loudly and gave several whoops.

'Rare dancing, Mrs Gilver,' she said 'Like something off the pictures.'

'Hardly, in these boots,' I said, then bit my tongue for almost all of the men and not a few of the women were dancing tonight in boots just as sturdy.

'I'd fair love to learn that dance there,' Janet said.

'A foxtrot,' I said. 'Mr Osborne could teach you.' At that she blushed to the tips of her ears and right down into the neck of her costume. 'Or I can,' I said hurriedly, 'if you'll be patient with me while I try to transpose everything.'

It took a few minutes for me to forget the lady's steps and try to force my feet to carry out the man's, although the boots helped admittedly, but before long Janet and I were clumping around, counting out loud and causing a great deal of amusement to the watchers.

'And slow, slow, quick-quick, slow, BEHIND,' we chorused. 'Spin, slow, quick-quick, slow, AHEAD.'

'Ignore them,' I said, as we passed a gaggle of Guthries, all of whom jeered and whistled. 'And finish. Now slow, slow, quick-quick, the-next, STEP. Is, to, quick-quick, talk-while DANCING.'

'Lovely weather we're having,' said Janet, making me laugh quite genuinely and causing both of us to lose our timing and have to stop and wait for the music to catch up with us again.

'I, want, to-ask, you-someTHING,' I said. 'Did, you, tell-those-Masons someTHING?'

She was quiet and we executed three perfect sequences of steps.

'I'll tell you why I'm asking,' I said, managing to talk in a normal rhythm now. 'The most interesting bits of fishing tradition to me are all the good luck rituals. And I can't for the life of me explain why the Masons and Gows are so level-headed about what happened to John. So I think they must have a good reason not to be sorry he's gone. And you were fasted to him and then you spent the last season with them all.' I was parroting Alec. I had no idea where it was leading.

'I felt sorry for Peggie and Nellie Mason,' she said. 'I knew they liked the Gow laddies. Not just for the good boat. And I didn't want to see them wasting their lives waiting. It was all they could talk about. Once Nancy and John were married Peggie and Robert were next then Nellie and Wullie after that and, in three years' time, they kept saying they'd all be wed, three sisters and three brothers like a fairytale. I just couldn't stand to hear them dreaming of something that would never happen.'

'Why not?' I asked.

''Cos after Nancy, John Gow would just move onto the next fasting and the next and the next again and his brothers would grow old waiting and Peggie and Nellie would have to fast to somebody else or grow old waiting too.'

'What made you think that John Gow would move on?' I said.

'A handfasting with no bairn at the end of it doesn't turn to marriage,' said Janet. 'And it's not your *hands* you need to join to make a fasting work out right.'

'My goodness,' I said.

'If you know what I mean,' said Janet.

'Indeed I do,' I assured her. 'Well, if you'll excuse me, Janet, I just need to go and have a word with my brother. I really do think you've got the makings of the foxtrot now.'

I left her with a crowd of her relations all clamouring to be taught what she knew and went to rejoin Alec, who was sitting very relaxed on one of the benches lining the walls, looking as easy as his outlandish costume allowed and with yet another sausage roll in his hand.

'Swine,' I said to him.

'Granted,' he replied. 'It was my revenge for having to telephone Mr Birchfield for the anatomical details of the body. I knew if you knew what you were asking you'd never ask. I guessed a-right, then?'

'You did. And it wasn't a . . . medical problem, I don't think. As far as I could infer from Janet, he never came near her. And I suppose the same goes for Cissie and presumably Nancy too. What do you suppose he was playing at?'

'Poor chap,' said Alec. 'He couldn't have told his father he had no desire to marry. I've been asking the men and there's no such thing as a bachelor fisherman, you know.'

'But, heavens above, couldn't he just grit his teeth and get on with it?' I said. Alec guffawed and inhaled a piece of pastry. He was still laughing when he had finished coughing it back out again.

'You sound more like Hugh every day,' he said. 'Hugh and Queen Victoria combined.'

'But where was it all going to end?' I said. 'What was the point? If he kept handfasting the cream of Gamrie woman-hood and then dissolving the unions for lack of results and then the self-same girls moved on and bore fruit with other chaps. They'd all twig eventually, wouldn't they?'

'Perhaps he meant to do things differently with Nancy,' Alec said. 'But either his brothers didn't know that or didn't believe him.'

'And so he . . . went off on his own and they came home and told their father he had drowned. Alec, that's just awful. It's *awful*.'

'It would be,' Alec said. 'But come off it, Dandy. We both think it's worse than that. We both think that somehow, John Gow ended up in those barrels in July.'

'I've been thinking about that,' I said. 'Perhaps they ran him off at Lowestoft or wherever and then he turned up again in the summer and threatened to take over being the skipper again and to make them all wait. Only by then it was too late because Peggie was already pregnant and actually,' – I counted on my fingers – 'Yes, so was Nellie. So they killed him.'

'And somehow managed to do it without anyone seeing?' Alec said.

'If only it had been spring. When that nasty gutter's van comes round, the town is deserted for easily long enough to fill seven barrels. But there were no rough seas in the summer. The guts went by boat. I asked.'

'They could have done it under cover of darkness,' said Alec.

'Pretty risky though.'

There was a sudden rise in the level of hubbub throughout the room just then and all of the fiddlers began to play a particularly jaunty tune. They came away from the end of the hall and walked about like minstrels while everyone around got to their feet and began to re-wrap themselves in their shawls.

'Here's the long reel,' said Rita Mitchell. 'You'll not want to miss this!'

'I can't believe you're really going to dance up and down those lanes in the dark in this weather,' I said, but the line was already forming, the first couples being edged out of the door into the street.

'Ach, it's nocht when you've stood gutting on deck on a high sea and still packed your barrel so's the checker gives it a bye!' she said.

'I suppose so,' I agreed, laughing. I stood beside Alec ready to join the reel line with him and then I stopped and turned back to Rita.

'What did you just say?' I asked her. 'You gut and pack on the boat in a rough sea?'

'Ocht, no!' said Rita. 'Not really. Just to slicht your ooty.'

Now Alec grabbed one of her arms and I grabbed the other.

'What do you mean?' I said.

244

'There's no harm in it,' she said. 'Everybody does it.'

'Of course, of course,' said Alec. 'But does *what* exactly?'

'When you're ooty erle you're ooty erle and you can do what you like.'

'Naturally,' I said. 'And so what is it that you do?'

'One last catch on your road home,' she said.

'Sailing home at the end of the season you catch one last catch of herring,' I said.

'And gut and pack it on the boat,' said Alec. 'Where do you get the barrels?'

'Fa the coopers,' said Rita as though speaking to rather slow children. 'The Gamrie coopers come round with the boats too.'

'Of course they do,' I said. 'So you gut and pack the herring and then . . .'

'You hang on to it to the summer and then when you're in arle and you have to catch for Mr Birchfield but the lobsters is right good, just for a day or two . . .'

'You catch lobsters instead but you take your out-of-arle catch all ready there in the barrels . . .'

'And you slicht it.'

'Of course you do,' said Alec. 'By sleight. In it goes, and no harm done and no one the wiser.'

'Aye,' said Rita. 'A herring's a herring. March or July makes no odds, does it now?'

17

Alec and I stood stock still as the villagers surged past us on both sides, joining the end of the line for the long reel.

'They killed him,' I said.

'And stored him until summer.'

'And slipped him into the summer catch.'

'Because he was blocking their way to wives and sons and boats of their own.'

'Wicked, wicked devils,' I said. 'They broke their sister's heart!'

'At least her heart,' said Alec. 'Who's to say she didn't guess what they had done and meet the same punishment? Not the barrels, but the killing anyway.'

'But why did they do something so grisly?' I said. 'So dreadful. Why on earth not just tip him overboard?'

'Bad luck,' Alec said. Then his eyes flashed.

'Fit's bad luck?' Robert Gow was behind me. 'Are you dancing the long reel? Come in the line ahint Peggie and me.'

Alec nodded. I did not manage even as much as that. I knew that I was staring at Robert Gow with solemn eyes and a face turned pale but I could not seem to shake any animation back into myself.

'Right you are,' said Alec heartily. 'If that's our last job as worst maid and man we are game, aren't we?'

Robert Gow gave me a long cool appraising look and went to rejoin his bride in the line.

'What shall we do?' I said.

'We've no proof,' said Alec. 'So for tonight we keep our nerve and hide our knowledge from them. Then tomorrow, by hook or by crook we'll get ourselves to the police station in Macduff and tell all.'

'We just let them dance through the town and go to bed?' I said.

'I'd say that's a splendid plan,' said Alec. 'With a crowd of their friends guarding the closed bed until morning, it's not as though they can run away. Now come on, Dandy.'

He dragged me by the arm up to the place in the long line where the Gows and their brides were waiting. They had joined hands, crossed at the wrists ready for the dance and I could not help staring at Peggie and Nellie's sturdy wrists and red knuckles. Had they really stood on the pitching deck of a boat at sea and taken their knives to a man's body? A man they knew and who their sister was tied to? Perhaps even loved, given the way she fled after losing him?

As soon as the first strains of music drifted in through the open door all the couples started bouncing lightly from foot to foot, ready for the off. The Gows turned their backs on us and I leaned close to Alec to whisper but he shook his head and drew away.

'In the morning,' he mouthed, and the dance began.

It was tremendous fun, at least one could see that it would have been fun without the driving rain, the aching cold and the thought that just ahead of us were four murderers.

The reel threaded its way out of the hall and down to the harbour, along the shore road, and up the furthest lane. By the time the head of the snake had turned into the lane and its tail was out of the village hall, we in the middle were soaked to the skin, our hair plastered flat, what rouge and eye-black we might have indulged in for this high holiday running in rivers down our faces and our boots squelching with every step. On the other hand, there comes a moment when one is so wet that one can just put one's head up and shoulders back, for there is no wetter state to avoid. Also, capering along stopped us succumbing to the worst of the cold and I was not the only one whose face was flushed tonight instead of being pinched and blue as in the days preceding. It was really just the Gows then, the four of them, jigging along ahead of us, laughing and prancing, not a care in the world, which troubled me.

At the Guthries' as the crowd jostled in to stand crammed in the tiny yard and those who could not fit hopped up onto walls and railings to peer over heads, Janet Guthrie as was and her new husband threaded their way through the arch the other dancers formed for them and stopped at the front door.

'Your wedding gift,' said an old man I took to be the groom's father, and he handed over to the young couple one of the walnut mantel clocks every householder in Gamrie seemed to possess. There was a cheer from the gathering and Janet and Robert ducked inside, followed by a little clutch of friends – the best and worst maids and men amongst them – who would stand outside the closed box bed all night shouting encouragement and sharing views of what passed within. Then the front cottage door shut behind them, the fiddlers began again and the long reel, slightly shorter now, moved on.

Cissie and Jimmy were next and Jimmy's mother presented the couple, at the door, with a box of Sheffield plate silver, all nestling in velvet slots, and glittering by the light of raised lanterns.

'A canteen of cutlery!' said Cissie. 'That's awfy posh! Thank you.'

'I'll teach you how to polish it right,' said the new mother-in-law, causing Cissie's smile to falter a little, and Mrs Walker's to contract as though someone had pulled on a drawstring. There was an awkward pause before the fiddles took up the tune again and the reel moved on.

The next stop was the Gows and old Mr Gow had evidently left the dance in good time and hurried home to put out a welcome, for lamps were lit in the cottage windows and the air was redolent of wood smoke and peat smoke when he opened the door. Both couples came crouched and laughing through the arched hands and stopped in the doorway.

'Welcome to your new homes, Peggie and Nellie,' Mr Gow said, beaming. 'We've been through dark times but here we are at a new beginning.'

There was a general assent from the crowd. It seemed that now the deed was done all these friends and neighbours, willing to dance in the dark and rain, were willing too to put the past behind them and give the young couples their blessing.

'I have a very special gift for you,' the old man said. 'A remembrance as well as a celebration. For I know,' here his voice broke, 'that you, like me, will never forget the one we've lost. Now wait you just a minute and see what I've saved for you.'

He ducked behind the door and the sound of him grappling with something large, as well as that odd word he had used – 'saved', these two things together alerted Alec and me just a minute in advance of seeing the thing with our own eyes.

Old Mr Gow rolled a barrel into the open doorway and looked at his sons with shining eyes. 'The very last of John's last catch,' he said 'I kept it for you.'

Alec gripped my arm so tightly that drops of rain were squeezed from my sleeve and I saw his face grow pale as I felt the blood drain from mine. Neither of the Gow boys, nor either of the Mason girls, moved. Then Robert Gow turned his head and stared at Alec and me. Peggie and Nellie caught the glance and their eyes flashed. William Gow frowned, glanced our way and knowledge sparked in his face. For a moment there was perfect stillness and then suddenly

249

the two couples surged forward, crammed into the cottage taking the barrel with them, and slammed the door. All at once everyone was moving. The fiddlers struck up, the villagers began to dance and the reel poured out of the little yard back to the lane. Only Alec and I were struggling to move the other way.

'There's no one to stand guard,' I said, shouting over the crush of dancing bodies which had separated us as soon as Alec let me go. 'They were each other's best men and maids and we're the worst.'

'You stay here,' said Alec. 'I'm going to the kiosk to telephone to the police in Macduff, storm or no, Christmas or no.' He turned and started to follow the snake of dancers out of the yard, pushing his way up the line and being jeered and jostled for it.

'Alec, no!' I shouted. 'There's a door on the gable-end and a door on the other side. They're not stuck in there at all. They'll get away.' I began to edge around the side of the house to the front, squeezing along beside the dancing couples, still laughing and singing, and I turned the corner just in time to see the barrel come bowling out of the lane on the far side of the house with Robert Gow chasing after it and his brother and the Mason girls scurrying along behind him.

'Stop,' I shouted. Some of the dancers turned to see what was wrong and, in the light of their lanterns, Robert and Willie Gow were caught, just for a second, their faces naked and haunted, before they turned a corner, kicking the barrel along before them and disappearing again. The Mason girls broke the other way, climbing the lane and whisking off into a stairway, gone in a second.

'Stop them!' shouted Alec, plunging into the lane mouth after the Gows. This was better sport even than dancing and a full third of the couples broke up, the men running after the Gows and the women, rushed and fluttered, settling into groups and breaking up again.

'Help me,' I shouted over my shoulder as I pelted after the Mason girls. The women were standing as though turned to stone. 'Help me!' I screamed again. 'They can't get away.'

But of course they could. They knew the labyrinth of these steps and lanes as well as I knew the grounds of my own house and I had not a chance of catching them. When I had rounded two corners I was completely lost, could see nothing but chinks of light around curtains in some of the cottage windows and could hear nothing except the drilling of rain on the roofs and cobbles, the wind moaning and snatching at any loose scrap of wood or slate, and the sea, the endless angry boom of the sea. I stood under the shelter of a gable end and let my head drop back. Just faintly I heard music. Here came the fiddlers again and with them the light of bobbing lanterns and the sound of stamping feet, from all the couples who had been too far away to see what happened and were carrying on with the dancing.

Then, as the reel drew nearer, only a yard away from where I stood, there was a sudden scraping noise and a blurred rush as the Mason girls fled their hiding place – they had been so close! – and made another dash to get away from me. This time, I ran towards the dancers and snatched a lantern out of someone's hand.

'Here, what are you at?' the villagers called after me.

'They killed John Gow,' I shouted as I threw myself down a crooked stairway the way the girls had gone, but the fiddlers had started up again and I knew that no one had heard me, or understood, or perhaps believed. They were dancing again anyway.

Would the Masons make for the shore or the land? The road was flooded but they could escape across the fields and hide anywhere in that empty landscape which stretched southwards for endless dark miles. Down at the shore they could break for Crovie or for the path to the church, or they could hide amongst the sheds in the boatyard until morning. I heard something and wheeled around, dodging into a tiny lane that opened on my left. Someone rushed forward and I snatched at the arm of a coat. It was Alec. He grabbed the lantern and raced ahead of me, took my hand and pulled me on with him.

'I've got men all along the bottom road,' he panted as we thundered on down the lane. 'We'll flush them.'

'They might go up,' I said. 'If the— Ahhh!'

Someone had flitted across our path, inches in front of us, and disappeared.

'One of the girls,' Alec said. 'Let her go. The men have the barrel. If they tip it into the sea the evidence is gone.'

It can only have been a few minutes at most that we were racing up and down those steps and lanes, for although Gamrie is a jumble it is not large. Still, in the cold and dark, as the rain lashed us and our breath grew ragged, our legs aching, it seemed as though the nightmare would never end. The women I had called out to were prowling around in pairs now, lanterns high, whispering and gossiping under their breath, and when we came upon them their voices sounded like prayers, or spells.

'John Gow. Aye, John Gow.'

'Dear save us.'

'Heaven have mercy.'

'Just *find* them,' Alec shouted as we tore past.

And still the nightmare went on. We passed the fiddlers and dancers again, the swinging lanterns turning the whole scene into a monstrous carnival; cackling faces, red from exertion and streaming with rain, leered up and fell away again and, as we tried to break through the chain of dancing couples, another dark shape flitted between two cottages ahead of us and was gone by the time we were through.

'What did you say to the men?' I gasped.

'Didn't have to say much,' Alec replied. 'I reckon deep down a lot of them knew.'

'And some of the women too,' I said. 'Alec, where *are* they?'

'We'll catch them,' he said, picking up his pace. 'They won't get away.'

Then at last we heard the first shouts. The fiddle music stopped and instead of the rhythmic thumping of feet in the reel, somewhere in the lanes beside us, we heard instead drumming footsteps as everyone began to run down towards the sea. They were all shouting the same word, over and over again, one we could not decipher. Alec and I looked at one another for just a moment in the light of the lantern and then streaked after them.

Down on the shore road, everyone was scurrying to the harbour, lanterns bobbing and swinging as they ran. Even some of the people who had left the reel and already shut their doors were appearing again, pulling on boots and hats, their faces drawn up with worry.

As we got to the harbour head, a bell began to clang, furious and deafening, and all around us the prayers grew to clamours and some of the women were weeping.

'Look, look, it's true,' said Rita Mitchell standing beside me. 'To Crovie, see!'

I leapt up onto the breakwater ledge and peered through the sheets of rain to where she was pointing.

Far away in the distance I could just see the faint smear of a yellow light growing and fading over and over again.

'What is it?' I said.

'Distress flare,' said Alec.

'Aye,' said Margaret Wilson. 'Somebody's in bother at Crovie and needs our help.'

'But what can you do?' I asked. I was having to brace myself against the wind and rain just to stay upright on the harbour wall. How could anyone get to Crovie tonight?

'Here they come,' said an old man standing by Margaret. We turned, just in time to see a crowd of men, half a dozen or so, come jogging down the steps from the harbour office, with ropes over their shoulders and lanterns in their hands.

'The lifeboat,' said the old man and he had a tremor in his voice.

'They can't—' I said, then I stumbled as a huge surge of wind swept me half off my feet. 'They can't put out to sea in this.'

But the men were moving in a pack, shoulder to shoulder, grim-faced, making towards a boatshed which sat alone with a short steep slipway, just to the far side of the harbour. The villagers moved behind them, some of them weeping loudly now, the wives and mothers of the men, one assumed. I made as if to follow but Alec clutched at me.

'Look,' he said and pointed. I shook the rain away from my face, blinked hard and peered. The harbour was packed solid with boats buffered against the storm by straw bags set all around them, but still creaking and scraping as the swell pushed relentlessly at them, even here in safe haven.

'What?' I said.

'They're on the boats,' he whispered. 'Look. You can see them.'

I strained my eyes and squinted harder down into the dark and this time I could make out several shapes, four of them, hunched and skulking, moving swiftly across the jostling decks.

'Could they even get a boat out of the harbour mouth?' I said.

Alec did not answer.

'Is there any way to close it off? Trap them?'

'They've got it,' said Alec, flinching at a sudden dull thump from down amongst the boats. 'They've got the barrel with them.'

Then the splutter and roar of an engine rose above the shouts and the sound of the hammering rain and some of the crowd turned back from the lifeboat slipway and peered towards the sound. 'Who is it?' someone shouted.

'It's the Gow laddies and their paraffin engine,' came another voice.

'What are you doing?' a third man yelled. 'The lifeboat's near launched.'

'They'll never get out!'

'Aye, they will. Their boat was in the mouth.'

'They put it there deliberately,' Alec said to me. 'They must have dreaded that this was coming.'

We began to run out along the breakwater. Alec cupped his hands at his face and shouted to them.

'Give yourselves up,' he said. 'Turn yourselves in. You'll never get away.' From here, against the lanterns and the lights in cottage windows, it was easier to see the figures moving, scuttling like crabs towards the boat whose engine whined and brayed, just barely holding back, waiting for the two women who were closer now, were almost there, were there! Bashing heedlessly against the neighbouring boats, the drifter turned and nosed out of the arms of the harbour, out into the black tumult of the sea.

'They've took their brides!' a voice yelled.

'Come back! The lifeboat's going out! Save yourselves!'

'No!' screamed someone and I thought I recognised Mrs Mason, leaning far out over the harbour wall, keening and weeping as her daughters were borne away.

Over at the slipway the lifeboat was rolling, with a deafening rumble which drowned out even the roar of the wind, until the little boat – and it did look tiny – shot onto the water and bobbed there like a cork, its prow rearing up and plunging down like a pump handle. The Gows' drifter, clear of the harbour now, driven by the swell despite its straining engine, was edging closer and closer to the little lifeboat, until for a moment they were only yards apart, and we could see the lifeboat men waving their arms wildly, yelling at the tops of their voices.

I could not bear to watch. With every swell and drop I was

sure that one or both of the boats would tip and be gone. I turned away, but it was only to meet the gaze of old Mr Gow standing there behind me, rain and tears mingling as they poured down his cheeks.

'It's meant to be,' he said. 'What's meant to be will be.'

At last the Gows' boat had turned full to the wind and began to pull out into the bay, walloping hard on every drop, water washing over into the deck. Three of the four were huddled in the stern, clutching the barrel to them.

The lifeboat men were drawing close in under the harbour wall now, shouting up at the crowd. They were shouting to Mr Gow, imploring him to tell them what to do.

He waved an arm, bone weary with all of it, just flapped his arm towards that distant yellow light, flashing and fading still at the Crovie headland.

'Save souls that want saving,' he whispered and turned away.

The lifeboat held, hard, pulled, somehow turned, and began to plough into the swell towards that light. The crowd was dumbstruck, standing stock still, gazing between the stern of the drifter, Mr Gow as he walked with faltering steps back along the breakwater, and the side of the lifeboat, coursing along now with all the men lashed by ropes to the sides and holding on grimly.

I ran to catch the old man but he was surrounded by his neighbours and I could not get near him.

'My own fault,' he was saying. 'If I'd have stopped it like I should have.'

'But fit are they at?' said a friend. 'They're not even set for Crovie. Why don't they turn and come home?'

'Ach, they're taking the black luck away with them,' he said. 'They tried to weather the storm of it and couldn't. They knew it was wrong.'

'But the fastings were blessed,' said a woman. She was

wringing her hands and the tears were pouring down her cheeks as fast as down the old man's.

'So it looked,' said Mr Gow, and a rustle of prayers and whispers broke out all around.

'What do they mean?' I asked the woman next to me. I had not noticed it was Cissie Walker, up out of her marriage bed, out in the rain with a shawl over her nightgown and boots on her bare legs.

'It wasn't right,' she said. 'If they bairns started after John Gow drownded, Auld Clootie could have had his way. Dear knows what was coming to them. They've saved us all the night. They've saved Jenny's laddie.'

'Your new nephew?' I said. 'But there's nothing wrong with him. Your auntie told you. He's fine.'

'He *looks* fine,' said Cissie darkly. 'But till they're kirked nobody can say.'

'They were sore tempted,' came a woman's voice louder than the others. 'Auld Clootie tempted them right well, did he no? But they turned their faces to the good at last and saved us all.'

I dropped back and fell into step with Alec.

'This is madness,' I said. 'Utter madness. They're making up some kind of hysterical story that . . .'

'The devil came in when John Gow died and he bewitched them.'

'The devil told them to handfast and the devil put babies in them? They got as far as the very marriage bed before their virtue stopped them? It's disgusting nonsense, Alec.'

He gave me a long cool look, gazing calmly at me, unheeding of the rain streaming down his face and dripping from his chin.

'Is it worse than the truth, Dandy? Really?'

''Twas the barrel that stopped them,' said the loud-voiced woman again.

'Aye, the goodness of John Gow lived on though he was gone,' said another.

'Auld Clootie couldn't hold them to the ill with John's last catch right there shining with virtue.'

'If only we had it still,' said Mr Gow.

Then we were at the harbour head and the crowd began to disperse into the lanes, up the brae, along the seatown road.

'Will we hear the news when the lifeboat returns?' I asked Jimmy Peltie who had put his coat around Cissie's shoulders and was drawing her away. 'Do they ring the bell again?'

'*You'll* hear,' he said. 'For the doctor's on it.'

'Dr Trewithian is a lifeboat man?'

'Aye and young Douglas, the minister's first boy, too.'

'Good God,' I said.

'Aye, it's not just fisherfolk might lose their lives tonight, Missus,' he said with a twist of a grin. I had no answer, for I deserved what he said to me. Then his attention was hooked away at the sound of weeping. It was Mrs Mason, crying hard, with aching ragged sobs that bent her double and left her retching.

'She can't go home alone,' I whispered to Alec. 'But she hasn't a friend in the place. I'll take her.'

'Not a friend in Gamrie?' said Mrs Wilson, drawing herself up and glaring at me down the length of her nose. 'Who are you to be saying such black lies? We're all her kin and her friends together.'

'They couldn't find anyone to be worst maid,' I hissed.

'Aye, well,' said Mrs Wilson, jerking her chin towards the sea. 'That's behind us now.'

Miss Clatchie was up and about at the hotel, bustling around the kitchen in her dressing gown with her scant bun unpinned and braided into a scant pigtail instead. Bunty was curled asleep in front of the range but woke up and yawned as I slipped off the worst maid's boots, which had begun to feel like boxes of bricks tied to my ankles.

'You need to get out of your wet things,' Miss Clatchie said, putting a cup of tea into my hands. It was hotter and stronger than any cup of tea I had seen in the place before. Her hands brushed mine as she was handing it to me and her eyes flashed.

'You're chilled to the bone,' she said putting the back of her hand against my cheek. 'You'll catch your death of cold if you don't get yourself warm.' Then she bit her lip and hesitated, cast her eyes upwards, then brought them down and looked at me again.

'Have a bath,' she said. I could not stop my eyebrows from rising. 'The minister and Mrs Lamont are up anyway, waiting for the lifeboat. So have a bath, Mrs Gilver. Only . . .' she hesitated again, 'you'd better run it good and deep and then I'll make up the fire. The water'll be hotter for the doctor and young Douglas when they get home if it's drawn off fully rather than leaving it lukewarm.'

'You're instructing me to go and have a deep hot bath at half past eleven at night, Miss Clatchie?' I said.

'And give me your dry clothes down to warm at the range here,' she said.

I nodded and turned to go.

'Leave the plug in, Dandy, and I'll hop in after you,' said Alec. Miss Clatchie boggled a little at that, but Alec grinned. 'Haven't done that since Nanny,' he added. 'I was always second because Dandy had to wash her long hair.'

Miss Clatchie's cheeks were a shade of pink edging into plum, but she smiled.

'I was always bathed with my sisters too,' she said. 'And my brother waited until we were done. It's on nights like this you're glad to have your family.'

I lay in the bath, floating in the depth of it until my conscience and the thought of Alec waiting started to prick at me. Then I put on my nightclothes, since Miss Clatchie was in hers, and started to make my way downstairs. I was arrested, however, by the sight of Mrs Lamont sitting on the bottom step, holding an untouched cup of tea and staring at the back of the front door. I drew away a little, trying to think of some words of comfort and so it was that I was unseen when Reverend Lamont opened the drawing room door and saw her there.

'Come away in to the fire, Betty,' he said gently.

'I came away from the harbour head,' she said coldly. 'Leave me be.'

'You should take comfort,' said her husband. '*For the Lord is full of mercy and—*'

'Don't!' she said. 'Tell me about the Lord's mercy if he shows it.'

'Oh, Betty,' said Reverend Lamont. He walked over and joined his wife, sitting beside her on the step and putting an arm around her.

'You said you'd talk to him. Forbid him. You promised me.'

'He's twenty-one, my dear,' said Lamont. 'I can't forbid him to the Lord's work if he's called to it.'

'If anything happens to him tonight, Douglas.'

'If anything happens to any of us tonight, we will all meet again in the sweet bye and bye.' I could hear Mrs Lamont's sigh like a gust of wind all the way up the stairs.

'I envy you sometimes,' she said.

'And I love you,' said Reverend Lamont. 'Always.'

They were silent for a minute and then he stood and held out his hands to her. She sighed again, slipped her hands into his and let him help her to her feet.

Once I was sure that they were gone I stepped forward again and had just put my foot on the top step when I heard a dreadful sound, somewhere between a moan and a sob, and saw Miss Clatchie come reeling along the passageway beside the stairs, tears pouring down her round cheeks. She sniffed and scrubbed at her face with her fists as she turned. Then she saw me.

'Did you hear that?' she said, her voice stretched tight with pain. 'Did you hear them?'

'I did, I'm afraid,' I said. 'No one should have been privy to it but so long as they never know it can't hurt them.'

Miss Clatchie was stumbling up the stairs.

'He loves her!' she said in a ragged whisper. I smiled.

'He seems to,' I had said before I caught the import of her words.

'He loves *her*,' said Miss Clatchie again. 'I didn't think he could. She's so harsh and so stern and she doesn't appreciate him the way—'

'Oh, Miss Clatchie,' I said, putting out a hand to pat her shaking shoulder. She was at the locked door, fumbling with her keys. Although my sympathy was genuine, and despite the shattering events of the evening and the grinding anxiety about the lifeboat men, I followed her closely, greedy to witness the sea-monster or steam-bellows at last.

'I'm a fool,' Miss Clatchie said, opening the door and bursting in. It was a very ordinary bedroom, equal in size to my own and equally sparsely furnished except that, at the window, there was a curious three-legged object covered by a velvet cloth.

'It's a telescope,' said Miss Clatchie. 'I can see his front door. I can see the way she follows him right to the step, nagging and scolding.' She caught her breath in a sob. 'I've wasted half my life standing here.'

'Oh, Miss Clatchie,' I said again. I could think of nothing more, except for one lingering question. 'What was the noise?'

She shook her head.

'A screeching noise,' I added.

'Oh,' she said. 'Just the window.' And she showed me, lifting the sash and letting it fall, unleashing the banshee howl. 'I open the window so there's nothing between us but air. Then it's almost as though we're together.'

'I see.' She was staring out into the black night and since I had no real comfort to offer I left her to her pain and trusted that her pride would come along soon and outdo it.

It was two o'clock in the morning, with the fire banked halfway up the chimney so that all of us except perhaps for the minister's wife were drowsing, when we heard the front door. Reverend and Mrs Lamont leapt to their feet but the doctor's voice boomed out the blessed relief of good news even before they were inside the house.

'All home safe and sound,' he said. '*Their stately ships go to the haven under the hill.*'

'*The Lord is the source of my light and my safety, so whom shall I fear,*' said Lamont.

Mrs Lamont caught my eye and did I only imagine that she raised hers to Heaven? Perhaps only to the upstairs where her younger boy was sleeping, wishing the men would murmur their quotations instead of bellowing them. Then she rushed forward into the hall and enveloped her older son in her arms. Upstairs the thunder of the bath taps announced that Miss Clatchie was already beginning the second round of succour.

'I'll steam in front of the parlour fire while you bathe,' said the doctor, waving young Douglas and his mother towards the bottom of the stairs.

'The tea will be stewed,' said Mrs Lamont over her shoulder.

'But there's nothing amiss with the whisky,' Alec said.

Even I took a little of the wretched stuff as we resettled in the front-room chairs. I was shaking from shock and exhaustion, feeling perhaps rather worse after my nap than I had before. Bunty slumped against my legs and put her muzzle in my lap, looking up at me with concern, devotion and just a little displeasure at how late it was and how much she wished she were not needed and could leave me.

'Did you . . .' I began. 'I'm not sure of the etiquette. May one ask?'

'We didn't,' said the doctor. 'We hadn't a chance.'

'Who was it out in this on Christmas night?' the minister said.

'Those Bennets from Crovie,' said the doctor and I gasped. Alec put out a hand and took hold of mine.

'The Bennets are dead?' I whispered, thinking stupidly that I still had her mackintosh.

'They put out on a boat,' said Dr Trewithian.

'Why on earth were they out in a boat?' the minister said, with far more disapproval than compassion. Alec stared in disbelief at him.

'It must have seemed safer,' said the doctor. 'Crovie village is all but washed away. The sea wall crumbled, rocks down on the roofs, doors and windows smashed to bits, and a mudslide washing them into the water from behind. So they put out in a wee boatie. Madness. Even if the man had had the faintest notion how to handle his craft.'

'Six years they were here,' the minister said. 'They painted every boat and lobster pot and gutting knife in the place and never spent a day on the sea.'

'Well, if any of their paintings survive this night, I'll be damned,' said the doctor. 'I'll be blowed, I mean, padre. But they're no loss. Outsiders without children.'

'That's rather unbending, isn't it?' I said, thinking I should offer a mild reproof before Alec produced a worse one or a punch on the nose, which he looked fair to do.

'Overly professional, perhaps,' said Dr Trewithian.

'I've often said your work will taint you, Trewithian,' said Reverend Lamont. 'And it's beginning to.'

'I know you don't approve—' Dr Trewithian began.

'I *cannot* approve,' said Lamont. 'But I will not quarrel

tonight with the man who brought my son home to his mother.'

'What *do* you do?' said Alec.

'Genetics,' said Dr Trewithian, then he laughed at my face. 'Genetics, Mrs Gilver, not eugenics. Inter-marriage and fertility. So Gamrie is the perfect place for me. I've got very adept at spotting connections.' Here he dropped one of his eyelids in a half-wink. 'Or the lack of them.'

All at once a great many of the doctor's hints and arch remarks made sense to me and I blushed. Of course I with my black hair and dark eyes and Alec with his tawny hair and eyes to match could not have convinced a geneticist that we were brother and sister.

'So the Bennets weren't amongst your guinea pigs,' said Alec, hastily changing the subject.

'If my boy had lost his life saving them,' said the minister, then he drew in a deep breath and swallowed. 'I'd have accepted God's will. As ever.'

'Will you accept God's bounty?' said Alec, holding the whisky bottle out to him.

The minister's stern face softened just a little. He did not go so far as to smile but his eyes creased a little in the corners. 'If the doctor advises it,' he said. The doctor nodded. 'But if Elizabeth comes down and catches me she'll want to see a written prescription.'

Alec smiled. 'And we must drink to their memory, Dr Trewithian,' he said. 'Whether you like it or not.'

'And that of the Gows,' the minister said. If it were possible, a heavier gloom descended upon us then. 'Did you see anything of them at all, Trewithian? While you were out there?'

Dr Trewithian shook his head and settled his chin onto his chest, staring down at the fire, a picture of dejection.

'What a waste,' he said. 'All these superstitions and traditions. Fair enough if they're harmless, although I doubt the padre would agree – but when it comes to four lives thrown away for nothing. It's a sad day.'

That was the moment for Alec and me to speak. Earlier, when the doctor and Lamont's boy were on the sea, their lives in the balance, we could not have added another, monstrous, note to the evening. Now, though, now was the time. I glanced at Alec only to find him looking at me. Neither one of us said a word. It was the minister who filled the yawning silence in the room.

'*Be sober, be vigilant,*' he said. '*Because your adversary the devil, as a roaring lion, walketh about, seeking whom he may devour.*'

This, if anyone was interested in my opinion, did not help. I went to bed and stared at the ceiling until Alec knocked and entered in the morning.

18

'Mr Birchfield will be relieved,' was Alec's opening. He went to the windows and unlatched the shutters. I had heard the gale relenting around three o'clock and the rain had gradually let up too, going from drilling to spattering until it stopped altogether, but it was still astonishing, when Alec had got the shutters open, to see a beam of sunlight, weak and milky but unmistakable, shining in through the lace curtains and landing in a bright patch on the linoleum.

'He will be unless the barrel washes ashore,' I said.

'They'd have unstoppered it and thrown it overboard,' said Alec, standing with his back to me, looking out.

'Why in the name of everything holy didn't they just throw *him* overboard?'

'Because they believed it all,' said Alec. 'My mother would let herself be eaten by tigers if the only escape was under a ladder.'

I sat up, struggling against the weight of Bunty who was still dozing beside me and pinning the blankets down. Alec turned, took my dressing gown from the hook on the back of the door and brought it to me.

'It seems like a nightmare,' I said. 'Did they hope to escape, do you think? Or did they really just sail out into a storm to die?'

'Better than the noose,' said Alec. He sat down at the foot of the bed and began scratching Bunty's flank in a half-hearted way. 'Heavens, she's rickety, isn't she?'

'What are we going to do?' I asked him. 'If we leave it to

Mr Birchfield, the truth will never see the light of day. If we go to the police, countless people will be harmed – Mr Gow and Mrs Mason will be destroyed! – and no good will come of it. And . . .'

'And what?'

'I don't know,' I said. 'I've just got the oddest feeling that we haven't got to the bottom yet.'

'If there's a lower level than four murderers bumping a chap off for not being the marrying kind and then pretty well deliberately killing themselves on their wedding day, I'd rather not get there at all,' said Alec. 'Fratricide and suicide are quite enough for me.'

I took in a great wuthering breath and felt the danger of tears as I released it again. Alec let go of Bunty and instead reached out to me, grabbing my ankle through the bedclothes and shaking me.

'You know what we need?' he said. I raised my eyebrows, eager to hear it. 'Quiet contemplation, spiritual guidance and a good old sing-song.' My eyebrows lowered again without my making them. 'Church, Dandy.'

It was clear from the knots of worshippers all walking away from the harbour towards the beach end of the seatown road that the path to St John's Church had been deemed passable again. It was clearer still, from the placid way they strolled past, looking out over the bay, air-force blue ruffles this morning just tipped with white, that Gamrie had taken the storm in its stride and had already made some kind of peace with six deaths overnight. The villagers were solemn but not stricken, not weeping. It was as much to turn away from their callousness as from the thought of the deaths themselves that I cast around for a different topic and found one.

'Poor Jenny,' I said, looking up towards the church. 'The chapel of ease would have been much easier for her. I wonder if she'll still go.'

'Hmm?' said Alec.

'Cissie Walker's sister Jenny who was delivered of a son last night had stated her intention to go and be kirked this morning.'

'Delivered of a son on Christmas Day!' said Alec. 'If she were Argentinean do you know what she'd probably call him?'

'I do,' I said 'and it always seemed like the very ends of blasphemy. As it is, she'll call him after his father's father and Gamrie will have another Gordon Wilkie, even if that makes seventeen in all.'

We walked on. The curtains were closed at Mrs Mason's cottage, and no smoke emerged from the chimney. I ached to think of her shut up in there contemplating a future without her two remaining daughters, not to mention the new sons-in-law, the good boat and the promise of prosperity and grandchildren in which she had been revelling when I met her. But it was more than just aching; I was troubled too. I was not aware that I was scowling until Alec challenged me.

'If the wind changes, Dan, you'll be stuck like that. What is it?'

'I don't know,' I said. 'I've the queerest feeling that we keep getting close to something and yet never seeing it. We might be talking of other things and there's just an echo or a rumble somewhere.'

'This again,' said Alec. 'I've heard you on this subject before. It never does get any clearer.'

'It might be no more than the irritation of not having answered all the questions,' I said. 'Why did Nancy Mason disappear? Was she killed? Why was she killed? And who were the strangers?'

'It doesn't matter who they were,' Alec said. 'We were sent here to find out who Mr Pick— Do you know, now that he has a name and a grieving father I can't quite bring myself to call him that any more, but we found out who he was and the strangers are neither here nor there.'

'But doesn't that irk you?' I said. 'Seven strangers, all of them men travelling alone, none of them typical tourists or workers or anyone who had a discernible reason to be here and all of them vanished into thin air. Seven people, Alec. Eight if you count Nancy.'

Then our conversation was forced to end since we had reached the fold in the cliff and had to start up the path in single file preceded and followed by more of the congregation.

At the top, the sexton was standing at the open doors of the church, like a proxy vicar, greeting the arrivals.

'Home again, Chalmers,' said Alec. 'Which way did you come?'

'Round the dead man's way, to see was it clear enough for the minister,' he said.

'And was there any sign of the Searles?' I asked. 'They never did turn up in the village.'

'No cart overturned nor any pony wandering,' said Chalmers.

'They turned back and spent the night at home, Dandy,' said Alec, ushering me inside. 'We can drop in after the service if it will stop you worrying.'

St John's Church was of the other persuasion from the chapel of ease down in the village; we felt the seeping chill of damp stone and an inadequate boiler as soon as we stepped beyond the vestibule and when we shuffled into a back pew and I put my feet up on the pipe running along at its base I could feel only the faintest glimmer of warmth, as from a hot water bottle which has been left in one's bed all day and is encountered upon a second night's retiring.

Nor was there much comfort to be had from the service. No mention was made of the two brides who should have been here and were gone except that Reverend Lamont read from Ephesians Chapter 6, of all things on a Boxing Day morning: loins girt about with truth and the breastplate of righteousness to wrestle the rulers of darkness. It was as much as I could do not to snort. After yesterday's utter let-down of a Christmas reading we all needed something seasonal and jolly today.

All in all, therefore, and not for the first time in a Church of Scotland pew, I slumped into a state of mind somewhere between a yearning and a huff. In Northamptonshire at Christmastime, the church would be bristling with all the adornment the ladies' flower committee could muster from every hothouse in the parish and the service would be filled with joy and song, as the glad tidings of great joy were proclaimed again from the pulpit.

At home, the kitchens would be filled with the sound of goose skin crackling in the oven, the sight of steam billowing out of a plum pudding puttering away in its basin on the back of the range and the intoxicating scent of every spice in the cook's cupboard, burnt sugar and oranges too, mixed up in a punch bowl, which we children would be forbidden and from which we would sneak sips anyway.

But the greatest excitement of all, greater than drinking punch or finding silver between one's teeth, greater even than chocolate mice wrapped in tinsel paper, was The Trunk.

When The Trunk was opened, each Christmas Eve, Mavis and Edward and I would drink in lungfuls of its beloved camphorous breath and our hearts would beat faster as the business of Christmas truly began with the children's nativity. The casting always took forever and the competition for the best roles showed little peace and goodwill for as to what the best roles were, all of we children agreed. Although Mary and Joseph were in most scenes, the angel undoubtedly had the best lines and the shepherds got to hold lambs, when it came to costumes the three wise men who travelled from the east, their crowns worn proudly if unsteadily and the little mustard pots pasted over with glass 'jewels' carried as reverently to the manger as though they held real treasure, were in a class of their own.

Something shifted. I came out of my daydream and looked towards Alec sitting beside me, but he was sunk in the kind of torpor a sermon can bestow after a late night and too much whisky. Whatever that sensation of being joggled was it had not been Alec nudging me. I shut out Reverend Lamont's words and returned to my thoughts.

Three wise men travelling from the east. Now why had that notion disturbed me, if it *was* that? Someone had said something in the last few days. I let my mind drift and into it came a memory of Jenny Walker's voice 'not Macduff, this was the Rosehearty bus, coming from the east.' And that was the bus which had the oriental gentleman aboard. I turned that thought around for a moment or two but it led nowhere.

Perhaps, I thought to myself, I was simply retreating into sentimental nostalgia because the present had only the poor dead Bennets, the poor dead Gows and Masons and this dreary church to offer me.

Perhaps, but I did not think so. Some aspect of those long ago Christmases when we three Lestons, the three Paigntons from the adjoining estate and our hated twin cousins from Lincoln had performed the nativity to our indulgent mothers and bored, fidgety fathers, something about it was tugging at me in a very particular way. I stared ahead, gazing without seeing at the black grosgrain ribbon around some unknown woman's best church hat, thinking of the braid which used to tether the shepherds' head cloths, and all of a sudden I had the most monstrous idea.

I did not move much, but I think I stiffened, for my shoe leather squeaked as my feet jerked.

'Dropping off?' Alec whispered. 'I should have brought peppermints.'

Seven strangers. A Chinaman, a swarthy man and a red-haired man of impressive proportions. A beautiful young man with the face of an angel. An unfortunate-looking young man, with the shaved head of ringworm, and a shabby sort with a grey beard; these two were lowly peasants. Which left the long-haired man. Three kings, an angel, two shepherds and Joseph.

A small moan escaped me and Alec glanced my way again. The monstrous idea was growing stronger inside me, budding and sprouting.

Wee horsies, cows with big horns and a fearsome beastie of which she had never seen the like. Little Nesta Chalmers had told me as plainly as she could from her short and narrow experience that the animals delivered to the Searles that summer had been donkeys, oxen and a camel. They had cut their teeth on the Garden of Eden, I told myself, and flexed their muscles with Noah's Ark, but the crowning glory of the Searles' life's work was to be a manger scene and, since the point of a manger scene was not really the few animals to be found there, they had abandoned Durban's mannequins and moved into quite a new realm. I knew that I was breathing heavily; I could see the front of my coat rising and falling and could feel my hands inside my gloves start to prickle with heat as waves of dread and horror washed over me. It could not be true. It could not possibly be true. I shook myself. They were all men. Where was the virgin? Where was the child? I tried to steady my breathing and pay attention to the service, anything to escape the torrid thoughts that filled my mind.

'Do you need to leave, Dandy?' Alec murmured.

Lamont had reached the blessings. The three brides, Cissie, Janet and Margaret, walked forward and stood at the altar with heads bowed while he spoke more of St Paul's words over them – 'Wives submit yourselves unto your own husbands as unto the Lord' – and laid his hand on each of their heads in turn. They returned, each blushing deeply, to their pews and then it was Jenny's turn. She lumbered up to her feet, smiled upon fondly by her mother and sister, and shuffling a little she trailed her rather weary way up the aisle to the altar. If one had not known different, one might have thought that she had spent the night in a tavern to produce that unkempt air and the slow rolling walk.

I was on my feet before I knew I had moved and was sprinting out of the church before I had even decided to go. I dashed past a startled Mr Chalmers and shot out of the door and across the churchyard to the gates. I was halfway there when I realised Alec was behind me.

'Dandy?' he said. 'Are you ill? Are you going to be sick? I'll avert my eyes, darling. You don't need to make it into the trees for cover.'

'I'm not going to be sick,' I said. 'Well, I might, but that's not why I left. Alec, I know why Nancy Mason ran away. And I know where she went. And dear God I know what's going to happen to her if it hasn't already.'

Alec was jogging along beside me as we passed the crow and owl gateposts and entered the woods. The storm had done fearsome damage and several trees had fallen over the drive blocking our way. I launched myself at the first one, scrambling up one side and down the other without regard to the twigs that snatched at my clothes and scraped my skin.

'Wait a minute,' said Alec, vaulting the tree trunk and landing beside me. 'Stop for just a minute and tell me.'

'Nancy Mason was warned about John Gow,' I said. 'She knew but she fasted to him anyway, because she had a plan. He might have been in on it and he might not. But her plan was to present him with a fait accompli when he came back on the boat last spring. She was going to tell him that their handfasting had been smiled upon, to use the delicate local phrasing. And even though he would know it was a trick – unless he was in on it, I mean – what could he do? She would have to time it properly and even at that perhaps pass the child off as an eight months' delivery, but what could he do?'

'Good Lord,' said Alec. 'But he didn't come back and there she was, stuck with it.'

'Exactly. So she ran away. But she didn't run far.' I pointed up the drive. 'The Searles' maid Helen is Nancy Mason. Nancy Mason's teename is Nancy Nell. Her full name is Agnes Helen Mason. It's her. That's why she doesn't do the shopping and why she stays out of the way when there are visitors. Her mother is half a mile away and doesn't know it!'

'It was very kind of them to take in a girl in that condition and give her work,' said Alec. I groaned.

'That's only a tiny bit of the story,' I said, 'and they are anything but kind. She had the baby. When I saw her on Christmas Eve she looked every bit as weary and slow as Jenny Walker looks today. She was safe until she had the baby, Alec, but now there's not a minute to lose and we might be too late already.'

'What are you talking about?'

'Something that's going to make a man chopped up in herring barrels seems like nothing in comparison,' I said. I took his hands in mine, looked straight into his eyes and told him all of it. The shepherds and kings and the angel and Joseph and, of course, the young woman and her child. He shook his head through most of it, then bit his lip, still frowning, still not believing, and then finally turned pale and rubbed a hand over his face, but nodded. It was the camel that did it. After that it was only a second until he was thundering up the driveway again, launching himself at the next fallen tree.

We were both scraped and bleeding when we got there and winded enough by the struggle to stand panting and aghast at what greeted us. The coloured signs and mannequins on the front sweep had been blown off their supports, splintering and cracking as they went, but from the front at least, Lump House looked to have survived the gales without harm.

It was when we went around to the kitchen door that we saw what the storm had done. The roof of the added rooms – Searles Realm of Bounteous Wonder – had been breached by an enormous pine which had crashed down and, finding only rafters and asphalt in its path, had cracked the roof like an egg. Whole sections of the tarpaper had blown away and lay littered over the yard and even some of the bricks had crumbled, leaving gaping holes in the walls. I could see part of the painted backing of the Garden of Eden display and I whipped my head away lest I see any more. I was sure we were right about what was in there, and I knew that we might *have* to look in the end. If it came to that I would gird myself and manage it somehow, but I had no desire to catch a glimpse of it now.

'Shall we knock?' Alec said. 'Creep in? Barge in?'

'One minute,' I said, stepping over to the stable. 'Let's see if the other pony's back. If the Searles aren't here then we just barge in and take Nancy to safety.' I opened the stable door and peered inside. One small pony was standing in a loosebox, looking back at me. I glanced to either side. None of the other boxes had straw on the floor or any hay in the rack.

'But if they only have one pony . . .' I said.

'That's not all,' said Alec, nodding towards the end of the row where we could just see the shafts of a cart resting on the cobbled floor.

'She definitely said they'd taken the cart,' I said. 'I suppose she might have been mistaken.'

'Either that or they're back,' said Alec. He sounded perfectly calm but before we left the stables he took a crop down from the tack wall and handed it to me, then took another for himself. With jaws grimly set, we made our way to the house.

There was a scuffle as soon as we entered and, sprinting across the passageway and flinging the kitchen door back on its hinges, we just caught sight of someone leaving by the door on the far side of the room. When we followed, though, there was no sign of anyone. Alec caught my arm and we stood still, listening, then at the sound of a door banging shut we raced off towards the noise. With a sickening sense of inevitability, I guessed where we were going and the warren of distempered passageway, linoleum underfoot, confirmed it. Whoever it was was not leading us to the front of the house and the public rooms; we were working our way through the domestic offices, back and back, to the museum. The doors we passed were locked – we tried them, Alec on one side and I on the other as we sped along – and so we kept going, as the passageway narrowed and the ceiling lowered, until we turned one last corner and came up hard against a closed door. Alec tried it, it opened and we burst through.

The holes in the roof let in enough watery sunlight, even through the pine branches, to show the wreckage of Eden, spoiled and sodden now with its painted backdrops broken and animals toppled. The serpent had stretched and split as the backdrop to which it was attached collapsed; back into some of its original seventeen parts, one supposed. I snapped my head away from the sight of its ragged edges and the coarse stuffing now revealed, even as I did so knowing that far grislier sights were shortly bound to come.

We edged our way around the debris and on to the next room. The half-open door bulged in its frame from the weight of the roof sagging down and even as we squeezed through there was a creak and the wall settled a little further, wet plaster dropping in clods all around us. Through here the damage was less; Noah and his family in their robes, with their ludicrous expressions more monstrous than ever, were mostly upright and the pairs of baby animals stood on the gangplank, frozen on their way into the belly of the ark. We stopped and listened again. There was no sound but neither was there anywhere to hide. No one was in here. We knew that. We knew we should have to open the door before us and enter the third room. 'Gift of Bounteous Light' proclaimed a banner which had not been there before, hanging just a little askew over a crack in the plastered wall. This door opened without sticking, fell open indeed as though to coax us through.

It was the stable familiar from those childhood Christmases: the straw roof, the walls made of logs, the hay underfoot, and all of them gathered around in their sumptuous cloaks and crowns, in their lowly robes. St Joseph stood with bowed head, his halo a small disc of bone white; the shepherds knelt, youth and age between them; the three kings, ruddy, swarthy and olive-skinned, held out the gifts towards the manger; and the angel was suspended above them all, resplendent in robes of gold, with wings as wide as the stable and a halo which seemed to shimmer in the dimness of the scene.

Alec and I stood as still as they. We were petrified by the sight of them, by their unmistakable, undeniable realness: their skin with the marks of lived lives – crow's feet, stubbled jowls, a bunion on one of the bare feet of a shepherd. And yet they were as far from real as Durban's mannequins somehow: their eyes glass, their parted lips dull and dry, and the quietness of them impossible and unbearable.

We turned our eyes from their stillness to the only movement, tiny as it was, and the only sound.

Beside the empty manger, Mary sat huddled and trembling, holding tightly onto the bundle in her arms, her shoulders rounded and her head lowered, her whole body curled in on itself to protect the child. It squirmed and began to cry the quavering cry of the newborn.

'Nancy,' I said, 'don't be frightened.' *Fear not*, said an echo in my mind. *Be not afraid*. I stopped speaking lest hysterical laughter burst out of me and terrify her even more, as she sat there quaking.

'We've come to help you,' said Alec.

'Hurry, Nancy,' I said. 'In case the Searles come back and find us here.'

'They'll no come back,' she said.

'But come away from there,' I added. My voice was unsteady and although I was steeling myself not to look at any of the figures, I could see their eyes shining. Those glassy, beady eyes. I felt the ground shift and feared that I would faint if I stayed a minute longer. 'Come out of here,' I said. 'Why on earth would you come here?'

She laughed at that, a dry empty bark of a sound without the faintest trace of amusement. Then the fight seemed to go out of her and, her legs buckling, she slid off the low stool until she was sitting with her skirts puddled around her on the floor.

'So's you'd see,' she said. 'Nobody could blame me if they'd seen this.'

'Blame you?' said Alec. 'Nancy, what have you done to be blamed for?'

Before she could answer there was another shifting underfoot and a great yawning creak of nails pulling out of wood and joints splitting under their own weight. Alec leapt forward, grabbed her and rolled away.

'Dandy, take the baby,' he yelled. Nancy held out the swaddled bundle towards me.

'Aye, take her,' she said. 'And run.' I ran flat out, faster than I had ever run in my life before, back past the ark and through the garden, almost tripping over one of the broken lengths of the endless serpent, tangling my feet in its coils so that, from terror and revulsion, I almost believed it was winding knowingly around me. I shook it off and ran back into the twisting passageway and along it all the way to the front of the house, bursting out through the servants' door into the hallway.

The baby was shrieking, wriggling and struggling inside its swaddling cloth. I raised it to my shoulder and hissed softly in its ear, jogging up and down and patting it rhythmically. It had quieted a little when the door opened again and Alec appeared, with Nancy in his arms. He set her down on one of the hall chairs and then stood bent over, panting. There was dust in his hair and a scratch on his face was bleeding.

'Is she all right?' Nancy said.

I drew the child gently away from myself and handed her back.

'She's just a little startled,' I said. Nancy opened the swaddling blanket and felt the baby all over, uncurling her tiny hands to inspect her fingers and straightening each of her red, wrinkled little legs in turn. When she was satisfied, she rewrapped the blanket and looked up at me.

'Thank you,' she said.

I smiled at her.

'Blame you for what?' said Alec again. Nancy's smile faltered and her shoulders slumped.

'Let's make ourselves comfortable,' I said. 'The kitchen is far enough away from where the tree came down. Let's go there.'

19

'I was at the station at Macduff,' said Nancy, 'waiting for a train to get away and the Searles were coming home fa one of their trips and they recognised me.' We were back in the kitchen now, Nancy sitting in the chair by the range, rocking to and fro and patting her baby gently to soothe it back to sleep again. I was sitting on the edge of the chair opposite, agog to hear the tale but ready to leap up at any sound from outside. She seemed very sure that the Searles were not around but I was as fidgety as a blood horse. Alec, with no great expertise it had to be said, was making cocoa.

'Where were you going?' I asked her.

'Anywhere!' said Nancy. Still, all these months later and after all the horrors she had lived through, the fright and despair was in her voice as she remembered. 'Anywhere I could call myself a widow. Anywhere but here where folk knew me. You've no idea what it's like here.'

'As bad as everywhere else, I daresay,' I said and could not help glaring at Alec since he was a man. He had the grace to look sorry.

'I'd been crying,' Nancy went on, 'and Mr Warwick was always a kind man.' She caught her lip in her teeth. 'He always *seemed* like a kind man. He asked me what was wrong. I didn't tell him but you'd not need a crystal ball to work it out, would you? A woman sitting greeting on a station platform running away fa home. It's not exactly a mystery.'

I did not interrupt to tell her that all week long it had stumped Alec and me.

'He offered me a position,' she said. 'He said the world was a harsh place and that's why him and his brother had no time for it. He offered me work and a bed and said they'd help me when my time came and find a good home for the bairn. Then I could go back down to my mammy and my family again. They were that kind. *Seemed* that kind.'

'Your family,' I said. 'Yes.' I did not know where to begin: her family had killed her betrothed and last night they had died. 'Tell me,' I said, trying to distract her lest she ask about them, 'did John Gow know what you were planning?'

'Him!' she said. 'Nah, he didn't. But fit could he say? When I telt him the bairn was coming he'd just have to button his lip, wouldn't he? That or tell the world what me and Cissie Wilson knew.'

'And Janet Guthrie too,' I said.

'Didn't you dread living with him on those terms?' said Alec.

'He'd a good boat and made a grand living,' Nancy said.

'And the father?' I asked.

'Old Gow's a good man too,' said Nancy.

'No, you misunderstand me. I meant what about the baby's father? Mightn't he have caused trouble for you?'

'Not him,' said Nancy. 'He's married and he'd not want his wife to know.'

'It wasn't a bad plan, all told,' Alec said.

I said nothing. Certainly I did not speak to disagree.

'I still cannot believe John Gow got himself drowned,' said Nancy. 'It was calm seas, folk catching their ooty and gutting on board. My sisters fine, Robert and Willie both fine. Do you know what I think really happened?' Alec and I waited in silence for her to continue. When she did, she spoke not to us but to the child which had wakened and was waving its fists and making little crooning noises. 'I think your daddy was feart to come home, cushie-doo. He could not see a way forward out of the guddle. If he'd known what I had planned, if he'd known you were already just begun, he'd have taken more care with himself.'

'Suicide?' I said. 'Oh, Nancy.'

She blinked tears away and raised the bundle to kiss the baby's cheek.

'When did you discover what the Searles were up to?' said Alec. 'Christmas Eve,' said Nancy. 'It was my time and I went to find them to let them know.'

'What happened?' I asked her.

'I'd never been in the new bit,' she said. 'That was one thing they telt me over and over. The new bit was private and I wasn't allowed inside. That and the icehouse too. Well, they'd no need to bar me fa that place.'

'The icehouse?' said Alec. 'Why?'

'That's where they put the bits they didn't need for stuffing.' Nancy said. 'It reeked to high heaven. So I'd not have gone in there for all the silver in Aberdeen. And I didn't much want to see what they were doing either. It was bad enough dusting them when they were finished. All they poor wee rabbits and that. Only, on Christmas Eve when I knew my time was here, it was hours since I'd seen them and I was getting worried. So I went to find them.' She took a sharp breath in as though sniffing smelling salts and the baby flinched at the sudden sound. 'And then I saw what they were at. Saw it but still couldn't credit it. I couldn't . . . I cannot even now I've seen it with my own two eyes. It was lamplight, ken, and for a minute I thought Mr Durban had got that much better at the painting and then I thought they were dummies and then I recognised one of them. I'd seen him in the summer at the back door.' She shuddered. 'I hope it rots away to nothing,' she said. 'I hope every tree in the woods falls in on it and it's buried for ever.'

'But,' Alec began. 'It can't just be left to rot away. We must telephone to the police. They need to start the manhunt for the Searles.' Nancy blinked, then she stood and walked over to a cradle in the far corner, away from the draughts and the fierce heart of the range.

'Manhunt?' she said. 'There's no need for that.'

'What happened when you surprised them?' I said, trying to take her back to recounting her tale. 'Did they just run off that minute?'

'Nah,' she said. 'They didn't hear me come in. I got a good swing at Mr Warwick before he could stop me and then Mr Durban was always such a spindly wee smout.'

'Nancy?' said Alec, 'are you telling us you killed the Searles? Is that what you're saying?'

'Nah,' she said again and she gave a chuckle which was horrifying for the comfortable sound of it. 'I bet they're wishing I did by now. They're in the ice house. I flang Mr Warwick down before he come round and I chucked Mr Durban in on top of him. He was no match for me.'

'What—' I began. I cleared my throat and started again. 'What were you planning to do next?'

'Pack my traps and go,' she said. 'Like I meant to nine months ago. Leave all this for whoever finds it.'

I could not look at Alec then lest my face show what I was thinking: that it seemed a perfectly reasonable course of action.

'Shouldn't you be resting, though?' I said. 'One can hardly believe what you've been through in the last day.'

'Been through?' said Nancy. 'I birthed a bairn like women do.'

'And the Searles,' I reminded her. It was a sickening thought somehow, that she had grappled those two men into the ice-house and then calmly gone to her childbed all alone.

'Speaking of the Searles,' Alec said, 'I shall go and see how they're faring. If you'll point out where the icehouse is, please Nancy.' I could tell from his voice, that he wished with all his heart he could simply leave this place and walk away. 'And then Mrs Gilver and I shall have to go back to the village,' he went on. 'And telephone to the police. Meanwhile, I suggest you do as you said and "pack your traps".'

'I cannot go back down the hill,' said Nancy. 'Not with a day-old bairn and the man that's meant to be her daddy gone a year.'

'I'll come with you, Alec,' I said. Staring into a charnel pit at two madmen was preferable somehow to sitting here with Nancy as she contemplated her future.

'I'll show you where it is,' she said. She gathered the baby up out of the cradle and led us to the kitchen door. Outside, I looked towards the brick exterior of the Circus of Wonders, expecting to see at least one other tree crashed in on it, but it looked exactly as before. Puzzled, I hurried to catch up with Alec and Nancy but I did not mention my puzzlement since she was speaking.

'It's not that easy to find,' she was saying. 'There's no path and it's overgrown, like.'

'Just point,' said Alec. 'You should be resting, not tramping about.'

'It's good to get some fresh air,' she said and then she stumbled. Or at least I thought she did and yet at the same time I thought I had been struck by a dizzy spell. The trees and undergrowth and the faint path leading into the darkness seemed to shiver. Alec turned towards me and frowned.

'What was that?' he said.

'Oh my God!' I said. I leapt forward and clutched at both of them. 'Run!' I screamed. In the museum minutes ago I had felt it without understanding. No tree had fallen; the ground had moved under our feet and now it was moving again and much more strongly too. 'The cliff's crumbling!' I shouted. 'We have to *run!*'

For the second time Nancy Mason showed the woman she was. She thrust the bundled baby into my arms again.

'Go!' she said. 'Save her!' I did not need to be told twice. Holding the child like a rugby football I barrelled away. 'I'm calling her Henrietta!' she shouted after me. I glanced backwards and saw Alec lift her again, this time like a fireman, doubling her over his shoulder and clamping her hard behind her knees with both arms. Then, as another shuddering rumble shook the ground beneath me, I turned around and raced away, clearing trees I would have clambered over on my way here, sailing like a steeplechaser across dents and ditches. Still Alec caught up with me just before the rumble became a roar and we all felt the sickening pull of the ground beneath us sinking as a great tranche of solid earth beyond it simply fell away.

We stood, gasping for breath and dumbstruck. Where Lump House had been minutes ago now there was a view of the bay, where the calm blue-grey sea stretched to the horizon and met the smooth pearl-grey sky.

Alec stepped forward to look over the edge.

'If there's any justice in this world at all,' he said, 'the next high tide will wash the whole lot clean away.'

We could hear shouts already. Perhaps there were still churchgoers at the kirk, or perhaps Chalmers was on his way. In either case, our most immediate problem was Nancy. Time had slowed down as I was racing away from the edge of the cliff and I had managed to think a great many thoughts in a very few moments. In a year's time, I had thought to myself, no one would know the difference between a child born on Christmas Day and a child born at the Harvest Festival nine months after John Gow had last sailed. She could come home then, comfort her mother, comfort old Mr Gow and bring up little Henrietta surrounded by friends. Harry Bennet, who had painted pictures of her hands and been so obliging, was dead and could not trouble her. Her choice of name had revealed that little morsel of the story to me.

But what about right now, as she stood there still slow and

tired from the birth, as the shouts of the villagers grew louder? All at once I knew what to do.

'Alec,' I said, 'I know it's a fearful trek, but could you go round by the dead man's path and fetch Bunty and the motorcar? Nancy and I shall wait for you at Dr Trewithian's.'

'Doctor T's?' she said. 'Why would he help me?'

'Because knowing the facts of your story will stop ten years of his work being wasted,' I said. 'Little Henrietta will be a most useful addition to his categories if he knows the truth about her and she'd scupper the whole thing if he didn't. Besides, he's only going to let you sit by his fire for an hour while Mr Osborne fetches the motorcar and then we'll be on our way.'

'Where are we going?' Nancy said.

'Perthshire,' I told her. 'To my house. Or perhaps to Mr Osborne's.' I had spent quite some time in Hugh's demerit book already for introducing waifs and strays to our household and Alec only had one bossy valet with whom to contend. 'There you shall rest for a while,' I went on. 'I have an idea I want you to listen to.' I had a great many things to tell her, in truth. The deaths of her sisters and of Harry Bennet were the most pressing, but in her condition she should still have been in bed sipping tea and having her pillows plumped by a nurse. She should not have been shoving evil men into icehouses and galloping around the woods to outrun landslides and I feared that one more incident in this day might floor her.

'Perthshire?' she said. 'Blooming miles from the sea. How long do I have to stay?'

Perhaps I was wrong then. Perhaps a herring quine like Nancy could take all of this and more in her stride without once blinking. I thought so until Alec arrived at the doctor's house half an hour later, bringing Bunty with him.

'There's all sorts of commotion going on out there,' he said.

'So I gather,' I said. 'Dr Trewithian dashed off to help with casualties and barely gave us a glance. I'd be surprised if he even noticed the baby.'

I glanced at Nancy as I said this. Bunty had ignored me, unusually, and gone straight to her, putting a paw on her arm and looking deep into her eyes. Nancy's mouth began to tremble.

'Give Henrietta to me,' I said, 'and you put your arms round Bunty's neck and have a good old howl. She'll join in and, besides, she's quite the most comforting creature ever born.'

Between the three of them – Nancy, Bunty and, of course, little Henrietta who started up in sympathy – the noise was fearful but absolutely fitting comment upon the events of the day.

Postscript

It was over a year later, during another case which I have yet to describe, that Alec and I found ourselves back in Gamrie again. We decided against accompanying Nancy home when she returned. Instead we put her on a train with Henrietta, a lusty ten-month old (whom anyone would believe to be past her first birthday), and had to settle for imagining the joy on Mrs Mason's face for the sake of not raising questions in the minds of any who would remember exactly when those two philly-oolies were last in town.

When we did find ourselves passing on the top road between Fraserburgh and Banff, however, it was only natural that our thoughts would return to Mr Birchfield, the conscienceless acts of the Gow and Mason siblings and, above all, to the Searles of Lump House. We hardly had to discuss it at all; Alec merely turned and raised an eyebrow, I nodded once, and then we were on our way across the flat land and over the edge of the world again, down the brae, brakes screeching, Alec's hands tight on the steering wheel, until we shot out at the harbour head as before.

The scene was very different from that foggy December night, though. It was one of those May evenings which the far north of Scotland does so well if rather seldom. The sky was an impossible colour between blue and pink with a smudge of purple on the horizon. Gulls wheeled lazily over the bay and some of Browning's startled little waves were leaping around at the edge of the shore, teasing the children who were playing there.

'This was old Bunty's last trip, wasn't it?' Alec said. I nodded, stepping down, ignoring the barking and scrabbling from inside the motorcar.

'He's scratched that door to bits,' said Alec. 'Really, Dan, when will you ever have a dog with some manners?'

'Does Hugh provide you with a script?' I said. 'You sound more like him every day. Except for speaking kindly of Bunty, I suppose.'

'As I remember, Bunty was rather more comfortable than us that winter,' said Alec.

'Yes, she spent the entire week curled in front of the range,' I said, laughing. 'Let's go and see if Miss Clatchie remembers her. Or us even.'

But when we arrived on the Main Street, after a wrong turn or two in the lanes, the sight which greeted us was of a Three Kings painted seashell pink and with its doors thrown open. A sign in one window advertised afternoon tea with piano accompaniment and a sign in the other said CHILDREN WELCOME.

'Miss Clatchie's gone then,' Alec said.

'Phemie?' said a voice behind us. We turned. A man in his thirties, dressed in the herring catcher's uniform of dark gansey with rolled sleeves and trousers made from barkit cloth, was standing there. 'Phemie Clatchie's away. She took off after the storm when the cliff over by gave way. Didn't matter how many folk telt her she was safe as hoosies here in the bay. Off she went, away to Crieff to stay with her sister.' He gave us an appraising look and rubbed his jaw. 'There's no boarding in Gamrie now. You'll have to try Macduff, or Rosehearty.'

'We weren't really looking for somewhere to stay,' I said. 'Just stopped in to watch the boats come in and the sun go down.'

He looked up at the sliver of sky visible between two of the buildings and nodded.

'Aye, they'll no be long now,' he said.

'You weren't out yourself today?' Alec asked. 'I'd have put you down for a herring man.'

'Ah,' said the man with a secretive smile. 'I was busy today right enough, just not with herring.'

'Ah,' I said back. 'And was it a good day for lobster?'

'Aye,' he answered, although his smile had gone.

'Splendid,' Alec said. 'Well, I hope you got a good "ooty catch" last February for you to "slicht".'

I took pity on the chap whose face had paled.

'Don't worry,' I said. 'Are you arled to Mr Birchfield? Well, we won't say a thing.'

He tipped his hat and slipped away from us up one of the stairways to the high cottages.

'Rather mean,' said Alec. 'But irresistible all the same. Shall we go, Dandy?'

'I want to stroll along the seatown road past the Masons' place,' I said. 'I'd love to catch a glimpse.'

We did more than that as it turned out. We met Mrs Mason taking in a washing from the line along the edge of the beach.

'Mrs Gilver!' she said. 'And Mr Gilver, was it? Your brother anyway.'

'My dear Mrs Mason,' I said. 'How good to see you again. How are things with you?'

Her face clouded and I kicked myself. How good could things ever be? It took only a moment for her expression to clear, however, and her smile to return. She indicated the washing she was unpegging and I looked at it properly for the first time, noticing the little nightgowns and the dazzling white nappies hanging there.

'I've got a grandbairn,' she said. 'And another on the way.'

'Grandchildren?' I asked, hoping that my frown of puzzlement was convincing.

'Nancy came home,' she said. 'And you'll never guess if we stand here till morning why she had run away?'

290

We gave in immediately and she regaled us with the tale of Nancy's panic when the father of her coming child was killed, her year away, her timid return and her joyous welcome from Mrs Mason and from old Mr Gow too, who saw more of John in Henrietta every day.

'And she has a good man now,' said Mrs Mason. 'He's tooken wee Etta to his own and old Gow says if this new one's a laddie and gets looking for a boat he'll not forget him.' She pressed one of the folded nappies to her bosom and hugged it. 'I'd as soon he went for a cooper or up country to the farm for work but even wee Etta loves the boats already. Nancy's away along with her the now to watch the fleet come home.'

'And no more geological upsets?' said Alec. Mrs Mason frowned.

'The Christmastime we were here was when the cliff collapsed and Lump House was lost,' I said.

'Oh, aye, I remember all right,' said Mrs Mason. 'That was some week. They Bennets drownded, my own lasses and the Gow laddies drownded and they Searles drownded too if they weren't killed in the fall. That was the blackest week Gamrie ever knew.'

'Better times now?' said Alec gently.

'I'd not have believed my heart could mend,' she said. 'But every new life helps a wee bit and a wee bit more.'

All three of us stood in silence for a moment, for there was nothing to say. Then Alec and I stirred and looked back the way we had come.

'I'll tell Nancy you were asking for her,' said Mrs Mason. I nodded before I managed to stop myself. Mrs Mason smiled even wider. 'She's a bright enough quine but just sometimes she gets it wrong. Once or twice she's forgotten she's not supposed to know they two English folk that were here thon time.'

'In light of that,' Alec said, 'we really must be getting along.

And I don't think we'll be back, Mrs Mason. Many things happened that week – that year – that are best let lie.'

'What lies on the sea floor won't wash on the beach,' said Mrs Mason, which was rather too horribly apt. Alec and I murmured our goodbyes and left her, turning back to the harbour head and the motorcar.

'Did we do the right thing?' I asked.

'That Christmastime?' said Alec. 'Undoubtedly. Can you imagine this place if Birchfield's had been put out of business by scandal and if we had told the world about the Searles? All these fisherfolk with no work to do except taking boatloads of ghouls out around the headland to look at where it happened. The place would be a freak show. We did the right thing, Dandy.'

'By everyone living,' I agreed. 'But those men. All those poor men.'

The Searles had been very careful and, although we had made discreet enquiries around the Glasgow doss houses, we had not met with much success. They were all single, all indigent, and none them much missed or mourned. Joseph and the shepherds had outwitted us completely, but the red-haired man and the swarthy man, not to mention the Chinaman, rang a few bells, and one young nun in the City Mission had nodded and flushed when I mentioned the chap with the face of an angel. She had repeated the phrase – 'face of an angel, madam; that he does,' and I had not corrected her.

'And you have become the Mission's greatest benefactor,' Alec reminded me.

'After Mr Birchfield anyway,' I said. 'And it's partly to annoy Hugh.'

'Enough of this, said Alec. 'We made our decision and it was the right one.'

And so because the sun was going down in a riot of orange and purple and the fleet was coming home like a flock of geese, the wakes of the boats dazzling; and because whatever the future might bring, I was sure there would be new troubles enough without raking over old ones, I simply took Alec's arm and for a brief moment forgot it all, breathed in the sea air and enjoyed the view.

Facts and Fictions

I've taken quite a few liberties with the geography of Gamrie, while trying to stay true to the spirit of the place: Lump House doesn't exist, people might be relieved to know, and neither does the Three Kings. I'm far from sure that any light in the window of a village house would be visible from a manse on the top road either. Also, St John's Church had ceased to be used before the time at which this story is set, although its position and the paths and roads leading to it are accurate.

Obviously none of the characters is real, although the name 'Euphemia Clatchie' was a gift from the family tree of my friend Catherine Lepreux.

Most of the background herring and wedding lore is my best attempt at authenticity but the shenanigans of the Gows and Masons with their out-of-arle catch are my invention.

Teenames were a feature of the fisherfolk of the northeast where shared last names, added to the habit of giving grandparents' first names to children, meant that there were multiple individuals with exactly the same names in any settled village. For example, in the 1901 census forty men in Gamrie were called James or Alexander Watt.

For the first time, in this book, I've departed from the calendar of the year in question. Boxing Day in 1930 fell on the Friday, not the Sunday, but after a lot of staring out of the window trying to reconcile the year, the dates, the story and the days of the week, I decided life was short and this was fiction. Forgive me.

Oh, and the skulls in the church wall? True.

The World of
Dandy Gilver

Grant's Seasonal Modes

At a Village Wedding

Every woman wants to look her best whatever the occasion, but a lady of fashion attending a village wedding has a ticklish problem, for no one should outshine the bride.

If the wedding gown is white with a veil and a train, there is no need to worry. A girl in love, in white, on her wedding day, has a bloom which no amount of taste and fashion can match. Even the lucky mistress of an excellent maid, versed in the latest news from Paris and discerning as to coiffure and maquillage, will be second to such a flower.

But what if the girl is of very modest means and white tulle, lace veils and long trains are beyond her pocket? The quaint old tradition of "something borrowed" can be turned to account by a generous-minded patroness. Instead of wearing her own fox-fur, diamond choker, pearl brooch or silken shawl, a true lady might offer these ornaments to the bride for the day.

But what if the church where the nuptials are to be held is the house of a narrow sect which frowns upon finery? What then? The lilies of the field are the only solution. The lady must offer a wedding gift of flowers: a circlet of buds for the bridal head, a posy for her hands, a buttonhole for her groom and nosegays for all her attendants. The dourest of the dour cannot take offence at the good Lord's own glory.

But say the wedding is in December, in Aberdeenshire, after the end of the last peony and before the first snowdrop of spring? Well then there's nothing to be done except wear brown and say no to such an invitation next time.

From Mrs Tilling's Recipes

HERRINGS IN OATMEAL

This is a lowly dish, not for the dining-room but healthful and tasty and hardly to be sniffed at on a cold winter's night.

Ingredients

Two fresh herring fillets per person

flour

milk

4oz fine or medium oatmeal per pair of fillets

Salt and pepper

Butter for frying

Lay out three large plates on one side of the range and one plate covered with crumpled greaseproof paper on the side.

In the furthest plate from the range, place a deep dredging of flour. Fill the middle plate with milk. In the plate closest to the range, have plenty of oatmeal, well seasoned with salt and pepper.

Melt the butter until it is foaming, but not browning, in a heavy frying pan.

Dip the fillets one at a time in flour, then milk, then oats, pressing the oats in firmly to both sides. Fry until golden and sizzling then drain on the crumpled paper. Keep going until all the fillets are ready.

A good cook with a good range, a sharp eye and a keen nose can fry twelve fish without the butter burning. Some cooks will have to wipe out the black butter and start again at least once. Let not your pride rule you: better to pause and clean your pan than waste the Lord's bounty.

Serve with a boiled floury potato and steamed kale.

**For more
Dandyish delights visit**
• • •
www.catrionamcpherson.com

Dandy Gilver and a Deadly Measure of Brimstone

Catriona McPherson

Perthshire 1929 and the menfolk of the Gilver family have come
down, between them, with influenza, bronchitis, pneumonia
and pleurisy. Dandy the devoted wife and mother decides it is
time to decamp; Dandy the intrepid detective, however, decides
to decamp to the scene of a murder she would dearly love to
solve.

The family repairs to the Borders town of Moffat, there to
drink the sulphurous waters straight from the well and to submit
to the galvanic wraps and cold salt rubs of the splendid Laidlaw
Hydropathic Hotel.

But all is not well at the Hydro. The Laidlaw family is at war,
the guests are an uneasy mix of old faithfuls and giddy upstarts,
and the secret of the lady who arrived but never left cannot be
kept for long. And what of those drifting shapes in the Turkish
bath? Just steam shifting in the air? Probably. But the Hydro
was built in the lee of a Gallow Hill, and in this town the dead
can be as much trouble as the living. . .

HODDER

Dandy Gilver and a Bothersome Number of Corpses

Catriona McPherson

Before she was a detective, before she was a reluctant wife and distracted mother, before she was even a debutante, Dandy Gilver spent one perfect summer with the Lipscotts of Pereford. The golden memories of it have sustained her through many a cold snap in Perthshire.

So when two of the Lipscott sisters beg her to help the third, she can hardly refuse. Sweet, pretty Fleur Lipscott: where is she now? The astonishing answer to this is that Fleur – still Miss Lipscott, indeed more Miss Lipscott than ever – is buried alive in the tiny seaside village of Portpatrick, working as a schoolmistress at St Columba's College for Young Ladies.

But she is one of the few remaining, for St Columba's has been shedding mistresses as a snake its skins and the exodus is far from over.

With mistresses vanishing and corpses mounting up, can Mrs Gilver, detective, pass herself off as Miss Gilver, English mistress, to solve the one and stop the other?

HODDER

Dandy Gilver and an Unsuitable Day for a Murder

Catriona McPherson

Friday 3rd June, 1927

Dear Alec,

'Careful what you wish for, lest it come true' is my new motto, and here is why. I was summoned to Dunfermline, that old grey town, in the matter of a missing heiress.

She had flounced off in a sulk over forbidden love and I, suspecting elopement, was loath to take the job of scouring guesthouses to find the little madam and her paramour.

Before I could wriggle out of it, though, there was a murder in the mix - or was it suicide? I had hardly begun to decide when it happened again. Then I was sacked. Actually sacked! By two separate people, and both dismissals in writing. And that's not even the worst of it, darling: matters here are careering downwards much in the style of a runaway train.

Please hurry - or who knows where it might end,

Dandy xx

HODDER

Dandy Gilver and the Proper Treatment of Bloodstains

Catriona McPherson

1st May 1926

Dear Alec,

Just when those who should be working are all downing tools for this wretched strike (and I still can't believe it – I mean to say: riots, Alec – in Edinburgh of all places) guess who is setting her virgin shoulder to its very first wheel?

I am dressed in serge and sensible footwear, sleeping in an iron bed and dining off pickled tongue at six o'clock each day. I am, in short, that nice young Mrs Balfour's new maid. But don't worry, Alec dear: things haven't got as bad as all that. It's just that that nice young Mr Balfour is going to kill his wife. At least, she thinks so, and the more I hear about him from butler, cook and bootboy the more I'm inclined to agree.

So I'm undercover, in disguise, bent upon foiling. And jolly hard work it is too – tomorrow is my half-day free if you'd care take me out for a restorative bun. (Every maid needs a beau to buy buns for her.)

Yours,

Dandy xx

p.s. Ask for Miss Rossiter: below stairs I am she.

HODDER